HOLD M

M.J. Ford lives with his wife ⟨...⟩ ⟨...⟩
Peak District in the north of England. He has worked as an
editor and writer of children's fiction for many years. *Hold My
Hand* is his first novel for adults.

Hold My Hand

M.J. FORD

avon.

This novel is entirely a work of fiction.
The names, characters and incidents portrayed in it are
the work of the author's imagination. Any resemblance to
actual persons, living or dead, events or localities is
entirely coincidental.

AVON

A division of HarperCollins*Publishers*
1 London Bridge Street,
London SE1 9GF

www.harpercollins.co.uk

A Paperback Original 2018

3

A catalogue record for this book is available from the British Library.

ISBN-13 (UK): 978-0-00-825882-5
ISBN-13 (US): 978-0-00-826266-2
ISBN-13 (CA): 978-0-00-829064-1

Set in Bembo Std 11.5/13.5 pt by Palimpsest Book Production Limited,
Falkirk, Stirlingshire

Printed and bound in Great Britain by CPI Group (UK) Ltd, Croydon, CR0 4YY

MIX
Paper from
responsible sources
FSC
www.fsc.org **FSC™ C007454**

HOLD MY HAND

Yarnton, near Oxford, July 26th, 1987

Somewhere, a girl was screaming, but the sound died on the air and became wild laughter. Josie spotted Kim and Bec by the Twisters the moment they were through the main gates, and started tugging at her brother's hand.

'Stay close,' said Paul, breathing two jets of smoke through his nostrils. He'd lit up the first ciggy as soon as Dad's car was out of sight, and finished it in the queue. Josie didn't get smoking at all – she'd had a puff on one once and it had almost made her chuck.

Dad had made her promise to stay with her brother, but Kim and Bec were only eight too, and she knew their parents didn't give a monkey's if *they* went off on their own. And why should they? *What does Dad even think is going to happen?*

She saw Kelly Adams with an ice cream, and waved.

The circus had been here all week, but tomorrow it was moving on to another town. In fact, there were already patches of discoloured grass, and she guessed some stalls had packed up already. The first few days had been really rainy and there was still the odd muddy puddle on the churned-up ground.

The 50p Gran had given Josie was sweaty in her palm. She wondered what it would get her.

Her brother suddenly stiffened, and Josie saw Helen Smith hanging around with a group of her friends. Everyone said Paul and Helen had done it, and Josie had helped spread the rumour, pretending to know what *it* was, and feeling slightly special for the respect her brother's actions conferred upon her. Helen was wearing a denim jacket, and her massive pile of blonde curls spilled over the top.

Paul threw the cigarette on the ground and twisted the heel of his trainer on top. 'Come on,' he said, taking Josie's hand.

She resisted. 'I don't want to hang round with you and Helen Smith,' she said.

Paul hesitated. He looked at his watch. 'Fine,' he said. 'Meet me back here at three o'clock. And don't you dare tell Dad I left you.'

Josie nodded. 'Wicked.'

Paul smiled at her. 'Be careful. And don't talk to strangers!'

Josie was already running off to where she'd seen Kim and Bec, but they'd moved on. She thought about jumping on one of the spinning cups – it was 10p a go – but stopped herself. She should check everything out first, and spend her money wisely.

She wandered slowly through the crowds, passing a load of stalls where you could shoot airguns, or throw tennis balls at coconuts, or fish for prizes with plastic rods. There were kids screaming on the dodgems, smashing into each other. In front of the haunted house, a bored man with grey skin and fake blood painted on the side of his face was taking money from the people queuing. Right in the centre of the field was the big top, a massive red-and-white striped tent with flags across two towers and long ropes fixing it to the ground. Josie made her way over to it. A clown on stilts tottered past.

There were barriers set up outside the big top for queuing,

but the gate was closed across the front. A sign outside read 'Magic and Mayhem', and there were shows every three hours, but the next one wasn't until half two. Josie had heard there was a dog that rode a horse, fire-breathing men, and someone who juggled chainsaws. Apparently, on the opening night, Tom Banks from fourth year had volunteered to be cut in two, even though there was a rumour that someone had died in another town and the circus had covered it up.

As she walked away from the tent, Josie saw a football stall. That was more like it. She hurried over, hand already searching for her money. You had to stand behind a line and chip the ball through different-sized holes at the far end. The lower ones were big, but the top one was barely larger than the ball itself. Teddy bears and sweets hung on the walls either side, ready to be won. One other boy was playing already. Josie thought he was probably about eight too, maybe a bit younger, and he wore a bright red Liverpool shirt from the new season. She'd asked for one like it for Christmas, much to her brother's teasing. He said they lived nowhere near Liverpool and she was just a glory supporter like the rest of them. He didn't care that she could name the entire squad, plus their numbers. In the end, it didn't matter anyway. Her parents had bought her a Man U shirt by accident. Of course, she'd never worn it.

Josie watched as the boy kicked the ball. It bounced off the rim of the top hole.

'Bad luck, lad,' said the man running the stall. He had a funny little beard on the tip of his chin, and a crooked nose. 'You want another go?'

The boy shook his head. His ginger hair was cut short and he had lots of freckles. His chin was plump, with a cleft down the centre. He looked like he was ready to cry.

'How much?' said Josie.

'Hello sweetheart,' said the man, smiling and showing off a

gold tooth. 'Five pence gets you two balls, ten pence gets you five.'

Josie handed over her 50p. 'I'll have five, please.'

The man dropped her money into his apron and gave her four ten-pence pieces in return. Then he fetched the ball.

'There you go, sweetheart.'

Josie placed the ball carefully and took a few steps back. The boy had stayed, and was staring intently.

Her first chip bounced off the board, not even close, and she tried not to let her disappointment show. From the corner of her eye, she saw the stallholder fold his arms. He didn't think she could do it – probably because she was a girl. The freckly kid was the same, most likely. She wished he'd get lost.

I'll show them . . .

Her second shot was even worse, and nearly went over the top. The man tossed the ball back to her.

'Take your time,' he said.

Josie knew he was being patronising, so she kicked the ball deliberately quickly. It nearly went through the middle hole! She threw the stallholder a glance to see if he was impressed. He was smiling at her.

'You can do it,' said the red-headed boy in a small, hopeful voice.

'I know I can,' she said, and he blushed more than she'd ever seen a person blush before. It was like a switch being flicked that changed the colour of his face completely. For her next shot, she did take it slowly, sucking in a deep breath before she kicked the ball. It arced straight up and dropped through the top ring, barely touching the sides.

'Yes!' she said, pumping her fist.

The stallholder was already fetching down one of the huge teddy bears from the top rail of prizes. 'You could be a pro, I reckon,' he said. 'There you go – pretty teddy for a pretty girl.'

Josie didn't like the way he said it, or the look on his face.

'I'm with my brother,' she said, adding, 'He's fifteen.'

She clutched her prize. The stuffed toy was almost as big as she was, and though she was much too old for teddies, that wasn't the point. She started to walk away.

'Wait up, lass – you've got another go.'

Josie turned back. The stallholder was holding out the ball to her. The ginger boy was hanging back.

'Let him have it,' she said.

'Thanks!' called the boy, reddening once more, then eagerly taking the ball.

Josie stayed and watched as he kicked and missed.

'Tell you what,' said the stallholder, 'have a prize anyway.' He took a lollipop from a jar and handed it over. Josie thought that was very kind.

Turning away, she spotted Kim and Bec queuing at an ice-cream van and ran over to join them.

They spent the next hour together. Kim got a Feast, but Bec and Josie went for crushed ice drinks – blue ones, that made their tongues change colour. They tried out the swingboat, throwing their arms in the air as the wind blasted through their hair. Then they went on a bouncy castle, until some bigger boys started being too rough. After a go on the dodgems, and some strawberry sherbets, Josie was down to her last 5p, and there was still an hour before she had to meet her brother again. She wondered if he might give her some more money – even 10p. Paul had a Saturday job helping at a barbers in town and that got him three quid a time. Their parents thought he was saving, but most of it went on cigs. First, though, she needed a wee.

Kim pointed her past the big top, towards a set of cubicles standing in a row. With all the crowds, the quickest way was through a load of caravans parked up behind the tent. She guessed it was where all the workers stayed, and the people who set up the shows.

'Meet you by the haunted house,' she said, and headed off.

Beyond the main circus tent, the ground was boggy, but here and there panels of rubber matting had been laid across patches of mud. Cables snaked between the caravans, and with bin bags and buckets strewn about it wasn't very nice at all. The caravans themselves looked deserted, their curtains drawn. Josie quickened her step, suddenly thinking she probably wasn't supposed to be in this area at all.

As she rounded a wheelbarrow filled with sandbags, a movement to her left made her heart jolt. A huge black and brown dog leapt right at her, only to be snatched back on a chain around its neck. It barked and strained, drool flying from its mouth. Josie normally liked dogs, but she could tell this one wanted to bite her. The caravan door opened, and a young woman in a blue satin dressing gown appeared at the top of some steps.

'Shut it, Tyson!' she said.

The dog immediately relaxed, sitting back and licking its lips.

'Sorry,' said Josie.

The woman stared hard at her – almost *through* her, Josie thought.

'You shouldn't be here,' she said. Then she went back inside and closed the door.

Josie's heart was still racing as she hurried on to the portable toilets. She didn't want to take her teddy inside, so left it on the grass, hoping no one would take it. The loos weren't as bad as she expected, but she made sure she washed her hands twice anyway.

When she came out, there was a small queue forming, and for a moment she found it hard to get her bearings. Which way was the haunted house? Then she spotted the main entrance again, and remembered it had been close to that. She grabbed her teddy and set off, passing the trees that lined the bottom edge of the field, and a shed with a corrugated metal roof that looked like it was falling down. A piece of old farming machinery – something that looked like it belonged on the back of a tractor – lay rusting amid the long grass.

A flash of red caught Josie's eye, and she saw the boy from the football game again, but he wasn't alone this time. Holding his hand was a clown, with red hair almost as bright as the Liverpool shirt. They were walking away, quite quickly, past a leaning bathtub stained with green and brown streaks. The boy was looking up at the clown and saying something, but she couldn't see the clown's face to see if he was talking back. And then they were gone, around the corrugated shed and out of sight towards the trees at the bottom of the field. It seemed an odd way to go – there weren't any rides or anything in that direction.

Josie stood still for a moment, a strange warm feeling rising from her chest to her throat. She considered going after them, just to check everything was okay, but something kept her feet rooted to the spot. Maybe the clown was his dad, or uncle. And she didn't have time to hang around anyway. Kim and Bec were waiting for her. She set off once more, and though she thought about looking back, she did not.

There was no queue at the haunted house, so they used the last of their money to go in together. It was scarier than it looked from the outside. You had to walk through, and it was really dark. Things jumped from the walls, and in one part, a hologram made it look like a witch was peering over your shoulder in front of a mirror. The noises were the worst – creaks, and shuffles and cracks that came from every side. Josie was secretly glad she was with her friends, and gripped the large

7

teddy tightly every time there was another shock. Kim's scream was so loud that Josie's ears were ringing as they bundled through the exit doors.

'Dylan?'

A woman about the same age as Josie's mum was walking in long strides past the front of the haunted house, calling out.

'Dylan!'

Her eyes scanned left and right, and her face was flushed. For a moment, her gaze passed over Josie and her friends, paused, then moved on. Josie saw her spot a man sitting at a fold-out table near the entrance. She made a stumbling, darting run towards him, pushing past two teenagers.

'I can't find my son,' she said.

The man, who had a bushy moustache and a ruddy, swollen face, looked taken aback for a moment. 'No kids have come out this way. How old is he?'

'Seven,' said the woman. She held out a hand at hip-height. 'This tall or so. He was wearing a red shirt. I only looked away for a second.'

The warm feeling blossomed again across Josie's chest. She felt itchy, her breathing shallow and strange.

'Let's find your brother,' said Kim. 'I *really* want to try the swingboat!'

'He's probably having it off in a bush somewhere,' said Bec.

'Yeah,' said Josie, vaguely. She was looking at the woman, who broke away from the table and put both hands up to her mouth.

'Dylan!' she shouted again, her voice panicky.

'He's probably with his mates,' said the organiser.

'He hasn't got any mates!' snapped the woman.

'Steady on, love. He'll turn up.'

Josie stepped closer to them. She felt tiny. 'Excuse me,' she said. 'I think I might have seen him.'

The woman turned to her, eyes confused and afraid, then suddenly focused. She advanced quickly and gripped Josie's shoulders so hard it hurt.

'Dylan? Where? Where did you see him?'

Josie managed to point to the buildings at the edge of the field. 'Down there. With the clown.'

'What clown?' asked the organiser, suddenly interested. He stood up from his seat, and Josie noticed a small patch of his belly showing from the top of his trousers.

'With red hair,' she said. 'They were holding hands.'

The woman released her, and her face moved in a way Josie had never seen before – a sort of crumpling – and she let out a wail that sounded like someone had ripped it from her stomach. She began to run. A few seconds later, the man at the desk waddled after her. Josie stayed where she was, wondering if she'd done the right thing.

'Come on,' said Kim. 'There's nothing we can do.'

'There's your brother,' said Bec, and Josie saw Paul carrying Helen Smith on his shoulders, like she was a prize he'd won on one of the stalls. She turned full circle, watching the rides and the games and the flags of the big top flying. She wanted to see a flash of a red Liverpool shirt, just to tell her that the orange-haired boy called Dylan was okay, even though, somehow, she knew he wasn't.

Chapter 1

FRIDAY

Jo tried to ignore the vibration in her jacket pocket and concentrate on what Dr Kasparian was saying.

'. . . the cost of the vitrification starts at three thousand pounds for one harvesting procedure, but there are discounted rates for subsequent treatments.'

'And would you recommend that?'

The doctor – well-tanned, athletic, expensive-looking wire-rimmed spectacles – spread his hands.

'In most cases, the initial hormone boost should allow us to harvest more than one egg. Of course, probability-wise, you are more likely to conceive the more cycles of fertilisation you undertake.' He looked at the papers in front of him. 'Based on your age, any single attempt yields a twenty-two per cent chance of a successful pregnancy.'

'One in five,' said Jo flatly.

'A little better that that,' replied the doctor.

Not great odds either way. Her phone stopped ringing.

The doctor cocked his head sympathetically and removed his glasses.

'Ms Masters, I realise this is a big decision for anyone, whether a woman of twenty years, or someone older. No fertility treatment is foolproof. But I can assure you that here at Bright Futures, we are solely concerned with providing you with the best possible care and outcomes. Our protocols are designed to the highest medical technology standards in the field. Our results reflect that – we're in the top ten percentile points of success.'

'So three grand?' said Jo. If she got the promotion to Detective Inspector, it wouldn't be a problem. 'Do the eggs have a best before date?'

The doctor smiled. 'Not in practical terms, no.'

'And can I pay in instalments?'

He looked taken aback. 'Erm . . . that isn't something we usually do.'

Jo stared at him. Told herself not to get flustered. Just be straight.

'Right, but *can* you?'

Christ, I sound desperate.

The doctor looked away first. 'There may be ethical considerations,' he said. 'If we were to freeze your eggs, then subsequently, through no fault of your own, the payments were to fall into default—'

'Is that a "no" then?'

The doctor placed his glasses back on. 'Perhaps you could excuse me for a moment? Hopefully I can discuss the matter with my colleague.'

Jo nodded and watched him stand up and walk out, leaving her alone in the plush room.

She let her gaze travel around the dark wood furniture, clean lines, books neatly stacked. Perfect, sanitised order. She wondered how much a gynaecological consultant earned. Probably a hell of a lot more than a DS for Avon and Somerset Police. There was a single photo frame on the desk, facing partly away. Jo leant forward to look. It showed Dr Kasparian with a man who must be his partner – dark-haired, well-groomed facial hair, maybe fifty, but with a carefree face that looked ten years younger – and two teenage boys. All hanging off each other on a leather sofa. They looked perfect too.

Good for them.

The door opened and she sat back in her chair.

'Good news,' said the doctor. 'Monthly payments for six months should be fine. Would you like my secretary to start the paperwork, or would you like to go away and think about it? There's really no rush.'

Isn't there? thought Jo. *Easy for you to say.*

She'd have preferred a year of payments, just to be safe, but she could probably afford it over half a dozen instalments.

'Yes, please,' she said, and though it galled her to add it, 'Thank you.'

The phone in her pocket was ringing again.

Just leave me alone, Ben. Just for ten fucking minutes.

★　★　★

The paperwork didn't take long, but the questions got more personal as they went along.

First, the basics. Name (*Josephine Masters*); address (she gave the rented place in the south of the city; didn't need Ben somehow getting mail about this); DOB (as if she needed reminding); occupation (copper). Then medical history. Clean bill of health, apart from the scare last year; alcohol unit intake (everyone lied, right?); do you smoke (no, but gagging for one right now); last period (the 18th); last instance of sexual intercourse (regrettable); last pregnancy (she paused a moment, wondering whether it was the conception date they wanted, or the date of the miscarriage, then opted for the latter). The secretary tapped deftly at the keyboard with manicured fingers. She was perhaps early twenties, a pretty, natural blonde, combining elegance and amiability in a way Jo could never have managed at that age.

Jo wondered what the young woman thought of *her*. Did she judge? What did she think of the going-on-forty-year-old sitting opposite, her hair needing a colour, her crow's feet obvious, her sensible shoes and middle-of-the-range navy suit? Did she wonder why Jo was here, why she didn't have a partner, if . . .

You're getting bitter, Josephine. Stop it.

The bank details came last, and then, when the printouts were signed, they set a tentative date for the hormone infusion. Jo knew she'd have to check her shifts and told them she'd be in touch. She was glad to be out of there, stepping onto a quiet mews street in the shadow of the cathedral. Though in the shade, the summer air was warm. She guessed the cottage would once have held a member of the clerical staff. Now the only sign it was a commercial property was the discreet Bright Futures plaque beside the listed front door.

She checked her phone and saw nine missed calls, all from Ben.

It was almost eleven. She'd blocked out three hours for the meeting, saying she was taking her mother to the doctor's in Oxford, so she still had forty-five minutes before she was due back at the station for the weekend briefing. It was Paul's birthday party that night and she still hadn't got him a present, though she knew exactly the thing. Her brother, like their dad before him, had started balding in his early thirties, and Bath was the sort of city that still had gentlemen's outfitters. A quick

Google had given her a promising place off Wallford Street. She walked across the cobbles, then stepped out into the throng.

Bath was never quiet, of course, but Friday lunchtime in the summer holidays was pretty close to Jo's idea of hell. An engine of commerce. Tourists jostling with street performers, gaggles of teenagers up to nothing. Workers – mostly Europeans and South Americans – on breaks from jobs at hotels. People spilling out of cafes, bars and shops. And here and there, the city's true denizens – Jo's bread and butter. The drug addicts, leaning towards their next fix. The pickpockets, swimming with the tides. The petty criminals who existed in every city; the grit in the machine.

Jo fought through the pedestrians outside the Assembly Rooms before slipping off into a narrower alley, a row of bikes chained up against a set of railings. She found the hat place, and though at first she thought it must be closed, when she pushed the door, it opened, a bell above her clanking. A small, very elderly man with luxuriant white hair and a stoop looked up from behind a counter.

'Good day to you,' he said.

Jo smiled at the unexpected chivalry, but just as she was about to speak, her phone rang again. This time the vibration was different.

'Excuse me!' she said, and she backed out of the shop to take the call.

'Why aren't you answering?' said Rob Bridges, her DCI back at the station. 'Ben's been trying for the last hour.'

It took Jo a moment to gain her composure. 'With my mum,' she said. 'It's in the diary.'

Bridges breathed a sigh. 'Fine, can you talk?'

'What's up?'

'We've got a body. Bradford-on-Avon. A kid.'

Jo looked at her reflection in the window of the shop, swallowed. 'Go on.'

'Thames Valley have already sent someone, but I want you there.'

'Why Thames Valley?'

'Something to do with identifying features. They think it's one of their mispers.'

'Text me the address,' said Jo. 'I'll call when I'm on my way.' She hung up. Paul's present could wait.

★ ★ ★

It took Jo three minutes to get back to her car, another seven to get out of the car park. She plugged in the address as she did so, but it looked like it was the middle of a random field. Bradford-on-Avon was a well-to-do market town about five miles out from Bath – all Cotswold stone and shops she could never afford. The sort of place her mum would've liked to spend an afternoon, before her world shrank to the four walls of a room in a residential care home. As soon as she was out of traffic, her phone rang again. Ben. This time she answered on the hands-free.

'I'm on my way,' she said.

'So what's wrong with your mum?' No pleasantries.

'Y'know,' Jo replied airily. 'What's right with her? She's old. I took her to the doctor's.'

'Really? When you didn't answer, I rang the home looking for you. She's there. You're not. They couldn't remember the last time you'd visited.'

Dammit.

'You should have called me on the station line.'

He didn't answer for a few seconds, then said, more softly, 'Can we talk later?'

Jo's hands tightened on the wheel. 'There's nothing to talk about.'

'It's been months, Jo. We can't just avoid the subject forever.'

'There is no subject,' she said. 'That's how breaking up works. Put Rob on.'

'He's already on his way as well.'

'Well, you fill me in then.'

Ben gathered himself and gave her the details. A skeleton had been unearthed in the grounds of a derelict house off the Frome Road. They'd found a body by the pumping house of the drained pool. From the size, it could only be a child.

'Any idea when the pool was put in?' asked Jo. The satnav said she'd be there in twenty-one minutes.

'We're looking into it – still trying to track the owners of the house. It's been a wreck for eighteen months. Electrical fault caused a fire, apparently.'

'So what makes them think it's an Oxford misper?'

'There's clothing that matches an old file,' said Ben. 'A Liverpool football club shirt.'

Jo's foot touched the brake involuntarily, and the BMW behind beeped as it drove up into her rear-view mirror.

'You okay?' asked Ben.

'I'll be there in fifteen,' said Jo. She stepped on the accelerator, feeling the engine surge along with her racing heart.

Chapter 2

The sign for the Hanover Homes development loomed large over the hedgerows at the side of the B3109. The space promised 240 units, 'built to house the local community', whatever that was supposed to mean, here in the middle of nowhere. The road was spattered with mud from the procession of vehicles using the site, and when Jo turned into the entrance, her small car rocked and bounced over the hard ruts in the ground. It hadn't rained for weeks, and the weather forecasters were saying it was already the driest summer on record.

She passed a couple of temporary cabins, several stacks of scaffold and a concrete truck. A squad car was parked up alongside her boss Rob Bridges' scarlet Volvo, along with a battered Discovery, a Toyota and a police-issue Vauxhall. DCI Bridges, in plain clothes, was talking to a woman in a hard hat, making notes in his book.

Jo killed the engine and climbed out.

'Can I see?' she said straight away.

'Who's this?' said an older, silver-haired man whose grey pallor suggested he was at least one heart attack down. His suit looked thick, maybe woollen, and completely wrong for July.

Jo frowned; there was something familiar about him.

'Detective Jo Masters, meet Harry Ferman,' said Bridges. 'There's a DS from Thames Valley round the back already.'

The older man held out a massive, paw-like hand, and Jo shook it.

'Follow me,' he said. His teeth seemed a little too big for his mouth, and she guessed they were dentures.

As he led her under the secondary perimeter police tape and around a bend between overgrown hedges, Jo wondered who he was. He had police written all over him, but he had to be at least sixty.

A substantial Georgian house came into view at the end of the drive. Though the stone was still pale in places, a lot of it was stained by sooty streaks, darker above the paneless window arches. The roof was a mess of exposed joists, many collapsed already. A uniformed officer took their details at a second line of tape by the side of the house and gestured them through.

'Who found the remains?' said Jo.

Ferman was wheezing a little. 'Skull came up in the claw of the digger when they were excavating round the pool. Must have been a hell of shock.'

It is a shame it's been disturbed, thought Jo.

At the side of the house, what had been a set of French doors opened onto a wide terrace with stone balustrades and steps leading down to the old pool. On the left-hand side, a two-person forensics team was already at work, erecting a white awning over the site. Jo greeted them, and they nodded back from behind their masks. A slight man, just a few years older than her, with dark, sharp features, was crouching nearby.

'You must be Masters,' he said, standing up.

'Call me Jo,' she replied.

The man straightened. 'Detective Sergeant Andy Carrick, Thames Valley. Pleased to meet you.'

Jo looked behind him. The bones were dark, clotted with mud, but still recognisably in the shape of a body. She could see a small skull. They lay there, half-wrapped in a piece of semi-transparent plastic, which, she thought, was probably what had preserved the clothing too – a scrap of dirty red material. The forensics team had an open case and Jo fished for a glove and booties from the dispensers. She donned the gear, then edged closer to the body to check the yellow lettering on the front of the shirt: 'Crown Paints' – and a Liverpool FC crest.

'You really think it's Dylan Jones?' she asked, peering at the bones. It was impossible to say much at all, but pathology wasn't her field. When it was all cleaned up, they'd get more answers.

'Looks about right,' said Ferman. 'You're familiar with the case then?'

Jo glanced at him, wondering what he was doing here. He didn't look at all well, and she'd guess he was way past retirement. But she was sure their paths had crossed before.

'Sort of,' she said.

'You look too young,' said Ferman. 'It was over thirty years ago.'

'Flattery will get you nowhere,' said Jo. 'I was a witness to the kidnapping. I was eight.'

'You serious?' said Carrick. Jo nodded, and he whistled. 'I'm not normally suspicious, but that's a coincidence and a half.'

'Bloody hell,' said Ferman. 'I remember you!'

His face had lifted, and the years fell off. And then Jo realised where she'd seen him.

'You were there, that day,' she said.

Ferman nodded. 'I was still training for CID. Came with my gaffer.'

Jo edged back as one of the forensics team approached with a camera. 'My brother made the call,' she said. 'Someone had cut the temporary line from the circus. He had to run to the nearest farmhouse. You came to my house and took a statement.'

'You couldn't stop crying.'

'I thought it was my fault.'

It was my fault.

Ferman came closer, moving with difficulty down the steps, until he was standing beside Jo and Carrick, looking at the remains.

'You were the only witness,' he said. 'And pretty reliable for a young girl. Still, it wasn't much to go on.' Though he was staring in the direction of the skeleton, he had a faraway look in his eyes. 'We interviewed over forty people,' he said. 'Didn't get a damn thing.'

Jo heard the scuffle of footsteps and looked up to see DCI Bridges.

'We've got an address for the parents, Jo,' he said.

'Still the place off the Banbury Road?' asked Ferman.

Bridges looked impressed. 'That's right. I think we owe them a visit.'

'Bit premature, guv?' said Jo. 'Shouldn't we wait for a positive ID?' She glanced at the child's skull. 'Dental comparison?'

'Dylan was seven,' said Ferman. 'I doubt there were any records. At least, I don't remember any at the time.'

'Ben's got Carter looking into when the pool was built,' said Bridges. 'We'll need some swabs from the parents.'

'And you want me to do it?' asked Jo.

'Given your connection with the case, I think there's a sort of poetry to it, don't you?' said Carrick. He sounded pleased to be rid of the cold case.

'What connection's that?' said Bridges.

Jo explained, briefly, staring at the remains. Nothing poetic there. It was a dead kid.

'Gosh – isn't that uncanny?' he said.

21

'Want a lift back to Oxford?' Carrick asked Ferman.

'I'll accompany Detective Masters to the parents' house,' said Ferman. 'If she doesn't mind, that is.'

'No problem,' said Jo. The thought of such a steady presence was comforting.

As Ferman and the others went to sign themselves out of the crime scene, Jo remained for a few moments. One of the forensics team was photographing the site from every possible angle, and Jo knew they wouldn't be done here until it was dark, would spend hours scouring the earth for any extra material. The body might get moved tomorrow, and they'd likely have it bagged and driven to Salisbury for the coroner to take samples and try to discern the cause of death. Jo stared at the skeleton, trying to imagine it as the little boy from the circus that day.

In truth, she could barely remember Dylan Jones, other than his red hair and the look of pure gratitude he'd given her when she'd let him take her final kick on the football game. In the weeks following the summer holidays had taken over, and then it was school again. Life had moved on, and though she'd occasionally thought of Dylan after, it was only ever fleeting, and mostly with an uneasy sense of guilt. She guessed her mum and dad would have done their best to keep her away from the unfolding investigation, moving any lurid headlines out of reach, switching over the channel if it came on the news. It would be next to impossible these days, but in the era of four TV stations and no internet, sheltering your kids wouldn't have been all that hard.

There'd been a bit of teasing at school, but kids could be pretty brutal without really meaning it. She wondered about the last time she'd seen Dylan, hand-in-hand with his abductor. Had there been fear on his face, or had he been struggling? She didn't think so.

Soon, she'd learnt the whole episode was like a bruise – if she didn't press it, it didn't hurt at all. The bullies had found other victims, other causes, and she was left alone.

She peeled off the gloves and boots as she went back round the house. Andy Carrick was already pulling away in the Toyota.

Bridges was sitting on the bonnet of his car, drinking tea from a Thermos cup. He handed her a piece of paper with an address on the north side of Oxford. There was a blue Audi parked across the road now, and a young woman sitting in the front seat on her phone.

'Vultures are circling,' he said.

'Already?' said Jo. 'Who tipped them off?'

'Probably one of the builders,' said Bridges. 'The official line is that we've found a body, but there's no indication of foul play. Ben wants to keep it all under wraps, and I agree.'

'Ben's leading?'

'Sure,' said Bridges, smiling. 'Got my best team on it.' He tossed the remains of the tea across the ground, and dropped the cup into the skip. 'Let me know how it goes with Mr and Mrs Jones.'

'Can you send me the original case files?' said Jo.

'I'll get Thames Valley to push it all over,' said Bridges. 'It'll take a while to dig out.'

Then he was in his car and reversing out of the site entrance.

Jo folded the address and climbed into her own car, which had grown stuffy in the brief time she'd been on the crime scene. She switched on the air con. As Ferman lowered himself into the passenger seat, the car dipped noticeably.

'You don't like this Ben fella?' he said.

Jo's eyes were on the mirrors as she manoeuvred out. 'It's complicated,' she said.

* * *

23

They joined the M4, skirted Swindon, and approached Oxford from the south-west. With so much on her mind, Jo would have been comfortable with silence, but Ferman was the chatty sort. And though his tone was conversational, Jo couldn't escape the feeling he was analysing everything she said, like she was a witness all over again.

'You worked for Avon and Somerset long?'

'I was at Reading after training,' she said. 'Moved across a couple of years ago.'

'But you're from Oxford originally.'

'That's right,' she said.

She watched him from the corner of her eye as she drove, carrying out her own appraisal. The suit he was wearing was way out of date, and though spotlessly clean, it was slightly worn on the knees. She wondered if it had come out of a dry-cleaning bag that morning. Shoes polished, but showing scuffs. His left hand (no wedding ring, but perhaps a patch of slightly paler skin where one would sit) clutched the roof handle the whole way, and she wondered if he'd not been in a car for a while. His right hand was yellowed at the fingertips, but she couldn't smell any smoke on his clothes, and he showed no inkling of wanting a fag now. There was a shaving cut under his jowls.

'What station are you with, sir?' she asked, as they came off the bypass.

He chuckled. 'You mean, what's an old fart like me doing on your crime scene?'

She smiled. 'Something like that.'

'Professional courtesy,' said Ferman. 'Retired a few years back. My name was on the file, I suppose. And I'm not "sir" – I retired as a DS.'

'You live locally?'

'Aye.' He didn't elaborate.

24

'Kids?'

'Not any more.'

She decided not to push. He wouldn't be the first police officer with unhappy family circumstances.

'What can you tell me about the original case?' said Jo. She remembered dimly that there'd been a suspect.

Ferman tried to stretch his legs, but there wasn't room.

'There's a seat adjustment thing at the side,' Jo said.

After a couple of goes he found it, and edged the seat back.

'Ah. That's better. Well, not much to say, really. There was zero physical evidence. We combed the fields down below the circus site – a few scuffed prints, but the grass was long down there and it was a well-known fly-tipping spot. Nothing biological we could use. We knew it wasn't a spur-of-the-moment thing. Like you said, someone had cut the phone line – they knew the police wouldn't get there and start tracking for at least twenty minutes. Must have had a car parked nearby, and loaded Dylan in. We drew up a profile that night. The kidnapper was male, probably local and knew the area, must have had a car, and had probably scouted the place in the preceding days.'

'The parents give you anything? Grudges?'

'Nowt. It looked completely random. We wasted some time going after dad – neighbours told us he could get a bit handy with Dylan, but there was nothing in it. And why kidnap your own child?'

'Though it would make sense that Dylan went with him.'

'That was our thinking. Alibi was cast-iron though. He was at a rugby match. The guy who ran the carnival – McTavish, I think he was called – wasn't very helpful at all. He couldn't even give us a definitive list of employees, because a lot of the workers were off the books. And thousands had been in and out, because the circus had been there for a week. The clown thing threw us – you were the only witness to the costume,

25

and the other staff said they'd have known if a different clown was hanging around. We figured the suspect must have put on the disguise at the site.' Ferman laughed. 'The gaffer had us empty out the chemical toilets – you can imagine how that went down. We found a bag with make-up – lipstick and face paint, the like. High-street stuff, and no way to trace it.'

'Sex offenders?'

'We did the rounds, but it was pre-'97, so no proper records of those sorts of crimes. We went on local intelligence back then.'

'But you made an arrest?'

'Oh, aye. We thought we had him too. Clement Matthews – lived less than a mile away. Previous convictions for indecent exposure. No alibi worth speaking of for the day in question. Said he'd never been to the circus, or near it, but when we flashed his picture to McTavish, he was sure he'd seen the fella. We stripped his place to the joists, took his car to bits, looking for anything to tie him to Dylan.'

'And nothing?'

'Not a bean, apart from some vids. But even they were borderline – the sort of thing you can find with a couple of clicks these days. Hard to determine the age of the participants. To be honest, I felt from the start he wasn't a good fit – he just seemed out of his depth. But the high-ups were on us like a rash to charge someone.' Ferman sighed. 'We went at him pretty hard, and in the end he admitted he'd driven past the circus a couple of times. We threw the book at him.'

Jo hadn't remembered any of this. She guessed her parents had done their best to keep the unsavoury details from her.

'It went to court?'

'I wish it hadn't. We really only had McTavish to put Matthews at the scene,' said Ferman. 'Bastard turned up half-cut just after lunch, slurred his way through his evidence and fell to bits under cross-examination. It was embarrassing for everyone.'

'So Matthews walked free.'

'I wouldn't go that far. The papers got hold of it. Called him "The Killer Clown". The locals didn't take kindly to finding out there was a perv living next door.'

'I can imagine.'

She remembered now, some of the specifics of that term at school following the kidnap. 'Clown's coming for you!' was the taunt of choice. To her shame, she'd even used it herself once or twice. Maybe it was just a way to process what had happened, but she felt a sudden rush of disgust.

'He was rehoused in the end, I think,' said Ferman. 'Taxpayer's expense.'

'Is it worth picking him up again?'

'He was mid-forties then and hardly in great nick,' said Ferman. 'He's probably popped his clogs.'

Jo focused on the road as they came off the bypass and towards the city. She wondered how deep Ben was in the case files. If Matthews *was* still around, Ben would sniff him out like a bloodhound. For all his personal faults, as a police officer he was tenacious.

Coming back into Oxford always left Jo with a feeling of unease. Despite the wide spaces and the grand buildings – the bloody 'dreaming spires', as people insisted on calling them – it had always felt claustrophobic.

They drove on in silence, past the looming 1930s residences north of the city, the Arts and Crafts cottages with their leafy gardens and 4x4s parked in the drives. The satnav took them into a small housing estate of 1970s bungalows, and they found 94 Curlew Close. There was a small electric car in the drive. Ferman looked a little tense, gnarled old hands resting on his thighs.

'You want to do the talking?' asked Jo. 'You know the family.'

Ferman shook his head. 'I'll just observe, if you don't mind.'

Jo would have rather he took over, but given she was the serving officer, she didn't quibble. It had been a year or so since she'd served a notice of death to the next of kin. The last time was a drowning accident. The parents had thought their teenage daughter was at a friend's studying for her GCSE chemistry, when actually she was drinking cheap cider by the local reservoir and decided to strip off and have a dip. This felt not a little different, given the time that had elapsed and the fact it was still conjecture that the body was even Dylan.

They walked up to the front door. There was a boot-scraper by the mat in the shape of a dog. Jo rang the bell, and a yappy barking started up at once. She composed herself, taking out her warrant card.

The woman who came to the door was tall, athletic-looking and stylish, with cropped, grey hair, baggy linen trousers and a matching shawl over a blouse. She wore open-toed sandals, and had a multitude of bangles down both arms plus a necklace of amber beads. Her fingers were slender, with a touch of dirt under the nails. At her ankles sat a Westie, wagging its stubby tail.

'Mrs Jones?' said Jo, wondering if this could be the same woman she'd seen rushing around the carnival ground screaming her son's name.

The woman nodded. 'Yes?' Then her eyes latched onto Ferman and a hand rose to her throat. 'Oh my God. You've found him, haven't you?'

Jo showed her badge.

'My name is Detective Masters, and I believe you've met Harry Ferman before. We need to speak with you. Can we come in?'

Mrs Jones backed into the hallway. 'Of course.'

Jo went first, with Ferman at her back, and Mrs Jones led them through to a conservatory at the back of the house. A man – Mr Jones, presumably – was sitting in a wicker chair, doing a crossword on a folded newspaper. He put it down as they entered.

'These people are police officers,' said his wife. 'Do you remember Constable Ferman?'

The years had not been as kind to Mr Jones as to his wife. He was stout, his face and scalp liver-spotted, and wore a pair of green corduroy trousers and a plaid shirt. He stood up, gathering himself, and extended a hand to Ferman, who shook it briefly.

'I remember,' he said.

Jo didn't get a handshake, and didn't let it bother her. 'I'm Detective Masters,' she said again. 'I've come to tell you that we have uncovered the remains of a body, and though we don't have confirmation at this stage, we have circumstantial evidence that suggests it's your son, Dylan Jones, who was reported missing a little over thirty-one years ago.' She paused, wondering if she'd struck the right tone, then added, 'I'm sorry to have to deliver this news to you.'

Mr Jones moved to his wife's side and took her arm. 'You're sorry?' he said.

Jo struggled to discern his tone. It sounded like a genuine question, so she forged on.

'We are carrying out enquiries and the coroner will be examining the remains.'

'Can we see him?' said Mrs Jones.

'Sheila . . .' said her husband.

'Mrs Jones,' said Jo, trying to be as delicate as possible. 'The body is in an advanced state of decomposition. It really is little more than a partial skeleton.'

She saw Mr Jones flinch, and small dots of purple appeared under each cheek. 'Then why in God's name do you think it's Dylan? Where was he found?'

Ferman spoke up for the first time. 'Apologies, Mr Jones, I'm very sorry we're breaking this news to you. But you remember what Dylan was wearing the day he disappeared?'

'The day he was taken, you mean?'

'Indeed, sir.'

'His football shirt?' said Mrs Jones.

'That's right,' said Jo. 'The body was found with a similar shirt. The remains were discovered in Bradford-on-Avon, but we're not sure at the moment if . . . where the victim might have died.'

The way the middle-aged woman's face collapsed in front of her took Jo right back to the day at the circus. She felt as if she was deceiving them by not mentioning her connection to the case, but now definitely wasn't the time to bring it up. Mrs Jones buried her face into her husband's shoulder, and he hugged her tightly, glaring at Jo all the while.

'Is there anything else we need to do?' he said.

'As part of the process of identification, we'll carry out DNA tests,' said Jo, pleased to be focusing on the procedural aspects. 'If it's not too much trouble, we will need to take a biological sample from both of you. It's a quick and simple enough procedure that involves taking hair follicles and cheek swabs. That can either be done here, in your home, or at your local station. I'll ask them to contact you directly, if that's all right.' Jo fished her card out and placed it on the table beside the newspaper. 'If you have any questions, don't hesitate to call me.'

'So that's it?' said Mr Jones, nostrils flaring.

'Until the body is formally identified through biological methods, we'll be following up a number of leads.'

Mrs Jones nodded, clinging to her husband.

'We'll be going then,' said Ferman, glancing at Jo. 'Once again, Mr and Mrs Jones – you have our condolences.'

He led the way back into the hallway, Jo following with the

Westie trotting at her side. They'd reached the door when Mrs Jones caught up. She was wiping her eyes with a tissue.

'Thank you,' she said. 'We appreciate everything you're doing.'

'Just our job, ma'am,' said Jo.

They walked back down the drive, and Jo was glad to turn her back on the house. What a strange day the Joneses must be having. Contented retirees one moment; the past rearing its head like a spectre the next.

'Well, that went as well as could be expected,' she said when they were back in the car.

'Did it?' said Ferman. His eyes betrayed a hint of bemusement.

'You think I was too . . . brusque?'

Ferman shrugged. 'What do I know?'

'Can I take you back to the station?'

'I file my reports at The Three Crowns on Canterbury Road these days,' said Ferman.

It took Jo half a second to register what he meant, but she didn't bat an eyelid.

'You got it.'

★ ★ ★

She dropped Ferman at the pub, turning down his offer to buy her a drink. Not only because drinking on duty was generally frowned upon, but because she still had to pick up a present for Paul.

She found a milliner's just off Turl Street, and drove right into town before realising she had no cash for the meter. She parked on double yellows a hundred yards from the shop and hurried in. Amelia had texted her Paul's size, and she selected a brown homburg without properly looking at the price. When the owner told her, she baulked, but paid out of embarrassment. It was a pittance to her brother, but she'd have to cut a corner somewhere else if she was going to make her monthly payments to Bright Futures.

When she got back to the car, a traffic warden was just taking a shot of her number plate.

'Oh, come on!' said Jo. 'I was two minutes!'

The warden shrugged, made a few more notes, and stuck the ticket to her window wordlessly. She'd been in the same situation with Ben once, years ago, and he'd used the badge, but that wasn't her way. Instead, she tore off the notice and threw it into the car like any other civilian.

Driving back out of the city, she went through some of her options. She knew she was overdrawn, but she still had credit. The immediate problem was this month's rent though. If she wrote a cheque and the landlord tried to cash it straight away, it would bounce. As for the Bright Futures payments . . .

A bike swerved out in front of her and she slammed the brake and the horn at the same time. The young man riding, wearing a student's gown, turned and smiled sheepishly.

Fuck Ben.

She told herself to calm down. If she took this into the station, it would only end badly. She attempted to breathe deeply, and tried not to think of the almighty shithole she was in danger of falling into.

Thirty-nine years old, renting a one-bed flat, and up to your eyeballs in debt.

She put on Classic FM to calm herself down, but it just reminded her of her mum, so she switched to some mindless pop instead.

It took an hour to get back to Bath, and as she parked up and climbed out, Ben was emerging from the station with DC Rhani Aziz close at his side. Rhani had been with them only a few months, but she was settling in well. Both were laughing.

'Oh, hi, sarge,' said the pretty young constable.

'Hi,' said Jo.

'How'd it go with the parents?' asked Ben. He was professional as always. Quite the actor. Even his eyes didn't give anything away.

'As well as can be expected, sir,' said Jo. 'They were shocked.'

'I'll bet,' Rhani said. 'Not often we get a lead after three decades.'

'Constable Aziz here managed to track down the former suspect. Chap by the name of—'

'Matthews,' said Jo, cutting him off. 'I know.'

'No flies on you,' said Ben, smiling in a way that made Jo want to kick him in the balls.

'Detective Ferman was pretty sure he wasn't involved,' she said.

Ben snorted through his nose. 'Is that the dinosaur who tagged along? Did he bring his magnifying glass and truncheon too?'

He was talking towards Jo, but looking at Rhani as he spoke. She duly obliged with a laugh, but Jo didn't want to give him any satisfaction. Was he actually trying to make her jealous somehow?

'Not quite – he just said Matthews didn't fit the bill. The case stank from the start.'

Ben straightened a bit, into exactly the same mixture of outrage and hurt he'd shown whenever she'd questioned him about his other dubious calls.

'Well, this is a new case,' he said. 'And it would be remiss if we didn't pursue all avenues of enquiry.'

'Very well, sir,' said Jo.

Rhani and Ben continued to a marked car. Jo thought about suggesting they take Ben's Jag, given the heat Matthews might get, but she suspected he wouldn't take any more advice kindly. As it happened, it was Ben himself who called to her.

'Jo?' he said.

She faced him.

'There's a journalist from the *Oxford Times*. I don't know how she's got wind, but don't give her anything, okay?'

Of course I won't, you condescending arsehole.

'Right, sir,' she said.

She greeted the front desk clerk and several other uniforms on the way to the CID room. DC Kevin Carter was playing some sort of golf game on his computer, which he promptly closed when Jo cleared her throat. The guy really was fifty years' worth of useless flesh, with two failed marriages and three kids he rarely saw. She'd actually come across his profile on Tinder about two months back, and going by the age of the picture he'd used, she could have done him for fraud.

'Anything on when the pool was put in?' she asked.

'Not yet,' said Carter. She saw him start the game up again with his mouse.

DCI Bridges was back in his office, on the phone, and a stack of papers lay in front of him. Jo wondered if her results were in the pile. It had been a fortnight since she'd undergone the half-day assessment for a Detective Inspector position, and she knew she'd done pretty well in the role play and interview board sections. It would likely come down to the written test result, and that was harder to judge. Bridges maybe knew already, and was just waiting for the right moment to tell her.

Jo checked her emails. Some phone records had come through in relation to a drug-trafficking investigation they were doing in Snow Hill, as well as a few CCTV files on a burglary carried out on a machine-hire warehouse out west. She saw someone called Heidi Tan from Thames Valley had already started forwarding her the entire contents of the Dylan Jones file in batches of scans, and added her to the distribution list on the case. *Efficient.*

Jo opened up the first few in no particular order. Most of it was clearly written on a typewriter, but there were some handwritten pages also. Witness statements, photos of Dylan, of Matthews, interviews. There was a recording of the original 999 call. She placed on her headphones.

'*What's the nature of your emergency?*'

'*A boy's gone missing. From the circus. I think he was kidnapped.*'

Hearing her brother's voice, raw and inflected with the accent of their youth, was shocking.

'*You're calling from Home Farm, Yarnton, is that correct?*'

'*Er, yeah, I think so?*'

'*And can I take your name?*'

'*Paul Masters . . . I ran here. Can you send someone?*'

'*A car has already been dispatched. The boy who's disappeared – can you tell me where he was last seen?*'

'*I don't know. At the circus. My sister—*'

'Detective?'

Jo looked up. Bridges was standing over her.

'Can I have a word?'

'Doesn't sound good,' said Jo.

Bridges wasn't giving anything away.

'In my office in five?'

Not good at all.

'Sure.'

She took a deep breath. Rob Bridges was a good bloke, and she trusted him to be straight with her whatever. He was an odd one in the force, having had a career in finance before making the switch to law enforcement. Somehow he'd risen fast, and now, mid-forties, had moved across from the economic unit into CID. It was he who'd suggested she go for the promotion in the first place, and she knew that if it came down to it, he personally would vouch for her. Though if she'd failed the test, no amount of senior support would push her past the post.

She turned back to the files, opening up the arrest details for Clement Matthews. The mugshot showed a pudgy man with curly dark hair. Clean-shaven. He looked bored, sleepy, with an edge of defiance in the way he stared down the lens. Jo resisted searching for her eight-year-old self's statement in the interview files. There was a picture of a Liverpool football shirt, said to be the equivalent of the one Dylan was wearing, a 1987 season with the Crown Paints logo in yellow. Jo felt a wave of sadness at the thought of the rag holding together the remains, caked in soil and other debris that would probably never be washed out. The shirt was what she remembered most about Dylan, the thing that had caught her envious eye that day at the fair.

Jo was about to close the picture when a thought arose.

Why leave just the shirt? Why not the other clothes? Underwear, socks, trousers? If you were covering your tracks, why not get rid of everything? She fired a quick email to the Salisbury lab, copying Ben, to see if they'd found anything else. It might simply be that the other clothes had become separated with the decomposition.

She left the computer and crossed the banks of desks towards Bridges' office. He'd left the door open and she knocked, then went inside.

'You may as well close it,' he said.

Jo did so, a sinking feeling in her stomach. Definitely bad news. She braced herself.

'Is everything all right between you and DI Coombs?' said Bridges.

'How do you mean, sir?'

'Humour me,' said Bridges. 'I let the relationship slide, because it hasn't affected your work, and to be honest, I don't want to stick my nose in. But if your personal life affects operations here, that becomes a problem.'

'Has he said something?' asked Jo, aware that she was being evasive.

'No,' said Bridges. 'And I haven't asked him yet. But I'm beginning to think I should.'

'We're not together any more,' said Jo, as flatly as she could manage, and she felt suddenly angry not just towards Ben, but towards Bridges too. *Why should I be saying all this? Ben's the lying sack of shit who got us into this mess. He's the one who flushed our entire fucking future down the drain.*

Bridges steepled his fingers. 'I thought as much. Okay, Jo, I'm taking you off the Dylan Jones case from this moment.'

'But, boss . . .'

'Surely you can see why. We're going to get a lot of attention on this. I can't let the investigation be compromised.'

'It won't be. Look, talk to Ben. He'll tell you—'

'The decision is made, sergeant. Follow up on the Thompson gang surveillance. Pass anything on Dylan Jones to Ben.'

'This is—'

'A done deal. Thanks Jo.'

Jo returned to her desk, fuming. She should have been grateful. The chances of identifying a suspect would be small, and in every likelihood whoever buried Dylan was dead anyway. It was the injustice that burned. The sense of powerlessness. She'd done nothing wrong.

And, in the back of her mind, there was disappointment. She wasn't sure about there being a *poetry* to her involvement, but she couldn't argue there was a kind of circularity. Ben and Bridges had taken away any chance she had to see the case through. To make amends.

The emails were still coming in from Thames Valley. She hovered the mouse over the delete button, ready to consign the case files to her Trash. *So much for making amends.*

Then her phone rang. An Oxford number.

She answered.

'What did you tell them?' said a man's angry voice.

'I'm sorry, who is this?'

'She was here, just now. *You* must have told them!'

In the background, Jo heard another voice. 'Calm down, Gordon. Please.'

Mrs Jones.

'I'll be making a formal complaint,' said Mr Jones. 'You come round here, pretending to be on our side. Dropping your little bomb and leaving us to pick up the pieces. This might just be a game to you . . .'

'Please, Mr Jones,' said Jo. 'Tell me what's happened. Has someone visited you?'

'A journalist. A fucking hack!' he said.

'*Gordon!*' came his wife's distant exclamation.

'Mr Jones, we didn't contact any journalists,' said Jo. 'Please, believe me. We're not sure how they've gotten hold of the news about Dylan.'

'Well, you're a detective, aren't you? How about you find out?'

The phone went dead.

Bridges, who'd obviously overheard, was standing in the doorway to his office.

'That sounded unpleasant.'

Jo rubbed her temples. Maybe she was better off out of the case after all. The *fucking hack* had to be the same woman who was at the building site. She'd thought it might have been one of the construction workers who'd sold the info for a few quid, but how had they made the link to Dylan Jones?

'I think we need to put out a statement to the press,' she said. 'The Joneses got doorstepped by a journo.'

Bridges nodded. 'Leave it with me,' he said. 'You're on the Thompson gang, remember?'

Chapter 3

Jo spent the next couple of hours piecing together the movements of the gang, cross-referencing the GPS from phone
records with on-the-ground surveillance reports from an under-
cover they had staying in the Snow Hill flats.

She had a voicemail from Bright Futures, and recognised the
receptionist's discreet tones before she remembered the name.
They wanted to know, politely, if she'd be able to call back in
to amend some paperwork, because there was a problem with
her bank details. Jo saved the message for later.

The Thompsons were three brothers, all with lengthy records
for theft, drugs and minor violence, but they never ended up
doing more than a few months at a time inside. It was thought
their network of mules, distributors and money men stretched
to about forty individuals, involving a complex series of drop-
offs and safe houses across the south of the city.

If Jo was honest, there wouldn't have been so much appetite
for the investigation if it weren't for a couple of deaths three
months earlier – two teens found stabbed in a burned-out car,
one of them a cousin of the Thompson brothers and the other
a known member of a rival gang. It looked like there might

be fractures in the family, and that meant a turf war was on the cards.

The intelligence was painstaking and boring beyond belief, but if they were ever going to build a case, it was completely essential. Most of the phones were anonymous burners, tossed every few days. The general consensus was that this was a case of identifying one of the middle rankers and bringing them in. Then, when they turned, everything above should fall like a game of Jenga. They didn't really care about the footmen – as Ben put it, they'd always find ways to get arrested another day. Eighty per cent of CID business came back to drugs, one way or another.

At about four p.m., Ben and Rhani came in. Through the glass, Jo saw them booking in an untidily dressed pensioner wearing low-slung tracksuit bottoms and a striped T-shirt that revealed his abdomen and had sweat patches under the armpits. His thinning wisps of hair were matted to his head, and from the droop in the left half of his face and a badly slanting shoulder, Jo guessed he'd suffered a stroke at some point. He was grotesquely fat, the years adding more folds under his neck and blubbery upper arms, but the disinterested, almost vacant way he surveyed the room gave him away as Clement Matthews.

They led him across to one of the interview rooms, before Rhani emerged again a couple of minutes later, making for the small kitchenette area and switching on the kettle.

'He saying much?' asked Jo.

'Wants a brief, sarge,' said Rhani. 'And a tea with four sugars.'

She made it quickly and carried it in.

Half an hour later, Samantha Gore, one of the duty solicitors, arrived and the clerk from the front desk showed her in too.

Jo waited a moment before heading to the AV suite where she could monitor the live feed to the interview room. Bridges had headed off for the day – some sort of meeting with the

Local Authority. His instructions about getting involved had been clear, but what he didn't know wouldn't hurt him.

Matthews cut a sorry figure, slouched in his chair. Sam Gore finished introducing herself for the tape, then Ben showed Matthews the photo of Dylan.

'I'm sure you remember this boy.'

Clement Matthews peered over and nodded.

'Can you speak up?'

'Yes.' His voice was slightly slurred. 'What's this all about?'

'You tell us,' said Ben.

Clement looked across at him with watery eyes, then at Sam, then shrugged. 'I'm not under arrest, am I? I can go if I want?'

'You're not under arrest at the moment, but how you co-operate now will affect our decision whether or not to re-arrest you at a future point.'

Ben next turned over a photo of the derelict house, and another of the drained pool.

'Recognise this place?'

Clement glanced down. 'Means nothing to me.'

'Have a closer look.'

The old man's eyes flicked down. 'Still nope.'

'Perhaps you could help my client with some more guidance as to what these images show,' Sam interjected.

Ben pointed to the second photo. 'That's where we found the body of Dylan Jones.'

Matthews seemed to wake up. 'You found him?'

'I'm afraid so. You should have buried him deeper.'

Clement Matthews chuckled. 'Is that all you've got? Jesus wept.'

He folded his arms and sat back.

'We've got forensics crawling all over the place,' said Ben. 'If there's even a hair there, we'll find it.'

'But at the moment?' said Matthews.

A pause.

'I should say,' said Sam, 'I'm failing to see any compelling evidence of Mr Matthews' involvement. He was acquitted of the abduction. The case collapsed. He came here today of his own free will.'

And from the way Ben clasped his hands on the table, almost in prayer, Jo knew he felt exactly the same way. He looked defeated, like the story he'd built was crumbling around him, and it was a gesture she was only too familiar with.

★　★　★

She'd found out by accident. Ben had been behaving weirdly for days. Not sleeping, drinking more heavily than usual. She'd thought it was work, stupidly, but then she'd checked the savings account and seen the truth. They'd been putting a bit away each month for three years to get the deposit together. Nearly thirty grand. And when she checked, the account was empty. Well, not quite. The balance was two quid something. She logged out and in again, but it was the same. Had to be a mistake. But when she viewed the recent transactions, her whole world dropped away. There were regular payments to a stock-trading website, a few thousand at a time. The last one was six days before.

Heart beating fast and fingertips tingling, she put the computer aside and tried to stay calm. All their money gone. Or maybe not. Perhaps it was sitting in another account still. He couldn't have lost it all. He wouldn't do that to her.

Ben had always been a recreational gambler. Fruit machines in the pub, sports events. It had been cool in the early days because he often won, and sometimes he won big. And when he did, he was generous with it. In their late twenties, two grand on a football accumulator had gone straight on a blow-out weekend in Copenhagen. Of course, the wins were easy to remember. They'd had one or two arguments, no more than squabbles really, when she thought he'd gone too far. It was normally after a loss, when he'd sulk for a few days, then she'd learn he'd placed another bet to try and recoup. She didn't get that – it reeked of desperation. And when she found a betting app on his phone, she'd put her foot down and demanded he delete it. He did so, but she'd suspected he'd reinstalled it not long afterwards. When they moved in together, in their first rented place, a condition had been that he stop gambling completely. Work had been crazy at the time, so there were plenty of other distractions.

In the days after she found he'd emptied the account, she watched him closely and the signs weren't good. He looked knackered and was only going through the motions at work. She checked his phone, and in his internet history found searches for short-term loans. She came close to confronting him, but something stopped her. She realised it was fear. Not of how he'd react, but of what his reaction would mean. If he really had lost everything, it was over. There was no way back. She couldn't help him, because he couldn't help himself. She flitted from anger, to pity, to despair.

One night she went out with a friend and got drunker than usual. When she returned home, she found Ben asleep. For the first time in weeks he looked at peace, his brow smooth, his breathing slow. He looked like he used to, and her body took over. She woke him and they made love wordlessly. Maybe it was the booze, or a part of her knowing it would be the last time. Afterwards, as she was about to bring up the unmentionable, he broke down and told her. He said he'd done something awful, but they could get through it. She let him talk, knowing they couldn't. She barely listened to his justifications, his retellings of the minutiae – the peaks and troughs of his early trading. She'd seen how the story ended already.

She'd packed her things and moved out the following day – one night in a B&B, then finding a place on Gumtree across the other side of the city. She could've kicked him out, and he would have gone, but she knew she couldn't afford the rent on her own and she couldn't bear the thought of being in any way beholden to Ben for financial support.

That was five months back. He'd given her the space she asked for. For the first few days, anyway. It was surreal at work, like a parallel world where nothing had happened. They even laughed and drank tea together in the canteen, but she found ways never to be alone with him for long. And she saw, in his furtive glances, that he was plotting something, and that in her every unguarded moment, he was watching her.

She still had a key to the old place they were renting, and went by to pick up a few more things a week or so after walking out. It was a tip – it looked like he'd been sleeping on the sofa, and the overflowing bin reeked. There was paperwork for a loan on the small dining table, and a crushed dent in one of the doors that must have been caused by his fist. After a flash of vestigial concern, Jo's mind turned to anger. What a fucking cliché. *And there goes our security deposit.*

She gathered her remaining clothes and left.

That night, as she sat in her bedsit, trying to work out her finances, he called, pissed out of his skull, and demanded to know why she'd been in *his* flat. She hung up straight away. He called and called, until she switched off her phone. Listening to his garbled messages the following day was brutal – the slow progression from alcohol-fuelled rage to conciliation and self-pity. She texted him, against her better judgement, at ten a.m., and told him to get some help. He didn't ring back.

Work became slightly more difficult after that. His senior ranking had always been something they joked about, but in the wake of the break-up, the joke soured completely. Ben

44

was never one for holding a grudge, and he didn't try to make her life difficult. It was quite the opposite. He went out of his way to alleviate her workload, even if it meant putting upon others. No one knew they'd split – at least, she hadn't spread the news – and Jo wondered if her colleagues noticed the shifting dynamic. It embarrassed her, made her feel like a child being looked after. If it was an attempt to ingratiate himself with her again, it could hardly have been less successful. When he put her forward for a commendation based on work on a burglary case, she confronted him outside the cell-loading bays.

'You need to stop this,' she'd said.

He'd looked bewildered. 'Stop what?'

'The commendation. All of it.'

He glanced over her shoulder.

'I don't know what you mean, sergeant. Your work was excellent.'

'Ben . . . please. I know we have to work together, but—'

'Sergeant . . .'

'Stop calling me that!' She realised she'd raised her voice, and when he next spoke it was very quiet in comparison, but slightly menacing too.

'This is what you wanted, isn't it? Purely professional. Well, that's how it's going to be.'

He walked away.

Another few days went by without incident, but then the texts began. *We need to talk. Can you call me? Can we talk later? I miss you. I can't bear this. Where are you staying?* She ignored them, and the calls too, usually late at night or first thing in the morning. More texts, sometimes disguised as practicalities: *Post for you. Where shall I send it?* and sometimes verging on accusatory – *Can't we be adults about this?*

Gradually, they wore her down. Maybe she *was* being childish.

Avoiding the issues. She decided to meet him for a drink, somewhere busy and neutral in the town centre.

'To clear the air,' he said, like they'd had a minor disagreement.

'To talk about where we go from here,' she'd replied.

He was there early, sitting at a corner table – he'd ordered her a cocktail. He'd dressed smartly, and as he arrived he tried to hug her awkwardly. Her heart sank as she smelled his aftershave. *He's still not getting it.*

He wanted to know where she was living, and when she wouldn't say, he took offence. He wasn't a *stalker*, he said. Jo knew that, she replied. She just needed her own space. He told her he was getting help, like she said. Gamblers Anonymous. She nodded, said she was glad for him, but it didn't change anything. He asked why she was being so combative. It was like she hated him, but she couldn't hate him. They'd been together for years. They loved each other. They'd almost had a child together.

And that was when she lost it.

'You're using *that* as some sort of bargaining tool?'

'No, I'm not. I—'

She leant across the table and spoke through gritted teeth. 'If we *did* have a baby, we'd struggle to afford nappies at the moment.'

He looked taken aback. 'I wouldn't have . . . I mean, if it had worked out, I never would have started.'

'I don't believe you,' she said. 'And you know what, I'm *glad* we never had to find out.'

That knocked him speechless for a minute or so and they sipped their drinks silently, two angry pugilists having a breather between rounds. The pregnancy a year before had been an uncalculated surprise that opened a future neither had planned for, but the subsequent miscarriage, right before the twelve-week scan, had hurt more than she'd expected. They'd agree to wait then until after they'd found a house before trying again. Life was suddenly full of opportunities.

Until he had thrown it all away.

She told him then and there, in no uncertain terms, that they were never ever getting back together. And she'd found Bright Futures online the following day.

* * *

The knot in her stomach grew tighter as she drove away from the city, following the signs to the pretty neighbouring village of Horton, with its single pub-cum-village-shop-and-post-office. For families with young kids it was ideal. Good schools, safe roads, countryside on the doorstep. For Jo, growing up car-less, it had felt like the back of beyond. She remembered vividly the feeling of relief as she'd left for uni at eighteen, swearing to herself that she'd never come back. Her dad had actually cried on the doorstep – *he* knew. Her mum had waved her away with a cheery smile. Perhaps she had known too. They'd never had the best of relationships.

Jo pulled off onto Blenheim Road, where the houses were all discreetly distanced from one another, with names rather than numbers. At the one called 'The Rookery', she turned up the gravel drive. The front of the house was already filled with cars. Her brother had painted the door red over the old blue, but otherwise the family home was just the same – externally, at least.

Paul, his wife Amelia and the kids had moved in after Dad died suddenly. It had happened without much discussion – they'd been thinking of moving to somewhere bigger anyway and it made sense while they found the right place. Jo was grateful at the time, too, because she had just transferred to

Bath, and there was no way she could make the commute and be there for her mother as well. Amelia had been thinking about going back to work as a teacher, but she put it on hold.

Paul's theory was that having family at hand and her grandkids running around would help their mum, but it hadn't. Stella was lost without her partner of forty-five years. First it was a series of falls, after which they made some changes to the downstairs to give her a room on the ground floor. Then her mind began to suffer as well. Paul's youngest, Will, was only three at the time, and thought it was all quite funny, but Emma, then eleven, started to find Gran frightening. She started wandering around at night too. Paul and Amelia took the decision to move her to a residential home. They'd never asked Jo for money, thank goodness, but as far as she knew they didn't have any mortgage or rent either. It had worked out pretty well for her brother.

Not for the first time, she wondered guiltily what would happen when her mum died. The house must be worth close to a million quid.

There were lights on across the ground floor, and as she walked up carrying the hatbox, she felt like a teenager again, sneaking back after a night out. Growing up, she'd hated the remoteness of the place, envying her friends who lived within walking distance of the city centre. At sixteen, her parents had finally given in and let her head into the city on a Friday night, with strict instructions to get the last bus home. She remembered once how she'd forgotten her key, and rather than wake up her parents, she'd climbed the drainpipe onto one of the front bays, then opened the sash window from outside to get back into her bedroom.

She rang the bell. On the other side of the door, she heard the laughter of adults and the shrieking of children. No one came. She thought about ringing again, but decided to go around the back instead. She passed the bins, reached over the side gate and pulled back the bolt.

'Hey!' a figure jumped back. 'Oh, it's you!'

Jo couldn't see the cigarette but she could smell it, and it set off a pang, even though she hadn't touched one for years. Her niece stood in the darkness of the side passage, illuminated only by the faint light from her phone's screen.

'Hi Em.'

'Why didn't you go through the front?'

'No one answered.' She saw the dying embers of a fag butt. 'Would it help to tell you those things will kill you?'

'Please don't tell Mum.'

'I'm sure she knows already.'

'I doubt it,' said Emma sulkily. She was taller than Jo already, even though she was only fifteen. 'Ben not with you?'

'He couldn't make it.' She wasn't even close to being able to tell her family. Ben had charmed them all from the start, like he did with everyone.

Emma pointed further down the passage. 'Oh, well – the fun's all round the back.'

There were people spilling out from a set of bifold doors. Paul and Amelia had redone the kitchen, she saw – extending it out another few metres with a glass-roofed orangery arrangement. It must have cost a fortune. Their guests, all effortlessly cool forty-somethings, were drinking from champagne glasses, lounging around a kitchen island and on outdoor furniture. Jo hated it already, but told herself to give it a chance.

William, her nephew, was charging past the legs of the adults, holding a very realistic Uzi machine gun. One of the guests was pretending to be shot, collapsing against a wall.

'How many times,' boomed Paul's voice. 'Stop killing people. The police will shut us down . . .' He caught sight of Jo and grinned. 'See, they're already here! Hi sis!'

William ran towards her and Jo put down the box and braced herself as the six-year-old leapt in the air. She caught him, but almost lost her footing.

'You weigh a tonne!' she gasped.

'Hi Auntie Jo,' he said.

Amelia wafted through the crowds, a glass in hand ready to give to Jo. 'Hello darling,' she said. 'Thanks for making the trip.'

'Wouldn't miss it,' said Jo. Amelia was hard not to like.

Paul was looking good.

'You've lost weight,' Jo said.

'He's doing a triathlon in September,' said Amelia. 'He'll be tapping you for sponsorship, so watch out.'

'I'm broke!' she said, managing a smile.

'I've given up cheese,' said Paul morosely. Then he pointed with his glass to the box. 'Is that for me?'

'I hope you like it,' said Jo.

Whether it was the booze or not, his face lit up when his eyes landed on the homburg, and he paraded the hat in front of his guests.

'You look like something out of le Carré!' said Amelia, laughing. William tried it on as well, to much amusement.

'Thanks sis!' said Paul, giving her a peck on the cheek. 'Actually, we could have done with you here a week ago. Car got broken into – they nicked my iPad. And my bloody squash racket of all things. Police didn't even come out and take prints!'

Jo could tell a few people were listening, so just said jovially, 'Sorry, bro – not my patch!'

She could have told them that the police force were suffering the deepest cuts since their inception, that manned stations were being phased out in all but the biggest towns, and that the few demoralised officers who did remain really couldn't give a shit about someone stupid enough to leave their iPad on display in their vehicle.

But that would probably sour the mood.

She'd never been great at small talk anyway, and less so when she was lagging several drinks behind the rest of the guests. So she drifted through the party. Several people professed intrigue about her line of work, declaring their own jobs intensely uninteresting, but when she offered few salacious details, she sensed their disappointment.

She sipped at a glass of champagne, feeling like a schoolgirl out of place at a disco. Amelia had offered her the bed in the spare room for the night, but she'd politely declined. It was weird enough just visiting for a few hours. She found the lounge had been renovated too. Gone was the old worn carpet, replaced by oak flooring and a plush Afghan rug. The furniture was leather and chrome. There were figurative daubs of paint on the walls instead of the conservative rustic watercolours her parents had favoured. She thought briefly of the stained sofa at the flat, with the numerous chips in the wallpaper. *How the fuck did I go so wrong?*

Eventually, she extracted herself through the back doors again, glad to be out in the warm evening air. The house's garden had always been her dad's pride and joy – dropping down towards a tributary of the River Cherwell at the bottom. Beyond, past a small orchard, the ground rose to abut the land of Cherry Tree Cottage, about two hundred metres away. Mrs Carruthers, Jo's former piano teacher, had once lived there with her husband. They were both surely dead now, or at least moved on. The evening light was failing as Jo made her way down the steps, away from the glare of the security light, under an overgrown trellis. Paul wasn't green-fingered at all, and there was something sad about the disarray.

The river had been fenced off, and Jo remembered Paul saying that Will had once had a bit of a scare down there, or perhaps it was one of his friends. It was a shame.

Jo climbed over, letting the chatter from the party fade into insignificance. There'd been newts and frogs down here when she was a girl. The ground was squelchy in places, but she reached the old beech tree, and saw to her astonishment that the swing was still there, hanging loose from one side.

She went further, using her phone as a torch, into ground that had always been a wilderness, where Dad had chucked the grass shavings and prunings to rot down into compost. Where, as a girl, she'd made up silly games about beautiful fairies and goblin kings, borrowing the plots from the Enid Blyton books she'd voraciously consumed.

Bats swooped over the old barn opposite like flakes of black ash. Jo couldn't believe it was still standing too. It belonged to Cherry Tree Cottage, a relic from when the place was still a farm. As a girl, it had always scared her a little, sitting out there alone and abandoned, with its tiny shuttered windows. Mrs Carruthers said it was dangerous, close to falling down, and one wall was bowed a little.

Jo was about to turn round and head back to the party when the barn door opened suddenly, and a figure came out, hunched and walking with a stick. An arc of torchlight flashed across the ground. It couldn't be, could it?

'Mrs Carruthers?'

The old woman stopped suddenly, and turned towards Jo with her whole upper body, as if her spine and hips were welded together.

'Hello there? Who's that?'

'It's me – Josephine,' she called.

'Oh my!' said the old lady. She had something in her other hand that looked like a tin can. 'Is that really you, Josie?'

Jo could have cried, so powerful was the wave of nostalgia that washed over her. How long had it been? Twenty years at least. She hadn't seen Mrs Carruthers since the day she'd moved out to uni.

The old woman hobbled across to her, over the uneven ground, still clutching the can in one hand and the torch in the other.

'No, stay there!' said Jo. She hurried over herself, the dewy grass soaking her feet. She shielded her eyes as she got close, until the beam dropped. She saw a fork sticking out of the top of the can and smelt something that might have been cat food. She remembered a little tabby brushing against her ankles by the pedals during her lessons, but that was long ago.

'Let me look at you,' the older woman said, peering awkwardly from under a bowed back. She was wearing a blouse and baggy cardigan, and wellington boots. Her wrists were narrow, her fingers knotted. Under her thin white hair, her face was painfully gaunt; her once sparkly blue eyes looked silvery pale like a winter sky.

'Goodness,' she said. 'All grown up.'

'My brother's having a birthday party,' said Jo, and as she said it she realised it sounded a bit silly, like there'd be jelly and ice cream.

'I see them from time to time,' she said. 'He's got two bonnie children, hasn't he?'

'That's right. Emma's fifteen, William's six.' She frowned at the dish. 'What are you doing out there, Mrs Carruthers?'

'Oh, do call me Sally,' said the old woman. 'It's my cat Timmy. He's turned quite feral since Mr Carruthers passed away. Lives in the old barn, won't come in the house.'

'I'm sorry to hear about your husband,' said Jo. In truth, she barely remembered Mr Carruthers. He'd been a large, taciturn presence at the best of times, drifting about, always doing indeterminate jobs. He'd used the barn as a workshop of some sort.

'Don't be,' said Sally, with a toss of her head. 'He was ready to go.' She reached across and touched Jo's arm. 'Now how's your practice coming along?'

The question threw Jo. 'I'm sorry?'

'Your piano!' said Sally.

'Oh, I'm afraid I don't play any more,' said Jo.

Mrs Carruthers wore a look of mock indignation. 'But you were such a talent!'

'I bet you say that to all your students.'

Sally Carruthers chuckled conspiratorially. 'Quite the opposite actually. But really, you've given up completely?'

Jo felt like she was letting her old teacher down. She'd had lessons weekly from the age of six through to eleven with Mrs Carruthers, rising to grade seven just before her twelfth birthday. It had been her parents' idea at first, though she'd quickly taken to it, playing for hours on the old hand-me-down her dad had found at a house sale. But after that, with secondary school and other distractions, the practice had started to slip. The piano had been passed on to cousins in Wiltshire. If she could talk to her teenage self now, she'd give her a firm telling-off.

'I'm afraid so. I haven't touched a keyboard for years.'

'I'm much the same, though not through choice,' said Sally Carruthers. She held up her twig-like fingers. The joints were swollen and misshaped. 'I can barely manage my own buttons these days.'

Jo wondered exactly how old Mrs Carruthers was. Pushing eighty, in all likelihood.

'Would you like to come and say hello to Paul?' she said on the spur of the moment. 'I'm sure he'd like to see you.'

As soon as she said it, she realised it would be next to impossible for the bent old woman to make it over the fence and back up the garden path.

'Ha!' said Sally. 'I'm too old for parties now. But you must drop in and see me. I'm in most of the time. Just find me in the phone book.'

'I will!' said Jo, and she meant it. Though she'd have to locate a phone book first. There was probably one in a drawer some-where at the station.

'Right, I must go and dispose of this,' said Sally, brandishing the can.

'Okay – see you soon,' said Jo.

She watched the old woman walk up the rutted path towards her house. Jo headed the other way, back through the garden, feeling lighter in her heart than she had for days. If she closed her eyes, she knew she'd be able to remember the exact lavender scent of the morning room in Cherry Tree Cottage as she played the piano under her tutor's watchful eye.

She didn't go back into the kitchen, but instead took the side gate again, climbing into her car. Perhaps leaving without saying goodbye was childish, but they wouldn't miss her. The music inside was louder, and she really didn't want to see Paul's dancing. She was starting the engine when her phone rang. Bridges. She grinned, for some reason sure it was about the promotion. Maybe he felt bad about taking her off the Jones case earlier. There was no other reason for the late-night call and she wasn't due on shift for another three days.

'Are you still in Oxford?' he said straight away.

'Yes, just leaving actually.'

'Well, don't,' he said. 'I've just had a call about a possible kidnap.'

'In Oxford?'

'From a circus in Port Meadow. A kid's been snatched.'

The mention of a circus gave her a moment's pause, but she regained her composure quickly. 'Okay, I'm close.'

'Jo – you're not going to believe this.' Bridges sounded much more animated than normal. 'It was a clown.'

Chapter 4

Jo drove quickly, trying to stay focused on the task in hand. But memories kept rearing up unbidden – the same roads she'd cycled along as a girl, past the houses once occupied by her friends, the pubs she'd drunk in on fake IDs, the alleyway off Walton Street where she'd had a forgettable encounter with Dave Philips. Or was it Mark Philips? Not that it mattered now. In front of the University Press, she heard her first siren, and a car sped past going in the same direction. Then another. Drinkers gathered outside the bars watching the blue lights streak by.

There were signs for the circus too – in town for one night only. Jo knew where she was going without them, and took a left on the way out of Jericho, past the tall student townhouses, over the canal. Port Meadow was a large expanse of farmland spreading right out to the city's limits, and bisected by a tributary of the River Thames. The first set of gates had been opened up to allow for parking. Two police cars were stationed either side, lights spinning, with officers stopping the queue of exiting vehicles. Jo pulled up just across the bridge, and a uniform came up to the window with a torch angled right in her face. Jo wound the window down.

'You'll have to go back,' he said. 'We've got an emergency situation here.'

Jo flashed her badge. 'I'm Detective Masters from Avon and Somerset,' she said. 'Who's in charge?'

'Sorry, ma'am,' said the uniform, angling the torch away. Out of its dazzle, Jo saw he was really young – maybe not even twenty-five. 'It's DCI Stratton from Thames Valley. He's on site somewhere, talking to the witnesses.'

'And DS Carrick? Is he here?'

'He's about, yes. I'm afraid I don't know where.'

Jo climbed out and locked up, then started towards the meadow. Beyond the cars she could see the garish lights of the circus rides.

It's just a coincidence. Has to be.

'We've got checks on all the exit roads,' said the uniform, 'Wolvercote, Binsey, Godstow, the canal towpath, and the bridges that cross the river.'

Jo greeted the other uniforms on the gates. They were opening the boot of an estate car, with two excited-looking kids in the back.

It's too late for that now, thought Jo.

She showed her ID again to the uniforms, and went through the gates. Carrick was talking to some men in high-vis jackets from a company called Securitex, who looked like they hadn't signed up for anything like this.

'. . . no detail is insignificant.' He handed them cards. 'I'll need a full list of personnel from your supervisor. You got that?'

He saw Jo, registered surprise, and beckoned her over.

'I was only in Horton,' she said. 'My gaffer said the suspect was dressed as a clown.'

'Weird, isn't it?'

'I guess so,' she said non-committally. 'What's the timeline?'

Carrick took out his notebook. 'We got the call at 9.43 p.m. Witnesses estimate the boy was taken at 8.30.'

'What took them so long to make the call?'

'Beats me.'

'You said witnesses plural?'

'Stratton's got them in a temporary office,' said Carrick, pointing across the site to a cabin a couple of hundred yards away. 'Kids. Hard to get much sense out of them. Looks like there was some sort of altercation. A lad called Niall McDonagh, eleven years old, got taken from somewhere over by the water at knifepoint. One of his friends was assaulted.'

'How bad?'

'Walking wounded.'

'And the suspect?'

'We're putting together a profile. The kids are all pretty spooked, as you can imagine. Doesn't help that they've been smoking weed. Most of them think he was middle-aged at least, from the voice and posture. But he was wearing a mask and wig, so we don't have much to go on.'

'You think he worked here?'

'Who knows? He was in jeans and a fleece.'

'Image of the missing kid?'

Carrick took out his phone. 'It's been shared electronically from one of his friends with all officers in Thames Valley and other agencies.'

Jo peered at the screen, which showed what looked like a selfie of a boy wearing a green rugby shirt with the collar up. He had spiky dark hair, a button nose and owl-like brown eyes and was staring moodily into the camera.

'He's only eleven?' said Jo. 'Looks older.'

'We'll be getting more images from the parents. Car's gone to pick them up and take them to the station.'

As Jo left Carrick and headed across to the office, she found she was quite calm. A dozen explanations were swimming through her head, but none of them involved a clown from three decades before, miraculously making a reappearance the very day his former victim was unearthed. The most likely seemed to be a low-level drug deal that had gone south. Maybe Niall and his friend tried to take the product without paying, or maybe someone else had stumbled on the transaction and things had gotten out of hand. The fact the suspect was in a mask, not made-up, suggested someone just trying to stay incognito, rather than an actual clown. Not that any of these circumstances made the situation trivial. The first hour after an abduction was always the most crucial, and that window had been and gone. Every second that passed made the outcome less promising.

The circus site was almost entirely emptied out, with a few workers standing around idly or picking up rubbish. Jo was surprised Stratton was letting that happen – who knew what evidence might be getting dumped along with the drinks cans and sweet wrappers. There were plenty of coppers too, moving between the rides and checking underneath or round the back.

Beyond the fairground was the river, but metal fencing had been set up along the banks. Across the other side, Jo knew, were miles of fields, crisscrossed by the odd country lane and footpath. If it was a genuine kidnap, there were a dozen places a car could have been parked and driven away. The roadblocks and checkpoints were probably useless by now.

The door to the office was open, with another uniform at the bottom of a set of metal steps. Jo showed her badge and asked to speak to Stratton, then waited while the officer went inside. He waved her in a moment later.

The place stank of marijuana, and three sorry-looking teenagers – two girls and a boy – were sitting side by side on a sofa. A fourth, another male, perhaps fifteen years old – was seated on a desk chair, wrapped in a silver thermal blanket while a paramedic bandaged his head. Jo took them in quickly with a sweep of the eyes. Expensively dressed – labels on clothes and shoes.

Three white, one Asian. The older of the girls had her hair swept up in an artfully blonde mess, the other wore some sort of beanie. She had a flush across her cheekbones that suggested she'd spent the day in the sunshine. The other girl was in tears.

Chief Inspector Stratton was in uniform, still wearing a cap. His face wore an impatient scowl.

On the table, between Stratton and the kids, was a mobile phone, and everyone, apart from the paramedic, was looking at it.

'Sir,' said Jo. 'DS Masters, Avon and Somerset. DCI Bridges sent me over.'

'Thanks for coming,' he said. Stratton glanced across at her. 'We've put in a request with the network to track Niall's phone. They should be back with us in the next few minutes.'

'Any more contact?'

'We had three messages altogether.'

'From Niall?'

Stratton nodded, and Jo gestured to the phone. 'May I?'

'Go ahead.'

Jo picked up the phone – a newer model than her own. It was locked, but the boy getting his head looked at mumbled, 'Ten twelve zero four', and Jo typed in the numbers. The texts were right there.

> *He's got me. Shit. In his car.*
>> *U serious? Call police.*
> *He'll hear. Scared.*
>> *Ive called police. Mate?*
>> *M8?*
> *We've stopped.*
>> *Where are u?*
>> *M8?*
>> *Ny?*

Jo checked the time of the last message – half an hour ago. She placed the phone back down on the table.

'Where did the assault happen?' she asked.

The bandaged boy hugged the blanket around himself. 'Down by the river path. There's a boathouse.'

He was well spoken. Privately schooled, she'd have bet. Face like the member of a boy-band she couldn't recall the name of – handsome, square-jawed and unblemished. These weren't your usual townie delinquents. As a girl, Jo would have found them intimidating. Oddly, despite her age, part of her still did.

'What's your name?'

'Art.'

Was he being difficult on purpose? 'Your full name.'

'Arthur Price.'

'Tell me exactly what happened, Arthur.'

'I've already told three of you,' said the boy. 'Shouldn't you be out looking for him?'

'You haven't told *me*.'

The boy looked at her, a look she'd seen a thousand times, and from kids even younger than this one. Contempt.

'We went over the bridge, me and Ny.'

'Why?'

'Why not?'

Jo was looking at him, but she could feel the others were suddenly more alert.

'Okay, Art. And then what happened?'

The boy shrugged. 'This guy comes up, dressed in a mask. He asks us for a fag. I say no. He hits me, and then pulls a knife. He tells Niall to come with him.'

'And you didn't know him? Never met him before?'

Art shook his head.

'You seem very sure. Skunk's terrible for the memory, you know.'

'What are you talking about?'

'Well, you all saw him, right? That's what you told my colleague. Did you all go over the bridge?'

Art blushed. 'Who said that?'

Jo smiled. 'Listen, Art. All of you. Your friend's gone missing, and if you're telling even half the truth, he could be in danger.' She sat on the table and focused on the girl who'd finally stopped crying. 'If there's more to this, now is the time to let us know. We don't care what you were doing—'

'We weren't doing anything,' said Art.

'So how come it took you over an hour to call us?'

They shot furtive glances at one another, but it was Art who spoke up. 'We weren't *doing* anything.'

'And we *don't care*,' repeated Jo. 'But it sounds like Niall's in a lot of trouble at the moment. I think you know more about this clown than you're letting on.'

The crying girl caught her eye and looked away quickly.

'If Niall ends up being hurt, and we find that you've lied to us now, it could be worse for you. Isn't that right, guv?'

Stratton, his arms folded, nodded.

The kids were all quiet.

'Okay, gang,' said Jo, standing up. 'We'll need numbers for all your parents or guardians. They'll be picking you up from the station and you'll all be cautioned for possession of a Class C drug—'

'No!' said the boy sandwiched between the girls. 'You can't!'

'Doing my job,' said Jo. She took out a notebook, and pen. 'You first.'

'Please, don't!' said the tear-streaked English rose. 'Art, just tell her!'

'Shut the fuck up, Eve.'

'Tell her or I will.'

Art was stony-faced.

Jo reached out and touched Eve's hand. Cold fingers, chipped aquamarine nails. 'Help us,' she said, 'so we can help Niall.'

Eve sniffed. 'He said he had some pills,' she said quietly.

Now we're getting somewhere.

'The man in the mask?' interrupted Stratton.

Eve nodded. 'Niall and Art went with him.'

Art was shaking his head, but Jo stood up and walked across the room towards him. He flinched back in the chair.

'This really is your last chance,' said Jo. 'Tell me *exactly* what happened, or I'll arrest you for obstruction of justice as well, and it'll be a lot more than a slap on the wrists.'

Art's eyes were everywhere but on her. 'He took us round a boatyard. Said the stuff was in his car.'

'You saw his car?'

'No. I was on the ground.'

'But you saw him take Niall away?'

Art nodded, his breathing a little panicked. 'He had a knife, a little one, under Niall's neck. They just walked off.'

Jo let it sink in. It didn't make a lot of sense to her.

'Did you try to steal something from him – take his pills without paying?'

Art shook his head.

'Did he take your money?'

'Niall had it,' said Art. 'In his sock.'

A knock on the door, and Carrick stuck his head in. 'Parents are on the way to the station,' he said. 'Ten minutes out.'

Stratton picked up his coat from the back of the chair and Jo went with him to the door. Outside, they spoke in low voices.

'Andy, go back to the station. I'll stay here and co-ordinate. Jo, good work in there. See if you can get anything else out of them. Anything relevant, keep in touch.'

'Yes, boss,' said Carrick.

'Sure thing,' said Jo.

Carrick stalked off towards the exit, past the snaking queue of cars. The vehicle searches would take hours.

'First impressions?' asked Stratton.

'Drug deal went south,' said Jo. 'They know the perp, and they owe money. They didn't call the police straight away because they were scared. Can you dig around and find out who might be dealing here?'

'I'll get Heidi Tan on it,' said Stratton. 'That's her world. Can you stick around? Till this is done, we could do with all hands on deck.'

Jo wondered what she could really do. She had the Thompson gang intelligence to sift through back in Bath. Plus, she wanted to be close to the Dylan Jones investigation, even if not formally involved, and she was sure this wasn't connected, despite the surface similarity.

'Not sure what my gaffer will say,' she said.

'It's Rob Bridges, right? Let me talk to him – we got some history.'

'Yes, sir. I might take a look at the boatyard, if that's all right? Take the kid with me?'

'Go ahead.'

Stratton went back towards the main gates and Jo put her head back in the door of the office.

'Can I borrow Art?' she asked the paramedic.

'He's taken a knock,' replied the young man, slightly disdainfully. 'We can't rule out—'

'Up you get,' said Jo, beckoning Art over. 'I need you to go over exactly what happened.'

Art pushed himself to his feet and followed her.

They crossed the site towards the river and the bridge. Jo flicked on her pocket torch.

'Have you known Niall long?' said Jo, keeping the tone light.

'He's my mate's little brother,' said Art. 'Our parents are friends.'

'And this sort of thing is out of character?'

'Getting kidnapped?' deadpanned Art. 'Yeah, I reckon.'

'The drugs, smart-arse,' said Jo.

'Dunno.' They crossed a bridge, passed a couple more uniformed officers with torches, and Art pointed right along a path. 'That way.'

'I don't really care what you were up to,' said Jo. 'I just need to know what's really going on here.'

'I've told you,' said Art sulkily.

'I hope for your sake you have.'

The boatyard was cast in deep shadow as she ran the torch over it. A dilapidated chain-link fence was leaning in sections, and inside were several dinghies covered with tarps, as well as a rack of canoes, plus an ancient Land Rover with a trailer attached. Two large sheds at the back, shuttered with metal grilles.

'Show me where it happened,' said Jo.

Art led her past the side of the fence, along a narrow path of caked mud under the shelter of overhanging trees. It was all perfectly hidden from view. At the far side, a tarmac single track led to the boathouse between hedges. Jo calculated the track would emerge in the Marston area. Beyond that, the bypass. Open road.

Art stopped. 'Right here,' he said.

There was no light here, and Jo took out her torch, shining it across the ground. Not so much as a scrap of litter. The grassy verge by the road was worn down, presumably where cars turned in front of the boathouse gate.

'Tell me again what happened.'

Art rubbed the back of his neck. 'We were walking ahead. He hit me. I fell – here.' He pointed at the ground.

She looked up the lane. 'And he took Niall this way?'

Art nodded.

'Did you hear a car?'

'I don't think so.'

'And you couldn't get up – why?'

'I told you. He hit me.'

'So how long were you on the ground?'

Niall shrugged. 'I don't know. Twenty seconds.'

'And then?'

'I got up. I went back.'

'You didn't go after Niall?'

Art stared at her, hard. 'No.'

Jo frowned. 'Why?'

Art swallowed, lip trembling. 'I was scared, all right?' He began to cry. 'I wanted to. He had a knife. Fuck – Niall looked so fucking scared.'

'It's all right,' said Jo. 'I'd be scared too.' She pointed at a tree stump. 'Wait there.'

She walked up the lane, torch lighting the way ahead. Arthur Price might be lying to her, but she thought not. He'd probably sprinted back to his mates as fast as his legs would carry him. And part of her was glad. At least they weren't dealing with a kid dead from a knife wound.

About fifty yards up she found a layby, with a gate to a field that was locked. If the kidnapper had a car, this was where he must have parked. A brief inspection showed nothing, but forensics could comb it. She went to the gate and climbed a few rungs to look over the hedges. The lights of houses twinkled about a quarter of a mile away. It might be worth talking to the owners. The road couldn't get a lot of traffic and someone might have seen something.

As she was getting down, she saw a tiny speck of red on the end gatepost, which had buckled slightly. Maybe a piece of poor manoeuvring?

Jo turned back, mind playing over the possibilities. If it was a dealer, this wasn't a bad place to park up. Out of sight, easy access. But that didn't really add up with the overgrown path. You couldn't stumble on it. Whoever used it knew the area very well, and Port Meadow didn't scream gang territory.

If you were a planning a kidnap, however, it made perfect sense. Quick exit, no witnesses.

She headed back, uneasy.

Chapter 5

Jo had never been in St Aldates police station before, but when she arrived it was exactly like every other city station at eleven p.m. on a Friday night. A squad vehicle in the car park, unloading a couple of drunks, one clutching a bloody tissue to his mouth. A steady flow of uniformed pairs coming in and out of the back exit. The waiting room was full, the custody sergeant looked harassed and someone was banging on a cell door demanding to be let out.

She showed her badge, signed in, and followed the sergeant's directions through the communal area, down a corridor to the CID office. A slight, Asian officer in plain clothes had a phone clamped between her shoulder and ear while tapping on a keyboard, and a swarthy athletic-looking man in cycling gear emerged from a side room with a bicycle helmet over his arm and two mugs of tea in his hands.

'Hello?' he said.

'Jo Masters, Avon and Somerset,' said Jo, holding out her hand. 'I'm helping on the McDonagh case.'

The cyclist put down the two mugs and shook her hand.

'George Dimitriou. Call me Dimi. They dragged me in too. Seems like an overreaction.'

'Let's hope so,' said the Asian woman, coming off the phone. 'Heidi Tan. Nice to meet you face to face.'

Jo had already spoken to Tan on the way over about the paint chips on the gate and the houses up the road from the crime scene.

'Is Detective Carrick here?' asked Jo. 'I'm supposed to co-ordinate with him.'

Tan had taken a mug and gestured to an interview room with it before sipping. 'He's got the parents in Room 2.'

'May I?' said Jo, heading over.

'Knock yourself out,' said Tan.

Jo knocked and entered. Carrick was sitting across from two understandably worried-looking forty-somethings. The man was pacing back and forth, and the woman clutched a handkerchief like it was the only thing keeping her sane. Both well-dressed – Mr McDonagh had a corduroy jacket and a knitted green tie over a checked shirt. Greying at the temples, his hair was a luxuriantly artful sweep. He was clean-shaven, with a small cleft in his chin. He looked like Richard Burton. Two untouched mugs of coffee sat in front of them, and an assortment of photos lay on the table, some still in picture frames.

'Can't you track his phone?' said Mr McDonagh. 'He's never off the bloody thing.'

'We're working on that,' said Carrick. 'What we need from you now is a list of family members who live locally. And any adults that Niall regularly comes into contact with.' He looked over his shoulder. 'This is Detective Masters. She's been drafted in from another force to help with the search as well. Jo – this is Professor Anthony McDonagh and his wife, Brigitte.'

The man stopped pacing and stood with his arms akimbo

before coming forward and offering his hand. He towered over her, and she received the impression of a former sportsman – a rower, or a rugby player. They shook hands – his were massive, the skin rough.

Jo offered a hand to his wife as well. 'Mrs McDonagh.'

'Doctor, actually,' said the woman. On closer inspection, she looked to be in her early fifties – she must have had her children late – with blonde hair turning to grey in the bouffant style of an eighties news anchor, slightly misshapen as though she'd been woken from sleep. She wore a stylish long cardigan and tailored trousers. Her mascara was smudged around the eyes, and Jo wondered if she'd applied it just to come to the station.

Jo registered the correction with a smile. 'Apologies. You're both academics at the university?'

'Gloucester College,' said Mr McDonagh.

Jo passed a glance over the other photographs they'd brought. Family gatherings, a school uniform shot, one with an older boy who might have been the brother. Niall looked a little different in every one, but the large soulful eyes were a common thread – luminous and innocent.

'I just don't understand why anyone would take Niall,' said Mrs McDonagh. She dabbed her eyes. 'He's just a little boy. What do they want with him?'

'And you have another son?' said Jo.

'Yes,' said Mrs McDonagh. 'Kieran's fifteen. He's not well – glandular fever.'

'Want to bring me up to speed, boss?' said Jo.

'I've been over the basic facts as we know them,' said Carrick. 'It's very early to form any conclusions, and at this stage our priority – all our resources – are simply focused on locating Niall.'

'What resources are those?' said Mr McDonagh, waving a

70

hand at the door. 'There's a chap out there making tea looking like he's about to start the Tour de France.'

'Tony, they're doing everything they can,' said Mrs McDonagh. Mr McDonagh grunted and began to pace again.

Jo leaned in, speaking softly. 'I'm sure you've been over this already, but did Niall have any enemies?'

'He's eleven, detective,' said Mr McDonagh. 'When you have enemies at that age, they tend not to kidnap you.'

'Darling, Detective Masters is just trying to help,' said his wife.

Jo felt Carrick watching her. She guessed he hadn't mentioned the drug angle at all, but she wasn't going to beat around the bush.

'Did your son owe anyone money?'

Anthony McDonagh snorted. 'This has something to do with Arthur, doesn't it? I *knew* it. Where is that little brat, anyway? Have you rung Simon and Penelope?'

'They're his parents?' said Carrick.

'Nominally,' said Niall's father. 'Not that they do much actual parenting.'

'Arthur Price is friends with your eldest?' said Jo.

'Despite our best efforts. We never should have let Niall go out.'

'Is that something you would normally do?' asked Jo.

'What are you suggesting?' said Mrs McDonagh. 'That this is somehow our fault?'

'Not at all,' said Jo. 'I'm just trying to get a feel for his life-style.'

Anthony McDonagh reached over and laid a hand on the table, as if to placate the room.

'We wouldn't normally have allowed it,' he said. 'But we had a departmental dinner. We knew there would be some older, responsible children accompanying him.'

'Like Arthur Price?' said Carrick.

Jo glanced at him, surprised he would press like that.

'Has Arthur been in trouble before?' asked Jo hurriedly.

'He's been expelled from two schools already,' said Mrs McDonagh. 'Drugs.'

Now we're getting somewhere.

'We think there may be a drug connection to Niall's disappearance,' said Jo.

'Well, slow down,' said Mr McDonagh. 'Niall isn't into anything like that.'

'Of course not,' interrupted Carrick. 'What we're saying is that it may be he was in the wrong place at the wrong time.'

And carrying the money, thought Jo.

Mrs McDonagh scrunched the handkerchief more tightly. 'Oh God. Will they hurt him? They won't, will they?'

Jo wasn't sure what to say, but Carrick leant across the table and touched Niall's mother's hand.

'I doubt it very much. We're exploring every avenue. If this is drug-related, I'd anticipate we'll get Niall back very soon. It's a small world, and we have plenty of intelligence about the groups involved.'

'Thank you, detective,' muttered Mrs McDonagh. 'We just want him home.'

'Call Simon and Penelope,' said Mr McDonagh. 'Or get them in here. If that little shit . . .'

'Don't worry,' said Jo. 'We'll be talking to Arthur at length. He's been very helpful already.'

'If you wouldn't mind waiting here for a moment,' said Carrick. 'I'd like to talk to Detective Masters in private.'

As they left the room together, Anthony McDonagh had both hands on his wife's shoulders. Once the door was closed, Carrick raised an eyebrow at Jo.

'They're in denial, don't you think?'

'Isn't that a survival strategy if you're a parent? They're real-ising that their little angel might have a dark side.'

'I think we need to push a bit harder on the friends,' said Carrick. 'The older boy, especially.'

'Agreed,' said Jo. 'He wasn't saying much to me, but if we get his parents in the room too, he might open up.'

Heidi Tan came over. 'We've got officers over at Blackbird Leys, Cowley Road and Abingdon. They're knocking on doors, talking to the usual faces. Plus I've put out feelers to the regular crowd. Nothing so far, but someone will talk. We've sent uniforms to speak to the owners of the houses near the boatyard, and to cordon off the area. Forensics can't get there till three a.m.'

Which reminded Jo about the body site near Bradford. It was probably too early for much of an update there, but she wondered how Ben was faring with Clement Matthews.

'If you don't need me for anything else right now, I'd like to make a call?' she said to Carrick.

'Sure – take yourself off and get some sleep,' said Carrick. 'Front desk will help you find a hotel.'

Jo baulked to think how much a city-centre hotel would cost. She could claim it back, but the process took a few days. Of course, there was another option. No cost at all, at least not a financial one.

'Thanks, boss. I'll see you first thing.'

On the way back to the car, she called Bath, and got DC Rhani Aziz, who sounded chipper as always. *Give her a few more years . . .*

'Ben's mad,' she said. 'He had to let Matthews go.'

'I thought it was a long shot. Was there anything at all?'

'Nope. Either the guy's an amazing actor, or he's innocent. He actually fell asleep during questioning.'

'So what's next?'

'Carter's tried to get hold of Land Registry to find out the owners of the wreck, but they say they can't get into their offices to find the clients till Monday.'

Jo sighed. 'And Ben's okay with that?'

Carter was widely accepted to be the weakest member in the CID. He'd probably even admit it himself. With two ex-wives to support, he was happy to drift towards mandatory retirement.

'Not really, but he's been too busy with Matthews to sort it out himself.'

Jo stopped talking for a moment as Andy Carrick led the McDonaghs towards his car. Both of them looked shattered, and why not? It was every parent's worst night nightmare. Despite Carrick's calm professionalism, it must have been dawning on them, as the hours passed by, that they might not see their son again.

'What about the council?' she asked, once they were out of earshot.

'Same story. Have you ever known a council worker to put themselves out at the weekend?'

'Fair point.'

'Anything on your kidnap? Was it really a clown?'

'No,' said Jo, decisively. 'It was just someone in a mask. We think it's drug-related, probably just a scare tactic. Ten to one we have the kid back before dawn.'

'Oh good,' said Rhani. 'Bit creepy though, right? I never liked clowns.'

Jo managed a half-hearted laugh, suddenly back in the toilet cubicle at school.

'Killer Clown's coming.
What you gonna do?
He'll drag you into the woods
And cut you in two . . .'

*   ★   ★

The party was winding up when Jo pulled up outside Paul's house in Horton just after two in the morning and with the clear night the temperature had dropped considerably from the high twenties of the afternoon. What a bloody day! She'd have gone round the back again, but her brother was on the doorstep wishing a noisy farewell to a pair of guests. He was wearing his new hat.

'Sis!' he slurred. 'You're back!'

Jo took the overnight bag from her boot. She always kept one, just in case she ended up sleeping at the station, something which had happened more than once.

'Wondered if I could change my mind and take you up on that offer?' she said.

'Eh?'

Amelia appeared, looking distinctly more sober than her husband. 'Of course! The spare room's made up.'

'Sorry I had to dash away earlier,' said Jo. 'Work.'

'You missed my dancing,' said Paul. He gave her a bear hug as she tried to squeeze past through the door. 'Want a drink? I'm going to have a drink.'

'I think I'd better just get some sleep,' said Jo.

'I think we all should,' said Amelia, steering Paul back through the door and closing it. 'Someone's going to have a sore head in the morning.'

Paul reached up, took the brim of the hat, and frisbee'd it across the hallway, clearly unaware of how much it cost. He always was a good-natured drunk, like Dad.

'Good night, everyone,' said Jo. As she took herself up the stairs, she crossed the landing, and before she even thought about it, she'd pushed open a bedroom door. Emma squealed and leapt off the bed. Jo caught a flash of underwear and flesh, but nothing more.

'Oh, God! I'm sorry!' said Jo, backing out.

A second or two later, her niece opened the door. She was holding a dressing gown in front of her.

'You could have knocked! I was getting changed!'

'This used to be my room,' said Jo. 'I wasn't thinking.'

'No worries. Spare room's down the hall,' said Emma.

'Night. Sorry again.'

Jo remembered the guest bedroom well, but it had completely changed. Gone was the huge old porcelain sink in the corner, and the horrible wallpaper and dark curtains. It was cool, the sash window open a crack. Her brother's wife had redecorated in pale colours. Mum and Dad had used it as a bit of a junk room, but now it was almost empty apart from a bed and bureau. Discreet fitted wardrobes lined the wall. There was an en-suite too, where once a mahogany wardrobe had dominated. Jo placed her bag on the end of the bed and began to unpack.

Two texts came through in quick succession. Both from Ben. *You still up?* and *Can we talk?*

Jo ignored them. When was he going to get the message? She took out her wash kit, her nightclothes and her laptop. Someone knocked at the door.

'Come in.'

She expected Amelia with towels, but it was her niece, now dressed in a hoodie and jogging trousers.

'Auntie Jo,' she said. 'You're probably not allowed to talk about it, but do you know about a boy going missing tonight?'

Jo noticed the phone clutched in Emma's hand. *News travels fast.*

'Niall McDonagh?' she said. 'Yes. You know him?'

'His brother,' said Emma. 'Everyone's saying he's been kidnapped. Kieran's going mental. His parents won't tell him anything.'

Jo looked at her niece, saw for a moment the infant she

remembered like it was only yesterday, excited about the tooth fairy, and realised she didn't know *this* young woman at all.

'You're right – I can't really talk about it,' she said. 'It's too early to say what happened exactly. But if you hear anything, Emma, anything at all, please come and find me. Doesn't matter if it's day or night.'

Emma nodded. 'I will. Sleep well, Auntie Jo.'

'Just Jo,' she replied. 'Auntie makes me feel sixty years old.'

Emma grinned. 'Okay.' At the door, she paused. 'Oh, we're going to see Gran tomorrow, if you want to come?'

Mum. The home was in Kidlington, maybe twenty minutes away, and Jo hadn't been for longer than she liked to admit. Last time hadn't ended well.

'What time?' she said, stalling.

'Mid-morning.' Emma grinned. 'Depending on Dad's hang-over.'

'Em, I think I'll be too busy.' It was – conveniently – true.

'Okay, no problem. Just thought I'd ask.'

After she'd gone, Jo finished unpacking. She was about to undress when she realised the curtains were still open, staring blackly at her. She first closed the sash with a creak and a bang. Looking out over the garden, the only lights came from the back of Sally Carruthers' house, beyond the orchard in the distance.

Mum had always been a little funny with her piano teacher, and now Jo thought about it, perhaps it was because Jo had shown such obvious pleasure in going over to their neighbour's house. Mrs Carruthers was everything her own mother wasn't. Warm, open, musical. *Maternal.* After the lessons, Jo had often returned home with something Mrs Carruthers had baked for her. Sausage rolls, apricot tarts, apple turnovers. But searching her memory, Jo couldn't remember her mother ever actually trying any of them. And when Jo had finally chosen to forgo the piano lessons, it had been their father who tried to dissuade her. Her mother had accepted the decision without protest.

She couldn't be sure, but she thought she saw the old woman's silhouette moving inside the house. She lifted her hand in a half wave, before realising it was extremely unlikely that Mrs Carruthers could even see her from such a distance. But the figure did stop, looking out.

I really should make the effort, she thought. It must be terrible, being there alone, though almost as soon as she thought that, she realised her own situation wasn't so completely different. Two lonely women, staring into the dark night.

And at least Sally Carruthers has a cat . . .

She closed the curtains, checked her work phone for any news, and saw none.

Niall was still out there, somewhere. Six hours had passed since he went missing. And despite the money in the sock, the pills and the weed, his mother was right.

He was just a little boy.

Chapter 6

SATURDAY

In the dawn light, Oxford appeared slightly bare and post-apocalyptic. Jo felt bruised, and exhausted, having woken at intervals throughout the night to check her phone for updates. There was nothing and she wondered if, somewhere, Niall was awake too. Terrified. Missing his parents and praying they'd come to find him.

The street-cleaners were hard at work, sweeping up the detritus from the night before. No one had been awake at her brother's house, so Jo had washed, dressed and left without a word, making the bed as though she'd never even been there. In the kitchen, strewn with bottles and glasses and the smell of stale alcohol, she had quietly made a piece of toast and chosen to eat it in the car. The hat she'd bought Paul lay half-crushed and resting on top of a yucca tree by the bifold doors. She'd straightened it and left it on the counter.

She needed coffee, and found a mobile stall opening up just off George Street. Parking outside, she ordered an Americano. Normally she didn't take sugar, but she had a craving today, so poured in two sachets. As she was stirring it into the cup, her eyes fell on a stack of bound local papers outside the newsagents next door. Her hand froze at the headline.

KILLER CLOWN'S VICTIM UNEARTHED.

What the fuck? Already?

'Do you have any scissors?' she asked the man who'd made her coffee.

He looked at her like she was mad. Drink in hand, she went to the bundle, and crouched. In her ankle strap, she carried a utility knife, a gift from Ben on her thirtieth birthday. She slid the blade under the bindings and cut through, unfolding the top copy of the *Oxford Times*. The byline was someone called Rebekah Fitzwilliam – and though the name wasn't familiar, the image stirred her memory. The main picture of the article was the smiling school photo of Dylan Jones, the colours muted, as well as a smaller inset of a Liverpool FC shirt.

Jo took a reflexive sip of her coffee, scalding her mouth. *Dammit.* She felt sick inside. The story would hit the national press, surely. It couldn't be long before Dylan's parents found out about it.

As she got into the car, she called DCI Bridges back in Bath.

'To be expected, I guess. We're fielding calls, and working up a statement to play it down. It'll make the tabloids tomorrow, but hopefully not front page.'

'Any confirmation from forensics?' Jo asked.

'Not so far – there might be usable DNA, but it's too soon to tell. The age seems about right though. They're saying six to eight based on bone density and teeth.'

'And dental records?'

'Not yet. Family practice closed years ago. Files were probably destroyed.' He paused. 'Listen, I've got another call. Phil

80

Stratton says he could use you until this kid turns up, so no need to check in here. You're Thames Valley for the time being.'

Jo wasn't sure she liked his tone. It sounded a lot like a criticism.

'Fine,' she said.

As Bridges hung up, Jo wondered what Ben had said about the split. He and Rob had never been close, but they'd played golf together a couple of times. If it came to keeping one of them on, Ben was senior, so it wasn't going to be her. So much for the promotion prospects. She slammed the car door closed.

The station at St Aldates was quiet now too. The board said that only one cell remained occupied. The custody shift had changed over, so Jo had to identify herself to a new, tired-looking sergeant. Tan had gone, but Dimitriou was now dressed in trousers and a shirt, shaving with an electric trimmer over the bin at his desk, with a small mirror. There was a uniformed constable standing by the printer. She wished them both good morning, before asking, 'Any leads?'

'Nothing concrete,' said Dimitriou, going up and down under his chin. 'Bloke in one of those houses saw a car driving slowly past about eight. Reckons it was red, or burgundy. An old model. He couldn't give us more.'

'Better than nothing. The mark on the gates was red too.'

'Carrick has arranged to get an official statement from Arthur Price, at his house. He's the best hope at the moment.' He switched off the razor and turned his head from side to side, inspecting his work. 'Oh, and we've got a sketch artist working with the kids, trying to get a visual on the suspect.'

'We're looking for Ronald McDonald,' said the uniform by the printer, before stabbing a button hard. 'Seriously, what the fuck is wrong with this thing?'

'The clown mask might be useful,' said Jo. 'The perp went

out of his way to disguise himself. We might be able to track down where he bought it.'

'If he bought it recently,' said Dimitriou.

It was a good point. Jo had to remind herself this wasn't connected to Dylan Jones. The clown mask was surely a co-incidence. Probably meant to scare the kids as much as keep him hidden.

Dimitriou must have taken her silence for being offended.

'But hey – let's find a list of costume shops. We could head out together if you want?'

'Is there a computer I can get on first? I need to look something up. Mine takes forever to get going.'

'Sure. Use mine.' He scooted back his chair, and Jo moved another across. In a few clicks, she navigated onto her Facebook page and found what she wanted.

'Sexy bloody Saunders.'

Dimitriou looked across. 'Hey, we have internet guidelines,' he said. 'When I said you could borrow my computer . . .'

Jo was looking at a picture of Rebekah Fitzwilliam (née Saunders) that seemed to have been taken in a nightclub. Easy enough to find – they had several mutual friends on Facebook. No wonder she'd known the face.

'I went to school with her,' said Jo.

'Who is she?'

'A problem,' said Jo. She remembered vaguely that Saunders had been captain on the netball team and had once made her cry, though she couldn't recall the exact cause. 'She was sniffing around the case I was on in Bath.'

'That cold case with the kid from thirty years back?'

Jo opened up the page for the *Oxford Times*, with the Dylan Jones leader.

'She was at the burial site, then pestering the parents. I think she might have an internal source.'

Dimitriou grabbed his jacket, glancing at the screen. 'She doesn't look all bad,' he said, grinning. 'Shall we head out?'

Jo treated him to a withering look and closed the Facebook window. 'Let's.'

★　★　★

There were four costume shops within a two-mile radius of Oxford city centre, but they drew up a list of all the likely toy shops too. After three hours of fighting through city traffic, of the same questions and answers, Jo was beginning to suspect the search was a futile one. All but one sold clown masks, but without a better description it was hard to pin down what they were really looking for. The shop staff were a mixture of owners and temps, and only one kept a detailed day-by-day inventory of sales by item.

Between shops, Jo kept her eyes on her phone, expecting at any moment news from the station that Niall had shown up. With every minute that he didn't, the nausea in the pit of her stomach built. What possible reason would a drug dealer have to keep him this long? The kid was eleven. They must have found whatever money he had on him almost straight away. And it didn't matter how streetwise Niall McDonagh was – by now he'd be terrified. As for what his parents were going through . . .

At 10.45 a.m., it was getting quite warm, and Dimitriou's five o'clock shadow was already darkening his jawline. They pulled up outside Kidz Costumz, a small, scruffy shopfront in Summertown. There was a coffee place next door, so Jo suggested she pick up a couple while Dimitriou did the routine enquiries in the shop.

'Mine's a flat white,' he said.

They parted ways.

Jo ordered, paid and was near the door with a cup-carrier when she heard shouts outside, then pounding feet. The next moment, three whooping teenagers ran past the window, all wearing plastic clown masks. *What the hell?*

She flung open the door with her free hand, nearly dropping the coffees, and hurried out onto the pavement. The kids almost knocked over an old woman and her wheel-along trolley. She was thinking about giving chase when Dimitriou arrived at her side.

'Apparently they've been doing a roaring trade,' he said.

'Because of last night?' said Jo.

'Kids have an odd sense of humour. Is that my flat white?'

Jo nodded, watching the teens round a corner and vanish.

'Anything pertinent?'

'Nope. Owner said there's a place in the Covered Market though. She's given me the number of the wholesaler who supplies them both. Might be worth a shout.'

'Hmm.' Jo was climbing back into the car.

'You don't sound convinced,' said Dimitriou as he did the same.

'I can't help but think we're grasping at straws.' She thought how quickly Emma had heard about the kidnap. The kids buying up clown masks just a few hours after the Dylan Jones story hit the papers. 'We need to bring in a few dealers. If Niall's found himself in that world, I guarantee dozens of people know about it already.'

'You're probably right. Let's visit the Market, then call it quits and head back to the station.'

★   ★   ★

Oxford's Covered Market, occupying a block between the High Street and the Cornmarket, had five street entrances. It was a mixture of traditional food stalls, clothes shops and tourist souvenirs, and bustled with footfall. Jo remembered coming in with her dad to buy meat from the butchers. The joke shop was tucked away with a row of tiny booths selling jewellery, scarves and purses. The sickly smell of incense from a neighbouring stall hung over the area, making Jo feel light-headed.

The owner was a shaven-headed, stocky woman wearing looping earrings and a vest. When she saw Jo and Dimitriou approaching, she gave a cackle.

'If there was ever a couple in need of a smile . . . '

Jo raised her badge briefly. 'A few questions,' she said. There were several masks hanging on the back wall. Frankenstein, Dracula, the US President . . .

The woman's cheerful face dropped. 'What's he done now?' she said, rolling her eyes.

'Who?' said Dimitriou.

'This is about my Elton, I'm guessing?'

'Sorry, not sure what you mean,' said Jo. 'We're making enquiries in relation to a missing child.'

'Who's Elton?' asked Dimitriou.

'My ex,' the woman said. 'Never mind. Here, let's have another look at that badge.'

Jo showed it again. 'Do you sell clown masks?'

'You as well? Afraid I'm all out. Hey, is this about that kid got snatched on Port Meadow?'

'Yes,' said Jo. 'And we don't want to buy one. We're interested in a person who might have purchased one recently.'

'Sold six or seven just this morning,' said the woman. 'Kids, y'know.'

'Further back than that,' said Jo. 'Say in the last two weeks.'

'Y'know what, there was a fella,' said the woman. Jo perked up. 'I wouldn't normally have noticed, but he was a bit older than my regular clientele. I said as much.'

'Yes?' said Jo. 'When was this?'

'Maybe five or six days ago.' She clicked her fingers. 'Actually, I can tell you exactly. It was Tuesday, because I was unpacking some new stock I'd picked up Monday night.'

Jo took out her pocketbook and started making notes. Chances were it was nothing, but it was something in a day of *absolutely* nothing.

'So Tuesday a.m.?'

'Yeah, early,' said the woman. 'Would've been first thing, before ten anyway.'

'And can you describe the man?' she said, scribbling.

The woman blew out her cheeks, and her earrings shook. 'You're putting me on the spot there.'

'Any detail at all might prove crucial,' said Dimitriou. He was glancing up and down at the ceiling, no doubt looking for CCTV. Jo had already spotted the camera at the far end. *Please, please, be working.* In her experience, one in three were unoperational – a deterrent rather than a recording device.

'He wasn't tall,' she said. 'I remember that. Maybe not much bigger than me, and I'm five-five.'

Jo immediately thought of the kids' description of the man at the circus. They'd said his posture had suggested someone middle-aged.

'How old, would you estimate?'

'Fifty, maybe a bit older? He had grey hair.'

Jo's handwriting was untidy because of her excitement. She forced herself to calm down. In all likelihood this was a grandfather buying a present.

'Clothing?'

'Definitely.' She cackled again. 'I'm sorry, I can't remember. I wasn't paying attention.'

'But the clown mask in question? Can you describe it?'

'I can do better than that,' said the woman, proudly. She bent down, rummaging under the counter, and when she came up she was holding a catalogue. She licked her index finger and flicked through several pages, before flipping it over and pointing to a listing. 'That's the one.'

There was a small picture of a clown mask – a leering over-sized bright scarlet mouth filled with gleaming, wrinkled skin and black daubs around the mouth. A wig of frizzy red hair.

Jo took it, glancing at Dimitriou, who wore a small, satisfied smile.

They asked more questions. Which way had the customer left? (She didn't know). His accent (maybe local, maybe not), distinguishing characteristics (nothing memorable). Jo sensed the helpful woman was losing interest, so decided to wrap things up and took her details.

'Can we keep this?' Dimitriou asked, holding up the catalogue.

'S'pose so,' said the owner, before gesturing with a hand at her wares. 'Maybe I can interest you in something for your children too?'

'I've escaped that trap so far,' said Dimitriou. 'Jo? You have any sprogs at home?'

She smiled as best as she could. ''Fraid not.'

The woman shrugged. 'Suit yourselves.' She looked Jo up and down, as if evaluating her fertility. 'Don't leave it too late though. They might be a pain in the backside, but they're worth it in the long run.'

I'll bear that in mind, thought Jo.

Afterwards, they took a turn of the Market, noting the location of all the other cameras. There were only two more, which was a disappointment, and Jo found a plate on one of the main doors listing the security company that looked after the building. The name gave her pause, but only for a moment. Securitex, same as the group at the Port Meadow circus. They were one of the bigger operations locally.

She put in a call to the number listed on the main entrance as soon as they were out. She got an automated switchboard, followed through several increasingly frustrating options, then the line went to an answerphone. She hung up and tried again, and this time managed to get to a message saying, 'If your situation is an emergency, please contact the police.' With a growl of frustration, she went back to the answerphone and left a message asking for a callback. She reckoned Carrick would have a direct line, for sure.

At the car, Dimitriou was grinning from ear to ear. 'You want to see something?' he said, flashing his phone at her. 'Composite sketch based on witness descriptions.'

She found herself looking at a pencil drawing filling the screen. It showed a clown's face, and was as close as dammit to the image in the catalogue.

'That's our man,' he said.

Chapter 7

Jo was hoping to get a call into Bath when they got back to the station. Rob Bridges had said she wasn't on the Dylan Jones case, but that didn't mean she couldn't show an interest. Anyone in Bath CID would give her the basics, unless directly ordered not to. She didn't want to put them in a tight spot though. She wondered, if it came to it, whether Ferman might be a better way to keep informed. She thought that she had earned his trust during their brief time together, but of course she hadn't got his number. Carrick would have it, probably, if he was the one who'd asked the old-timer to tag along when Dylan's body was discovered.

Heidi Tan and Andy Carrick were at their desks at St Aldates, but as soon as Jo and Dimitriou came through the door, DCI Stratton summoned everyone for a debrief in his office. They all compared the sketch with the catalogue and agreed it was the most promising lead. The links to known drug dealers idea was drawing a blank.

'Almost none of that fraternity is aged over thirty-five,' said Tan.

'What about releases?' asked Carrick. 'Someone coming back into the fold?'

'We had one,' said Tan, checking her book. 'Nigel Merryn, fifty-two. Previous for dealing amphetamines and GBH. But he's wearing a tag and checks out.'

'An addict then?' said Stratton. 'They get some hopeless junkie to lift Niall, payment in kind?'

'I think that's unlikely, sir,' said Jo, drawing a couple of glances.

'You do?' said Stratton, with a cock of the head.

Jo persevered. He wasn't her super, after all. 'It was reckless, I'll give you that, sir. Desperate even. A lot could have gone wrong. But to buy the mask a few days in advance, to take on two kids, to drive away, all that takes planning, and, dare I say it, guts. There are so many variables – things that could go wrong. He was careful and precise.'

'Not if he crashed into that gate,' said Stratton. 'That was your theory, if I remember?'

'*Just* a theory, sir,' said Jo. 'And why take the risk at all? If this is drugs – if it was just a message – they could have cut one of the kids. Chances are we might not even have heard about it. Now they've got half of Thames Valley resources out looking.'

Stratton crossed his arms and looked at her hard. She didn't break eye contact.

Someone's phone was ringing, and Carrick fished in his pocket. Looking at the screen, he said, 'About time. We've got the phone placement.'

He left the office, headed to his desk. After a second or two the rest of them followed. Before he started clicking, Jo saw on his monitor a brief screensaver of his family at the beach. Three mixed-race kids, a wife who looked like a supermodel. She knew it was only a snapshot – an edited highlight – but the sheer joy and colour of the photo made her feel suddenly monochrome and worthless.

'Hold on a second,' he said. 'Bingo.'

They crowded round. The screen showed a satellite map,

placing the final three texts Niall had sent, according to triangulation from phone masts, as small circles radiating pale green to red. They formed pretty much a line along the road west from Port Meadow, a track leading to a village called Swinford. The last, labelled with the time 21.29, was far from any main road. Carrick read the accompanying message.

'They lost the phone at 21.31,' he said. 'Switched off, one way or another.'

'Andy, get out there,' said Stratton. 'Take Jo with you. Heidi, George – follow up with Securitex and get the CCTV from the Market.'

As Carrick and Jo jogged to his car, she tried not to think about what they might find. She thought of the McDonaghs, brittle, unhappy and in denial, and wondered how they might cope with the news she might soon have to deliver. She prayed for a different outcome.

Carrick switched on the lights as soon as they pulled out of the station car park, and cut through the traffic expertly, almost brushing a couple of slowing cars. She recognised an ADQ when she saw one, having only passed the Initial Pursuit certificate herself. Advance Driver Qualified involved hours on a skidpan in powerful vehicles, and travel in excess of 130 mph with commentary. Ben had failed twice then given up.

And while she marvelled at Carrick's deft acceleration and manoeuvring, she didn't share the optimism his speed implied. Whatever was waiting on that lonely farm track in the middle of the Oxfordshire countryside, it probably wasn't going anywhere.

★ ★ ★

As they drove, Jo checked the map. The road where the messages had come from ended a good mile from Port Meadow as the

91

crow flew, but with its twists and turns through the fields, it was maybe a mile and a half. Still, with the head start he had, the kidnapper had had plenty of time to make his getaway. Again, she was struck by the planning. Instinct told her he was no addict.

They turned into a single-width track, and the Toyota started to bounce along the uneven ground. Carrick slowed down and switched off the sirens, but he was still driving more quickly than seemed sensible, and she heard the stones pinging off the chassis. There were no street lights off the beaten track, but after dark, the perp would have been very unlikely to meet anything coming the other way. Dust rose around the tyres as they made their way between overgrown hedges either side. They passed a couple of gates leading to distant farms and outbuildings.

'We're getting close,' said Jo, comparing the phone company printout with the car's satnav.

Suddenly she was thrown forward in the seat and caught by the belt as Carrick hit the brakes. A tractor loomed ahead. Carrick beeped the horn impatiently, but the driver looked over his shoulder, shrugged, and waved them back.

With a growl, Carrick put the car into reverse. Jo held her breath as he shot back at speed for about fifty metres and curled into a layby.

'Come on!' he said. 'Get a flippin' move on!'

The tractor rumbled past, and the farmer gave them a salute.

Carrick's wheels skidded as he set off again at breakneck speed. After another minute, Jo told him to pull over.

'We're here,' she said.

He edged the car up a bank, leaving it on a tilt. Jo climbed out, and Carrick had to clamber from her side too, to avoid exiting straight into a bush. He straightened his jacket and looked around. The smell of sun-baked earth filled Jo with a sudden pang of nostalgia for simpler times, of walking with her dad through the fields.

The spot couldn't have been more innocuous. Hills in the distance, hedges six foot high on either side, with fields beyond. No footpaths, no gates, no turn-offs. Jo scanned the track for tyre marks, but there was nothing amiss.

'Let's split up,' she said.

They took opposite directions. The phone company said the signal data was accurate to about a hundred feet, but Jo walked twice that far before turning back. She peered under the hedgerows, but apart from a bag of dog shit (she checked) and a prehistoric crisp packet, there was nothing. Gradually, all the adrenalin she'd felt back at the station drained away.

Finding nothing is better than finding a body.

'Masters!' called Carrick.

She broke into a run, and spotted him crouched thirty yards up from the car. 'Bring an evidence bag,' he said. 'In the door compartment.'

She fetched a bundle, and two pairs of latex gloves from the same place.

'What is it?' she said.

'Not really sure. I think it might be a phone screen.'

And when she saw what he was looking at, she was inclined to agree. There were three small fragments of glass, thin, with curved sides leading to a point. But the edges were clean. It looked recent.

'So where's the rest?' said Carrick, scanning the area.

Jo approached the hedge.

'Give me a boost,' she said. He frowned. 'So I can look over,' she added.

'Oh, right.' He cupped his hands, close to the hedge, and Jo checked her shoes before placing a foot on them. He heaved, and she had to hold one shoulder to stop herself toppling. She supported her other hand on top of the hedge. The far side was a field of maize, two feet tall, green and wispy.

'See anything?'

'Nope. Let's find a gate and get in.'

The roar of an engine made them both look over; the tractor was making its way back down the track in their direction.

Jo let Carrick lower her partway, then his hands were on her waist and helping her down. Their bodies slid together, just for a moment. Was he actually blushing?

The farmer stopped, leaned out of the tractor's open side, and took the pipe from his mouth. 'I've told you lot,' he said. 'You can take your business elsewhere.'

'We're police,' said Carrick. 'We need to have a look in this field.'

The farmer eyed them. 'Now I've heard it all. Look, what's wrong with a bed like normal folk?'

'You what?' said Carrick, and then he seemed to understand. 'Listen, that's not . . . we're not . . .'

He was definitely blushing now.

From the bemused look on the farmer's face, Jo guessed he was probably one of the few people who hadn't read about the missing boy. She pulled out her badge.

'We can get a warrant,' she said, 'but it might just be quicker to show us the nearest entrance.'

The farmer squinted. 'A'right. Keep your hair on. Up the track — there's a gate. It's locked, but you two young'uns can climb over. Are you going to shift this car? Can't get the tractor past.'

'No,' said Carrick, clearly still smarting from the embarrassment. 'And if you so much as scratch it, I'll take you in. This is a crime scene, by the way.'

He set off, and Jo, grinning, followed.

They found the gate and climbed over, then doubled back along the fallow trench between the crops and the hedge towards the spot they'd left the car. Cloying mud stuck to Jo's shoes, making each step laboured. Carrick didn't seem to care. Jo knew she shouldn't judge a book by its cover, but now she was forming a picture despite herself. The lack of swearing. That schoolboy blush. Regular churchgoer. Perhaps a teetotaller. She wouldn't be surprised if he was wearing a cross under that shirt. The current beautiful wife was his first real relationship, and they must have had kids early based on the ages on the screensaver. All missionary, birthdays and Christmas.

No, I'm being mean . . .

Roughly opposite where they'd found the glass, Carrick broke off into the crops, trampling a path, and she took a parallel route a couple of metres up.

In less than a minute, she found it, lying in the long grasses. The carcass of a mobile phone. She called Carrick across.

'There could be prints,' he said.

'No doubt,' said Jo. She took a photo with her own phone, then pulled on her gloves and began to gather all the pieces she could see into an evidence bag.

'Why here?' said Carrick, moving up and down, combing the rest of the ground. 'He must have stopped the car, got the phone, smashed it in the lane and tossed it over.'

'Maybe he didn't think of it until that point,' said Jo. 'From what Arthur said, he might have been panicking a bit. He wanted to get away, then remembered the kid might have a phone.'

'Does that fit the profile?' asked Carrick. 'He took enough care with the rest of it. The phone would be the first thing you thought of.'

'Not if you're of a certain age? Perhaps he wasn't a mobile phone user.'

'We're talking middle-aged, not Victorian.'

Jo had to admit it didn't make a lot of sense, but what did at the moment? A kidnapper who was meticulous in planning, but careless in execution. The drug angle was looking less likely by the second.

After a thorough search, they found nothing more. On the way back to the car, Carrick called it in, then asked how the CCTV was coming along.

'Bugger,' Jo heard him say. 'What about nearby businesses? There must be other cameras covering the exterior . . . Yes, sounds good. See you soon.'

He hung up.

'Let me guess,' said Jo. 'Cameras a no-go.'

'Two switched off awaiting servicing.'

'The one overlooking the joke-shop kiosk?'

'Sadly, yes. Nothing for the time frame on the one that actually works.'

'I suppose that narrows down his exit route from five possibilities to four. There are banks on two sides of the Covered Market though. They'll be more promising.'

'They're on it already.' He opened the car door on the passenger side, and climbed back across. 'That was good work this morning, by the way. With George Dimitriou.'

'Just lucky,' said Jo, but she allowed herself a smile.

As they headed back, the tractor was waiting, pulled up in front of a farm. Jo waved thanks but didn't get anything back.

'Andy, have you got a contact for Harry Ferman?' she asked.

Carrick looked surprised. 'Er, yeah. Yes, on my desk at the station. I think he took a shine to you.'

'What's his story anyway?'

'We only crossed over for a couple of years,' said Carrick. 'He was a good copper. Too good, really. Not sure he was quite ready for what the world's become, you know?'

'How do you mean?'

Carrick lowered his voice. 'Just that he held on a bit too long. Had demons he couldn't shake.'

Jo remembered Ferman's shambling, heavy gait through the doors of the pub when she'd dropped him off the day before.

'Drink?'

'Certainly,' said Carrick. 'But that was probably a generational thing. The chief super hated it, of course. Spoke to him more than once. From what I heard – and this didn't come from me – Ferman had some family problems. A daughter who died. Not sure he ever really got over it.'

Jo thought of the look on the sonographer's face when they couldn't find the heartbeat. Ben squeezing her hand.

'Understandable.'

She thought of the Joneses too, with their conservatory furniture, their trimmed shrubs, the ornamental boot-scraper, their quality, functional clothes. All the accoutrements of middle-class formality. If you were their new neighbours, moving in, you'd think they were the most normal couple in the world. You might wonder if they had children who lived in another town, or country. Or you might assume they were childless by choice. There wasn't a part of you that would suspect their only child, their dear little boy, had been snatched away, murdered, and buried under a swimming pool plot. Because if you learned what had happened to them, the most normal of suburban couples, you'd know it could happen to you as well.

Jo hoped again, with all her heart, that the McDonaghs would have a happier ending.

★　★　★

At the station, they catalogued the phone and sent it off by courier to the lab. If the kidnapper was clever, he wouldn't have touched it, but something told Jo that the man they were looking for wasn't clever at all. That he was clinging on by his fingertips.

And if that was true, it was a mixed blessing. It meant they might well find him, but it didn't mean they would find Niall.

'We've got four units on the likely businesses with CCTV in the vicinity of the market,' said Tan. 'Dimi's co-ordinating on site. Forensics have got a paint sample from the gate near the crime scene too. They can't confirm yet, but they're ninety-nine per cent sure it's enamel-based.'

'And that means?' said Carrick.

'Fifteen years old at a minimum, apparently. You can still buy the stuff online, but it stopped being used for mass-production years ago.'

Jo went over to the board. The images of Niall had been pinned up down one side where the victim's details were collated. Under the 'Suspect' column, where someone had scrawled 'Vehicle' she wrote 'pre-2003?'.

'I'm going to read through the kids' full statements again,' Carrick said, sitting at his desk. 'Oh, and Jo?' He ripped a Post-it off the side of his monitor, and handed it over. 'Ferman's contact.'

Jo took it. An Oxford landline, and an address in Abingdon.

'Be back in a second,' she said.

She went to one of the interview rooms and dialled, not holding any great hopes he'd be in.

He picked up on the fourth ring. 'Hello?'

Was he slightly slurred? She wasn't sure.

'Mr Ferman, it's Jo Masters. We met yesterday.'

'Of course. How are you?'

'Very well, thank you. I thought I'd touch base on the Dylan Jones case. I wondered if you'd heard anything?'

'Read about it,' he said. She thought she heard a hint of belligerence.

Jo chose her words carefully. 'I've been seconded to another case with Thames Valley,' she said, 'so I'm out of the loop a bit.'

'This have something to do with, what was his name? Ah, yes. Ben.'

'I'm not sure what you mean.'

'Never mind,' he said. 'Short answer is no. That journalist was round here though. Don't know how she got my address.'

Again, perhaps the slight tone of accusation.

'Did you tell her anything?'

'She knew a bit already. But no, I didn't. Is there something specific you wanted?'

'Ah, no. I was just seeing if they were keeping you up to date. Or, y'know, if there was anything you'd thought of . . . that might help.'

'If you're coming to me, you must be desperate.' He chuckled.

'A little, maybe.' He didn't say anything else. 'Well, sorry to bother you.'

With no other option, she called Bath and got DC Kevin Carter.

'Hi Kev, it's Jo. I'm in Bath on this kidnap – just following up a lead, and . . . well, it's probably a waste of time. Wondered if you had anything more on a suspect for the Jones body?'

'Hold on a minute,' he said, sounding bored. 'I'll put you through to Ben.'

'Hey, no, wait—'

Too late. The phone was already ringing, and then Ben was there.

'Jo,' he said.

She hadn't replied to his texts the night before. Dammit – she wasn't going to apologise. *If he can't get it into his head . . .*

'I could do with you here, Jo,' he said, and he sounded genuine. 'We had to let Clement Matthews go. Rob's breathing down my neck on this.'

Jo went along with it. Maybe he was playing her for a fool, maybe not. With Ben, you never knew, she'd learned that the hard way. Perhaps he didn't know Rob had taken her off because of their split.

'Have you got anything on the previous owners yet?'

He lowered his voice. 'Carter couldn't get water out of wet sponge, so I called and went through the utility company for the former owner. Told them I'd have to turn over their office on Monday if they didn't assist as a matter of urgency.'

Jo smiled, despite herself. When Ben was just Detective Coombs, she could remember why she'd first admired him so much.

'Chap got us a name within ten minutes. A Mr and Mrs Moulden. We did a trawl of the phone book, and found all the Mouldens. There's one who still lives near Bradford-on-Avon. Turns out it's the daughter who grew up in the house. She said her parents moved to France years ago. Dad's dead now, but we got in touch with Mrs Moulden. She said they employed an architect, first in '82, when the east wing of the house needed some underpinning work, under an extension. Then again a few years later. That's when they wanted the terrace remodelled with a pool. They remembered the architects they used – RTA partners – but not the building contractor RTA employed.'

'Sounds like you've been productive,' said Jo.

'Constable Aziz did some outstanding legwork.'

He paused and let out a laugh. Jo felt oddly hot as she realised Rhani was probably sitting next to him. His voice was more distant, away from the mouthpiece. '*Compared with Kevin, you're Hercule fucking Poirot!*' he said.

The volume returned. 'Sadly, it goes a bit dry there. RTA folded years ago, and we're trying to locate the owner via Companies House. Until we do, it's a dead end.'

'Sounds promising though,' said Jo. 'Whoever put that body there must have done so when the pool was put in. They must have had access to the site, and known it intimately. Mr Moulden check out?'

'We think he's unlikely. He'd been paralysed from the waist down since he was twenty-five. Horse-riding accident.'

'Christ.'

'Indeed. The pool was put in chiefly for physio work. *Thanks, Rhani. Milk no sugar.*' There was a long pause. 'I meant it, you know. I want you here.'

'Sounds like you're doing okay. Anyway, I think we're close here. It's a good team.'

'I didn't mean like that,' said Ben. He was speaking louder now, and she imagined he'd moved into another room, making sure no one could hear. 'I want to *see* you.'

'Ben, Rob knows,' she said.

Half a beat of hesitation. 'You told him?'

'He asked me. I had to.'

Silence, then, slightly fearful, slightly threatening: 'What did you say?'

'Nothing about why, if that's what you mean.'

'Nosey fucking bastard,' said Ben vehemently.

'He's just doing his job,' said Jo, though part of her agreed.

'So this is why you transferred.'

'I didn't,' said Jo. 'Rob took me off.'

'But I bet you didn't put up a fight, did you?'

Jo felt a rush of anger. *How fucking dare he blame me for this?* She tried to stay calm, not to react. There was a knock at the interview room door, and Carrick opened it.

'We got something,' he said.

'Who's that?' said Ben.

'I've got to go.'

Temper still high, she followed Carrick back to the incident room, where Dimitriou was plugging a memory stick into his computer. He placed a second one on the desk. Everyone was weirdly quiet, but Tan was tapping her foot anxiously.

'We've got him,' she whispered.

Dimitriou's computer opened a video file, and black and white footage filled the screen. 'This is from outside the chemist on Market Street,' he said.

Dragging the cursor until the time said 09.40, he let the footage play. There were a few pedestrians and bikes. A delivery van pulled up, then at 09.41, a short man exited the Covered Market entrance, holding a single carrier bag and wearing a baseball cap. Dimitriou paused the tape.

'We checked with the stall owner again – that's the same as the bags they use – blue polythene.'

He played on, and the man walked off the opposite way. Too far away to get anything useful on his face. Jo was about to say as much, before the man stopped, turned, and headed back. Straight towards the camera. Dimitriou stopped the tape, took a screen grab, then opened it in another program. He zoomed in, losing resolution.

'That's our man?' said Carrick.

Jo estimated his height of five-six or five-seven tops, with slightly hunched shoulders. He seemed to have a limp. He was wearing jeans, some sort of work boots, and a jacket zipped up to the neck. It was hard to see much of the face because of the angle and resolution, but it looked fleshy and clean-shaven. The cap had some sort of logo.

'It's pretty vague,' said Stratton.

'Wait – there's more,' said Dimitriou.

He took out the memory stick and plugged in the second. 'We got this from HSBC. It's better quality.'

Dimitriou was right. The CCTV was crisp, in muted colour, and showed Cornmarket, where the flow of pedestrians was much heavier. However, Jo spotted the suspect straight away. He walked quicker than those around him, and there was a definitely awkward lift of his right leg. He hurried up the street, the bag clutched in front of him. His top was actually dark blue or black; a fleece, she thought. Though he looked afraid, and nervous, there was something in his broad shoulders that suggested power, perhaps someone used to manual labour. The picture on the cap was a crest of some sort.

'Get a close-up on the headwear,' she said.

It took a few moments, but when it came up Jo grinned. It was indeed a shield motif, with coloured stripes.

'Those are college colours,' said Dimitriou.

'Yes, they are,' said Jo.

'Anyone know which one?' asked Stratton.

'I'll hazard a guess, sir,' said Jo. She gestured at the keyboard. 'May I?'

'Knock yourself out,' said Dimitriou, vacating his chair.

Jo typed in 'Gloucester College', the one where Mr and Mrs McDonagh taught, and located their page on the university site. Sure enough, the crest at the top of the page was a beige background, with blue and red detailing.

'You think he's staff?' said Tan.

'He's a little old to be a student,' said Dimitriou.

'It can't be this easy,' said Carrick.

Stratton patted him on the back. 'Don't look a gift horse in the mouth,' he said. 'Anyway, what are you talking about? It's solid police work that's got us this far. Heidi, organise a couple of cars at the main college exits. Tell them to stand by. Andy, Jo – you two take the picture and get over to the college for an ID. Name and current address. As soon as you've got something, report it.'

Chapter 8

Gloucester College was less than five hundred metres from the station, and it was quicker to walk than take the car. Carrick was right – it felt too easy, too convenient.

'You think this could be a grudge against the parents?' said Jo, as they walked under the colossal gothic façade of Christ Church.

Carrick gave her a lopsided grin. 'I know academia's a cut-throat business, but kidnapping someone's child is a stretch, isn't it?'

The startling connection with the college had thrown her. The McDonaghs didn't even live there, so it was hard to see how the suspect would even have come across their young son.

The sign at the front said Gloucester College was closed to visitors, but the studded medieval door was open and they stepped inside. Jo had never even thought about applying to the university, mainly because since the age of thirteen all she'd wanted to do was get as far away as possible from Oxford; all her friends had been the same. So it had been History at Sussex, and three wonderful years where she'd learned very little about Tudor England, but an awful lot about life.

Paul, being the perfect son he was, had stayed in the city of their birth, studying PPE at Balliol College. Somehow the fact that he returned home to get his washing done once a week had proved his filial worth, whereas her decision to go it on her own had been just another example of her lack of gratitude. At least in their mother's eyes. Her dad, she thought, had respected her choice.

The gates opened onto a cobbled courtyard, and through a broad arch she saw a neatly mowed quadrangle of grass with a sign telling people to keep off. There was a small door on the left, with a glass-partitioned desk, and an old man in a bowler hat and blazer suit behind it. Jo, sensing Carrick was as ill at ease as she was, went in first.

'Good afternoon,' said the man, tipping his hat.

Jo showed her badge. 'We're from Thames Valley police,' she said.

The man held up a hand to stop her. 'Is this about the poor McDonaghs?' he asked.

'Our enquiries are related to that, yes,' said Jo. 'If you could just take a look at—'

'The dean was very clear – all enquiries through him,' said the man, his hand still in place. 'I'll summon him. A moment, please.'

Jo could hardly reach across and stop him as he picked up a bulky phone and dialled three numbers on an internal line.

'Dr Silcott. Yes, it's Howard here. I have the police . . . Of course, doctor. Of course.' He placed down the receiver, then pointed at a ledger on the desk. 'If you wouldn't mind signing in . . .'

'Is that really necessary?' said Carrick.

The porter replied with a smile that suggested he might look like a doddery old man, but he was used to dealing with more difficult customers than them. Jo took the pen and signed in their names.

The porter scanned the book, gave a satisfied nod, and said, 'Would you like to follow me?'

He led them around the cobbles at a stately pace, then along the northern side of the quad, which was lined with ivy-clad, three-storey buildings that must have been medieval. It was the summer holidays, so there weren't many students around, but a gaggle of suited businessfolk, probably using the college for a conference of some sort, wandered past. The porter turned abruptly into an open doorway to a corridor with a rickety wooden staircase. A board at the bottom listed a number of names, including, she noticed, a 'Dr A Silcott, Dean of Studies', on the second floor. The porter started up, his body looking almost as creaky as the steps themselves.

'We can find our way,' said Jo.

'No, no, no,' muttered the porter. 'Wouldn't hear of it.'

So they were forced to follow him, painfully slowly, up two flights of switchback stairs.

At the door to the dean's rooms, he knocked ponderously, and a slightly feminine voice called on them to come in.

The porter opened the door, then stepped aside to let them through. 'The police officers, sir,' he said. 'A Ms Masters and Mr Carrick.'

Jo was impressed once again – she hadn't even written their names all that legibly, and he'd barely looked at the badges. The man didn't miss much, and she made a mental note to question him afterwards, whatever the dean gave them.

The room was lined with bookcases, with an internal door on the left and a huge fireplace. The man who sat across a large mahogany desk inlaid with leather was around fifty years old, with baby-smooth skin, and thinning blond hair combed violently across his scalp. His eyes, a cutting blue, sat a tad too close together over a delicate nose and full lips. He wore a pale green shirt with a yellow bow tie just visible under a racing-green jumper.

'Thank you, Howard,' he said, softly.

The porter nodded deeply, and left backwards, closing the door.

'Dr Silcott,' said Carrick. 'We're investigating the disappearance of Niall McDonagh, the son of two of your faculty members, and we'd like to ask you a few questions.'

'Me?' said the dean. 'Gosh. Of course, I'll do all I can to help. The McDonaghs are good friends of mine.'

He stood from behind the desk, and walked across to a bureau under the mullioned window with odd, small steps, almost like a dancer. His feet looked barely bigger than her own, and she took a size six. He opened it up to reveal a decanter, a couple of bottles and crystal glasses.

'Drink?' he said, his back to them. 'I normally take one before lunch.'

Jo glanced at Carrick. Was this guy for real?

'No, thank you,' said Carrick, on their behalf.

The answer seemed to give the dean pause, then he poured himself a glass of what looked like sherry. He took a sip and turned back towards them. Jo guessed he was around five-eight.

'Do you know their sons?' said Jo.

A cock of the head. 'Whose sons?'

'The McDonaghs,' she replied. 'Niall and – ' She took out her pocketbook, pretending to consult the names – 'Kieran.'

It always paid to look a bit absent-minded. If people thought your questions were routine, they tended to be more open.

The dean took another sip, and from his knowing gaze, Jo sensed he'd seen through her misdirection.

'Not well,' he said. 'Kieran used to sing in the boys' choir until his voice broke.'

'And Niall?' said Carrick.

'Not so much. He had a beautiful soprano, but . . .'

'Had?' said Jo.

107

'When he sang,' said Silcott. 'He did a term with us, but you know kids these days, there are so many other distractions.'

Jo made some notes. 'When did you last see him?'

'Oh, months ago,' said Silcott.

'Can you be more precise?'

'Let me see . . .' His eyes travelled up and to his left. 'It would have been Michaelmas.'

'In English, please,' said Jo.

'The autumn term,' said the dean, eyes flashing. 'That's when he left the choir.'

'Because of his . . . other distractions?' said Jo, tapping the page with her pen.

The dean finished his drink. 'I'm sorry, detective, I really don't think I can help you. Niall isn't a student here. He doesn't live here. He's simply the son of two faculty members.'

'So why have you asked for all enquiries to come through you?' asked Carrick.

Silcott placed his glass down, and for the first time smiled, knowingly.

'The university houses over ten thousand students,' he said, 'but in some ways it's a small community. We prepare our charges for the future, but despite everyone's efforts, we're locked into the past. Our tradition, our arcane titles, our rituals. I dare say it all appears rather strange to outsiders such as yourselves. But the smooth functioning of a college relies on institutions and rules. It doesn't take a lot to upset the ship.'

'I don't follow,' said Jo.

'Perhaps you don't,' said Silcott. 'But not two hours ago, we had a lady here. She managed to get past Howard, somehow, and she was taking pictures and asking questions of our foreign guests. I encountered her myself. It turned out she was from the city's newspaper. I was forced to ask her to leave.'

'Rebekah Fitzwilliam,' said Jo.

The dean's face darkened. 'Indeed. My point is that I will not allow the reputation of this college to be tarnished by association with whatever it is Niall McDonagh and his friends are involved with.'

'Which is what?' said Carrick.

'I do not know, and I do not care. I'd suggest you speak with his parents.'

His cheeks were quivering a little, and Jo decided it was time to take some of the heat out of the conversation.

'We'll be out of your hair soon,' she said. 'There's just one more thing we need to run by you.'

'By all means.'

Jo took out the printout of the suspect in the bank CCTV. 'We'd like to speak with the gentleman in this image. Do you know who he is?'

The dean looked at the picture, and Jo watched him, trying to gauge his reaction. He showed no panic or recognition at all.

'Is that a Gloucester crest?' he said.

'Yes,' said Carrick. 'We wondered if this man was connected with the college in some way.'

'I'm afraid I can't help you,' said the dean. 'That sort of headwear would be available in several shops across the city. They sell them to tourists, mainly.'

'We thought as much,' said Jo. 'Thank you for your time.'

'I'm sorry I couldn't be of more use,' said the dean, walking to the door. There was nothing in his step that reminded her of the man in the footage. He trod delicately, as if afraid of making a noise.

Carrick left first, Jo behind. As she was passing through, she stalled.

'Dr Silcott,' she said, offhandedly, 'could you tell us when you first heard about Niall's disappearance?'

'It would have been this morning,' he said. 'I read the *Oxford Times* when I can. You know, to find out what is happening in our city.'

'And last night?' said Jo, working nonchalantly towards the killer question. 'Where were you?'

'Ah, I was at home, writing up a lecture for next term. Early Norse folklore, if that interests you?'

'Those the ones where children get snatched by strange monsters in the forest?' said Carrick.

Silcott chuckled, but there was no unease in it.

'Touché, detective,' he said. 'I worked until eight, after which my partner of twenty-six years and I attended our local bridge club. Would you like to know our score?'

'That probably won't be necessary at the moment,' said Jo, refusing the bait. 'Thanks for your time.'

'Good day to you,' said the dean, closing the door behind them.

Back in the fresh air of the quad, Jo asked Carrick what he made of Silcott.

'I think he's a little odd, but that's what you get living in a place like this. He'd got the measure of us towards the end. The guy in the photo is about the same height, but the body type's all wrong.'

'Can't see him in a baseball cap either,' said Jo. 'Might still be worth Heidi testing the alibi though. She can dig up the address.'

Carrick nodded. As they passed the porter's office again, Jo went inside. Howard was placing several pieces of post into separate pigeonholes on the wall. There was a cleaning lady, a young woman, polishing the glass partition.

'Back already?' said Howard, opening the door to his small office. 'I'll sign you out, don't worry.'

As he pulled the ledger towards him and took up the pen, Jo placed the printout on top of the page.

'Do you recognise this man, Howard?' she asked.

The porter set down the pen, and picked up the paper, drawing it closer to his face. 'Should I?'

'We wondered if he worked at the college,' said Carrick.

The old man squinted. 'Can't say I do,' he said. 'There's not a lot of face to see, is there?'

He handed back the paper, but Jo shook her head. 'Keep it,' she said. 'And here's my card. If anything comes to you, give me a call.'

They left the college, and Carrick took out his phone to call Stratton back at St Aldates and give him the news. Or lack thereof.

Jo looked up and down the street. An American couple – or at least she guessed that by the man's size, and his trainers and socks combination – were taking pictures with a selfie stick; and a young woman was struggling with her pram over the cobbles. Jo went to help her on the steep lip of the pavement. In the pram, a girl barely a month old was somehow still blissfully asleep.

'Thank you!' said the woman.

'Your baby's beautiful,' said Jo. 'What's her name?'

'Madeleine,' said the woman.

Jo fought back a sudden rush of nausea – it had been top of her and Ben's shortlist – and the shock must have shown in her face, because the woman looked worried.

'Are you okay?' she said.

'Yes,' said Jo. 'I'm fine. Sorry, I've got to . . .'

She walked back towards Carrick, who was on the phone, and saw the woman pushing her pram quickly in the other direction. She was regaining her composure when the cleaning lady from the Porter's Cottage came out of the door. In her hand she was holding the printout. Looking both ways, she spotted Jo and rushed towards her.

Jo's heart, still finding its rhythm, quickened once more.

'Can I help you?' she said.

The woman pointed to the photo. 'I know this man,' she said, her accent Eastern European.

'Are you sure?' said Jo. Carrick had seen them talking and was jogging over.

'He is working at the college. He is gardener.'

Carrick must have heard, because he spoke into the phone. 'Hold fire, boss,' he said. 'We might have something.'

There were no games this time. Silcott wanted them to come back to his office, but Jo made it clear things were on their terms and he was to come at once to the porter's lodge. To her credit, the young woman, Maria, didn't wilt under repeated questioning. Asked again by Silcott if she was sure, she insisted the man in the picture had worked at the college – on and off – for as long as she had. She didn't know his name, though.

'I'll need a full list of groundspeople and gardening staff,' said Jo.

'Of course,' said the dean. 'I'll speak with Mrs Manderley, the college secretary, at once.'

'There'll be gardeners working today,' said the porter. 'In the provost's rose garden, I believe.'

'Show us,' said Jo.

'Now wait a moment,' said the dean. 'Professor Graves is on leave at the moment. We'll have to get permission before we go—'

'Mr Silcott,' said Jo. 'We're talking about a missing child. I don't give a fuck about permissions, or traditions, or college rules. Take us there – now.'

The dean was leaning back slightly in the face of her onslaught.

'Very well,' he said. 'The quickest way is through the side entrance. Howard, the key please.' His hand was shaking as the porter handed it to him.

They left the college again, and headed along the street outside, then reached a sturdy-looking door. The dean inserted the huge iron key, and opened it onto an exquisite walled garden where dozens of different roses blossomed. On the other side was a man in a green uniform – sixtyish, sitting in the sunshine and smoking. He took a long tug, and remained seated.

'Just on a break, dean,' he said.

'It's all right, Pete,' said Silcott. 'These people are police officers. They need to ask—'

Jo held out the paper in front of him as the man slowly stood. 'This man works here. What's his name?'

With his cigarette hanging from his lips, the gardener looked at the page and frowned. 'Looks like Al to me.'

'Al?'

'Al Trent.'

'Do you know where he is now?'

'What's he done?' he asked casually.

'He's wanted in connection with a missing child,' said Jo, her patience wearing thin. 'So it's important we find out where he is.'

Fag ash tipped onto the paper.

'You serious?' said the gardener.

Jo took the cigarette and tossed it on the ground. 'Deadly.'

'I dunno,' he said. 'Haven't got an address or 'owt. He's cash-in-hand. A lot of the lads are. Comes in when we need him.'

Jo turned to Silcott. 'Does this mean he won't be on the books?'

'Erm, it sounds as though that may be the case,' said the dean.

'I got a number for him,' said the man called Pete. He fished a phone from his pocket, started scrolling. 'Here you go. I can call him if you want . . .'

'No!' said Carrick, snatching the phone.

'Hey! Hold up!'

113

'No one contacts Trent,' said Jo. 'Got it?'

The gardener nodded.

'Might any of the other gardening staff know where he lives?' asked Carrick.

'Maybe,' said Pete, with a shrug. 'He didn't really hang around with us, though. Never came out for a pint after work.'

'We'll need you to come to the station now so we can collate possible contacts,' he said. 'We'll still need those personnel files,' he said to the dean.

'What about the roses?' said Pete. 'Provost's got a reception tomorrow afternoon. He wants it all cleaned up.'

These people . . . thought Jo.

'Gardening can wait,' she said, through gritted teeth.

Chapter 9

They left the dean at the college with strict instructions not to contact the McDonaghs under any circumstances. Maria gave them her details, but Jo said there was no reason to stick around. Carrick and Jo escorted the gardener, full name Peter Whittaker, back to the station. Jo believed it when he said he was no friend of Trent, so wasn't likely to tip him off, but they couldn't afford any fuck-ups. It was as they reached the gates onto St Aldates that Carrick said he thought they were being followed.

'Four o'clock,' he said.

Jo turned to see a woman with a camera, about thirty yards back, pointed straight at her. She looked like an office worker in a well-cut beige suit and a pair of pale shoes with short heels.

'Wait here,' she said, and left Carrick with Whittaker.

She strode past a fountain, half expecting the woman to turn and run. However, she just lowered the camera.

'Hi Josie,' she said as Jo approached.

'No one calls me that now,' said Jo. 'You're interfering with police business, Ms Saunders.'

'No one calls me that either. And nice to see you too. It's been a few years.'

'This is an active investigation,' said Jo. She wondered how long Saunders had been on their tail. 'You're jeopardising it.'

'I'm just taking pictures.'

'Don't be fucking smart, or I'll take that camera off you.'

'No you won't,' said Rebekah, with a grin that took Jo right back to the school corridors, to cliques and PE and short skirts and the unreadable minds of teenage boys. 'Look, I'm just doing my job.'

'And if you stop me doing mine . . .'

'You walked over here,' said Saunders. 'I'm curious, though. Yesterday you're in Bradford digging up Dylan Jones. Today you seem to be working on the Niall McDonagh disappearance.'

'You're fucking spying on me.'

'Spare me the melodrama. They're connected, aren't they? I heard about the clown mask.'

'Bye Rebekah,' Jo said, turning. 'I wish I could say it was nice to see you again.'

'Do you think it's the same person?' Saunders called after her.

'Don't be ridiculous,' snapped Jo.

'Can I quote you on that?' asked Saunders.

Jo headed back to Carrick without answering.

'What was that all about?'

'Nothing to worry about,' she said, hoping it was true.

'Feels like things are moving fast, doesn't it?' said Carrick. 'We're close.'

Not fast enough, thought Jo.

★   ★   ★

But back at the station, things had changed completely. That at least was good news.

As ever, the devil was in the detail.

'Prints from the smashed phone of Niall McDonagh confirm we have our suspect,' said DCI Stratton. Heidi Tan handed him a piece of paper fresh off the printer, and he tacked it to the centre of the case board. 'Alan Trent.'

The police mugshot showed a square face, eyes wide, with red rings beneath suggesting extreme fatigue, or maybe even tears. The demeanour of a man caught in the headlights and not knowing which way to run.

'Arrested at his home in Aylesbury in 2013, as part of Operation Yewtree, when Bucks police received consistent and credible complaints concerning activities when he was cub scout leader in the early noughties. Victim came forward later, said that Trent sexually assaulted him as a nine-year-old. Subsequently, two other accusers emerged. Trent was convicted, given six years and served three.'

Nothing unusual there. As long as you kept your head down, a half stretch was typical.

'Parole officer?' Jo asked.

'I'm tracking her down,' said Tan.

'Trent's last known address was social housing in Tring, Bedfordshire, but the council say he vacated several months ago, after some harassment.'

'Heart bleeds,' said Dimitriou.

'Known affiliates?' asked Jo.

'He was a loner, as far as we can tell,' said Stratton. 'No listed occupation on his arrest. We contacted the DVLA though, and he's listed as owning a maroon '93 Vauxhall Cavalier Estate, which gives us a match on the paint too. We're circulating the reg to all traffic units across all surrounding counties, checking the ANPR too, but we think he's still in the area.'

'We might have a lead on current whereabouts,' said Carrick.

He explained what they had from Gloucester College, and the plan to round up all contacts from the college gardening staff.

'Excellent work,' said Stratton. 'Niall has been missing for almost twenty-four hours, but we still have the element of surprise. I don't need to say, I'm sure, but the main thing is that this doesn't get out.'

Carrick was looking across at Jo, and she realised he was waiting for her to say something about Rebekah Saunders. She held up a hand.

'Sir, we may have a problem with a journalist.'

'The one from the *Times*?' said Stratton. 'That's Avon and Somerset's problem, not mine. She's on the Dylan Jones story.'

'Maybe not, sir,' said Jo. 'She seems to have latched onto my presence here.'

'How's that?'

'I know her. Knew her anyway. Years ago.'

Stratton sighed through his nose. 'Okay. We keep things tight. Stonewall her. It's still a local story, and the editor at the paper will want to keep it that way. I might be able to get us some breathing room. Everyone clear?'

Nods and mutters of 'Yes, boss' echoed across the room.

The meeting broke up.

With the sun going down outside, the incident room buzzed with quiet work for the next hour or so. Tan managed to get hold of Trent's parole officer, who agreed to come in from High Wycombe.

'She insisted there was no way it was Trent,' said Tan. 'Said she'd bet her life on it.'

'Lucky she doesn't have to,' said Dimitriou, leaning over the desk. 'Trent wouldn't be the first perp to pull the wool over his parole officer's eyes.'

'I'm not sure,' said Jo. She'd spent the last thirty minutes looking over Trent's file. 'There's nothing in the notes that marks him as manipulative. He confessed and pleaded guilty at the first questioning. The judge actually praised his "candour and honesty" in the summation.'

'Thank the Good Lord for upstanding paedophiles,' said Dimitriou, laughing mirthlessly.

Jo caught Carrick flinch.

'You don't think this fits?' he said to her.

Jo shrugged. 'His historic offences were pretty opportunistic,' she said.

'The ones we know about,' said Dimitriou.

Jo persisted. 'The incidents all follow a pattern. Boys he knew well, who trusted him. They all took place on outings – camping trips, activity holidays. And they were quite a bit younger than Niall.'

'So what?' said Dimitriou. 'It was years ago. Maybe his tastes have moved on. Give him another twenty, and it might be legal.'

Carrick glanced across. 'How are we doing tracking the other ground staff, Dimi?' he asked.

Dimitriou seemed to get the message and continued to the interview room.

'He can get a bit black and white about these things,' muttered Carrick.

'He might be right,' said Jo. 'I'm just not seeing it. If you'll forgive me, this snatch took balls, and that's not the Alan Trent I'm seeing. He was involved, but . . .'

'. . . maybe wasn't working alone,' said Carrick.

'It's a possibility, right?'

A constable put her head round the door and called across to him. 'Sarge, we've got data from the ANPR. Nothing from the Friday, but we've got something twelve days prior on the A40.'

They brought up the results on screen. The Automated Number Plate Recognition system had been up and running for several years, and was expanding all the time. Two cameras four miles apart had picked up the Cavalier heading west on the A40 Northern Bypass then returning by the same route three hours later, almost a fortnight before the kidnap.

'Visiting someone?' said Jo.

'Hard to say,' Carrick replied. He clicked through to the images. Trent, his face barely visible, appeared to be alone in both sets.

'Probably nothing,' said Carrick. He thanked the constable.

Jo returned to the file. The physicals fit for sure. Five-six. Stocky build. Distinguishing features included a tattoo of an eagle on his left forearm, with the letters 'PAAA' across its wings (whatever that was supposed to mean). A long scar to the back of his right thumb.

DOB was 17/10/61, which made him almost sixty.

Despite herself, she did a mental calculation. He'd have been twenty-six when Dylan Jones went missing. The file didn't have an address further back than 2001 though, and there was nothing there to link him to Bradford-on-Avon. The manual labour sat well with the landscaping angle, but she knew well enough the feeling of trying to push a square peg into a round hole.

Her personal phone beeped. A text from Emma.

Mum wants to know if you're staying again?

'Shit,' said Jo. She should have called them. She didn't know what to make of the fact that Amelia had deputised correspondence to her daughter.

Don't worry. Still at work. See u tomorrow maybe.

She'd pressed send before she wondered if that sounded ungrateful. Then she was angry with herself for even worrying about it. Why was *she* the one feeling like a teenage girl staying out past her curfew?

'Jo?'

Stratton was looking over the desk, and she slid the phone away guiltily. 'Sir.'

'The parole officer's here. Andy's taken her into Room 2.'

'On it, boss,' she said.

She passed IR1, and saw Dimitriou was taking down notes from the college gardener.

Trent's probation officer was younger than Jo by a couple of years at least. She was dressed casually, in jeans and a long macintosh coat belted around the middle.

She held out a hand. 'Laura Phelps.'

'Josephine Masters,' said Jo. 'Thank you for making the trip at short notice.'

'No problem,' said Phelps. 'Kids are in bed. Other half's under strict instructions to keep them alive.' She blanched suddenly. 'Sorry, bad taste. I didn't mean . . .'

'Don't worry,' said Jo.

Carrick returned with a mug of tea, which he placed on the table in front of Phelps.

She thanked him, removed her coat, and sat down.

'When was your last contact with Mr Trent?' asked Carrick.

'About three months ago,' said Phelps. 'Listen, I don't know the full story, but I know Alan Trent. Your colleague, Heidi, she said there was a missing child. Alan just wouldn't be capable of that.'

'We're just following the evidence at this stage,' said Jo.

'Which is?' She spoke earnestly, rather than with any belligerence.

'We'll get to that,' said Carrick. 'Heidi – Detective Tan – said you had no up-to-date address? Aren't you supposed to keep a tab on your parolees?'

'Trent was low-risk,' said Phelps. 'He had a place, but the locals drove him out. It was horrible for him.'

Jo was glad Dimitriou wasn't in the room. She could only imagine what his reaction would have been.

'How did they find out about his record?'

121

'Who knows,' said Phelps. 'Social media makes the world a small place, right? And Aylesbury to his new place in Tring is only ten miles. Word spread quickly. It started off as name-calling and vandalism – dog crap smeared on his car, broken windows. Escalated to assault when he called the police. Someone broke his nose. He said he knew who it was but didn't press charges. Moved out soon after.'

'To Oxford? He had friends here, did he?'

Phelps shook her head. 'He knew the area,' she said. 'He didn't want it getting out where he was. Asked me to continue to list the Tring abode. I didn't see a problem with it.'

Jo let the silence linger until it was uncomfortable.

'I guess that was wrong,' said Phelps quietly. 'I had his phone number. We spoke a couple of times.'

'We just need to find him,' said Jo. 'Did he have money?'

'A small pension, yes,' said Phelps.

'So what makes you so sure he wouldn't kidnap someone?' asked Carrick. 'Maybe he bottled up his urges for so long, and now he just . . . cracked.'

Phelps sipped her tea. 'He wasn't like that. He just wanted to live his life. He had a bad time as a youngster with his stepfather, and I'd managed to get him referred to a counsellor in Bedfordshire before it went bad for him. I thought it might help him move on. It was working, just talking to someone. That was one of the worst parts for him when he left. He needed that sort of help. Professional, you know?'

'And when you last spoke to him – sorry, when was that?'

'Maybe a month ago.'

'Right. How did he seem?'

'Fine,' said Phelps. 'Positive. He had work, gardening. He told me he was looking into a new counsellor, and he'd found this new group that met once a week, a kind of support network for victims of abuse.'

Carrick looked up sharply, and Jo knew his mind was in the same place as hers. *An accomplice.*

'Where do they meet?' asked Jo.

Phelps looked flustered. 'I don't think I could tell you that, even if I knew.'

'Ms Phelps – you said you weren't familiar with the case,' Jo said, 'so I'll help you a little bit. We have no doubt that Alan Trent first spotted his victim, Niall McDonagh, at the place he worked. He discovered that Niall would be at a local carnival, yesterday evening. Having purchased a disguise from a shop in Oxford town centre on Tuesday morning, he drove his car to a hidden spot, entered the circus, and lured Niall McDonagh away, assaulting another child in the process. Those are as close to facts as we can get, with a clear chain of evidence. We also believe that he did not work alone. So please, spare me your scruples and tell us what you know.'

Phelps smiled, all the warmth gone. 'I *don't* know.'

'If we find out . . .'

'Detective, I didn't have to come here,' said Phelps. 'And I won't be here very much longer if you threaten me.'

Jo sat back in her chair. Perhaps – despite the soft, Home-Counties mum–of–two exterior – there was more to Laura Phelps. Being a parole officer, she'd probably seen her fair share of the darker elements in life. *Time to change tack.*

'I apologise,' said Jo. 'We're all simply worried about Niall and, in all honesty, I don't think that Alan was acting in character either. We think he may have been working with someone else – hence our interest in any known associates.'

Phelps' guard, she could see, was still well and truly up. 'And like I said, I honestly do not know anything about the group he attended.'

'But you think it's genuine?'

'Whatever Alan Trent is, or was, he's not a liar.'

With a double knock at the door, Stratton came in. 'We've got an address from one of his work colleagues. We're going in.'

Chapter 10

Jo had been on armed responses before, always planned drug raids, almost always pre-dawn. The intelligence was normally gold standard. They knew what they were getting. This couldn't have felt more different.

They took her car, because there was no way it could be tagged as police by locals or Trent. The AFO unit was travelling from the other side of the city, while Heidi Tan and George Dimitriou were with Carrick. Together they would converge on Warwick Close in the Headington area of the city. It was an area she'd visited once before, for a house party that got out of hand when she was sixteen. One of her mates had her stomach pumped. She remembered Mum's dread silence as she'd come to pick her up from the hospital.

Following Whittaker's list of contacts, one of the other gardeners – a Lucas Hardy – revealed he'd dropped Alan Trent at home after work a few weeks ago. He couldn't remember the house number, but he knew the road, because it made him think of the singer Dionne.

'*This is AR7*,' came the voice over the earpiece. '*We are in position. Over.*'

'We're approaching Warwick Close now,' said Carrick, as Jo slowed the car.

'*This is Unit 1,*' said Stratton. '*Unit 2, ID the house if you can. We're looking for a maroon '93 Vauxhall Cavalier Estate. Once you're positive, call it in. AR7, await my signal. Over.*'

'This is Unit 2. Roger,' said Carrick.

'*This is AR7. Roger,*' said the armed response leader.

Jo switched off the engine and they climbed out.

The estate was only a couple of miles from the city-centre grandeur, but couldn't have been more different. Pokey sixties terraces with tiny windows. Messy front gardens strewn with rubbish. Jo saw an elderly couple walking a dog dragging one of its back legs, but otherwise the road was deserted. A side road opened onto a row of garages.

'Let's take a look,' said Jo.

She and Carrick walked slowly through, and she saw the car immediately. A dirty reddish estate of a make and model you rarely saw on the road. It even had a chipped dent just above the fender on the right-hand side. The garage it was parked beside had no number, but the one next to it belonged to 12.

Carrick spoke into his chest mic. 'This is Unit 1. He's number 14 . . .'

'*Confirm one-four,*' said AR.

'Confirm, one-four. Over.'

'*This is Unit 1,*' said Stratton. '*Stand by Unit 2 at the rear of the property. AR7 – primary objective is extraction of Niall McDonagh. Eleven years old. Secondary objective is the arrest of Alan Trent. After that, secure anybody else in the house. Over.*'

'*This is AR7. Roger.*'

'*This is Unit 1. You have permission to go. Over.*'

'*This is AR7. Roger and out.*'

Jo's heart was pumping as she followed the alley running between the row of garages and the rear gardens of the properties. A discarded washing machine lay on its side, and a child's plastic trike blocked the way.

On the other side of the house she heard the rumble of the AFO van before it stopped. Then about ten seconds of silence. She held her breath.

A door smashed, and then the shouting started.

'Armed police! Armed police!'

Screams.

'Get on the ground. You! On the fucking ground!'

A moment later, there was a cry of pain at the rear of the house, just over the fence, then a young Asian man burst through the gate in front of her, bare-chested and wearing tracksuit bottoms. He crashed into the wall on the other side, saw Jo and Carrick and sprinted the other way down the alley.

'No you don't!' said Carrick, after him in a flash.

The kid tried to vault the fence at the far end, but Carrick grabbed him by the legs and hauled him down, accidentally exposing his backside at the same time. There was blood spattering thickly on the ground, but she couldn't see where it was from.

'Get off me, man!' shouted the kid.

'Stop fighting then,' said Carrick. He prised an arm back and knelt in the small of the suspect's back.

'*This is AR7,*' crackled the radio. '*We have Trent.*'

'*And Niall?*' said Stratton.

'*Negative, sir . . . House is secure.*'

'You got him?' said Jo, nodding to the bare-arsed young man. 'He's injured.'

'Yes,' said Carrick. 'You go.'

Jo headed into a small back yard laid to flagstones. Other than two bins and a crate of empty glass bottles, there was nothing but a washing line. More fresh blood on the ground, presumably from the youth in custody.

An armed officer looked out at her through the kitchen window and she held up her badge.

'We got one running through the back,' she said.

She went through the open back door into a kitchen heavy with the smell of spices. A narrow corridor with a thick carpet. Gold-framed family photos on the wall. In the front room, a man and a woman in their fifties, Indian heritage, lay on the ground, the TV showing a talent show. They looked petrified to be surrounded by gun-wielding officers.

Tan and Dimitriou, both vested and helmeted, came through the smashed front door ahead of Stratton.

Jo held back as they headed up the stairs, then followed.

She dreaded what she'd find, but her feet carried her onwards. An open door straight ahead led to a bathroom, then on the right was a master bedroom surrounded by copious wardrobes. Two armed officers stood by the far door, at ease, and looking in.

There was no noise on the other side.

Jo passed a room with a door smashed off its hinges. Inside, the window was open, and there were various movie posters on the wall and the faint smell of cannabis. Jo quickly put two and two together. The open window, the blood out back. The stupid kid had jumped.

She walked on, to where the other detectives were disappearing into the final room.

'Bugger,' said Stratton.

Jo caught up and looked in.

On the floor was a mattress, and beside it a sports holdall and a few items of clothing. A transparent plastic bag contained a toothbrush, paste and a bar of soap. The only furniture was a plywood wardrobe.

A bare bulb cast everything in harsh light and dark shadow, including the man hanging from the wardrobe pole, almost in a sitting position – legs out in front of him, heels on the floor, but backside a fraction off the ground. He'd tied a sheet around his neck and the pole, and his head was lolling to one side. Despite his face being almost blue, it was clearly Alan Trent.

★   ★   ★

Ben and Jo had once engaged in a macabre competition: who'd seen the most dead bodies in the line of duty. Looking back, it was grossly insensitive, but when they'd started the game, they'd both been relatively new to the job. You could even call it small talk, a language of courtship that came naturally to two young police officers. It was probably a coping mechanism more than anything, a way to face the horrific things the day-to-day threw at them. Auto accidents, electrocutions, the elderly who'd met their end alone and neglected. Jo recalled a date in the early days when Ben had arrived an hour late, only to announce he'd taken the lead, having come from a scene where a tree surgeon had misjudged his balance and broken his neck falling from fifteen feet.

As the years wore on and the single-digit scores grew to double, then into the twenties, they'd both stopped playing. But, as she looked at the bloated, strangulated face of Alan Trent, Jo found herself vaguely wondering who was winning now.

An ambulance had come to take the injured boy to hospital – he had a laceration to his upper leg and a suspected broken ankle. There was some drug paraphernalia in his bedroom, which might have explained the otherwise idiotic decision to leap from a first-floor window. Heidi Tan and George Dimitriou were downstairs talking to the boy's mother and father. It looked like they were in the clear. Jo heard their protestations from the upstairs landing.

'He was just renting the room,' said the husband. 'We put an ad in the window of the newsagents.'

'He always paid on time,' said the wife. 'What is it he's done?'

'He's wanted in connection with a missing child,' said Heidi. A gasp. 'Not the boy at the carnival in Jericho?'

'Yes, I'm afraid so. We're going to need to ask you a few questions, to see if we can establish his movements over the last few days. Why don't you take a seat?'

'Is our boy Balreick in trouble?'

'We don't think so,' said Heidi. 'It looks like we startled him – he'll be looked after.'

'Alan was just a lodger, you know? Kept himself to himself.'

'Of course,' said Heidi. 'Shall I make us all a cup of tea?'

Stratton told them to get started without forensics. This was in all likelihood a secondary crime scene. As Carrick and Jo worked, the mood was sombre and mostly silent, not owing to any respect for the recently departed, who for the moment remained as they'd found him, but because of what it undoubtedly meant for Niall McDonagh.

Alan Trent had few possessions. A couple of sets of spare clothing, a pair of work boots, and the trainers his corpse was wearing. His Gloucester College baseball cap was hanging from a peg on the back of the door.

DCI Stratton, having dismissed the AFO unit, was pacing the hallway outside, probably wondering how he was going to break the news to the McDonaghs.

The wardrobe pole, a wooden rod spanning three feet across, was bowed under Trent's body weight, but he'd managed to tie the torn sheet to two anchor points in a V shape, to split the load and avoid it breaking. It struck Jo as almost comic. Carrick carefully unhooked the pole and let the body sag to the ground.

Jo patted down Trent's pockets. In one she found his wallet, which contained a driving licence, a bank card and a blood donor card. In the other was a mobile phone, which had clearly run out of battery. There was no charger that she could see.

His back pocket contained a set of car keys, a Yale which she guessed opened the front door and a small key that looked like it was for a padlock or bike lock.

'We need to check his car,' she said.

They formed a slow procession downstairs, through the back door and out to the garages where the Vauxhall Cavalier was parked. The central-locking electrics had gone, so Jo opened the car manually. Carrick walked purposefully to the boot and popped it open. It was empty apart from a toolbox, a pair of gardening gloves, and some bolt cutters. Carrick pulled up the shelf over the spare wheel.

And there, looking back at them, was a clown mask.

'Get this whole place cordoned off,' Stratton said to the uniforms. 'No one else touches it until the forensics get here.'

It was close to midnight, but lights had come on in pretty much all the surrounding houses. There were a few people out in dressing gowns, and a group of teens in hoodies with their bikes. Someone asked if 'Bal' was in trouble, to which Jo replied he wouldn't be jumping out of another window any time soon. It didn't look like he had any involvement at all, but a few routine questions at the A&E would clear that up.

They regrouped with Tan and Dimitriou back in the kitchen.

'What now?' said Stratton.

'We check the phone for recent records,' said Carrick.

'We'll get proper statements from Mr and Mrs Singh,' said Dimitriou. 'They're understandably a bit confused at the moment, but they must be able to give us more on Trent's movements over the last week.'

'I'll talk to Niall's parents in the morning,' said Stratton, and Jo didn't envy him for a second.

★   ★   ★

Stratton said she could go home, but there was no way she'd go knocking on her brother's door at this time of night. For one thing, she couldn't face their questions. She said she'd go back to the station and see if there was anything else in the files that could help indicate where Trent might have taken his victim. No one said it explicitly, but she sensed the shift: the search for a living, breathing boy was over.

We're looking for a body now.

As she walked back down Warwick Close, she caught a flash, and looked up. And there, across the road, was the sporty Audi she'd seen back at the Bradford-on-Avon worksite.

'Oi!' she said, but the window was already winding up. She marched across the street, only to see the car pull away at speed. 'Fucking bitch!' she whispered, memorising the plate for good measure.

When she got back, the front desk clerk said Laura Phelps had left an hour ago, but with a message saying that they could call her day or night. The clerk also said that Lucas Hardy was still in IR3.

'Sorry, who?' said Jo.

'The bloke who gave us the address,' said the clerk. 'I wasn't sure if we could cut him loose.'

Jo went through to the back, and found an athletic-looking man with golden curly hair asleep at the table, head resting on his folded arms. She nudged him awake and he straightened up blearily. He looked to be in his late twenties and there was a comforting, sun-kissed smell about him.

'You can go home now,' she said.

'Did you find Al?' he asked.

'We did,' she said. After the day she'd had, she almost told him straight, but something about the concern in his voice softened her. 'Are you close?'

'Nah – he's a good worker though.'

'I'm sorry to tell you he's deceased,' said Jo.

The man blinked, mouth agape. 'You're having a laugh.'

'Depends on your sense of humour,' said Jo grimly.

'Bloody hell. You're serious. Al's dead?'

'Afraid so.' She was knackered. Ready to drop, but she felt a sense of responsibility after breaking the news. 'How well did you know him?' she added conversationally as she held open the door.

'Barely at all,' said Lucas. 'Drove him home a couple of times, that's all.' Jo waited by the door as Lucas shambled over. 'Fella could tell a story.'

'Such as?' Jo remembered the victim impact statements in the file. *I bet he didn't tell you about the time he snuck his hand into little kids' sleeping bags at night, stealing their childhoods away.*

Lucas grinned, looking like a puppy. His green eyes were quite startling against his tanned skin.

'Oh, y'know. About his time in the forces.'

It was a detail she hadn't been expecting. 'Alan Trent was in the army?'

'No, RAF. So he told me. Went all over the world on aircraft carriers.'

'And you believed him?'

'Sure. Why not?' Lucas tapped his forearm. 'He had this flier's ink. On his arm. A bird or something. Said he got it in Morocco. *Through hard work we reach the stars.*'

'I'm sorry?'

'P.A.A.A. *Per ardua ad astra.* It's Latin. Written under his tattoo.'

'Oh . . . right.'

Lucas smiled. 'I get it. You're surprised a gardener knows Latin.'

'A little.'

'I don't,' said Lucas. 'Just so happens it was my school motto. Sorry, what's your name? I'm Lucas.'

'Er . . . Jo. Jo Masters. Thanks for your help, Lucas.' She fished out a card and handed it to him. 'If there's anything else you think might be important, or if you need to get in touch.'

He looked at his watch, smiled apologetically, eyes crinkling at the edges.

'I'm stuck in town for a while. You fancy a drink, Jo? I know a Moroccan place that's actually not full of idiots this time of night.'

Jo wasn't at all prepared for that. She couldn't remember the last time someone had asked her out.

'Er . . . oh . . . no, I can't.'

He blushed. 'Of course not. Silly me. You're probably married. Or you hate Moroccans. Joke, by the way.'

He made his way to the door, tried to open it, and bounced off.

'You need to press the buzzer,' said Jo, smiling to herself. 'Here, let me.'

'This is getting really embarrassing now,' said Lucas.

She pressed the button to open the door. 'Everyone does it,' she said. 'And I'm not married. It's just bad timing,' she said. 'Middle of a case and all. If you need a ride home, we can arrange one.'

'No need,' said Lucas, as he pushed open the door. 'My humiliation is complete.'

And with that, he was gone.

Jo, shaking her head, returned to the incident room alone. *I should have taken him up on the offer.* It wasn't often she got asked out in the flesh, rather than a simple swipe on a smartphone. She couldn't imagine Lucas Hardy using a dating app – he seemed a bit more old-fashioned. Her own brief attempts had been disastrous. The first guy seemed okay, for all of five minutes, but as soon as he heard what she did for a living the conversation had soured. Turned out he had a record. And the second had been great for three days – until his girlfriend had showed up while Jo was still in the shower.

She found herself flicking back through the Trent file. There was nothing in there about time in the forces, but then there was nothing listing his occupation at all. She wondered when he'd retired, and if it had been voluntary. There was one person who might know. It was close to one o'clock in the morning, but Laura Phelps probably wasn't home yet. She found the parole officer's card.

She didn't answer, and Jo didn't leave a message, because she couldn't get her thoughts in order. She didn't really know what she wanted to say.

Phelps rang back. 'Hello?'

'It's Detective Masters. We spoke earlier.'

'Sorry, I had to leave. My little girl – she likes to get in with us in the early hours.'

Jo smiled to herself. 'No, of course. I was just wondering – is it true that Alan Trent was in the RAF?'

'Yes, served twenty years. Retired in '99. He was some sort of signalman. I think he was based at Brize Norton.' She sighed. 'He said it kept him on the straight and narrow. It was only after, when he was back on civvie street, that it went bad for him.'

Jo had no time for the wistfulness.

'We found him by the way. Looks like suicide.'

'Oh, no . . .'

'No trace of his victim though.'

For a few seconds, Phelps didn't speak.

'Are you sure you can't give us anything else about the support group he attended?' asked Jo.

'Look, I told you everything I know.' A pause, then she sounded more reflective, maybe even as though she was fighting tears. 'That poor, poor man.'

Jo ended the call.

Chapter 11

SUNDAY

At four in the morning, Jo caught forty winks on the sofa in the rec room, vaguely aware of the comings and goings during the morning shift change. She dreamt fitfully of her father, and cycling down the canal towpath in Oxford. It was a happy time – they'd headed all the way out to Wolvercote, where he'd sunk two pints at the Anchor, and she'd had a lemonade and black. There was an old stone packhorse bridge to cross, and Dad had always claimed a troll lived beneath it. She'd never dared to look, but this time, in this dream, she did. The water was still, opaque, but as she peered in, something floated to the surface and she knew it was a body. It rolled over, a white face, eyes gone, the skin of its lips distended and sloughing away . . .

'Thought you might want this?'

Dimitriou was sitting on the table in front of the couch, holding a steaming cup of coffee. Jo prised herself up. Her neck felt locked in place, but a few flexes cranked it back to life. The clock read 06.15. Pale light behind the closed slats of the blinds.

'Thanks,' she said.

'You could've gone home.'

'Did you?'

'No chance. Overseeing the work on the car.'

'Find anything?'

'There are hair fibres in the boot, and some blood. Loads of prints. We're guessing there'll be a match for Niall somewhere.'

'Fuck. Where the hell did he take him?'

'Drawing a blank at the moment. Trent had been staying in the house for four months. The Singhs were letting out the room to earn a bit of extra cash. Trent replied to an ad in the window of the local newsagent. They said he was a gentleman, no trouble, paid the rent in cash a week in advance.'

'Visitors?'

'None they knew of, and Mrs Singh doesn't leave the house much.'

The dream of the floating corpse wouldn't leave her alone.

'Maybe we check the river?' said Jo. 'It runs through Port Meadow.'

'You think he killed him straight away?'

'I'm not really thinking clearly at all yet. Give me a minute.' She sipped the coffee. 'Anything from the phone?'

'Pay as you go – no credit, and the call record wiped. We're seeing what we can get from the network.' He ran his hand over his stubble. 'I don't envy Stratton this morning. He's going to update the parents at eight. There's no pay rise you could give me to make that call.'

'Tell me about it. Is there a place I can wash?'

'Sure – shower in the basement. Ignore my Lycra hanging up. I like to give it an air down there.'

Jo took her overnight bag down, showered and brushed her teeth. She'd packed one more clean set of underwear, but she had a feeling that today would bring a conclusion one way or the other. Either they'd find Niall's body, or the operation would scale back and she'd be returning to Bath.

And Ben.

Funny, in the last twelve hours she'd barely thought of him, or Dylan Jones.

She wiped the steam from the mirror and got the same moment of cognitive dissonance as always when she saw the reflection looking back. *When did I get so fucking old?* She started applying make-up, but overdid it, so washed it all off. Sod it – there was no one here she needed to impress.

As she reached the top of the stairs, opening the door into the corridor, her feet slowed, and a heartbeat later she knew why. The voice from the incident room was one she knew well.

What's he doing here? It was like her ruminations downstairs had somehow summoned him.

Ben was leaning casually against a wall, drinking a mug of tea. He looked fresh as a daisy, in his best suit, chatting to George Dimitriou. He smiled when he saw her.

'Detective Masters.'

'Sir,' she replied.

The confusion must have been obvious on her face.

'The DCIs have been sharing intelligence – looks like the links between our cases are becoming a little more than super-ficial.'

'They are?'

'Alan Trent, manual labourer, clown mask. He'd have been twenty-six when Dylan Jones went missing.'

'It's a long shot,' said Jo. 'He was at sea a lot. Aircraft carriers, I think.'

'It's currently our only shot,' said Ben, shortly. 'And don't worry, we'll look into his service record.'

The sudden development had taken her by surprise, and her head was filled with doubts.

'The suspect in the Dylan Jones kidnap was tall,' she said.

'According to the one witness,' said Ben. 'Who was, if I remember, an eight-year-old girl.'

Jo knew more than most how dodgy a person's memory could be, especially with stress added to the equation. In her remembering, the clown who'd walked off with Dylan had been practically a giant.

'Point taken,' said Jo, 'but I'm not sure Trent's right for Jones. His MO was more cautious – the kids he molested . . .'

'I read the file, detective,' said Ben. 'But he didn't look right for Niall either. Maybe something went wrong with Dylan. Maybe he fought back or made the wrong noise. There are a hundred variables we'll never know.'

'Of course, sir,' said Jo. She was struggling to put her objections into words, because they were coming from instinct rather than logic.

'A shame the bastard grew a conscience and killed himself,' said Ben.

Dimitriou nodded in agreement, and Jo felt herself shrivel up. *He can't just walk in here and take over.*

'My money is that we find he was on shore leave. Maybe took a part-time job for the contractor who dug the pool at Bradford and used the opportunity to bury the body.'

'That would be pretty conclusive,' said Jo. 'But we don't even know the exact date the pool went in, do we?'

'We're getting there,' said Ben.

'Nice to meet you, sir,' said Dimitriou. He turned to Jo. 'I'm going to head home and get some rest. Maybe you should do the same?'

'I might,' said Jo, knowing that she wouldn't.

Dimitriou left the room, leaving Ben and Jo alone.

'You look tired,' he said. 'Paul said you were staying at theirs.' His use of her brother's Christian name riled her for some reason. Maybe that wasn't fair though. She couldn't expect him to return to a more formal address, just because they'd split. And asking him to delete her brother's number from his phone would look completely heavy-handed.

'I kipped there one night,' she said.

Ben edged closer and she backed away.

'Wow!' he said, holding up both hands defensively. 'Do you hate me *that* much?'

'I don't hate you,' she said. 'I just want to know why you're here.'

'I've told you. We're looking into the possibility that the two missing kids are linked.'

'That's bullshit,' said Jo. 'And even it were true, you didn't have to drive thirty miles to find out. We have these things called phones now.'

Ben shook his head. 'Be professional, for God's sake.'

'*Professional!* Are you kidding me? What would you know about—'

The phone rang on Heidi Tan's desk and Jo snatched it up, sliding into the chair, glad of the distraction.

'I'm trying to get hold of Detective Tan,' said the man. 'I know it's early, but . . .'

'This is Detective Masters,' said Jo. 'Can I help?'

'I'm phoning from the morgue at John Radcliffe,' said the man. 'We're processing a deceased male. Name's Alan Trent.'

'Go ahead – I'm working that case.'

'It might be nothing, but we're bagging the clothes, and we found a receipt in his back pocket. The files said personal possessions had been removed at scene of death, so I thought I'd better flag it. It relates to a purchase made only two nights ago. For fuel at a petrol station outside the city.'

'Can you photograph it and send it over?' said Jo. She gave the man her email address and hung up.

141

'Lead?' asked Ben.

'I doubt it,' she said, trying not to show any flicker of excitement. The last thing she wanted was Ben tagging along. She remained at Heidi's desk, with her back to him. 'Listen, I'll be asking for a transfer as soon as this case is over.'

'You don't have to do that. *I'll move.*'

'I don't want anything from you,' she said. 'You have to understand that.'

Ben hitched up his chin, so he was looking at her with a hurt pride. 'Fine,' he said. 'You're a good detective, Jo. I don't want to stand in the way of your career.'

'Thank you,' she said, ignoring the implication in his words that he was doing her some sort of favour.

Jo slid her laptop out of her bag and logged on to her force ID. When the receipt came through, she quickly brought it up on screen: £5.14 for fuel, purchased from the Shell garage on the A40, near Witney. *Either he was broke, or he knew he wasn't going far.* But it was the time that set her heart racing: 01.26 on July 28th, about four hours after Niall was taken. She searched the location quickly and saw it was only a mile from one of the ANPR cameras that had picked up his vehicle twelve days earlier. Somehow he'd avoided them on the night of the kidnap, or he'd been in a different car.

'I'm going to go to my brother's for a bit,' she said, gathering her coat and heading for the door. 'Call me with any developments.'

'Sure,' said Ben. He was looking through the parole board papers for Trent, sent over by the prison service.

As soon as she was in her car, Jo called the service station, and said she'd be over in half an hour to look at the CCTV. She thought about ringing Stratton, but he was probably with the parents already, so she decided against it. Plus, she didn't want her whereabouts getting back to Ben.

She drove quickly out of the city, taking the Northern Bypass westwards – a lonely straight road shielded from the surrounding countryside by trees on both sides. She passed the odd lorry stop or layby, and a few turn-offs to small towns, but mostly it was empty black tarmac. It wouldn't have been busy the previous Friday night, but there would have been some traffic. It was hard to imagine Trent stopping anywhere and doing anything with Niall's body on this stretch.

The Shell garage was on the opposite side of the road, the eastbound carriageway, and she pulled in. There were two staff on duty, a portly thirty-something manager and a young female assistant. The former seemed relatively excited, but Jo had been vague on the phone. He took her through a back office that reeked of body odour, to a small desk. He began to show her how to use the equipment.

'It's fine,' she said. 'I'm familiar with the set-up.'

'Oh, right,' he said. 'Can I get you anything?'

Jo found the right section of the digital recording. 'No, thanks. Were you working two nights ago? Early hours of Saturday morning.'

'No – that would have been Brie,' he said, with a backwards toss of his head, indicating the girl he'd left on the till. 'She does most of the night shifts.'

'I need to speak with her then,' said Jo.

The man – his name tag read Ronnie – looked put out.

'She's not the sharpest tool in the box,' he said, shielding his mouth mock-theatrically.

'You can shut the door behind you,' said Jo.

The CCTV was a twin-feed showing the forecourt with a small section of the road beyond, and another angle from behind the counter, pointing through the service window. The time in the receipt narrowed it down precisely and she found the point in question in less than a minute. Trent's Cavalier pulled off the main road, entering the middle lane of pumps. She squinted at the jumpy footage as he got out. There was no sign of anyone in the passenger or rear seats, but the angle made it impossible to be sure. Trent filled the car for less than fifteen seconds, then dropped out of sight, reappearing as he limped up to the counter. He paid in cash, looking around as he did so, then climbed back into his car. All in all, maybe a minute and half had passed. He looked a little agitated, Jo thought, but maybe she was projecting. She rewound again – the car was coming off the nearside, heading back towards Oxford. He'd been somewhere else with Niall, now he was returning. Her sixth sense told her the boy wasn't in the boot any more.

Where did you take him, you sick fuck?

The door opened and the girl entered. 'Hi, Ron said you wanted me?'

Jo rewound the footage until she paused it on the man. 'You were working the night shift on Friday?'

'Yeah.' The girl looked at the screen. 'It's boring as shit and you get all the freaks. But hey – it's double time.'

'And do you remember this man?'

'Yeah, proper weirdo. At least he wasn't jerking off though. That happens, believe me.'

Jo made a 'yuck' face. She liked Brie a lot more than Ronnie. 'Why was he a freak?'

'He was crying,' she said. 'Like, proper sobbing.'

'Did you talk to him?'

'Er . . . what do you think? No way. I've got a panic button, in case anyone, y'know, gets aggressive. But he was just crying.'

'Thanks Brie,' said Jo. 'You can get back to work.'

Brie paused with her hand on the door. 'Is this about that missing kid?'

'You know about that?' said Jo. 'Let me guess, Facebook?'

Brie frowned. 'Nope. It was on the radio just now. Ronnie only lets us listen to . . .'

Oh shit. No. Jo interrupted. 'What did they say?'

'Some woman was talking about the Killer Clown.'

★ ★ ★

Back at the station, Heidi Tan met her at the back door.

'I'd vest up before you go in there,' she said. 'Stratton is not a happy bunny.'

Thankfully the DCI was in his office, though the blinds were only partially drawn, and she saw him through the glass wall on the phone. He caught Jo's glance with a look of unadulterated contempt as she walked in. Ben was sitting with Carrick, looking at a computer monitor. Both looked a little grim.

The page was one of the tabloids, and the headline lurid.

KILLER CLOWN STRIKES AGAIN, with the subheading, *Police search for body as suspect commits suicide.* The author of the piece was Lindsay Makepeace, 'with additional reporting by Rebekah Fitzwilliam'.

'Tell me Stratton got to the parents before they saw this,' said Jo.

'Wish I could,' said Carrick. 'She's the woman we saw yesterday, right?'

And then Jo realised what was going on. 'Stratton doesn't think that I—'

'Masters, my office please.'

She turned to see the DCI glaring at her. 'Sir, I—'

'In private, I think.'

He turned and waited for her to follow.

'Good luck,' muttered Carrick. 'His bark's worse than his bite.'

Sometimes it's better just to get the bite over with, thought Jo, steeling herself.

She closed the door behind her. 'Sir, I don't know how she got hold of—'

'Have you got children, detective?'

The question threw her. 'No, sir.'

'Then you have absolutely no fucking clue what it's like to lose one.'

Jo felt her gut physically stir, a reflex. She shut that part of herself down.

'Professor and Doctor McDonagh were going through hell enough already. They were relying on us, and we let them down in the worst possible way.'

'Sir, if I can explain. Rebekah Saunders . . . Fitzwilliam . . . We went to school together. We're not friends – I've not seen her for years.'

'Another startling coincidence.'

Jo didn't like the insinuation. Boss or not, she knew if she let the accusation pass, that was it. It would dog her for years.

'Sir, you have my word I haven't told Fitzwilliam, or any other journalist, anything about the case.'

'We didn't tell anyone he hung himself,' said Stratton.

Jo thought back. She just told Phelps it was suicide, she thought. And she hadn't spilled it to the gardener, Lucas Hardy.

'Maybe it was one of the Singhs? The son?'

Stratton looked unconvinced. 'I only took you on here because of Rob's recommendation,' he said. 'He said you were one of his best, but now I'm beginning to doubt that. From where I'm standing, your personal connection to the cases looks like a liability.'

'Sir, if you want me to take a step back, I can.' It galled her to say it, but there were some battles you couldn't win. *First Dylan Jones, now this. What a fucking week.*

'In some ways, that would be the easiest thing,' said Stratton. 'But we're in damage limitation now. The media team will be flat out shielding us, but our job is to find Niall McDonagh and put this whole thing to rest quickly and professionally. We need all hands on deck to do that, yours included. You can go.'

Jo, bruised but not beaten, headed for the door.

So much for my transfer request.

Chapter 12

None of the rest of the team mentioned Saunders at all. It was heads-down. Stratton was called away to speak to the Chief Constable in Kidlington, and left like a man on his way to the scaffold.

Heidi Tan and George Dimitriou were back in just after noon, establishing a timeline of events. Trent's movements up until the kidnap were becoming clearer. According to Peter Whittaker, the head gardener, he never worked Monday mornings at the college, but he'd come in Monday afternoon through Thursday. It was around three p.m. on the Monday that Professor and Doctor McDonagh had brought their son to the college while they collected some items from their respective teaching rooms. During that forty-five-minute window, Niall had been given free run of the college grounds. Another of the ground-staff, working with Alan Trent that day on the cricket pitch, reported meeting Niall by the nets, where he was messing around with the automatic ball launcher. While he went to get the roller from the pavilion, it looked like Trent was alone with Niall for perhaps ten minutes. It seemed likely that they discussed the circus that Friday coming, because on Tuesday morning, before work, Trent purchased the clown mask. Wednesday and Thursday, Trent behaved normally. Friday was something of a blank, until the kidnap itself. According to Mrs Singh, Trent left before eight a.m., returning briefly around dinner time, and she wasn't sure what time he returned. The pathologist was estimating, from the advanced rigor mortis, that Trent killed himself in the early hours of Saturday morning, not long after Brie from the Shell garage reported him being upset as he purchased just enough fuel to get him home.

The whats and wheres were all there, the pieces slotting into place, but for Jo, the jigsaw made no sense without the whys. Was this really a case of a man driven by unnatural passion? Had Trent taken Niall somewhere, performed some unspeakable act, then killed him?

The only person even slightly satisfied was Ben, and he drifted in and out of their investigation like a half-interested spectator. He'd taken a visit to the morgue, to get some preliminaries on Alan Trent. It seemed unlikely they'd get a DNA match with the body of Dylan Jones, but it needed only one shred of concrete evidence and his case was closed. Jo heard one half of a frustrating telephone conversation with Mr Robertson, the former partner at RTA, the architects on the Bradford house. It sounded, unsurprisingly, that he was having trouble remembering the contractors he used who'd put in a swimming pool almost thirty years ago. The name Alan Trent apparently meant nothing either.

On the wall of the incident room hung a framed, 1:25000 Ordnance Survey map of Oxford's urban sprawl and its rural environs, the A40 a red line snaking horizontally through the centre. Jo took a black marker, ringing the glass above the pertinent locations. Port Meadow, the Singhs' house in Warwick Close, Gloucester Close, and then further afield. The Shell garage near Witney. It was thirteen miles give or take, but the ANPR suggested Trent had not used the A40 on Friday night.

Maybe, two weeks before, he'd clocked the cameras and selected a different route. Given the time of the petrol stop, just after midnight, it was fair to surmise that Trent had driven straight from Port Meadow to a location where he'd disposed of Niall McDonagh's body, before returning home, apparently in despair, and taking his own life.

'I hope that wipes off,' said Carrick. 'Not saying it's a sackable offence, but you probably don't need any more black marks next to your name.'

'Where was he going?' said Jo.

'Or who was he going to meet?' said Carrick. 'You still think he had an accomplice?'

'I don't know.'

She did the maths in her head – the kidnap at 20.30, the Shell garage after midnight.

'How far could he get in two hours?'

'Wales, at that time of night,' said Carrick. 'Needle in a haystack springs to mind.'

Jo's eyes snagged on a place name. 'Brize Norton,' she read aloud – she circled it.

'Air base,' said Carrick. 'Not sure it would be the best place to dump a body. Quite a lot of people with guns hanging around.'

'The parole officer – Phelps – she said Trent was based there, before he retired.'

'I read the file,' said Carrick. 'Hidden depths and all that.'

'Might be worth a call to them,' said Jo. 'Maybe he still has contacts there?'

'Can't hurt,' said Carrick.

Jo started rubbing off the ink when she saw the reflection of a looming presence in the glassy reflection.

'What can we do for you, Harry?' asked Carrick.

'Front desk let me through,' said Ferman. 'Wanted to speak with Detective Masters, if that's all right.'

Jo arranged her face into a smile as she faced him. She hadn't forgotten his brusqueness on the phone the day before.

'I'll leave you to it,' said Carrick. 'Jo, I'll call Brize Norton. See what I can dig up.'

She nodded. 'Detective Ferman. How are you?'

'Oh, call me Harry,' he said. He was wearing the same suit and shirt as the first time she'd met him, though she thought he'd polished his shoes again. 'I wanted to apologise,' he said. 'You caught me at a bad time yesterday.'

Despite whatever aftershave he was wearing, she could smell the drink on him. Brandy. Just like her dad.

'It's not a problem,' she said. 'Been a tough couple of days for all of us.' *Surely he hasn't come in just for this.*

'I saw the news this morning,' he said. 'They're saying it might be the same suspect.'

'It's one hypothesis,' she said, being as low-key as possible.

'Is that the same as a guess?' said Ferman. His eyes twinkled slightly. She imagined he would have been a handsome man, thirty years ago. She wondered briefly about his wife, and if, like the daughter, she was dead too.

'There are some circumstantial similarities,' she said.

He nodded knowingly. 'Keeping your cards close to your chest,' he said, looking a little hurt. 'I understand.'

Jo felt a pang of sympathy. 'It really isn't that,' she said. 'Does the name Alan Trent mean anything to you?'

He shook his head. 'I've racked my brains, but no. Is there any link to the burial site?'

'We're still looking,' said Jo. 'Between you and me, I'm not convinced the cases are connected at all. Dylan was much younger, for a start. I wouldn't want to get your hopes up.'

'And between all of us,' said Ben, 'Detective Masters thinks too hard.' Jo hadn't even realised he'd returned. He thrust out a hand. 'Ben Coombs, Avon and Somerset.'

A slow smile spread across Ferman's face, and his eyes all but disappeared into creases. 'I've heard the name,' he said, extending his own hand slowly and shaking Ben's.

Ben's eyebrows shot up. 'All good, I hope.'

'Oh yes. You're on the Dylan Jones case, then?'

'Hopefully putting her to bed very soon,' said Ben.

The smile on Ferman's face was slightly disconcerting. 'This fellow – Trent – you really think he was the one?'

The tone – bemused, patriarchal – left no doubt that Ferman wasn't buying the theory, and Jo saw from Ben's dead stare he hadn't missed it.

'A few pointers that way, Detective . . . Sorry, remind me of your name?'

'Ferman. But you can call me Harry. Not on the payroll any more.'

Ben nodded. 'Live locally?'

'Fairly,' said Ferman.

'So you drove here?' Ben made an exaggerated sniff. He'd smelled the booze too.

Ferman's face darkened. 'No, I got the bus,' he said.

An uncomfortable silence followed, and Jo knew from the interview room that Ben was adept at those.

'I only came in to say, we had a list, on the original case – persons of interest. Thing is, we dropped everything pretty fast once we'd brought Clement Matthews in. Might be worth taking another look, cross-referencing with the Bradford-on-Avon house.'

'Don't you worry about us,' said Ben, in a particularly condescending way.

'Well, I do hope you've got your man, detective,' said Ferman. 'Good day to you, Josie.'

No one called her that any more, but she didn't react to the name. She watched as Ferman turned and walked back through the door towards the front desk.

'You didn't have to be rude to him,' Jo said.

'Was I?' said Ben. 'What's he hanging around for anyway? Guy's a soak.'

'We all have our demons,' she replied. 'If you'll excuse me.'

She headed to the loos, because it was one place he couldn't shadow her. On the way, she passed Carrick, and heard a snatch of his conversation on the phone.

'It would have been in the nineties . . . yes, do. I'm not going anywhere.' He cupped the phone away. 'They're going to pull his personnel file.'

Jo headed on towards the toilets, passing the incident board where Trent's mugshot looked back at her. The oddly vulnerable face. *God, Phelps is rubbing off on me . . .*

In the toilets she heard the unmistakeable sound of retching, and was about to turn and walk out again when the toilet flushed and Heidi Tan came out.

'Sorry about that,' she said. She cradled her stomach. 'Morning sickness is a bitch.'

'Congratulations,' said Jo. 'First?'

She nodded. 'Haven't told Stratton yet, if you wouldn't mind keeping it under wraps.'

'Of course.'

Tan began to wash her hands.

'Detective Coombs seems nice,' she said, meeting Jo's eyes in the mirror. 'You worked together a long time?'

'Too long,' said Jo. Had she somehow picked up that they had history? Time to change the subject. 'Is Stratton always so uptight?'

'He's a fair-weather boss,' said Tan. 'When things are going great, he's your best friend. He'll be putting you up for a medal next week – you'll see.'

Jo laughed. 'Can't see that happening.'

Someone knocked at the door and Carrick stuck his head round. 'Jo, Heidi – I might have got something.'

They left together, and Carrick was already over at the map on the wall. Ben and Dimitriou were up too, sensing the shift of adrenalin in the room.

'So I spoke to a warrant officer over at Brize Norton. *Someone* does work on a Sunday. Trent checks out. Exemplary record before honorary discharge. But get this – he wasn't at Brize Norton for the full service term.'

'His colleague said something about being at sea,' said Jo.

'No,' said Carrick. 'He was seconded to another airbase – Bampton Castle.' He pointed to a position on the map about two miles south-west from Brize Norton and three south of the Shell garage at Witney.

'Never heard of it,' said Ben.

'You wouldn't,' said Carrick. 'It was wound down in the nineties. Completely abandoned since 2006. The officer said it was like a ghost village, tucked away in farmland.'

'Holy shit,' said Jo, and she knew she spoke for everyone. 'That's the place.'

★ ★ ★

They travelled in convoy, three unmarked cars and a squad car, and made the twenty-mile journey in just under half an hour, arriving shortly after one o'clock. RAF Bampton Castle, used predominantly in the Second World War, was a sorry-looking place, reached by a single-track country road and adjoining vast acres of flat pasture. Two rows of ten-foot tall chain-link fencing ringed the site, topped with rolls of barbed wire. From the road all Jo could see were rows of single-storey wooden and brick cabins with reinforced glass windows amid gravel-coated concrete and burned-up patches of pale grass. Beyond was a tall signal mast. The flat countryside around shimmered with a heat haze.

It's perfect. Not overlooked. Completely private. I could scream my lungs out here and no one would come.

Jo swallowed thickly. The whole place felt lonely and forgotten. Devoid of life.

She checked the imposing front gates, thinking they must be secured. But a closer inspection showed the locked bolts had been cut through. She pushed them open with a creak. There was a guardhouse, the windows smashed. Inside, a desk remained, strewn with broken glass and a few scraps of newspaper.

The others followed her in.

'Split up,' said Carrick. 'Look for any signs of activity.'

'You mean like car oil,' said Dimitriou, pointing at a shimmering patch on the ground. It might not be from the Cavalier but it was recent.

Ben latched onto Carrick and herself, while Tan and Dimitriou took an opposite path around the main building. They tried the doors as they went, but they were all secure. Jo wasn't losing hope. The disguised bolts made it clear someone had been here and didn't want anyone else to know.

She tried to peer through the windows of the buildings, but all the glass was reinforced and filthy. They had a battering ram in one of the cars, and if it came to it, they'd take the doors down one at a time.

A weed-infested car park sat behind the main building, empty and desolate, and the remains of a raised helipad too, with ground lighting spaced around the square. Beneath the main signal tower was a large semi-cylindrical Nissen Hut of corrugated metal. Jo wasn't sure why she was drawn to it, or why she had the sudden urge to call out.

'Niall!' Her voice vanished into the air, muted and desperate. She felt a little foolish too.

The dead can't hear.

She saw Dimitriou and Tan coming from the other direction. 'Nothing yet,' he called.

Twenty feet from the hut, Jo saw the padlock and chain on the double doors at one end and called back to the uniforms. 'We need bolt cutters! And a torch!'

She broke into a jog, her breathing already laboured. The others converged.

The padlock and chain looked new – no sign of rust or weathering. Her mind wandered to the third key in Alan Trent's back pocket.

Jo tried the doors anyway.

The uniform came running up with the bolt cutters. Jo jammed the cutting edge into place and, with a single slice, the lock fell off. She hauled out the chain, then opened the door.

Inside, the air was musty, and organic. The hut was about fifty feet long. She saw several rats scurrying away at the far end. It had been used as some sort of workshop by the looks of it. There were a number of wooden benches and trestles, stacked untidily near the door. Jo shone the torch to the far end, where there was more furniture, and what looked like the remains of an engine or pump on a wheeled trolley.

But no sign of Niall McDonagh.

'Hello?' called Jo.

Her voice echoed off the steel ridges of the walls and roof.

She followed the torch arc inside, playing the light over a broken bulletin board, and a stack of metal-framed chairs.

'He has to be here,' she mumbled.

'Maybe he was at one point,' said Carrick.

'Let's check the other buildings,' said Dimitriou.

Jo killed the light and turned, following the others out. She was about to shut the door when she thought she heard the faintest of sounds. She flicked it back on.

'Niall?' she yelled.

And there it was again. A human cry, indistinct but desperate, pleading – a muffled wail.

Holy fucking Christ . . .

'He's in here somewhere!' she said.

They bundled back in, picking up anything from the floor and tossing it aside. With the hut's strange resonance, it was hard to tell where the muted sound had come from. Jo's eyes fell on the trolley. It was big, twice the base of a shopping cart.

'Under there!' she said. She dropped the torch and gripped the edges of the trolley. The thing weighed a tonne. Ben joined her, and together they managed to shift it on ruined castors. There was a hatch, three feet wide, beneath.

'We're coming, Niall,' she shouted. 'Don't worry – we're coming!'

She got her fingertips under the hatch, and it came up easily, opening onto a metal ladder. She saw Dimitriou gag, and then the smell of faeces, pungent and stomach-twisting, hit her too.

'I'll go first,' said Ben, and before she could object he was swinging himself down.

She grabbed the torch again and hurried after him.

'Niall!' Ben called, and the same muffled cry came back. This time it was closer.

Jo's feet hit the ground, and she shone the torch up and down a concrete corridor, bare but for lead pipework along the one wall. The air was thick, and warm, and the stench made her eyes water. She pushed past Ben, splashing through a puddle. The ceiling dipped, and she had to duck her head too. The world had shrunk to the arc of light and the sound of the footsteps at her back. And the all-pervading smell of shit and terror.

At a T-junction, one tunnel was blocked by a pile of what looked like the carcasses of typewriters, so old they made her

157

think of film props. In the other direction, the pipework came to a junction of complex bolts and sprocket heads, matted with cobwebs. And there was a metal door, with tiny slats and a single bolt across it. When the torchlight found the gaps, she saw movement on the other side – the flash of an eye.

Jo tore the bolt aside and flung open the door.

Niall McDonagh lay on his side, barefoot but otherwise clothed, curled in the foetal position, ankles and wrists tightly bound with gaffer tape. There was more wrapped around his mouth, pressing into his cheeks. As he saw them, he wriggled and shrank away, pressing his body into the corner of the room. His hair was matted, his skin covered in a sheen of sweat, and one eye was swollen grotesquely shut.

But the other eye gleamed wildly, right into the torchlight, fixing them with a stare that didn't belong on the face of a child. A stare that said he had looked on death, made his peace with it, and now couldn't quite believe he was alive.

Chapter 13

'Give him some space,' said Jo, handing Tan the torch. She redirected the light, throwing everything into deep shadow.

'Niall, it's all right,' said Jo. 'My name is Josie. I'm a police officer. You're safe now.'

He stared at her and no sound came from his taped lips.

'Niall, we're going to get you out of here, back to your mum and dad.'

Whether it was a deliberate or unconscious choice, a tacit recognition of what Niall may well have gone through at the hands of Alan Trent, the male detectives retreated while Heidi Tan and Jo stayed with Niall. He pushed himself against the wall. *He'd claw through it if his hands were free*, Jo thought.

She reached out, gingerly, and he let her touch his hand.

'I'm going to get this tape off you,' she said. 'I'll use a small penknife.' She crouched to reach for the utility knife at her ankle, then extended the blade slowly. All the time, she reassured him. Kept talking. She wasn't sure if he was really listening. What he heard.

He froze as she cut through the tape, and even when his wrists and ankles were free, he remained balled up.

'No one will hurt you any more.'

Up above, she heard Carrick on the phone for an ambulance, giving the address details carefully.

She thought Niall would complain as they eased the tape off his mouth, but he didn't say a word. God, he looked so young.

Once he was free, she quickly checked him over for injuries. It was almost impossible in the dark to inspect him closely. His knuckles were badly scuffed, and from the extensive bruising spreading around the swollen eye, she wondered if the socket was fractured. There'd be a proper examination later, by trained professionals, and Jo tried not to dwell on what they might discover.

'Can you walk?' she asked.

Still nothing.

'Let us help you then,' said Tan.

Together they eased Niall onto his feet. He was compliant as they helped him shuffle back down the corridor towards the ladder and hatch. Dimitriou waited above, leaning in and extending a hand. Niall shrank back into Jo. She tried not to let his rancid scent enter her nostrils.

'It's all right. This is George. He's with us,' she said.

Niall put a foot on the bottom rung, and then let Dimitriou hoist him up.

Back in the Nissen Hut, Niall gazed at the gathered detectives like they were from another planet. He squinted at the main door, daylight showing the bruising up in all its florid technicolour. He began to cry, and his legs buckled.

Jo caught him. 'Hold onto me, Niall. I've got you.'

He let her hold him, crying into her shoulder, until the sound of the ambulance siren eased into the group's consciousness.

Paramedics helped Niall onto a stretcher, then wheeled him across to the emergency vehicle. Dimitriou drifted to Jo's side.

'Someone should call the parents,' she said, glad to be back in the open air.

'Andy's on it. They'll meet us at John Radcliffe.'

Jo looked back towards the hut. Her gaze fell on the broken chain and padlock.

'My bet says that third key of Trent's is a match,' said Dimitriou, eyes following hers.

'I was thinking the same,' she said.

'So why the frown?'

Jo hadn't realised she was.

'Why'd he kill himself?' she said, articulating her thoughts slowly. 'I mean, Niall's still alive. I've done a couple of murder–suicides, but never a kidnap–suicide. If he felt *that* guilty, surely he'd release his victim?'

Dimitriou gave her a pat on the back. 'You're overthinking. The parole officer said he was trying to go straight, right? He gives into temptation, can't live with himself.'

'Maybe.'

'Maybe's good enough for me. We've got him for the kidnap, we've got him for transporting the body here, and we'll have him for the padlock too. Everyone's a winner.'

Jo nodded towards the ambulance. 'Not everyone.'

★   ★   ★

'Great work, Jo,' said Stratton for the fourth or fifth time. He'd been smiling like a Cheshire cat since she returned to the station, fielding calls from the top brass. Andy Carrick was still at the hospital with the parents, and Dimitriou and Tan were on their way back from the former RAF base, where they'd been liaising with the MoD officer regarding the status of the site as a crime scene, and gathering evidence with forensics before it got dark.

Jo felt like she was in limbo, as the tension of the last twenty-four hours seeped out of her like a slow puncture. However many times she'd washed her hands and face, she could still smell Niall McDonagh's terrified effluence. No one else seemed to pick it up, though, least of all Ben, who had pulled her into an embrace as soon as she came in through the door, at close to seven p.m. And though for a split-second it felt okay, she had a rush of claustrophobia and stiffened. Perhaps he felt it too, because he let her go quickly.

'Cheer up,' he said. 'The kid's alive. You know how unlikely that looked two hours ago? You're a hero.'

Jo managed the thinnest of smiles. Ben was right in his own way. The result was the main thing. Maybe she'd have wanted Trent to face his day in court, but the statistics and surveys were pretty clear – more than half the British public would have happily seen a man like that hung anyway. Maybe it was just the detective in her that wanted all the questions answered. She couldn't accept that some secrets had probably died in that dingy wardrobe on Warwick Close.

Dimitriou and Tan arrived back, and Stratton clapped the former on the back.

'Great work, George.'

'Any news on the kid?' asked Tan.

'Only heard from Andy briefly. Parents were over the moon, obviously. Once the docs have finished examining, a specialist counsellor will go in. Lord knows what happened down there.'

'That sick bastard is lucky he's dead already,' said Dimitriou. 'He wouldn't have lasted two days in prison.'

Ben nodded enthusiastically, and even Tan didn't look shocked at the vitriol. Not for the first time, Jo felt like she was out of sync with the room. Had any of them read the Trent file and taken it in? She glanced over at the mugshot still on the board, and tried to marry what she'd read, and seen, with the facts of the case as she knew them. This opportunist who suddenly became a planner, this man trying to put his life back together, then throwing it all away with a kidnap so audacious, so unlikely, so desperately in over his head. The sad, cornered countenance looked back at her.

But maybe that's just a mask too.

'Hey, Dimi?' Dimitriou looked up. 'You get anywhere with those numbers from Trent's phone?'

'Nope. They can wait though, right?'

'Mind if I take a look?'

'Sure.' He took out his pocketbook, flipped a few pages and tore one out. 'Times and dates are all there.'

'We're heading out for a drink,' said Tan. 'You coming?'

'I'll join you in a bit,' said Jo.

'What about you, boss?' said Dimitriou to Stratton.

'I'll come for one,' he said, picking up his jacket. 'I'm not going to try and keep up with you youngsters though.'

'Phew! I wondered who was paying!' said Tan.

She and Dimitriou were first out of the door, and as Stratton followed, Jo went across to him. 'Sir, can I have a word?'

'Of course, Jo.'

'Sir, I'm not feeling it. About Trent. Does this really stack up?'

'Go on?'

She was still thinking about the suicide. 'Even if he did do *something* to Niall, and even if it was too much for him, why would he leave the kid down there?'

Stratton sat down on the edge of a desk, and folded his arms. At least he was listening.

Jo continued. 'I mean, he must have pushed that trolley back over the trapdoor. He didn't want Niall to escape. He must have known it was a death sentence. That's cruel, unbelievably so. It's hardly the act of someone suffering with guilt.'

Stratton nodded thoughtfully. 'Jo, you're trying to examine a twisted mind with your own logic. Have you thought – perhaps he was planning to go back? I know it's horrible, but maybe he hadn't *finished* with him.'

'So why kill himself at the Singhs'?'

Stratton spread his hands. 'I doubt we'll ever know for sure. Maybe he knew we were on to him.'

'How?' she pressed.

The DCI straightened up, and Jo could see from his expression that he'd had enough. 'Jo, you've been great on this, but it's time to drop it.'

'Sir, I'm just saying. If there's a chance Trent wasn't working alone – that someone else knew – we can't ignore that, can we?'

Stratton shook his head. 'No. But there's no evidence that points that way, is there? And our job is to follow the evidence.' He let his statement linger, then smiled. 'You coming for a drink?'

So that's it – conversation over.

'Sure,' she said. 'Be there in a bit.' He turned to leave and she couldn't help herself. 'Maybe we should expedite prints from Bampton though – just to see if anything comes up?'

He breathed heavily and she feared she'd pushed him too hard. 'All right. I'll ask Andy to get on it first thing.'

When he'd left as well, Jo looked at the call list from Alan Trent's phone. He'd had a limited social life. Seven numbers in all, four landlines and three mobile numbers. Dimitriou had noted that one of the phones belonged to Whittaker, the head gardener at Gloucester College, the second to Mr Singh of Warwick Close, and the other was as yet unidentified. The landlines were a taxi firm called A2B and the central switchboard for the Buckinghamshire parole board, plus a phone box situated on Pleasant Grove, and a Chinese takeaway.

He's dead. Spirit flown. Case closed. No point chasing a ghost.

And a drink did sound good, sinking into normality among normal people.

Jo picked up the phone and called the taxi firm.

'A2B taxis? Where you going please?'

'Actually, I'm a police officer. I have some questions.'

'This is the booking line.'

'Is there a supervisor I could talk to?'

'Hang on . . .'

After a pause.

'Hello, who is this?'

Jo introduced herself and her rank. 'I'm trying to find out about a pick-up,' she said. She checked Dimitriou's note. 'Maybe from Warwick Close, almost two weeks ago. Monday night.'

'Sorry, darlin'. We don't keep those sorts of records.'

'Maybe you could ask the drivers?'

'Er . . . sure.'

Jo gave her name and number again, slowly, and made the supervisor read it back. 'It's important,' she added.

'Got ya,' said the man, and hung up.

She rubbed her eyes, knowing with almost complete certainty that the piece of paper in that taxi office with her number on was at that very moment hurtling towards the waste-paper basket in a screwed-up ball.

★   ★   ★

The pub by the river already looked busy, drinkers crowding the terrace, jugs of Pimm's on several tables. Lives going on. She spotted her posse on the far side; Ben was laying down a tray filled with glasses. She absently wondered if somehow he was flush again.

She turned, suddenly dispirited, and walked back to the station car park.

She drove through the dark streets, back towards Horton, stopping at a drive-through burger place, where she ate too quickly. By the time she pulled up at Paul's she had a knot of indigestion in her gut.

'We really must give you a spare key,' said Amelia, as she came to the door.

'Auntie Jo!' squealed William from the top of the stairs. He was in his pyjamas. 'Watch this!' He sat down, rolled over, and slid down in a succession of thuds on his stomach. 'Ta-da! Can you do that?'

Jo did her best to look aghast. 'When I was little, I used to slide down the bannister,' she said.

'Don't give the little scamp ideas!' said her brother. He was, disconcertingly, wearing only his underpants when he appeared from the bathroom door at the top of the stairs, towelling his back. Jo was shocked to see he had the beginnings of a six-pack. 'Congratulations, by the way!'

His smile threw her. 'I'm sorry?'

'The McDonagh kid. You found him.'

'How did you . . .?'

'I told them,' said Emma, coming from the kitchen into the hallway, drinking a can of Diet Coke. 'Kieran told everyone. His parents are at the hospital now.'

'Does he know what happened?' asked Jo nervously.

'What *did* happen?' asked Emma.

Amelia picked up on the tension. 'Come on, Billy-O, off to bed.' She shepherded Jo's nephew back up the stairs.

Jo waited until they were out of earshot. 'Listen, Em, I'm not allowed to talk about it. It's still an active investigation.'

'Niall's all right, isn't he?' said Emma.

Jo had a flash of the twisted, swollen face. 'He's been through a pretty tough time,' she said. 'We're not really sure at the moment, but he'll need to be looked after.' She gestured to

166

the phone. 'It's probably best to let the family have some space.'

'The guy who took him is dead though? The Killer Clown?'

Jo sighed. 'You shouldn't call him that. But it does look like he took his own life.'

'Woah! Did you . . . see it?'

'I attended the scene, yes.'

'How did he do it?'

'I think that's quite enough!' said Paul, jogging down the last few stairs, now in his dressing gown. He looked at Jo accusingly. 'I'm not sure we need the full post-mortem.'

'Dad, I'm old enough to—' said Emma.

'—Clean your bedroom? Good to hear. Now might be a time to start.'

'But, Dad . . .'

'Em – give us a moment, will you?'

Emma sighed and headed upstairs. Paul headed into the kitchen, where his running shoes rested up against the back door. Jo followed.

'Sorry,' she said. 'She asked and I didn't want to lie.'

'No, it's fine,' said Paul. 'I sometimes forget she's not a little girl any more.'

Jo thought about the smoking and wondered if her brother really didn't know. 'She seems to have her head screwed on. More than I did at that age anyway.'

Paul chuckled, grabbing a beer from the fridge and twisting off the cap. 'You were a bloody nightmare. You remember that time you went to that party out near Woodstock and tried to walk home?'

'No money for a taxi.'

'Mum and Dad went mental. Had all the neighbours up at two in the morning. I kept telling them you'd be fine, but they made me get on my bike and join the search.'

'I wasn't fine,' she said, allowing herself a small grin. 'I had hypothermia.'

Amelia came in, and went straight to the fridge too. 'Glass of wine, Jo? Sounds like you had an eventful day.'

Whether it was sibling envy at seeing her brother's physique, guilt at the fast food, or simply because she wasn't ready to rehash the details of the day, Jo waved her hand in a no.

'I might go for a run too, actually. Need to let off a little steam.'

'Oh, right.' Amelia poured herself one. 'Does this mean you'll be heading back to Bath soon?'

'I imagine tomorrow,' said Jo. 'I really appreciate you putting me up by the way.'

'Don't be silly,' said Paul. '*Mi casa, tu casa.*'

She thought she caught a glance from Amelia to her brother, and made a show of looking the other way.

'So how's Ben?' asked Amelia. It was a terrible attempt at changing the subject.

'Oh . . . fine,' said Jo. 'Y'know, he's Ben.'

'William never stops talking about the time he let him switch on the siren. He wants to be a policeman, y'know? He puts his toys in his wardrobe and calls it "the prison".'

'He's good with kids,' said Jo, and she meant it.

Paul swigged his beer. 'So, do you think you two might . . .'

'Paul!' said Amelia. '*Not* appropriate!'

'Come on, we're all family,' said Jo's brother.

'It's fine,' said Jo. Paul could be thoughtless, but there was no malice. She was even touched, though mystified, that he felt they were close enough to broach the subject. She hadn't told either of them about the miscarriage. They barely spoke anyway, and a text message was hardly the right medium to pass on that sort of news.

'The answer is no,' she said, and her throat dried up around the words. 'I'm not sure it's for us.'

Paul nodded, and lifted his bottle in a toast. 'Fair enough, sis. Don't blame you. Save a packet, for one thing.'

'I'll drink to that,' said Jo, raising an imaginary glass. Amelia, she noticed, looked a little disappointed. 'Anyway, how was Mum?'

'Not great,' said Paul. 'She was pretty confused. Amelia took the kids outside. She'd lost a lot of weight too. You should drop in, while you're here. It might give her a lift.'

Or it might do the absolute opposite.

From Jo's perspective, the problem wasn't the dementia, it was the moments of lucidity. That was when her mother tended to let Jo know how she really felt. There was always a ten-minute period of grace before the criticisms started, the sniping, the digs, the comparisons. The last time she'd visited, she'd left after twenty minutes. A stupid argument about her choice of holiday destination.

'Hopefully I'll have some time,' she said.

Paul fixed his eyes on his beer. 'The carers say she's not eating much at all any more. It might not be long.'

'I said I'll go,' said Jo.

Chapter 14

Dusk was falling, and in the well-to-do residential streets around her brother's house, the street lights were flicking on with eerie synchronicity, like nocturnal animals stirring to life at the scent of prey. Being a Sunday evening in a semi-rural village, most people were in their homes, and Jo caught flashes down the capacious driveways of families or couples together in lit windows.

She wasn't sure exactly how far she'd go, but she took a route that led away from the houses, until she was running uphill along a single-track road without a pavement. As always, she went off faster than she'd intended, and her chest was soon burning, the lactic acid leading her calves. She pushed harder, sucking in huge lungfuls of air. The odd car passed, but she saw their approach in the distant glow of headlights and stood up on the verge to let them pass. She wondered if Stratton really did leave after a single drink and if the others were still going. Ben would be. He must have been staying in a local hotel.

She continued down the hill on the other side, thighs protesting as they took the brunt of the decline.

I'll have to tell them about me and Ben at some point, she thought. *They're my family.*

And it wasn't fair on Will. The sooner she broke it to him that Uncle Boo wouldn't be coming round any more, the better.

In the distance, she could see the bypass, lights snaking across the countryside. She knew she could either turn round, returning by the same route, or take a longer track that ran past the old Horton waterworks, then cross a dismantled railway before looping back to the estate. She and her mates used to hang around over that way as kids, even though it was the sort of place mothers told their innocent teenage daughters to avoid. Maybe that explained why they went there.

But she was a thirty-nine-year-old woman, with moderate-to-good self-defence skills, and her mother probably didn't even remember her name. She opened a kissing gate and set off along the track.

The ground was uneven, and without the benefit of the street lights, she found herself stumbling a little, unsure of her foot placement. Any thoughts she'd had, about Ben, about the case, about Dylan or Niall, tried and failed to take root because all her attention was on the path and not falling over. With the hedges either side deepening the darkness further, judging distance was difficult as well. She wondered if her memory was letting her down and actually this was a track she'd never come down before. She couldn't tell if she was running fast or slow, and cursed herself for not bringing her phone. At least it had a torch setting.

Just as the odd sense of disquiet was morphing into some-thing more visceral, she saw the squat towers of the waterworks ahead, behind a metal fence. The path along its edge was as she remembered too – but narrower, with the bushes overgrown and overhanging. She slowed to a walk, pushing the tendrils out of the way, forging on almost blindly, until she broke through at the other side. Despite the walk, she was out of breath.

'Well, that was stupid,' she muttered to herself.

The railway had been taken up some time in the early 1900s, and now it was a straight path laid to tarmac, and much easier to run on. She settled back into her stride, glad to be out under the open sky once more. There were even a few stars peeping out between the shreds of cloud.

She wondered again about the transfer request. Oxford seemed too close to home now. Too close to Bath as well. There'd be other forces. Maybe Kent or Surrey? A completely fresh start. Greater Manchester had vacancies, and she had old friends up that way too. All coupled up, with growing broods, of course. Which brought the other stuff to the surface. Bright Futures would call again in the morning. She couldn't put them off forever. The one in five chance would only get smaller the longer she waited.

There were figures up ahead, on top of a small road-bridge. She could hear them, and her eyes made out four or five people, leaning over. She kept her pace steady, focused on the path. She heard their voices drop, and knew before it happened that one of them was going to say something.

'Get those knees up!' came the shout.

She glanced up, and saw there was something strange about their faces. With a jolt of unease, she saw they were all wearing clown masks.

'Evening, lads,' she said. *Keep running. They're just kids.*

Her peripheral vision saw them peeling off the wall of the bridge, moving towards its ends.

'Hold on! Wait up!'

She clenched her fists. *Just what I need.* She didn't slow at all, but didn't speed up either.

As she reached the bridge, the first of them slid down the bank onto the path right in front of her. He was wearing a white mask with swollen bright red lips. She thought about trying to dodge around, but suddenly her legs felt completely sapped of strength.

She slowed to a halt. 'Excuse me,' she said.

The mask stared back. She could hear him breathing behind it. Two others emerged onto the path too. She wondered how old they were. The clothing – tracksuits and hoodies – suggested under twenty. Maybe even teens. Aside from one, they were all bigger than her.

'Leave her alone,' said someone above. 'You're scaring her.'

'It's all right,' she said. 'I'm not scared. I just have to get through.'

'You look scared,' said the one in front of her. 'Is it the masks?'

Despite the fear, her training kicked in. *Establish a connection.* 'What's your name?'

'Why do you want to know my name?'

Okay, try again.

'Just being polite.' She looked right into the eye sockets of the mask. 'I'm Jo,' she said.

'And I don't give a fuck, Jo,' said the young man. Some of the others tittered.

'Can you move please?'

Straight question, no more subtleties. Her mind was calibrating, her body poised, depending on his answer. A straight 'No' and she would kick him so hard in the balls he'd be pissing blood.

'I'm Dara,' he said, his tone sleazy, entitled, like they were meeting in a bar and he thought his luck was in. Maybe, in a bar, if the girl was desperate enough, it occasionally worked.

'Hi Dara,' she replied. 'I'm a police officer.'

It was fear that made her say it, and she regretted it at once. Because the kid in front of her laughed.

'Where's your badge?'

'I don't carry it,' she said.

'Maybe it's in those shorts?' said another voice.

'Let's have a look,' said the leader. He moved closer – too close – hand already reaching, and whatever slim thread of hope that had been restraining her snapped. She took a fraction of a step back, and perhaps, dumb kid that he was, he mistook it for fear. She drove her forehead up into his nose. Basic training. The skull at the front of the cranium was thick, and hard as rock. His nose cracked, sweet as a nut, and his almighty howl of pain echoed off the underside of the bridge.

Jo ran, and a second later she heard the sound of their footsteps in pursuit. She looked back and saw just two. One was still with his broken-nosed friend, and the other on the bridge shouted, 'Leave her – for fuck's sake!'

Please listen to him. Please leave me alone . . .

And still, despite the terror, her mind fingered through the options like they were filed in a Rolodex. Two men. If they caught her, she might be able to disable one. Perhaps she'd get a finger in his eye socket, or a groin strike. If they got a hold of her hands, it was trickier. She'd scream blue murder, that might be enough. But if it wasn't, she just had to kick and thrash and make it as hard as possible. If they had a knife, then that was it. It was about biting, clawing, anything to get a DNA sample. She had to remember accents, characteristics, facial hair, body types. While her body propelled her, fuelled by nature, her rational mind was already working ahead, to a scene she'd attended more times than she really wanted to count as an investigator. The cool, professional paramedics, the witness statements. She promised herself she wouldn't feel the shame – she wouldn't give them that – and hoped it was a promise she could keep.

The path ahead stretched on forever, a straight-line sprint she knew she couldn't win. So she scrambled up the bank, clawing with her hands, and crested the top. There was a wooden fence, woodland beyond.

'Fucking get her!' called a voice.

The two young men began to climb as well.

Hands on the top rail, Jo vaulted the fence, and plunged into the trees. Staggering over roots, with unseen branches whipping her face, she didn't look back. She'd no idea where she was going, but her internal map told her it was roughly back towards the road where she could wave down a car. If there *was* a car. Their footsteps crunched behind her.

'Come back!' one shouted. 'We're just messin' wi' ya.'

Fuck you and your messing . . .

She slipped into a dell, skidding onto her backside, then charged up the far side. One of her trainers sank in a patch of squelching mud, and as she pulled up her foot, the shoe came loose. She hobbled on, barefooted. Up ahead, it looked like the trees thinned. And perhaps there was only one pursuer now, a good distance away.

She almost ran right into a barbed-wire fence and stopped herself just in time. She placed her good foot on the middle strand and flung herself over, but her clothing snagged and she landed hard on the other side, breaking her fall with her hands. It took all her strength to stand, then she staggered on, across a small field over overgrown meadow grass. There was something familiar about the land, and through the fug of fear she realised she was on the other side of the barn at the bottom of Sally Carruthers' land, about a hundred metres from the house itself. She could've cried with relief. She passed the raised beds where once Mr Carruthers had tended to his courgettes, onions and carrots, the bounty of which she'd tasted in the delicious soups Sally used to give her to take home after her piano lessons.

Her legs carried her up the flagstones to the back door, and she rapped loudly on the glass. There was soft piano music inside, which stopped abruptly.

Jo shot a glance back over her shoulder, then pounded on the door again, 'Please! Let me in!'

A light came on inside, and a moving shape appeared, fractured and blurred by the distortions in the glass. It coalesced as it grew closer, becoming the figure of Mrs Carruthers.

'Who is it?' she said, her voice tremulous.

'It's Jo. Josie Masters.'

The door opened. Sally was clutching a rolling pin in her right hand. There was the smell of something sweet in the oven.

'Oh, my!' she said, taking in Jo's single bare foot and her sweat-streaked face.

'Can I come in?'

Sally moved aside. 'Of course! Of course!'

Jo stumbled inside, noticing belatedly that rivulets of blood were trailing down her ankle and onto the wooden floorboards. There was a gash on the side of her calf.

'You're hurt!' said Sally. 'Can I call someone?'

'That's not necessary,' said Jo. 'Do you have somewhere I can clean myself up?'

'There's a bathroom,' said Sally, pointing along the hall. 'Second door on the right.'

Jo thanked her and hopped along the corridor, then into the bathroom. She found the cord and switched on the light.

'Josie, what happened?' said Sally, waiting at the door.

'I got lost running,' said Jo, peeling off her bloody sock. 'Tried to come back through the woods and slipped.'

'I could go over to your brother's house?' said Mrs Carruthers.

'No!' said Jo. 'No need. I'll be out in a mo.'

She looked at herself in the mirror. Her face was bright red, and there was more blood on her forehead. There didn't seem to be a cut though, so it must have belonged to the young man in the mask. The last thing she needed was to worry Paul or Amelia.

Maybe it would be an idea to call the police. They might well be able to track them down. She decided against it. In all likelihood the clown masks would be dumped somewhere by now and the young men would have vanished. Plus, she felt like a fool, even though she knew she shouldn't. She'd file a report tomorrow, if there was time.

Jo splashed water in her face, then dabbed the cut on her leg until it stopped bleeding.

The bathroom was decorated in peach shades, with a walk-in bath and handles bolted to the wall for support, though there was congealed dirt around the plughole.

In a couple of minutes, she emerged, holding a grubby, blood-streaked hand-towel.

Sally offered a mug of tea. 'Thought this might help?' she said.

In truth, hot tea was the last thing Jo wanted, but she forced herself to take it. Her hand was shaking slightly as the adrenalin worked its way out of her system.

'Thank you,' she said. 'Sorry about your towel.'

'Never mind that,' said Sally, taking it. 'I'll add it to the whites. Come and have a sit-down in the kitchen.'

Limping a little – her leg was throbbing now – Jo followed the hunched form into the country kitchen. It was exactly as she remembered it, even down to the bird ornaments on the pine dresser and the lace on the curtains. A grandfather clock said it was 21.05.

She sat down at the table. 'Sorry to intrude like this,' she said.

'I was just doing some baking,' said Sally, bending stiffly to look through the oven door.

Jo saw the flour still dusting the counter, a few scraps of pastry.

Looking through the glass double doors, her attention was caught by the piano in the living room. The keyboard was open.

'You're not as bad as you said,' said Jo.

'Sorry, sweetheart?'

'On the piano,' said Jo.

Sally blushed. 'I'm not what I was,' she said, looking at her knotted hands. 'Blasted arthritis runs in the family. Do you really not play any more?'

Jo shook her head, trying to remember the last time. It had been at a friend's wedding, when everyone was half-cut. She and Ben had been wandering through the rooms of a country house, and they'd found the piano tucked away in a drawing room.

She'd surprised herself with how easily it came back. It must have been the drink, but she hadn't even realised a crowd had gathered until she finished the first movement of Schubert's Sonata No. 21. Ben looked gobsmacked. She'd taken requests for the next forty-five minutes, moving through a variety of genres from ragtime, to jazz, to interpretations of the latest chart hits. By the time they went home, high on romance, booze, and youth, she'd promised herself she'd look into more lessons the following day. The hangover, and the reality of life, soon put paid to that idea.

Sally shuffled across to the counter, where she began to wipe up the mess. Jo noticed that there was a smashed plate on the sideboard, and wondered if Mrs Carruthers was coping all right. There was a slightly rotten smell too – it reminded her of a care home, or a public toilet. Poor woman probably just needed a cleaner.

'Will you play something for me?' said Sally, all of a sudden.

Jo grimaced. 'I couldn't. It would be embarrassing.'

'Nonsense,' said Sally. 'And it would make me very happy. I don't have a lot of visitors these days.'

Jo was going to keep protesting, but there was something pleading in the old woman's tone. She stood up stiffly.

'Don't say I didn't warn you!'

In the living room, she sat on the stool. It was a little lower than she expected, and she boosted it higher.

'What do you want me to play?' she asked, flexing her fingers.

'Whatever you like, dear,' said Sally, smiling in the doorway.

The sheet above the keys was Debussy, the music Sally had been playing when Jo interrupted her evening. It wasn't too challenging, and Jo let her fingers find their starting position. The smell was a bit worse in here, a definite tang of ammonia that she was all too familiar with from entering the houses of the elderly.

God save me from ever getting old.

She began to play, hoping the old synapses would fire as they did that night at Shane and Hannah's wedding. When they didn't, she stumbled discordantly to a halt.

'Take your time,' said Sally, her voice patient as always.

Jo began again, more hesitantly, and though she hit a few keys a fraction off-tempo, she found a purer sound. Her eyes were on the score, but she sensed Sally smiling behind her. And she actually began to enjoy herself, even finding a few places to lend greater expression to the notes. But a few minutes in, a clock chimed the quarter hour, and it brought her out of the music. She stopped abruptly. Her brother would be worried.

'I'm sorry, Sally, I should be going.'

'I quite understand. You must take some apple pie? I can't eat it all – perhaps the children would like it?'

Jo stood up, smiling. Though Will could still be classed as a child, Emma probably wouldn't appreciate the description.

'That's very kind.'

'Wait here, I'll get a tin.'

Jo did as she was told, wandering across to the bookshelf. There were several thick volumes on psychology, addiction and healing therapies that seemed quite out of place, but on the wall above the shelves was a certificate stating that Sally Carruthers had qualified as a talking therapist eleven years ago.

'You're a dark horse,' she called.

'What's that?' asked Sally, a little worried.

'Your second career,' said Jo.

The old woman entered, holding a tin.

'Oh, that! It's just listening to people, really. Same as the piano teaching.'

'Don't you have to weed out their darkest secrets?'

Sally laughed. 'It's odd – most of my clients are quite happy to tell me their secrets with no weeding. Half the battle is getting them here in the first place.'

Jo remembered her own GP had suggested she might want to see someone too, after she'd lost the baby, but she had flatly refused the offer, unable to see what could possibly be gained.

'I imagine you're very good at it.'

Sally offered the tin. 'I don't have a lot of clients these days,' she said, sadness in her voice. 'Not a lot of company at all, really.'

Jo noticed her hands again, holding the tin, the fingers twisted. *She must be in pain all the time.*

'You know, you could pop up to Paul's any time. The kids – they don't have any grandparents, not really.'

Sally smiled. 'Josie, you are a sweetheart. But I couldn't intrude like that. They wouldn't want a strange old crone turning up on their doorstep. It would frighten poor William.'

'Nonsense,' said Jo. 'You're a natural with children.'

Sally beamed. 'That's such a nice thing to hear. It's one of my biggest regrets, not having a family of my own.'

Jo smiled back. She wondered if Sally and her husband had had medical problems too. It seemed rude to ask. Instead, she wagged her finger like a schoolmistress.

'Well, I'll speak to Paul and Amelia. You're not getting off that easily. Perhaps Will could come here and learn the piano. Goodness, he needs something other than toy guns to distract him!'

'That would be quite wonderful,' said Sally. 'They do say talent is genetic.'

They walked together back to the front door. Jo wondered if part of the reason for the lack of clients might be the odd scent. It came to her in waves.

'You're wondering about the smell,' said Sally.

This time Jo blushed. Had she been so obvious?

'Oh, no . . . what smell?'

'It's the cat,' said Sally. 'Before he moved out for good, he decided to use the carpet in here as his toilet. I've done my best with it, the patches I found, but can't seem to work it all out. The hot weather doesn't help.'

Jo grimaced. 'Sounds nasty. Couldn't you get the carpet replaced?'

'I keep meaning to,' said Sally, opening the door. 'My husband used to take care of all that sort of thing.'

Jo stepped out. It wouldn't be difficult to make some enquiries about flooring herself – not that she wanted to intrude.

'How long's it been since Mr Carruthers passed away?' she asked.

'Oh, almost two years now,' said Sally. 'It was for the best, really. He wasn't such a nice man, towards the end.'

'I'm sorry to hear that,' said Jo, remembering what her mum had been like, the last time she visited. It must have been over a year ago now.

Sally waved as Jo backed down to the front path towards the road. 'You will come again, I hope. It would be wonderful to catch up properly.'

'As long as you promise not to analyse me,' said Jo.

'It really doesn't work like that,' said Sally, and Jo worried that she'd offended her.

'Thank you for the pie,' she said.

The pavement was cold on her bare foot as Jo headed home, and the clear night air brought up goose pimples on her arms. But she clutched the warm tin to her chest, cradling it as carefully as a child.

Chapter 15

MONDAY

Jo was the first in – hardly surprising given the celebrations of the previous day. Ben had texted just after ten with an emoji of wine glasses chinking together and a note: *You're missing a good night!*, to which she had replied, civilly, that she was spending time with her family. A lie, of course. She'd had a shower and gone to bed as soon as she got home, making up a lie about tripping over in the dark. Amelia, she thought, had looked unconvinced, but Paul had started tucking into the apple pie. She'd slept like a log until about two in the morning, when William had woken up screaming in the room beside hers. Apparently he'd started suffering night terrors around Christmas time. Monsters under the bed, in the garden, that sort of thing.

Jo dumped her things beside her desk and called the hospital for an update on Niall. She managed to get through to a Dr Parvinder Srai, but was told the hospital couldn't give out any information over the phone due to patient confidentiality.

'He's all right though?' said Jo, adding, 'I was the one who found him.'

Dr Srai sighed. 'Physically, he's fine,' she said. 'I'm sorry, but you'll have to come to the hospital in person.'

As Jo hung up, the front desk clerk came through. 'There's someone in reception for you, detective,' he said.

Jo was still wondering what 'fine' meant, but she was intrigued by the summons, and followed the clerk back through to the reception. The dean of Gloucester College was waiting patiently, clutching a document case.

'Morning Dr Silcott,' she said. 'What can I do for you?'

'Ah – I was hoping to speak to DCI Stratton,' he said.

'It's just me, I'm afraid. Want to come through?'

He gave a brisk nod. 'Very well,' and trotted past as she held open the door.

The CID room was as they'd left it the night before, with papers scattering the desks and dirty mugs dotted about. Silcott wore a look of slight distaste as he sat down. It was a long way from his salubrious study.

Jo was struggling slightly to understand why the dean was here, and why it was Stratton he'd wanted to speak with. When he wasn't forthcoming, she initiated.

'You've spoken to the McDonaghs?'

'Briefly,' said Silcott, the document case clasped in his hands. 'They're relieved, of course. Thankfully, with it being the holidays, they have very few teaching duties to attend to. I've suggested it might be best for all the family to put the college to the back of their minds for the moment.'

'Of course.'

'He wasn't officially a member of staff, of course,' said Silcott.

Jo took a moment to realise his eyes were lingering on Alan Trent's face, still tacked to the board across from them.

'I'm sorry?'

'Not on the payroll, I mean,' said Silcott. 'I understand our

184

head gardener Mr Whittaker had an informal arrangement with him. Cash in hand.'

He spoke the words with a twist of his mouth, as though the transaction had been in some way beneath him.

'I got the same impression,' said Jo. 'Anyway, is there something specific—'

'That practice will be coming to an end,' added Silcott, pursing his lips. 'You can rest assured of that.'

'That's really none of our concern,' said Jo. 'How the college pays its staff is a civil matter.'

Silcott sighed through his nose impatiently, as if she was an undergraduate answering a question incorrectly.

'That's exactly my point,' he said. 'The college really had nothing to do with Alan Trent.'

Jo leant back in her chair. '*Mister* Silcott,' she said, deliberately not using his academic title, 'Alan Trent was a convicted sex offender working at your college, and we have every indication he met his victim on college premises, in all likelihood using his access to plan his crime.'

'Do you have any proof of that?' asked Silcott, jutting out his chin.

'Proof of what?'

'That the college is the place Alan Trent first met Niall?' He began to open his document case.

'I can't see how that is relevant at the moment. Trent is dead, and Niall is safe. Thank goodness we were able to put the pieces together in time, because I can tell you from experience that these cases don't always turn out so well.'

'It might not be *relevant* to you, but I can assure you the college takes the welfare of all students and occupants very seriously. If we as an institution were to suffer reputational damage because of spurious press claims . . .'

So that's why he's here . . .

The letter he took out, written on heavy paper, had some sort of embossed crest at the top.

'. . . This is correspondence from the college's legal representatives. It lays out in some detail the unfortunate circumstances under which Mr Whittaker brought Alan Trent onto the college premises. It also makes clear our position going forward . . .'

'Let me stop you there,' said Jo.

But Silcott was still going – 'As I say, I hoped to deliver this personally to your superior, but given his absence, I submit it to you on the understanding that it will find its way to him before anyone says anything erroneous to the press.'

Jo took the letter. He must have had this drafted the night before, maybe even before the outcome of the search was known. When everyone else was focused on looking for a missing child, the dean of Gloucester College was trying to cover his own backside. She hoped her look of disdain was clear.

'I'll see that DCI Stratton gets your letter,' she said coldly.

'Very good,' said Dr Silcott, closing the case with a flourish and standing up. 'Then I'll wish you a good day, detective.'

Jo walked him to the door. 'We don't yet know the extent of Niall's ordeal, by the way.'

'That's business for the family,' said Silcott. 'I would never think to intrude.'

'You're not a family friend then?' said Jo.

Silcott stiffened. 'Not really.'

'You didn't know Niall well?'

'He sang in the choir for a few months,' said the dean. 'One of the sopranos. I know I mentioned that.'

Jo opened the door, but stood in front of it. 'He left, didn't he?'

'You know what children are like. They lose interest.'

'This choir – it includes adults? All male by any chance?'

186

The dean frowned. 'Yes. I myself sing tenor. What exactly are you implying?'

'Perhaps you could furnish us with a list of members?'

Silcott blanched. 'I'd have to speak to . . . I really don't see . . .'

Jo let the door close again behind her.

'No, you wouldn't see,' she said. 'But there's still a chance Trent might not have been working alone. Given his clear connections with your college, we'll be investigating every avenue. I've asked nicely, but I can come by the college later if you'd like, with a warrant and couple of officers in uniform. Not very low-key, but this was a serious crime . . .'

Silcott glared at her as he took a deep breath. 'I'll have a list drawn up,' he said.

'Thank you for your co-operation.' She didn't believe it herself, not really, but he'd pissed her off enough to make a point.

Jo stepped aside and let him leave, just as a somewhat unkempt George Dimitriou came the other way. He barely registered Silcott until after he'd bundled past.

'What's up with him?' he asked.

'Never mind,' said Jo. 'Looks like it was a good night.'

'God, Detective Coombs can put it away,' he said, flopping into his chair, peering curiously into a mug half-full with cold coffee, then swigging it down. 'He filled us in on your sordid past.'

Jo blushed, feeling suddenly trapped. 'He did?' she asked.

Fucking arsehole. How dare he?

'You're a tough one. Said you got stabbed working under-cover a few years ago, but maintained the alias. Insisted on staying on the case. Went back out. Kidnapping and sex offenders must pale in comparison.'

Jo felt the tension ooze out of her. Ben had been the first face she'd seen when she woke up in hospital, three pints of new blood pumped into her system, and an impressive three-inch scar across her abdomen. She'd cried her eyes out while he held her.

So maybe he had kept their private lives to himself, after all.

'He exaggerates,' she said.

Dimitriou took out his electric razor. 'By the way, Stratton's briefing the press at ten a.m. at the town hall.'

'Do we need to be there?'

'I think so. Decorating the troops and all.' He began to shave over his bin, grimacing at his reflection. 'I hope the cameras are forgiving.'

* * *

She'd never worked on anything big enough to warrant a press conference before.

Jo had never liked the limelight. From her earliest school performances, young Josephine Masters had always been listed as 'third soldier', or 'handmaiden', letting those in possession of almost preternatural confidence take centre stage. But Stratton was very specific she was to be at his right. Dimitriou and Tan were there too, along with a young man from the Thames Valley Comms team who probably earned twice as much as Jo but looked ten years younger. Carrick, who'd been on duty for nine days straight, was enjoying a day of enforced leave. That hadn't stopped him from calling in a couple of times already, though – apparently he was at a theme park with his kids.

Stratton's rank badges were sparkling, his shoes polished as they filtered behind a row of tables at the town hall. Jo felt hopelessly underdressed, and despite dabbing at the tea stain on her lapel, it was still obvious. About two dozen journalists had gathered, with as many camera operators. Jo wasn't sure where to look, because everywhere a lens stared back. And, right at the back, talking to a colleague, was Rebekah Saunders. Jo purposely avoided her eye.

The chief inspector gave the outline of the case: that the suspect was deceased, that the boy, Niall, was alive and well, and then read a statement from the McDonaghs asking for privacy.

Fine chance of that, thought Jo, as the cameras rolled.

Stratton ended by thanking his committed and resourceful officers, specifying each of them by name and rank, and then opened the floor to questions. He hadn't mentioned the Gloucester College connection, she noticed, even though he'd only grunted non-committally when she'd handed over Silcott's letter earlier.

The first questions focused on Alan Trent's previous criminal history, and the police intelligence on his whereabouts prior to the crime. Stratton, with the briefest of glances at the Comms rep, answered that Trent had recently moved to the area, but that he was deemed to be a low-level threat based on his old convictions. That brought a sarcastic follow-up about the integrity of police intelligence. Stratton summoned a pained expression.

'We feel that failure acutely, and we'll be looking into the procedural shortfalls to ensure this won't happen again. We'll be liaising with the parole board and prison services to re-examine our protocols.'

The questions moved on to the victim, which Stratton expertly batted aside, citing privacy, and Jo felt the energy of the room dip. What was there to say, really, other than the barest facts?

'So the Killer Clown is dead.' It was Saunders. 'Does this mean the murder of Dylan Jones is solved as well?'

Stratton placed his hands on the table. 'First of all, we'd appeal to the press not to use that term. There's no evidence that Alan

Trent's disguise was anything but an opportunistic way to conceal his identity based on the location of the kidnap – at a carnival. Nor, it appears, was he a murderer.'

'So you're still looking for the killer of Dylan Jones?' Saunders caught Jo's eye as she spoke.

'That investigation is complex, due to the time that has elapsed, and it's likely to be some time before we have any definitive answers. I'm afraid you'll have to address any specifics to Avon and Somerset, as they're carrying out those enquiries.'

Jo was impressed – he was a smooth operator.

'I think it's time to wrap up,' said the Comms rep.

'Hang on a moment,' said Saunders. 'These are important questions, and it so happens you have a representative from Avon and Somerset sitting to your right.'

'Detective Masters was helping us with the investigation into Niall McDonagh's disappearance,' said Stratton, 'and it was due to her solid police work that he was found alive.'

'So you expect us to believe her presence is a coincidence?' said Saunders.

The Comms guy was twitching, and Stratton spoke more brusquely. 'Thank you for your time,' he said, standing up and straightening his uniform.

Jo and the others followed suit, but Saunders wasn't giving up, and cameras flashed above the screeching of seats.

'Are you hiding something?' she asked. 'The public need to know, chief inspector. Is the real Killer Clown still on the loose? Is there a paedophile on the streets preying on our children?'

Stratton marched out, and Jo, eyes down, followed.

'What happens when he strikes again?' came the journalist's final call.

Jo really had no time for Saunders' sensationalism, but it didn't prevent a twinge of unease. *There's a chance she's right.*

And maybe it was the way Stratton had dismissed her

theories the day before – so perfunctorily, so condescendingly – but as she walked down the stairs, out of the building's rear exit, she wondered if there might be more to the clown mask after all. It made no sense that Alan was Dylan's killer. He'd started to plan the kidnap of Niall days before Dylan's body was even found. But if there was an accomplice . . .

If Dylan's killer was still out there, somewhere – if he'd somehow been involved – the clown mask wasn't just a sick copycat or a coincidence; it was a modus operandi – the method of a man who'd got away with it once and thought he could again. But this time he'd used someone else, a person he'd coerced, or paid.

She tried to think logically. It was improbable, for sure. Why use a proxy, with all the risk that entailed? Far simpler to carry out the abduction yourself, and cut out the middle man. But if it was the original kidnapper, he was old. Maybe the thought of carrying out such a crime was too much.

Stepping out into the busy street, she shook her head to clear it. It wasn't just improbable. It was really, really, hard to swallow. Why the hell would Alan Trent agree to anything so foolish and likely to fail?

She watched the faces of the pedestrians going about their business. Any one of them could be carrying a terrible secret, planning a crime, wearing a mask. She could be looking right at murderers and thieves and perverts.

The problem was, until they slipped up, you never knew.

Chapter 16

'Well, that went well,' said Ben. He was waiting for them back at the station, with the small TV still on. Stratton and the Comms rep had disappeared straight into his office and closed the door. Jo couldn't help but feel she was being blamed in some way, even though she'd never wanted to be there in the first place. The sooner she got back to Avon and Somerset, even with Ben there, the better.

'This came through, by the way,' said Ben. He looked surprisingly chipper as she handed her an envelope – it was addressed to 'Detective Ferman'.

'What is it?' asked Jo.

'Invite to a memorial service on Tuesday,' said Ben. 'Dylan's parents brought it in themselves. They said that we were welcome too.'

'Has the body been released?' asked Jo.

'No,' said Ben, 'and I've sent a team back to the site for another look, in case we missed something.'

'Something linking to Trent?'

Ben nodded. 'I know you're not convinced, but that reporter's got a point. It's a pretty weird coincidence.'

'They do happen,' said Jo. 'You know I went to school with her?'

'Dimi told me last night,' said Ben. 'I take your point.'

It struck her quite suddenly, as they spoke, that some things hadn't changed at all in their relationship. There was still a part of each of them that existed outside their past – two professionals shooting the breeze.

'The parents just want to put it behind them,' said Ben. 'Say a proper goodbye. I suppose they don't need a body for that.'

Jo remembered the drugs they'd sent her home with after the miscarriage, with the leaflet about what to expect next – physically as well as emotionally. Not that there had been a body, really. There was a section on grieving too, which she'd been too dazed to read. She wondered if Ben had, and if his memory was, in that moment, playing over the same topic.

She heard the door open behind her, and Stratton leant out. 'Masters, could we borrow you a moment?'

He didn't wait for a reply, and closed the door again. Though the tone was light, Jo had a bad feeling.

'No fear,' said Tan, as she walked past.

The Comms rep was still present, arms folded, and smiled reassuringly as Jo entered.

'Detective Masters, we all want to thank you for the work on the case,' said the chief inspector, 'but we think, in light of the rampant press speculation, that it might be best for you to be less obviously involved.'

'You're taking me off,' she said flatly.

'The case is closed,' said Stratton. 'Ben Coombs can follow up on any potential link to Dylan Jones – there's no immediate danger to civilians, so I'll be deploying our resources here back to ongoing investigations.'

'With respect, sir, there's still a question over whether Trent worked alone.'

Stratton and the younger man shared a glance, and the latter answered. 'Unless concrete evidence arises of that, it's not our official line.'

Jo forced a smile. 'Concrete evidence tends not to jump into one's lap. You have to look for it. Sir, did you ask Andy to chivvy on the print lab?'

Stratton's glance told her she was pushing her luck, and the media rep grinned back toothily. Jo wondered if he was actually a lawyer of some sort – it was a look she'd seen before, in cross-examination by barristers just before they sank their claws in.

'This Rebekah Fitzwilliam,' the Comms rep said. 'You know her, I believe.'

It was stated baldly, not as a question.

'I've already told the chief inspector, we *knew* each other, years ago. We have no personal connection now.'

'Yet she appears to have intimate knowledge of the case,' he added smarmily.

Jo felt her skin redden. 'If you have any evidence, anything whatsoever, to suggest that I've leaked information, present it to me now. If you haven't, then I suggest you fuck off and let me do my job.'

Stratton held up his hands. 'Things are getting a little heated.' He looked pained. 'Jo, nothing personal. We have to deal with the optics on this as well. It just doesn't look good. Surely you can see that?'

She wanted to scream, but she bit her lip. She couldn't even look the Comms rep in the face, so addressed herself to Stratton.

'I see, sir,' she said. 'But it would be negligent not to follow up behind the scenes, wouldn't it? I mean, the optics will be a lot worse if we miss something and it comes back to bite us.'

'Fair enough,' said Stratton, 'but you're back seat from now on. I want everything run through a superior officer. No more surprises. We'll work on giving Fitzwilliam something to keep her happy, but you two are to have no more contact.'

'Sir, I haven't—'

'Detective, if she asks you anything, if she even says hello, it's a "No comment".'

'Yes, sir. Can I go, sir?' she asked.

'Dismissed, detective,' said Stratton, cheerily. 'And thank you again for all your work.'

Jo did her very best not to slam the door on the way out.

Outside, Tan eyed her warily. 'That looked painful.'

Ferman's invite was still on the desk and Jo picked it up.

'I'm going out for a while,' she said, then made for the door without looking back.

Ben was in the car park, on the phone near his car. He shot her an inquisitive look, but she mouthed, 'Got to go,' then climbed into her own car. Tossing her bag on the passenger seat, she took a few deep breaths, then fished out her phone and searched for Ferman's number.

It rang and rang. No machine. She called again, just in case he needed some encouragement to pick up the phone. She doubted he was still in bed at eleven thirty in the morning. Eventually she killed the call. There was another place she could try.

★ ★ ★

Canterbury Road was a row of tall Edwardian terraces, and The Three Crowns pub was in the bottom corner. This far from the city centre, she guessed it probably didn't see much student traffic, and her suspicions were confirmed when she opened the front door and stepped inside. A russet carpet, threadbare in places and marked with countless indeterminable stains, clearly hadn't been changed since the smoking ban. Her eyes passed over brass ornaments, bar mats glued to the ceiling, a brick-laid fireplace filled with fake flowers. With dark wood furniture, green brush-satin cushions, it was a pub stubbornly stuck in the past, and trying to please nobody. The sort of place her dad used to drink. Jo liked it at once, but she couldn't see Harry Ferman.

She stepped over an Alsatian's tail by a flashing quiz machine. At the bar, a single customer sat nursing a half-filled glass of bitter. Behind the counter, wiping a bottle then reattaching it to the optic, was a fifty-plus buxom woman with dyed blonde hair.

She turned to Jo. 'All right, love, what can I get you?'

Jo was about to decline, then she remembered the look on the Comms Stasi's face and changed her mind. Plus, work-wise, there was nothing pressing.

Normally she had red wine in pubs, but her trained eye had already spotted the bottle on the counter, and it was a quarter full. God knows when it had been opened, but she didn't fancy a glass of vinegary Cabernet Sauvignon.

'Vodka, please,' she said. 'No ice.'

The barmaid took down a glass, inspected its cleanliness, then lifted it to the optic. The single looked pitiful, but a double would make driving questionable. The barmaid didn't ask for payment as she set it on the bar, and returned to cleaning.

'How much?' asked Jo.

The woman waved her cloth off to the left. 'Harry's got it.'

Jo took the glass and turned, seeing Harry Ferman tucked away at a table in the corner, almost completely cast in shadow.

'Cheers,' she said. 'I was looking for you.'

'Well, you caught me.'

She walked across to him, and sat on a stool. He had two drinks in front of him, a short of amber liquid that she guessed was brandy, and a remaining half-pint of Guinness.

He lifted the tumbler. 'Congratulations are in order, I believe.'

His voice was oddly flat and mirthless, and Jo wondered if he'd been drinking at home before the pub opened.

She returned the toast, then slid the invite across the table. 'This came to the station. There's a service tomorrow, for Dylan.'

Ferman didn't touch it, instead taking a sip of his drink. As he tipped his head, a shaft of sunlight penetrated the frosted windows. He looked dreadful, his pale eyes watery.

'If I've come at a bad time . . .' she said.

His Adam's apple sank and rose, then he chuckled, as if she'd said something unintentionally amusing.

'You think this Trent fella did it?' he said gruffly.

'Almost certainly,' said Jo. 'We haven't spoken to the victim yet, but we're expecting him to confirm it.'

'I don't mean McDonagh,' he said, then tapped the envelope with a thick finger. Nails chewed down. 'Dylan.'

'No. Do you?'

Ferman's finger continued to tap, as though in time with his thoughts. 'Doesn't matter what I think,' he said.

'Come on,' said Jo. 'Help me out here. You know the Jones case as well as anyone. Better than anyone, maybe. Trent had a conviction for some lewd behaviour much later. I'm not saying it doesn't matter, but it's a long way from kidnapping and murder. The timeline's weird too. Why come out of the wood-work now, after so long?'

'You want my opinion?' said Ferman. 'This world constantly surprises me. If it was Trent, he's not going to serve time. May as well chalk it in the win column.'

'You can't really mean that. Surely it matters that the right person is held responsible.'

'Why?'

'So justice is served. And to make sure it doesn't happen again.'

He swallowed the rest of the brandy. 'It will happen again. And justice doesn't bring back dead children.'

Jo wondered if he was always like this, or if the find under the pool in Bradford had stirred some muddy water in his own soul, where other tragedies and unhappiness lurked.

'Do you think you'll go – to the service?' she asked.

'Think they really want *us* there? A reminder of what happened?'

'I suppose we gave them some answers,' said Jo. She almost said *closure*, but she didn't think he'd appreciate the term.

He was moving his empty glass in circles. Jo hadn't touched her vodka, and now she really didn't want it.

'Have a good day, Harry,' she said. She got up, and walked away, but as she neared the door, he spoke again.

'Tell you what, Masters. I'll go, if you do too.'

She hadn't been planning to, but there was something pleading in his voice. A sense of doomed duty that he had to fulfil.

'You got it,' she replied.

Back in the car, she felt deflated. She wasn't sure exactly what she'd wanted from Ferman. Some perspective perhaps, some deeper understanding from the wise old head who'd seen it all before, and who didn't care about 'optics', or departmental wrangling, or the day-to-day of police politics. Someone who simply cared about getting to the truth. But Harry Ferman clearly had his own issues to deal with.

She had a missed call on her personal phone, from a mobile number she didn't recognise, and a voicemail.

'Hello. Is this Detective Masters? Emma gave me your number. This is Kieran. Kieran McDonagh. Look, I need to talk to you.' The voice was clipped, with an urgency to the delivery. *'Don't tell Mum and Dad, please. Just give me a call. It's Kieran. I'm Niall's brother.'*

Jo saved the message, then listened to it again. Her heart was racing, but she didn't know why. Jo imagined what Stratton would say. *Under absolutely no circumstances.*

But as far as Stratton was concerned, the case was closed. She wasn't actively interfering, was she? And the call had come through on her personal phone. *Personal phone, personal business.*

She called back, feeling light-headed.

'Hello?'

'It's Jo Masters. I got your message.' Keeping it professional. 'How can I help?'

'Hang on a minute, Daz,' he said. 'No, Mum – it's Dasha . . .' After a pause of about ten seconds, he came back on the line. 'Sorry about that. Mum doesn't know I'm calling.'

'Are you in some sort of trouble, Kieran?' she asked.

'No, but I will be if they find out I'm speaking to you.'

'Go on.'

'It's Niall,' said Kieran. 'No one's listening to him.'

'Your brother is in hospital, isn't he?'

'They've got him doped up,' he said. 'But I saw him last night. He won't stop talking about the clown. He's so fucking scared. He thinks it's coming for him again.'

It was hardly surprising. Being kidnapped and locked in a dark hole for two days was enough to give anyone nightmares.

'The man who took Niall is dead,' said Jo.

'That's just it!' said Kieran. 'He's saying it's not Trent. He says there was someone else down there. This clown.'

Jo felt a warmth spreading down her neck.

'Trent wore a mask,' she said, keeping her voice level. 'A clown mask.'

'Why won't you listen to me?' said Kieran. 'I'm telling you. Niall's not confused. He keeps telling Mum and Dad. There were two of them down there. Trent *and* the clown.'

Jo tried not to let herself get carried away. She knew where that could lead. 'Kieran, believe me, I'm listening to you. But you have to understand, we don't know what happened to Niall during the forty-eight hours he was missing.'

'So ask Niall, for fuck's sake.'

'It doesn't work like that,' said Jo. 'Your brother is a minor.'

'Emma said I could trust you,' said Kieran, 'but you're just like the rest of them.'

'Steady on,' said Jo. 'I want to help.'

'Then help!' said Kieran. 'Look, I've got to go.'

He hung up.

Jo sat for a moment, phone in her lap. *You're not even on the bloody case.*

She started the engine, her body moving independently of her mind. She weighed up the possibilities, the chances that this was just a dud lead, that she was getting carried away. There were dozens of examples, both apocryphal and based on real case studies, where confirmation bias had led investigators down rabbit holes of their own imaginings. Just because she wanted it to be true, didn't mean it had more validity than any other theory. If she got there, and Professor McDonagh was present too, what was the likelihood he'd let her talk to Niall? Slim to non-existent, surely.

She pulled away from the pub, plotting her route mentally to the hospital.

Of course, if Stratton did find out, the next meeting in his office would be a lot more painful.

Chapter 17

Dr Srai was younger than she expected, a striking Asian woman in her early thirties, with eyes the rich colour of polished horse chestnuts, and a sweep of otter-pelt dark hair in a ponytail. Jo showed her ID, and the doctor took her time inspecting it. Most people didn't bother, even those with something to hide. *Especially* those, actually. Handing the badge back, she shook Jo's hand.

'I'm afraid you can't see Niall just at the moment. His father has nipped out and we'll need permission.'

'Understood,' said Jo. 'Do you know when he'll be back?'

'Not long, I expect,' said Srai. 'He's gone to find a newsagents. Apparently our shop doesn't stock the *FT*.'

The doctor's delivery was dry, but Jo caught a hint of disapproval. Srai led her to an elevator. The first was full with an empty trolley and several nurses in uniform.

'You okay with stairs?' Srai asked.

'Sure.'

As they entered the stairwell, Srai continued. 'Mum went home last night. They have another son to look after. Niall will be going home soon – we have a few final obs to carry out.'

'You're discharging him?' said Jo. 'So he's okay?'

'That depends on your criteria,' said the doctor. 'Physically, he's doing as well as can be expected. We've given him plenty of fluids and small amounts of food.'

Jo needed to know. 'So no signs of sexual assault?'

'Sorry,' said Srai. 'We can't talk about that without the parents' permission.'

'Of course.'

'He's quite confused,' said Srai. 'Late last night he was very upset, shouting at his parents. He said someone was coming for him. We had to sedate him. It's principally his psychological state we're concerned about now, but that's not something we can address in this environment.'

'He was practically catatonic when we found him,' said Jo.

On the third floor, Srai buzzed them into the paediatric suite, and they passed several large colourful wards filled with children. There were a few parents too, in small huddles around the beds, but most were alone. Jo caught the eye of a child with a completely hairless head – she couldn't tell if it was a boy or girl. She winked and the kid waved back.

'There's a waiting room in there,' said Dr Srai. 'Help yourself to tea and coffee, though I wouldn't recommend the latter.'

Jo sat down, looking at the posters on the wall, with cartoon characters and smiling kids espousing the benefits of washing hands or advising on the early signs of meningitis. A box of knackered-looking toys sat in the corner, next to a stack of magazines and boardbooks. Over the years, Jo had spent plenty of time in hospitals in the line of duty, waiting to question victims and suspects alike. They were all the same, right down to the scuffed speckled lino on the floor, and the smell of the disinfectant not quite masking the scents of bodies doing what bodies did when they were compromised. Her dad had been admitted at the end to this very hospital, after losing consciousness. Mum had done nothing but talk in complete denial about a time 'when we get him home', and he'd died two weeks later without ever opening his eyes. Jo's mum had said it was a good way to go, somehow forgetting that he'd been 'going' for the last two years, and that it had been anything but good.

McDonagh appeared about ten minutes later, his paper tucked under his arm.

Jo stood up. 'Professor.'

'Detective,' he said. 'Is something the matter?'

'Not at all,' she replied. 'I dropped by to see how Niall's doing.'

'Oh, right. Of course.' He glanced along the corridor, then looked back at her. 'My wife and I . . . we owe you our thanks. Your colleague, Detective Carrick, he told us it was down to you.'

'It was a team effort,' said Jo. 'I'm just happy we found Niall.'

McDonagh looked momentarily pained. 'He won't talk to us,' he said. 'Won't tell us what happened.'

'That's understandable,' said Jo. 'It might be that he doesn't remember things clearly.'

McDonagh's fists clenched and unclenched. *He's not equipped for this*, she thought. Few people were.

'The doctors say . . . well, they examined him. They say that monster didn't *do* anything.'

Jo smiled, encouragingly. Small mercies.

'Would it be all right if I spoke to him?'

McDonagh looked perplexed. 'Why?'

Here we go, crunch time. Get this wrong and the opportunity's lost.

'We're just closing off enquiries,' said Jo. 'There's a possibility that Alan Trent is involved in a wider network of criminal individuals. As he's deceased, there might be something Niall can tell us – even if it seems inconsequential – that can further those enquiries.'

McDonagh's frown deepened. 'I don't know, detective. He's

very confused about things. We haven't told him Trent is dead, and he keeps saying . . . well, it doesn't matter. He's just getting things muddled up.'

'Muddled up how?'

'I don't think Trent was right in the head,' said McDonagh. 'That's stating the obvious, I suppose, but it sounds like he might have been, y'know, sort of schizophrenic. Niall says he wasn't that bad sometimes, but when he put on the mask he was different.'

Jo picked her words carefully. 'It would really help if I could talk to him,' she said. 'We just don't want this to happen to anyone else.'

'Yes,' said Niall's father, with the tiniest bob of the head.

She followed him to the last door in the corridor. In a smaller ward, only a single bed of the four was occupied. Niall was half reclined, facing away from the window, and Jo assumed he was asleep. But at the sound of their footsteps, he turned. In the hospital nightshirt, he looked very young, his eyelids droopy.

'Hi Dad,' he said.

Professor McDonagh kissed his son on the cheek. 'Niall, there's someone here to talk to you. A policewoman. Her name is Detective Masters.'

'Josie, please,' she said.

Niall didn't reply.

'Is that all right?' said Jo.

'You were down there,' he said. 'You found me.'

'I did. And I'm very glad you're safe now.'

Niall appeared to be processing the information.

'Dad, can I have a drink please?' he said. His father reached for a plastic cup. 'Maybe a Coke?' said Niall. 'From the machine?'

McDonagh glanced at Jo, then at Niall. 'You'll be all right on your own?'

Niall nodded.

'I'll stay right here with him,' said Jo, taking a seat next to the bed.

'Okay,' said his father. 'The vending machine's in reception. Back in a minute.'

He left the room.

'Were you the one who arrested Al?' said Niall, as soon as the door closed.

Al?

'Alan Trent?' said Jo. 'I was.'

He stared at her with an intensity that made her look away.

'He can't hurt you now,' she said.

'I know he's dead,' he said. 'Kieran told me.'

Jo, knocked off guard, didn't know what to say.

'Dad keeps saying how evil he was,' said Niall, 'but he wasn't. He was scared too. Cried more than me.'

'Scared of what?' asked Jo.

'Him. The clown.' Niall swallowed, and his eyes brimmed with tears. 'They won't listen to me. Dad just gets angry.'

'I'm listening,' said Jo.

'You believe me?'

'Of course. This clown, what was he like?'

'He was big,' said Niall, staring into space. 'Bigger than Al. Kind of hunched though.'

Jo was suddenly back in Yarnton, trying to find her friends, and seeing the two figures walking away from the fair – the giant and the child.

She resisted taking out her pocketbook. Niall's eyes were unfocused. He was back underground, in his memory. She wondered how long McDonagh would be getting to the vending machine and back. If he'd take the lift or the stairs.

'And he wore a mask too?'

'Not a mask. I think it was . . . make-up or something.'

205

'Clown make-up?'

Niall swallowed again, and his breathing seemed to catch. 'I don't know. His face was white. Like, really white. All of him was.'

Jo flinched. 'All of him?'

'All his skin. He didn't have any clothes on.'

Her stomach was turning. She knew she should stop. 'He was naked?'

'No. I couldn't see his privates. He had a . . . a cloth or something. I couldn't really see. It was dark, and I didn't want to look. It was cold down there, but he didn't care.'

Jo forced herself to refocus. 'So he was a tall, white man. How old do you think, Niall?'

'I don't know.'

'Older than your dad? Younger?'

'It was dark, I told you. He had bad teeth. Bad breath. He got really close. He kept sniffing.'

'And did he hurt you?'

Niall pressed his lips together, looked heavenward, like his eyes were searching for a way out of his memories.

'You don't have to tell me,' said Jo. 'It's all right.'

'It wasn't like that,' said Niall. 'He didn't fiddle with me or whatever you're thinking. My shoulder. He bit me. It wasn't that hard really. It was like he was . . . I don't know, tasting me or something.'

Christ.

'I shouted at him, told him to fuck off and leave me alone.'

'And did he?'

Niall swallowed. 'He hit me. A couple of times. I thought . . . I thought he was going to kill me. And I was just shouting at him to leave me alone. Then he did. He was just gone.'

'Did he say anything? Did he have an accent?'

Niall shook his head. 'I don't think he could speak.'

'What makes you say that?'

'He made noises, like he was an animal.'

The hair on Jo's neck was on end. It sounded to her like there was some element of ritual, or performance even. The strange attire, or lack of, perhaps body paint. It wasn't a pathology she was familiar with, but it was something a behavioural psychologist might be able to shed light on. Though she doubted Stratton would sign off on anything like that.

'Niall, this is really important. Did you ever see Alan Trent and this other man at the same time?'

Niall blinked the tears away, suddenly, and fiercely. 'They weren't the same person!' he said. 'I told you that!'

Jo heard the click of the door at her back.

'Is everything all right?' said McDonagh.

'You said you believed me!' shouted Niall.

'I do, I do,' said Jo.

'What's going on?' asked his father, rushing towards the bed holding a can of Coke.

'She told me she believed me,' said Niall. He was sitting bolt upright. 'But she's lying. You're all lying.' He hit the bed with his fists. 'I know about Al. I know what you all think, but you're all wrong. You weren't there. You didn't *see*! He was down there. He's probably still there now, but you won't listen. You won't listen to me!'

He was practically screaming as McDonagh took hold of both shoulders, saying, 'Calm down! Look at me, Niall,' before pulling his son's head into his shoulder. Niall was making a wailing sound, from somewhere deep in his gut, and McDonagh closed his eyes as he held his son.

'I think you should leave,' he said to Jo.

Jo stood, silently, and left the room.

★　★　★

Walking back across the hospital car park, she felt light-headed in the fresh air once more, as if she too had been locked up somewhere dark, only to be released suddenly into the glare of day. She wasn't sure what to think. It was plain that Niall believed what he said, but what he'd described was something informed by nightmares – a creature dredged up from folklore rather than fact.

The affection for Alan Trent made a sort of sense. She'd seen instances of Stockholm Syndrome before, mostly in cases of domestic violence, when despite bruises, broken teeth and black eyes, the victims point-blank refused to make a formal complaint about their spouses. This felt different though, and she couldn't buy the multiple personality theory. The physical details were the thing. The tall man, the strange clothing, the teeth, the skin. Trent was none of those things. And if he *had* dressed up, and changed his appearance as some sort of tactic to distance himself from his actions, where was the evidence of the make-up and strange clothing? They'd found the clown mask in his boot, and nothing else.

Which left the answer she'd been suspecting for some time. This person, this *freak* who liked to bite little boys, was still out there, and there was no saying what the fuck he wanted.

At her car, she sat weighing the options. Dimitriou and Tan would probably hear her out, but they'd need to follow up, and that could only end up bringing Stratton down on her. He had to listen now, surely. But getting close to Niall again, for any sort of official statement, would be next to impossible. She had to play her cards close, at least until there was something more concrete. There was the RAF base. She could go back and take another look around. There might be something there – *anything* – to link to the mystery suspect. She wondered where the prints were at.

First though, she went through her recent calls, and dialled Laura Phelps. It was worth one more try.

'My lawyer told me not to talk to you,' came the reply. She sounded furious.

'I'm sorry?'

'I've been suspended pending a formal enquiry.'

'Because of Alan Trent?'

'Of course because of Alan Trent.' Her voice cracked a little. 'They're saying I should have notified them of the change of address. Jesus. I was *trying* to do the right thing. He was fucking suicidal. Just look what happened if you don't believe me.'

'I understand,' said Jo.

'I've got to go.'

'Please,' said Jo. 'I don't think Trent was responsible. There was someone else.'

'I told you that,' said Phelps. 'Right from the start. You people don't want to listen, though, do you? You just want to bang someone up. I saw you on the news this morning. You're going to pin this other thing on Alan too, I suppose?'

Jo needed her to calm down, somehow earn her trust.

'Some of my colleagues want to,' said Jo.

A short pause. 'And you?'

'Someone was using Alan,' she said. 'And it might be the same person who killed Dylan Jones.' She let it sink in. 'That's why I need you to tell me about the group Alan went to.'

'Not this again. I told you, I'm bound by a code of profes- sional ethics . . .'

'Listen,' said Jo. 'It sounds like you're going through a tough time. As it happens, so am I. If we can prove that Trent was a compromised party in all this, it clears him to an extent, and it clears you too. I'm not asking for you to point someone out in a line. All I want is a location where these people meet.'

'I can't . . .'

'You did the right thing before,' said Jo. 'Do the right thing now. Do it for Alan, and do it for the next poor kid, before he gets taken and something worse happens.'

She'd started out trying to manipulate Phelps like a suspect in the interview room, but by the time she finished, Jo believed it herself, and she knew her desperation was obvious and she'd likely overplayed her hand. She expected to hear the line go dead.

Instead, Phelps sighed. 'It's a Quaker hall,' she said. 'I'm sorry, I don't know where, exactly.'

'In Oxford?'

'I really don't know, I promise. When Alan told me, I didn't pry. I was pleased that he was getting help. He really was, you know. He knew he had a problem, and he wanted to fix it.'

'Thank you,' said Jo.

'Look, this didn't come from me, all right.'

'No,' said Jo.

She was already on her work phone as Phelps hung up, searching for Quaker halls in Oxford. There were two. One was on St Giles, a busy thoroughfare near the centre, but it had a subsidiary meeting hall, off the Iffley Road. The website said it was available for use by members of the public, for a donation.

She called the number listed for the secretary, lied about a creative writing group she ran and enquired about availability for Monday nights.

'Sorry, we're booked on Mondays from seven until nine. Some sort of residents' group.'

Jo's skin tingled. 'What a shame.'

'We have a Wednesday, if that works for you.'

'It's Mondays I'm interested in,' said Jo. 'Not to bother. You've been very helpful.'

Chapter 18

Jo arrived just after six p.m., fighting through the traffic of the town centre, out along the Iffley Road, then taking a left on Magdalen Road. Local shops shared the street with terraced housing, and if she hadn't had directions, she'd have missed the Quaker hall. It was set back from the street slightly, an unassuming 1930s single-storey building with a hip roof. There was a well-tended front garden behind a small gate, and a flagged path which ran up the centre to a wooden porch. Ivy obscured most of the letters over the porch's arch – 'Friends Meeting House'. She drove past the first time, and with a little searching, discovered there was a back entrance too, serviced by a small car park on the next street over.

Two ingresses then. She figured the people she was waiting for would probably use the most discreet entrance, and reversed her car into a space opposite, twenty metres up the road.

Only an hour to wait, tops. Jo was used to much more gruelling stake-outs – the time-slowing mundanity, the sore back, the coffee cups and sandwich wrappers, the news bulletin repeats on the radio, every hour, the inane conversations with whatever colleague happened to be assigned the same watch.

A good ninety per cent of them came to sweet fuck all, but like most things in life there were occasional bright spells.

And, sometimes, she'd learned, you even fell in love.

Though it was twelve years ago, she remembered the case well. A local dealer, Harim Marek, Tunisian by birth, was thought to be using his girlfriend's grandmother's council flat in Whitley to store product. They had a bug in the neighbouring vacant flat, drilled into the wall, but it wasn't picking much up, so Jo was assigned to watch the eastern entrance to the block, noting the comings and goings of the suspect and his known associates. When her regular running partner, Hardeep, was called off to a family emergency, the passenger seat was filled with Benjamin Coombs, who ticked the tall, dark and handsome categories with an almost eerie precision. He'd brought a cafetière and portable kettle, plus croissants, and she'd joked that she hoped Hardeep's family continued to suffer. Ben, to her relief, had laughed.

Before the coffee had even brewed, she'd known he was the one. She'd been on a few dates to that point, in pubs and bars around Reading, and hated how forced it seemed. But being in that car, sometimes for ten hours at a stretch, wasn't forced at all. She felt giddy. And four or five days later, when Hardeep did return, his mother having passed away, Ben knew more about her life, her history, her childhood fears and adult dreams than any other person.

And if you'd asked twenty-seven-year-old Jo, she'd have said she knew him just as well.

As it happened, the drugs in the flat were just the start of it. On day six, the people in the apartment below complained to the council about a leak in their ceiling and a bad smell. It turned out that Marek's girlfriend's grandmother had been dead (natural causes) for close to a month. Instead of reporting the death, Marek and his heroin-addled partner had wrapped her in bedding and left her on the floor, clearly untroubled by the morality of the situation or the stench of her liquefying corpse. Marek had served four of eight years then been deported. The girlfriend, as she remembered, had OD'd while he was inside, leaving an eighteen-month-old to the 'care' of the state. Jo wondered vaguely how the little boy was doing now.

Movement on the other side of the road shook her from her thoughts. A middle-aged man with grey hair at the temples in a zipped-up Puma jacket arrived at the hall and walked straight to the rear door, crushing a cigarette into the wall. He tried the handle, but it didn't open, and Jo watched him look around with an annoyed expression on his face. The car's clock said it was ten to seven.

Jo stayed in her seat, lifting her phone just above the door frame and taking a picture through the window.

No one else came onto the scene for a few minutes, but at seven on the dot two men walked up together, greeting the first with nods. One was young – perhaps early twenties, with a narrow face and a ponytail, maybe six-one. His companion looked to be twice his age, bald, wearing an open leather jacket with a gut straining his T-shirt beneath. He took a key from his back pocket, and opened up the door. The three of them went inside. Jo photographed it all.

The minutes ticked past. Did they know Trent? If they did, and if they hadn't been living on Mars, they were probably talking about him inside. She hadn't really known what to expect, but was still a bit disappointed at the low turnout and the lack of menace the men exuded. It was still by far the most promising lead though, and if Trent's accomplice did belong to the group, there was a chance he was lying low.

Ben would probably have banged their heads together. He'd have burst in, made them panic, and got a list of names. But that wasn't her style. Plus, as a lone female, it maybe wasn't the best course of action. Chances were they'd run at the first sign of trouble and that would be it. Her best angle was to go back with the photos, cross-reference with the other detectives, and go through the mugshots. It was a longer game, but more likely to bear fruit. Stratton would approve. She decided to sit tight, get a few more shots as the men left.

A movement in her rear-view mirror caught her eye. Jo froze. On her side of the street, walking quickly, came a man. It was the height she noticed first – he must have been six-four at least. He wore a long beige coat, buttoned right up to the collar. A tonsure of white hair, closely trimmed white beard. A severe, ascetic face, the lips a thin line. Mid-sixties at a minimum.

She sank into her seat as he passed. He stopped a few metres up the street, then looked across at the Meeting House, frowning a little, then glanced left and right, before leaning off the kerb and stepping into the road. He had a loping stride, like he was leaning into a headwind. Jo watched him enter the building before even realising she'd been holding her breath. It came out in a rush.

And suddenly, sitting tight and checking mugshots wasn't an option.

She reached into her pocket and found her phone. She called Ben, who picked up.

'What's up?'

'I need your help.' She gave him the broad details quickly, and her location, and to his credit he listened without interrupting.

'You think it's him?' he asked.

Jo tried to remember exactly what Niall had said. Tall, pale skin, hunched.

'I don't know.'

'Under no circumstances go inside,' he said. 'Jo, I mean it.'

'I won't,' she said. 'How soon can you get here?'

She could hear his car door. 'I'm on my way. Ten minutes. Promise me you'll stay put.'

'Promise. And Ben – between us, okay?'

'Just stay in your car.'

He hung up, and she took another deep breath. No one was going anywhere for ten minutes. Only as she managed to relax a little did it occur to her that Ben was the first number that came to mind. Whether it was their history, or just because she wanted to keep Stratton at a distance, she didn't have time to dwell. She watched the clock, then the Meeting House, then the street.

At 7.09, a blue car was drifting slowly along the street. It took her a second or two to realise she'd seen the plate, and the model, before, and there followed another few seconds of confusion.

What in God's name is she doing here?

The car mounted the pavement and parked right across the rear entrance of Meeting House, completely blocking it.

No . . . no . . . no. Not now. What are you doing, you fucking idiot?

The passenger door opened first, and a man climbed out with a camera. He tipped it at the building, filming from the off. Rebekah Saunders must have scrambled across from the driver's seat, because she emerged from the same side, and marched towards the door of the Meeting House.

Jo was out of her own car quickly, and running across the road.

'Hey! Stop!'

Saunders turned, saw her and frowned, then said something to the camera operator. He directed the lens at Jo herself for a few seconds, then focused back on the hall as Saunders reached the door and tried the handle. It didn't open, so she banged it several times with the flat of her palm.

Jo reached the blocked gate. 'What the fuck are you doing? We've got this place under . . .'

The door opened a crack, and the ponytailed young man looked out.

'How well do you know Alan Trent?' asked Saunders immediately.

The man tried to close the door, but Saunders had her foot in the way, and used her weight to shoulder through. The cameraman followed. Jo heard shouts from inside.

Jo vaulted the bonnet of Saunders' car, and headed after them. She was met by the first man who'd entered, coming the other way. He had his head bowed, covered by a magazine, as he barrelled past. Seeing the car parked across the gate, he spun on the spot.

'What is this?' he said.

'Hey, you can't do that!'

Jo saw the leather-jacketed man pushing the cameraman against a wall just inside the doorway, bellowing, 'Get that thing out of my face!' Saunders was already inside, shouting something, and Jo ran in after her. The camera fell onto the ground and smashed.

In the sparsely furnished hall, Saunders was thrusting a Dictaphone in the face of Puma top, saying something about Dylan Jones. Across the other side of the room, the ponytailed younger male was standing on a bench, his upper body already through a window. Jo tried to get there in time, but he overbalanced and his feet disappeared. The man in the leather jacket had opened a fire door and was gone.

'Are you getting this, Clive?' said Saunders. She looked back, saw the camera in pieces. 'Oh bugger!'

Jo shoved Saunders aside, harder than necessary, and went straight for the tall man who'd arrived late. He watched her calmly, too calmly, and she pressed a hand into his chest, pushing him back into the wall.

'I think there's been a misunderstanding . . .'

'Name?'

'I'm sorry, who are you?'

'Detective Masters, Avon and Somerset. What are you doing here?'

'That's none of your business.'

'I note that you're declining to answer my questions, so I'm arresting you on suspicion of conspiracy to kidnap and the false imprisonment of a child.'

'I'm sorry?'

She read him his rights. 'You'll be questioned at the station.'

Turning around, breathing hard, she saw it was just Saunders and her companion who remained. Both were open-mouthed.

'What the fuck are you looking at?' said Jo.

Jo heard a car screech up, and then pounding footsteps. Ben ran into the building.

'Are you okay?'

'Fine,' said Jo.

Ben took it all in. 'What happened to staying in the car?'

'These two fuckwits decided to show up,' said Jo.

That seemed to snap Saunders out of her stupor. She held the Dictaphone up.

'Would you like to make a statement, detective?' she asked.

If Jo hadn't been holding the suspect, she might have grabbed the thing and done something stupid.

'Switch that thing off and get out,' said Jo. 'You're interfering with police business.'

Saunders stared back defiantly, but Ben took her roughly by the arm and steered her towards the door.

'You heard the detective. Out.' The camera guy followed meekly.

'You can't do this!' said the tall man, looking outraged.

'Want to tell us your name now?' said Jo.

'Timothy Ingliss,' replied the man. 'Really, you've made an error.'

'We'll see about that. Are you going to come with us nicely, or do I have to cuff you?'

'Lead the way,' said the man. 'I look forward to sorting this out, Detective Masters.'

Outside, Saunders was on the phone already, climbing into her car. Jo left the suspect with Ben and went over.

'What were you doing here?' asked Jo.

'Investigating,' said Saunders. 'Same as you.'

'But how did you find out about this place?'

Saunders tapped the side of her nose. 'We all have sources. Let's just say I got a tip-off about Trent's movements.'

'Wait, this is about Alan?' said the tall man.

'Save it,' said Jo. She turned her attention back to Saunders. 'The taxi firm, right?' she said.

Saunders merely lifted an eyebrow and pursed her lips. Ben looked nonplussed.

'I called them to follow up one of Trent's calls,' Jo explained. 'My guess is that she got a call earlier today from a driver who wanted a few quid for information pertinent to her recent articles. How's my guesswork?'

Saunders shrugged. 'So can we go?'

The sudden sound of sirens approached, and a squad car pulled up. Someone must have called them, and Jo opened her badge to the uniforms as they jogged over.

'Ma'am,' said the first.

'It's all under control,' said Jo.

Saunders was lingering.

'You're not needed any more,' said Jo. 'Please move your vehicle – it's obstructing the public right of way.'

'You know we're on the same side?' said Saunders. 'The public have a right to know their kids are safe.'

'Then let us do our job,' said Jo.

She managed to convince the uniforms that the disturbance

218

was related to ongoing CID business, so they could cite her on any formal reports, but asked them to remain and get in touch with the Meeting House's emergency contact. Ben put Ingliss in the back of his car, then came over.

'You're a bloody idiot,' he said, but he said it fondly enough that it didn't anger her.

'It went pear-shaped,' she said.

'So what makes you think that guy's involved?' asked Ben, nodding towards her car.

'He matches the description that Niall gave me,' said Jo.

Ben frowned. 'Jo, it was hardly thorough . . .'

'You think I'm overreacting?'

'Does Stratton know?' When she shook her head, he blew out his cheeks. 'You have been busy.'

He didn't sound entirely approving.

'I'm not going to just sit around,' she said, 'whatever Stratton says. If there's someone out there still, if he finds another kid . . .' She stopped, realising she sounded almost exactly like Rebekah Saunders at the press conference.

Ben touched her shoulder. 'Look, let me handle the DCI,' he said. 'We'll say it was a joint thing.'

'You don't have to cover for me.'

'I'm not doing it for you,' he said. 'I want to put this thing to bed too. If there's a chance this guy ties into Dylan too . . .'

'It's a possibility,' said Jo. He had to be pushing seventy. 'Nothing that links Trent yet then?'

Ben shook his head. 'I finally managed to get hold of the Building Inspectorate. Figured the pool would have needed planning permission. They've given us the name of the firm who put it in. Owner's selling solar panels now. Anyway, he's going to draw up a list of the guys who worked for him back then – all cash in hand, ad hoc stuff, and no Alan that he could remember. Doesn't rule him out, and we'll run the mugshot by him too. Carter's liaising with the daughter of the former owner – we're just trying to get all the paperwork lined up concerning the pool-work itself – in case there's anything there. But unless we get something biological from Salisbury, I don't see that we can link it up. Rhani's digging up everything on Trent from the eighties, but no known connections with the area at the moment.'

'Sounds like you've got it covered. We'll see if this guy's got any links to Bradford-on-Avon as well.'

'See you back at the station then?'

'Thanks, Ben,' she replied, and she meant it.

Chapter 19

Ingliss was waiting patiently in the custody suite when Jo returned. She had to double-take. He was eating a biscuit.

'He's diabetic,' said the custody sergeant apologetically. 'Had to let him test his blood.'

'I was a little low,' said Ingliss.

Jo rolled her eyes, and led him to the desk. 'Anything in his personals?'

The sergeant flipped round the screen. A packet of tissues, a set of car keys, some mints and a leather wallet with an assortment of cards. He'd declined legal representation, but that didn't mean anything in her experience.

'What's the charge?' asked the custody officer.

When Jo told him, the officer arched an eyebrow.

'What about my car?' asked Ingliss. 'I only paid for two hours. It's on Iffley Road.'

'You don't need to worry about that now,' said Jo, not a little unnerved by his demeanour.

He's playing it very cool.

It was only Carrick in CID, and Ben was filling him in as

Jo led Ingliss to an interview room. She seated him, and Ben came in too, closing the door.

Jo started the tape and introduced everyone for the record. Ingliss smiled throughout the process. His teeth, though a shade discoloured, looked even enough and the doubts in Jo's gut intensified.

'Mr Ingliss, can you tell me what you were doing at the Friends Meeting House on Magdalen Road today?'

'I was offering support to a group who meet there,' he said.

'Offering support how?' asked Jo.

'Spiritually, I suppose you might say,' said Ingliss. Ben scoffed, but Ingliss looked unperturbed. 'Maybe it would be simpler to say I offer an understanding ear.'

'And that's how you know Alan Trent?' said Jo.

Ingliss nodded. 'It's a terrible thing. I didn't know until I saw it this morning. And, to my shame, a part of me wanted to abandon today's meeting. But I reasoned their need was greater than mine, and so . . .'

'Where were you last Friday evening, between say ten p.m. and Sunday morning?'

'Over the weekend? I would have been at home, mostly.'

'In Thame?' said Jo. Ingliss nodded. 'Anyone who can verify that? A wife?'

'Widowed,' said the man.

'Now there's a surprise,' muttered Ben.

For the first time, Ingliss looked annoyed. 'You're being impolite, and my patience is wearing thin. You arrest me on a ludicrous charge, with no evidence that I can see . . .'

'Save it,' said Jo. 'We've arrested you because Alan Trent had an accomplice who matches your description, and along with your behaviour and your refusal to give us your name when initially requested, I deemed that a reasonable suspicion you were involved.'

'*My* behaviour?' huffed Ingliss. 'Well, I really couldn't tell you anything about an accomplice. But if it will help to eliminate me from your enquiries, I should tell you I'm a former prison chaplain, and it's in that context I first met Alan.'

Jo tried not to look surprised. 'You're a priest?'

'Indeed.'

He might have been lying, but it was as level a performance as Jo had ever seen. Besides, he wouldn't be the first man of God to have a penchant for young boys.

'So why does the group describe itself as a residents' organisation?' she said.

'Surely you can appreciate a level of . . . concealment,' said Ingliss. 'The men are rightfully worried about the repercussions should their former crimes be public knowledge. Alan himself suffered terribly in the past.'

'Hold on a minute,' said Jo. 'Their former crimes? They're all ex-cons?'

This was looking more promising.

'I prefer to focus on their potential for the future,' said Ingliss. 'Whatever crimes these men committed, they're dealing with them, and God never turns away from . . .'

And as he was talking, Jo realised why the men had all run. Why one had been shielding his face.

'They're sex offenders,' she said.

Ingliss stopped. 'I never liked the term, but yes.'

'You're ministering to a group of perverts?' said Ben.

'To a group of men,' said Ingliss, looking pained. 'If I may say, I've met dozens of law enforcement officers in my career, and many exhibit the same, how can I put this, blunt understanding of this subject. Are you aware of Alan's past, detective? His upbringing?'

'I thought we weren't dealing in the past,' Ben fired back. 'Anyway, my job is to protect the innocent, here in the present, and Alan Trent showed himself to be a dangerous man.'

Ingliss nodded, as if weighing up Ben's response. 'I'm not familiar with the details of the case,' he said, 'but I struggle to fathom Alan's involvement.'

'We have a clear line of evidence that he abducted a little boy, locked him up, and then killed himself,' said Jo. She couldn't help but notice that Ingliss' opinion of Alan Trent was almost identical to that of Laura Phelps.

'And all I can tell you is that is wholly out of character,' said Ingliss.

'Thanks for the insight – but it doesn't change anything,' said Jo. 'Let's go back to your whereabouts this last weekend.'

'Let's see.' He looked skyward, then counted off on his fingers as he spoke. 'I went shopping on Saturday morning. There was a fete in the village, and I ran the raffle. Following that, I went home. I would have seen my neighbours around eight – we press flowers. On Sunday morning, I went to church, and following that I visited a nursing home where I read to the residents on a fortnightly basis.'

'A verifiable saint,' said Ben.

'Make any trips to the west of Oxford?' asked Jo.

'I did not,' said Ingliss. 'And I am no saint, detective. To err is human, as you will know. It's how we address our mistakes that matters most in God's eyes.'

A heavy silence filled the room, and Jo felt the blood rush to her cheeks.

Finally, Ben spoke. 'Is that what you call making a child wank you off? A mistake?'

Ingliss took his time. 'I suppose it depends on your perspective. What the church calls a sin, you call a crime. A psychologist might say it was an inevitable outcome based on the fact Trent's own father raped him as a child. In anyone's eyes, however, Trent was punished. Don't you believe in second chances?'

Jo glanced at Ben. His eyes were burning.

★   ★   ★

Jo suggested a break so they could ascertain a few things, and left Ingliss in the IR.

'What do you reckon?' she asked Ben, staring at the monitor in the AV suite. Ingliss sat straight-backed in his seat, staring straight ahead. She ignored her gut, which was telling her that this was the wrong tree to be barking up.

'Alibi's hardly gold standard,' said Ben.

'We could search his vehicle,' said Jo. 'Maybe his house.'

'You think Stratton will go for that?'

Jo doubted it. 'Not on the current intelligence.'

'Well, let him sweat a bit,' said Ben, 'then we take another crack.'

For the next hour, they followed up on Ingliss' story, going in from time to time for clarifications. One by one, the facts checked out. Ingliss had worked at HMP Bullingdon until a couple of years ago, the very place Trent had served his time. His neighbours expressed great concern on learning he was in custody, and confirmed the flower pressing, plus other movements. Jo drew up a timeline, and slowly the window for a round trip to RAF Bampton Castle shrunk. To her eye, there was no obvious match to the prints found there either. She asked Ben to look also, and his face said it all. Still, they had them scanned to the lab for confirmation. And to cap it all, Ingliss had worked as a missionary throughout the eighties in South America, attached to a church in Kent, with zero links to Bradford-on-Avon or even Somerset and the surrounding counties.

At close to ten p.m., they decided to release Ingliss. He took it with surprising grace, choosing to make his own way back to his car rather than waiting any longer for a squad vehicle. His parting shot was to enquire politely where he could find reimbursement for any parking fines he might have incurred.

'It was worth a try,' said Ben.

'Was it?' said Jo. 'We're no closer to finding Trent's accomplice.'

Ben stroked his jaw. She'd seen the gesture a hundred times, at work and at home, and she braced herself.

'If he had one,' he said.

'You can't still think he worked alone.'

'All you've got is what Niall said. A kid who's been through an unbelievable trauma. He's not reliable.'

'I'm very aware of that,' said Jo. 'But Phelps, Ingliss, the colleagues from the college, none of them think Trent was capable.'

'No one ever does.'

'*I* don't either,' said Jo. 'What was all that, in there, if you don't believe me?'

'It's not about what I believe,' said Ben. 'It's about what we can prove. You look knackered, Jo. Take a break. There's nothing to be gained from killing yourself.'

She wanted to argue, but she didn't want an argument. 'Maybe you're right,' she conceded.

'Aren't I always,' he said, brighter. 'We could get a drink if you like. My hotel bar's pretty decent.'

He said it lightly, but the question gained weight as it hung in the air. Jo glanced at the clock, sorely tempted. In the last few hours, the awful history of their relationship had barely entered her mind. They'd just been two colleagues, getting on with the job.

'Look, no thanks. I wouldn't be good company. I'll finish up a few bits here.'

Ben looked disappointed, and she knew she'd made the right choice.

'See you tomorrow then,' he said.

Jo waited until he'd left, and she knew she must be tired; she'd been so close to going with him. *And Christ knows where that might have ended up.*

She went straight to a computer and logged on to the database, filtering for registered SOs in the area. There were fifty-three within a five-mile radius of Oxford city centre, and with her phone at her side, she cycled through the files.

She fully expected not to find anything, so it was a pleasant surprise that one of the images near the end of the list was undoubtedly the young man with the ponytail who had fled through the window. Lee Burgess was twenty-six years old, and had a conviction from five years prior for a single count of sexual activity with an underage girl of fourteen and causing a juvenile to be exposed to sexually explicit material. He had served four years. Jo took in the details with a dispassionate eye – the child in question had been his stepsister, and he'd also been having a simultaneous sexual relationship with her mother. The mind boggled. Jo was not unused to seeing such dysfunction, but it still took her a moment to fathom what she was reading.

'What a charmer,' she muttered to herself.

There was an address listed for Burgess, who wore a tag while out on licence. He was forbidden from contacting either his victim or her mother, and had to sign in at his local station – Cowley – weekly. They listed his employer as Prefecta Processing, based on the Botley industrial estate.

She phoned the place, pretending to be his mother, and learned his next shift started at six in the morning.

With a few hours to kill, she went back to her brother's in Horton to have a wash and grab some clean clothes. They'd had a slipper bath put in, and she could just imagine sliding into the bubbles. But as she turned into the drive, her heart sank at the sight of the BMW already pulled up.

Ben.

What was he playing at? Jo left the engine running and sat for a few moments. She could turn around and drive off, but where to? And they'd have heard the car. Better to be a grown-up.

She switched off the ignition and climbed out, heels crunching up to the front door. So much for the hot bath.

The adults were all in the living room, with the double-doors to the entrance hall open. They looked up as she came in. Ben stood from the sofa.

'Evening, Jo.'

'Is something the matter?' she asked.

'Not at all,' said Ben, coming towards her. Amelia and Paul remained seated. 'I just dropped by – would you believe Carter's come up with something useful?'

She folded her arms. It had been less than an hour ago when she'd said goodbye at the station.

'You could have called.'

The look on Paul and Amelia's faces was sombre, and she felt guilty. They didn't need this in their house.

'What is it?' she said.

'We'll leave you to it,' said Paul, standing up to close the living room door, leaving Ben and Jo in the privacy of the foyer. She had the horrible feeling they were listening from the other side.

'What have you got?' she said.

Ben looked hurt, but his voice didn't betray it. He took out his phone.

'The daughter of the owners – she went back by the house. Anyway, there was a tonne of junk mail – amazing what still gets delivered. She was chucking it all out, and she found this.'

He flipped the phone over. 'Some sort of architectural drawing by the looks of it.'

'Are those plans?'

'Indeed they are,' said Ben. 'A layout of the house in Bradford-on-Avon.'

Jo used her fingers to zoom in on an 'X'. It was beside a rectangular shape that must have been the pool.

'That's where the body was found. Sorry, where's this from?'

'That's the thing,' said Ben. 'It was postmarked April, nearly two years back – came through the Oxford sorting office. It's just been sat on the doormat of the house all this time. Anything with the family surname was on a re-direct, but this just had an address so it got delivered along with all the other crap. But I haven't shown you the best bit yet. On the reverse . . .'

He flipped to the next image, where there were four words, cut from fractured newspaper print.

PLEASE BURY HIM PROPERLY.

'That's a hell of a guilty conscience,' said Jo. 'Prints on the envelope?'

'Probably several,' said Ben. 'It's at the lab now.'

Jo stared at the image. It was a confession, just not a signed one, and it ruled one thing out.

'Trent would have been banged up then,' she said, airing her thoughts.

'But whoever sent this is likely to still be around now,' said Ben. 'Your accomplice theory is looking more plausible.'

'Stratton has to at least give it a hearing,' Jo agreed. 'If these are the plans from the architects that makes it pretty certain it was one of the workers on the site.'

'That's what I'm focused on,' said Ben. 'The Trent mugshot

didn't ring any bells with the pool guy though? Maybe let me talk to Stratton.'

'Man to man?' said Jo, with a smile.

'It's not that — I just know things have been awkward.'

'Fine,' she said. 'I've got this funeral tomorrow. Give me a call and let me know what he says.'

'Sure. And sorry — you're right. I should have called.'

His conciliatory tone caught her off guard. 'No — it's fine. It's been a long day.'

He stuffed his hands in his pockets. 'I'll be off then,' he said. 'Say goodbye to your brother and Amelia for me. And look, I'm sorry.' He jerked his head back towards the living room doors. 'I thought they knew.'

As he passed her, towards the door, he touched her arm fondly.

What he'd just said sank in. As he left, and the door closed, she went into the lounge to face the music. Paul and Amelia weren't standing with their ears to the door, but were together on the sofa again, Paul on the iPad, Amelia with a paperback.

'He shouldn't have come here,' she said.

'I'm glad he did,' said Paul. 'Why didn't you tell us?'

Jo felt like she was being cross-examined. She hadn't even taken off her coat. She wished she *had* booked into a hotel now.

'It's no big deal.'

'You've been together for over ten years.'

Hand still on the door frame, she half looked their way. 'Did he tell you why?'

'The gambling,' said Paul. 'He didn't go into detail, but he said he'd lost a lot of money.'

Jo laughed. 'He lost *all* our money. Everything we saved.'

'Christ,' said Amelia.

Jo wondered if he'd mentioned the miscarriage too. She wasn't going to bring it up.

'He cares about you,' said her brother. 'A lot.'

'It's too late for that,' said Jo. She started up the stairs.

'He's getting help, you know,' said Amelia. 'Gamblers Anonymous.'

'Is that what he said?'

'I don't think he was lying. He knows he's got a problem.'

'Look, I'm tired,' said Jo. 'Can we do this another time?'

'We don't have to do it at all,' said Paul. 'We're just worried about you.'

'I'm fine, honestly,' said Jo. 'And so is Ben. When this case is finished, we'll be going our separate ways. It's just a bit complicated at the moment.'

As she traipsed up the stairs to her room, she wondered if she was lying to herself. Leaving Ben, moving out, it had all seemed so simple at the time. But here they were, months later, and still the connections were there, like little tangles impossible to unravel.

It was a bit like the two clown cases. They were linked, just in ways she couldn't see at the moment. It was like trying to untie a knot in the dark.

Whoever sent that note, if he was the same person who had co-opted Alan Trent – he was out there, now. He might be desperate, he might be scared, he might be invigorated.

He could strike again at any moment.

★   ★   ★

She should have been exhausted, but with the fresh air blasting through her window she felt wide awake as she drove into the industrial estate in Botley just before dawn. It was the sort of place that never slept. Floodlit yards and warehouses lined each side, many with loading doors open, men – and it was *only* men – smoking outside, or operating forklifts in hi-vis clothing.

She followed the signs to Prefecta Processing, a vast grey windowless structure at the edge of the estate. She entered the fenced-off area, past an open truck being filled with pallets. There were parking spots designated to various names, but all were empty, so she pulled up across two, right outside a door to the reception area.

She found the front desk empty, but there was a buzzer, which she rang. No one came, so she opened the counter and was about to let herself through a rear door when a man in a boiler suit carrying a toolbox came the other way. She heard the clank of heavy machinery from the other side.

'Can I help you?' he said.

Jo opened up her badge. 'I need to speak to one of your employees. Name of Lee Burgess.'

The man squinted at the badge. 'Stay here – I'll find someone. You can't go back there – health and safety.'

Jo waited in the tiny reception area, vaguely scanning the certificates on the wall, all related to hygiene and cleanliness. She gathered Prefecta dealt mainly with supplying canned goods to supermarkets. She didn't know what Burgess' role was, but she imagined it was the sort of thing that would be automated within a decade.

The man himself arrived only a couple of minutes later, dressed in a hairnet, blue booties and gloves, as well as white overalls. He could have been a crime scene officer, if he didn't look so absolutely terrified. He was accompanied by a fat man with substantial sweat patches emanating from his armpits.

'What's this about?' Burgess' companion asked.

'I need to talk with Mr Burgess, in private.'

'Is he in trouble?'

'I ain't done nuffink,' Burgess said.

'No,' said Jo. 'He's just helping us with some enquiries. It shouldn't take more than a few minutes.'

Burgess' boss looked contemptuous. 'See that it doesn't. He's only just come on.'

'Shall we go outside, Lee?' asked Jo.

He nodded, pulling off the gloves and boots, folding them in his hands and placing them on the desk.

Outside, he looked around sheepishly, unzipped the overalls and pulled out a packet of cigarettes with a lighter inside. He had a thin fuzz on his cheeks, and a sickly pallor over old acne scars. As he lit his cigarette, the flame trembled.

'You ran away before I could talk to you earlier,' she said.

He took a long drag. 'What do you want?'

'I need to talk to you about Alan Trent.'

'Who?'

Jo let him smoke. Sometimes silence was the best weapon, and only ten seconds passed before he added, 'Look, I didn't even know him that well.'

'How long had he been coming to your little Monday circle jerk?'

Lee bristled, flicked the cigarette in a dancing shower of sparks. 'Go fuck yourself.' He started walking back towards the door.

'Your colleagues know about that tag you wear?' she asked.

Burgess stopped. For a moment she thought he might even go for her, but he just turned slowly.

'Yeah, they do actually,' he said.

Jo stared back.

'What'd you tell them? That she looked eighteen? Thing is, you knew she wasn't, didn't you?'

Burgess shook his head, looking at the ground. 'You fucking people. Just can't leave it alone. I did my time.'

'Four years?' said Jo. 'I bet there are people on your shift who'd cut your dick off if they knew.'

Burgess shot a glance back towards the door, then edged nearer to her. 'I'm just trying to get my life back,' he hissed.

233

'And I don't want to stand in your way,' she said. 'So tell me about Trent.'

'I told you, for fuck's sake. I saw him once a fucking week.'

'For how long?'

'I dunno. A couple of months.'

'We spoke to Ingliss earlier. Interesting chap.'

'What did he say?'

'Oh, he thinks you're all troubled souls,' said Jo. 'To hear him talk, you'd think Trent was the victim, not the boys he fiddled with.'

'I don't know nuffink 'bout that.'

'I'm sure,' said Jo. 'So what did you talk about, at your meetings?'

Burgess stooped, picked up the butt, and relit it.

'Stuff,' he said.

'You'll have to do better than that, Lee. Come on, give me a clue. Was it football? Was it God and forgiveness?'

'You wouldn't get it.'

'Try me.'

'We talked about our lives, I s'pose. Tim says it can help.'

God bless Tim!

'And does it?'

'I dunno.'

'What did Alan say about his life?'

'He didn't say much at all, the first few times. He was nervous. Thought people would find out. He had to leave the last place they put him. Got smashed up by some kids.'

'I heard about that.'

'I never knew what he'd done. I don't care really. He was a good bloke. Funny.'

'So when did you last see him?'

'A week ago.' The cigarette was almost done. Burgess seemed to be relaxing, leaning back on the wall. 'He was different.'

'Different how?'

'I dunno. Sort of sad. I thought maybe he'd had some bad news. Y'know – like someone close had died. He said he couldn't keep coming to the group. Said he was in trouble.'

'Did Ingliss know this?'

'No – it was after he'd left. He'd have tried to talk to Al, and Al wasn't much of a talker. Not with a chaplain anyway.'

'Did he give any indication to you what the trouble was?'

'No,' said Burgess, 'but—'

The large foreman emerged from the door. 'All right, break's over, Lee. You know the rules.'

'Just give us another minute,' said Jo.

'This is a business,' said the boss. 'One minute, no more.'

He dipped inside again.

'You were saying – about the trouble . . .'

'I'm guessing, okay, but I reckon someone had found out about him.'

'You think he was being blackmailed?'

'Maybe.'

Ingliss jumped into her head, but she dismissed it almost as quickly. The prison chaplain turned blackmailer didn't pass muster.

'I need the names of the other people at the group,' she said.

The look he gave her was so utterly devoid of emotion she found it unnerving. 'I'm no grass.'

'Just names, Lee. No one will know they're from you.'

But she knew she'd lost him as he began to walk away. At the door he paused.

'Look, do what you like. But I need this job. I've got a kid on the way.'

God help them, thought Jo, as he disappeared back inside.

As Jo drove away, with the dawn light breaking across the warehouses, she thought about where to start with Stratton when she saw him next. She'd be able to bring Burgess in to give an official statement, if he wanted. But it was still, infuriatingly, just conjecture.

They had nothing else. Ben was right that Niall's credibility was next to nought, and his nightmare recollection was more like a horror story than anything else. The print lab might come up with a match still, from down under the Nissen Hut.

In the meantime, she had a funeral to attend.

Chapter 20

TUESDAY

Back at her brother's, Jo packed her things quickly, and was checking her reflection in the mirror when Paul passed the guest room on the landing. He knocked on the already open door.

'Hey,' she said.

'Hi, sis,' he said. 'I wanted to say sorry – about last night. It's really none of our business about you and Ben. We're just sorry it didn't work out.'

'Don't sweat about it,' she said. 'It happened months ago, and I should have told you then.'

Her brother spotted the bag. 'You're not leaving, are you?'

'Case is closed,' said Jo. 'I'm due a few days' leave. Out of your hair and all.'

Paul came into the room. 'Where are you staying now then?'

'I've got my own place in Bath. Nothing special.'

To put it mildly.

'Oh, right.' He lingered. 'It's just, well . . . *actually*, I've got a bit of a favour to ask. Our babysitter's let us down. We're due at the firm's annual summer party tonight.'

'No problem,' she said, straight away. She'd hardly been relishing returning to the flat, and even if it only masked the disappointment of the case for a while, the distraction of children's TV and bedtime stories was a welcome one.

'You sure? We'd ask Em, but she's got some party that apparently she can't miss.'

'It'd be a pleasure. What time do you need me?'

'Say seven thirty?'

'Perfect.'

'You're a lifesaver,' said Paul.

★   ★   ★

St Edward's was a dark, gothic-looking church crowded in by houses. Jo walked up the front path just before ten a.m., between leaning gravestones clustered among overgrown grass. She'd worn, for lack of other options, her work attire, and as she approached the front porch, she felt distinctly underdressed.

Mr Jones was waiting by the open doors, wearing a blazer and suit trousers, with a stack of papers in his hand. His neck swelled across the top of his collar, and combined with the broken veins across his nose and cheeks, he looked distinctly uncomfortable. Jo wondered if this whole thing had been his wife's idea. When he saw her, she caught a slight defensive flinch of surprise before he nodded.

'Detective,' he said. 'Good of you to come.'

'I wanted to pay my respects,' she said. 'How is Mrs Jones doing?'

He shrugged. 'To be honest, she's enjoyed having something to do. Please, do go inside. We'll be starting soon. And have one of these.'

He handed her the order of service, on a folded piece of

thick card. The front cover read 'In Memoriam: Dylan Edward Jones', with his birthday and the day he went missing.

They have to tell themselves that, I suppose.

Jo entered, and it took her eyes a moment to adjust to the darkness of the church's interior. The musty smell of the wooden pews and ancient prayer books took her back at once. Her mother had been an ardent worshipper, dragging Jo along until the age of twelve or thirteen, and Jo could almost hear the rap of Mrs Masters' Sunday-best heels on the stone flags now.

The place was well attended with some twenty or thirty guests, most of a similar age to the Joneses. Jo ran her eyes over the assortment of thinning hair, walking sticks, costume jewellery and dark clothing. There were one or two in their late thirties as well, and she wondered if they were perhaps school friends of Dylan. Given his age when he went missing, they surely couldn't remember the disappearance as anything other than a distant novelty.

Most people were seated already, but Mrs Jones was holding court near the front of the church with a couple. As her husband had said, she looked cheerful, and her outfit was incongruously bright considering the sombre occasion, with a fuchsia skirt and matching jacket, and a stylish hat. *And why not?* She was probably making up for all the ceremonies she'd never had the opportunity to attend – the graduation, the wedding, maybe the christenings of grandchildren too.

And there was Ferman, seated almost out of sight behind a pillar, alone at the end of a pew with his head bowed. Jo walked down the aisle, then filed in along his row. He didn't seem to notice her until she had taken the seat beside him.

'You came,' he said, unclasping his hands from his lap and gripping the front of the pew in front.

'I said I would,' she replied. 'How are you?'

'Same old,' he replied. 'You look tired.'

'Thanks,' she said. 'I think I'll be heading back to Bath soon.'

He nodded sagely, as though understanding on some deeper level that their strange, second encounter had been as inconsequential as the first thirty years before, and that the vagaries of her case, the disappearance and rescue of Niall, and the violent death of Trent were ultimately meaningless. His gaze travelled to the front of the church, and Jo's eyes followed to the blown-up picture of Dylan on the trestle at the front, the black and white smiling face that would forever memorialise him. There were other, smaller images as well, but from the back of the church, Jo couldn't make them out.

The church stilled and quietened as the last of the guests took their seats and a cassocked priest emerged. He was at least a septuagenarian himself, so perhaps he too remembered Dylan. He spoke softly to Mrs Jones for a few seconds, then took her hands in his. She smiled before sitting beside her husband.

Jo had always found faith mystifying and childishly benign, but in odd moments she'd seen first-hand the solace it could offer, and in those fleeting glimpses, a sort of envy stirred in her gut. When her dad had gone, so suddenly, Paul said their mother had stepped up her attendance at their local church, but Jo had sensed it was for appearances rather than genuine comfort.

The ceremony began with words from the priest, about a life being cut short, about the shock and fear, about injustice and questioning God. Jo respected the crafty circumlocutions that the church could offer – almost lawyerly in their approach – and the way of using the liturgy to protect the congregation from the grim reality of his death, to deter the inevitable speculation of what had happened to Dylan between that summer's day at the circus and whenever he had met his end shortly afterwards. No single mention was made of the kidnap, no reference even to an unnatural death. Jo found herself thinking of Ingliss – he would have no doubt approved of the approach.

There was a reading by a family friend, of the Liverpool FC anthem 'You'll Never Walk Alone', and Jo found herself welling up at the words, because in that moment she was back at the circus admiring Dylan's football shirt. Afterwards, a sacred hymn was sung, and Ferman mumbled along, and then another guest read a passage from John, about Lazarus rising from the dead.

As the tone became more spiritual, her mind wandered back to Niall, speculating why the print lab was taking so long. She followed the service absently, until she saw Ferman turn the cover of the order of service. On the back there was a black and white image of Dylan, sitting at a piano. The text below the picture read 'Final prayers', with a further line, 'The church pianist will play the congregation out to Chopin's Prelude in E-Minor'.

Jo turned over her own order of service, fingers tingling oddly. Dylan looked tiny against the full-size keyboard, but Jo could see at once from his poise that this was no playful shot. His back was straight, the stool raised high, and his fingers were balanced on the keys.

Ferman muttered 'Amen', as the prayer finished. Then the familiar notes of the Prelude began to play. The guests shuffled in their seats, some rising. Jo leant across to Ferman.

'Did you know Dylan played the piano?' she asked.

Ferman shrugged. 'I think so, yes. No, definitely. He was quite the prodigy apparently. Everything all right?'

The aisle was filling up as people made their way towards the doors. Dylan's parents were at the head of the group.

'Oh, yes,' she said. 'I just need to have a chat with Mr and Mrs Jones.'

They joined the back of the procession heading for the exit. *It's probably nothing.* But still, a presence loomed on the edge of her consciousness. A broad back, a dark face cast in shadow. It didn't make a lot of sense, but . . .

The receiving line moved slowly, each guest clasping hands with Dylan's parents, or offering hugs along with their words of commiserations. Jo found herself tapping her foot impatiently.

'You sure you're okay?' asked Ferman, beside her.

'Did Dylan have a teacher? A piano teacher?'

Ferman frowned. 'Probably.'

'You didn't follow it up at the time?'

'Why should we?'

They reached the front of the line. Mr Jones looked wrung-out, but his wife appeared much more content.

'I hadn't realised,' she said, 'that it was you, by the way.'

'Excuse me?' said Jo.

'That day,' said Mrs Jones. 'You were the little girl, weren't you? The one who saw it happen. I didn't know until Detective Ferman told me this morning. Isn't that strange?'

There was no accusation in the tone, just a kind of beatific calm, as if Jo's presence was cosmically ordained, and somehow fitting, not just a walk-on part in someone else's tragedy.

'Mrs Jones, I'm sorry to bother you with a question, today of all days.' She felt Ferman bristle beside her. It *was* inappropriate to ask, but she could clear it up in a second. 'I just wanted to follow up on something.'

Mrs Jones looked perplexed. 'Yes, of course.'

'Dylan played the piano . . .'

'Yes. He was ever so talented, you know, considering his age. *He* said he wanted to be a footballer, but his piano teacher said he had potential to make a name for himself.'

Jo felt a little light-headed. 'His teacher?'

'Lovely woman over in Horton. I did send her an invite, but perhaps she's no longer—'

'Her name wasn't Sally Carruthers by any chance?'

'That's right!' said Mrs Jones. 'How did you know that?'

'I grew up nearby. She tutored me too.'

'Goodness! Another coincidence. Then again, can't be that many piano teachers in North Oxford.'

'I suppose not,' said Jo.

'Dylan just adored her,' said Mrs Jones. 'Of course, that may have had something to do with the scones she used to bake.' She chuckled.

'I remember them too!' said Jo, feigning cheer. 'Well, I'll leave you to it. And thanks again for inviting me today – it really was a beautiful ceremony.'

After saying farewell, Jo quickened her steps towards her car. She'd almost completely forgotten about Ferman until she heard his heavy breathing at her back.

'Running off?' he said.

She fished for her keys. 'Sally Carruthers – she had a husband. He's dead now.'

'Priors?' Ferman sounded suddenly more alert.

'I don't know.'

'So what makes you think he was involved?'

'Sally taught me from about six years old through to fourteen.'

'You must have been good,' said Ferman. 'I'm not following you though.'

'She was teaching me in '87,' said Jo. 'Exactly the time Dylan went missing. She never mentioned him. Not once. Isn't that odd?'

He frowned. 'You were young.'

'I've seen her a couple of times since I've been here too. She didn't bring it up.'

'Maybe she hasn't seen it in the news.' Ferman spoke perfectly reasonably, but it didn't dispel Jo's unease.

'I'll ask Andy Carrick to pull the file – see if he was ever questioned.' She opened the car door. 'Want to tag along?'

'Where are we going?'

'To scratch an itch.'

As Jo drove, she called Carrick on the hands-free and asked him to look into the persons of interest in the Dylan Jones investigation, specifically a Mr Carruthers of Cherry Tree Cottage in Horton. She couldn't remember the Christian name of Sally's husband, and wondered if she'd *ever* known it. At a set of traffic lights, she closed her eyes for a moment, trying to picture the man who'd walked Dylan away from the circus. She had no idea if the image in her head was accurate after all this time, but hadn't he been the same build as Sally's husband?

Her heart was beating fast as she played back the conversations she'd had with her former teacher over the last few days. Dylan had been all over the news, but Ferman might be right. Perhaps Sally didn't pay much attention. They certainly hadn't spoken about it. Jo never did like to discuss active cases. She thrust deeper into her memories, to the weekly lessons as a child. No one had ever said a thing, she was sure of it. Yet Dylan Jones had been learning on the same stool, on the same instrument, a few hundred yards from her house.

They were on the A34 heading for Horton when Carrick called back.

'Turns out Carruthers, Stephen, was a person of interest,' he said, 'but way down the list. Had some minors for affray, D & D. Uniforms went out and spoke to the wife, but he wasn't home. I guess once Clement Matthews was in custody, it wasn't followed up.'

'Well, better late than never,' said Jo.

'He's still around?'

'Died a couple of years ago apparently, but Sally Carruthers is in the same house. We're almost there now.'

'We?'

'I'm with Harry Ferman,' said Jo.

'Hullo,' said Ferman tentatively, leaning towards the steering wheel.

'Might be worth a look, I suppose,' said Carrick. 'Keep me in the loop.'

He hung up, and Jo took the exit off towards Horton.

'I came out this way to interview you as a girl,' said Ferman. 'Big house, I recall?'

'My brother's family live there now,' said Jo.

'Parents passed away?' asked Ferman.

'Pretty much,' Jo replied. 'Mum's got quite advanced Alzheimer's.'

'I'm sorry. I remember her being quite . . . what's the word?'

'Intimidating? Formidable?'

'The opposite, actually,' said Ferman. 'She was very upset. I got the impression she didn't want us there, asking you questions.'

'She liked routine,' said Jo. 'Things she could control.'

'I think perhaps she was angry with herself,' said Ferman. 'For letting you go too that day.'

'No offence, but that doesn't sound like Mum. She wasn't big on introspection.'

Ferman smiled. 'And no offence to you, but if that were me, I'd be thinking it could have been my daughter who went missing instead of Dylan. When you're a parent, it tends to change your perspective on things.'

Jo focused on the road, slightly cross that he was insinuating he knew her own mother better than she did based on a short meeting.

'Well, she certainly kept a close eye on me after that.'

245

They arrived at Cherry Tree Cottage and parked outside. As soon as she cracked the car door, Jo's nose pricked at the scent of jasmine and honeysuckle that spilled from Sally's front garden, taking her back suddenly and powerfully to her youth with a wave of poignant nostalgia that almost stopped her in her tracks. She asked herself again if she was going crazy coming here, and again couldn't answer. Possibilities lurked in her head.

Jo rehearsed her lines as they walked up to the front door, seeking just the right balance between professional formality and friendliness. Ferman smiled warmly. When Sally opened the door, she was wearing a pair of marigolds. The left side of her face was one large bruise.

'Oh my goodness. What happened?' Jo's first thought was the goons in the clown masks, her brother's car and the missing iPad.

Sally waved a hand dismissively. 'My own stupid fault,' she said. 'I slipped on the blasted runner in the hall.'

'Have you seen a doctor?' asked Jo.

'What's the point?' said Sally, with another. 'I know what they'll say. I'm not going into a home.'

'But—'

'I'm not listening!' said Sally, with another wave. 'Now, did you enjoy that pie?'

'It was lovely,' said Jo. She'd get back to the bruise afterwards. 'Sally, this is my colleague, Detective Ferman. Can we have a chat?'

Sally flinched. 'It's a bit of a mess . . .'

'We won't take much of your time.'

Sally looked back into the hallway. 'Well, come in then,' she said.

She turned and walked stiffly towards the living room. Ferman gestured for Jo to go before him, and she did so. In the living room, her eyes were drawn straight to the piano, the keys concealed under the lid. There was little sign of any mess that Jo could see, but there was a cat perched on the sofa arm. Ferman reached out a hand, but it hissed at him and he drew back.

'You managed to get him inside then?' said Jo.

'Oh, yes,' said Sally. She bent to the carpet, where a bucket sat on the floor. Taking a cloth, she began to scrub at a patch. 'He's decided he's not house-trained any more though.'

'Can I help with that?' asked Ferman, moving closer.

'There!' said Sally. 'Done. But thank you for offering, Mr Ferman.'

He took her arm and helped her to stand, which she did with a grimace.

'So what can I do for you both?'

'We wanted to talk about Dylan Jones,' said Jo, coming straight to the point.

Sally's thin eyebrows rose half an inch. 'Yes, I saw that was on the news and wondered if you were involved. Didn't want to pry, you know.' She pulled off the gloves awkwardly. 'He was a lovely young man. Fine pianist too. I knew from his first lesson that he had promise.'

'So you remember when he went missing?' said Jo.

'Of course! It was all over the news. Good parents too. Must have been so, so hard for them.'

'Can I ask you about your husband?' said Jo.

For the first time, Sally's demeanour changed, and Jo was sure a seasoned detective like Ferman would have spotted it too. Her eyes gave a furtive jerk, an animal sensing danger.

'You didn't say what this was about?'

'Maybe we should all sit down?' said Ferman, gesturing towards the sofa.

'I might look like a senile old thing,' said Sally, 'but I don't like being treated like one. How is Stephen possibly connected with the Jones boy?'

'He probably isn't,' said Jo. 'But we've looked into the files, and it seems there was an oversight. The police at the time intended to question Mr Carruthers and never did.'

'They'll have a job now,' said Sally, frostily.

Jo smiled, hoping to take some of the tension out of the room. Sally was wringing her hands.

'This is really just a formality,' said Jo, even though she was beginning to suspect it wasn't.

'Is it now?' said Sally. 'Because it looks to me like you're forcing your way into my house, telling me my late husband is suspected of some sort of crime.'

'You let us in, Mrs Carruthers,' said Jo.

'So it's *Mrs Carruthers* now, is it?'

'Sally, please. You're not in any trouble.'

'I want you to leave.' She stood by the door. 'I want you both to go now.'

Jo remained where she was, and glanced at Ferman. She'd seen enough.

'Sally, I'm going to have to ask you to come with us to the station. These questions are important.'

'You're arresting me?'

'No. No one wants that. We'd like you to come of your own accord. We can drive you, and bring you straight back.'

Sally Carruthers huffed. If she refused, Jo didn't know if she would have arrested her or not.

'I hope you're ashamed of yourself,' said Sally.

And Jo was. Even though every instinct told her that Sally Carruthers was hiding something.

Chapter 21

Luckily, Stratton was absent, and it was Andy Carrick who came from the back to greet them at the gate while Sally waited at the front desk reception.

'Well, well,' he said. 'You two *are* a sneaky pair, aren't you? Does the chief inspector know?'

'Not yet,' said Jo. 'Look, we just need room.'

'Jo – this is very irregular. You know the witness. Stratton's on edge already about all the press stuff.'

'This isn't connected,' said Ferman.

Carrick shook his head. 'Did you put her up to this?'

'Andrew, I think she might have a breakthrough.'

'If I'm right, this could be one in the win column on Dylan Jones too,' said Jo. 'An hour, tops.'

'I'd better not regret this,' said Carrick. 'Stratton's out for another couple of hours over in Kidlington. Take IR1.'

'Thanks,' said Jo. 'Is Ben about?'

'Not sure where he's got to,' said Carrick.

'Can you give him a call? He was in touch with the building contractor who worked on the Bradford site. Could be relevant.'

'Sure thing.'

Ferman made Sally a cup of tea. In the stark light of the interview room, the bruising on her face was a lurid purple blotch.

'Are you sure you don't want to see a doctor?' said Jo, as she settled in the seat opposite.

'I really just want to go home,' said Sally. She'd lost the steeliness from her tone and looked tiny in the chair. Fragile. The rooms weren't designed to make people comfortable.

'Are you warm enough?'

'I'm fine,' said Sally. She cupped the mug in her frail hands. 'I'm sorry if you thought I was being rude. I know you're just doing your job.'

'We've just got a few questions,' said Jo. 'Shall we start?'

'Please do. I want to help.'

'How would you feel if we recorded the interview?' said Jo. Sally sipped her drink. 'Go ahead.'

Jo switched on the equipment, introduced them all for the tape, then began.

'Your husband, Stephen Carruthers. When did he pass away?'

'About two years back now.'

When the note was sent . . .

'And you mentioned to me once before that it was difficult towards the end of his life . . .'

'Did I?'

'You said he wasn't a nice man sometimes.'

'Yes, he suffered dementia for the last few years. He could lash out a bit.'

'But before that, was he ever violent?'

Sally paused before answering. 'No. Not really.'

Jo didn't miss a beat. 'You mean, he was violent sometimes?'

'Never with me.'

'With others, then?'

'He had a temper,' said Sally. 'Got in a few fist-fights, when he was younger. He came from an army family. Had a tough upbringing.'

'Did Stephen ever have any contact with Dylan Jones, your piano student?' asked Ferman.

Sally glowered. 'What do you mean by *contact*?'

'Forgive me. Did they ever meet, at your house?'

'I'm sure they might have. Stephen would have been out working, most of the time. But there may have been occasions when he was home at the same time as Dylan's lessons.'

'And on those occasions, would they ever have been alone?' asked Ferman.

Sally shook her head angrily. 'I hope you're not suggesting—'

'We're not suggesting anything,' Jo interrupted. 'We're simply trying to establish the prior contact your late husband may have had with Dylan Jones.'

Sally pushed her tea away. 'Well, the answer is no. Dylan came for piano lessons. I would have been with him from when he arrived to when he left. Stephen – my husband – he wasn't musical.'

It struck Jo as an odd answer, but she could see what Ferman was doing, trying to deflect Sally's hostility towards himself with a prurient line of questioning.

'What was it your husband did for a living?' asked Jo.

'He could turn his hand to anything,' said Sally, her eyes flashing with pride. 'Did odd-jobs for people. Strong as an ox – he liked physical stuff.'

Jo noted it down, but her mind was already racing. Ferman hadn't reacted, but there was no way he could have missed the electricity in the air. He tapped his pen on the paper.

'Such as construction? Gardening?'

'That sort of thing,' said Sally.

'And did he have a regular employer?' asked Jo.

'He worked for lots of people over the years.'

'In the late eighties?' asked Ferman.

Sally snorted. 'That's thirty years ago. What were *you* doing?'

'I was looking for Dylan Jones,' said Ferman with an edge Jo hadn't seen before.

There was a knock at the door, and Ben looked in with Andy Carrick. 'I hope you don't mind me interrupting,' he said. 'A word, please?'

Jo excused herself, and she and Ferman left Sally Carruthers alone.

'You've been busy,' Ben said to Jo. 'Want to bring me up to speed on *my* case?'

There was no real irritation in his tone, just a bemusement as he gazed towards Ferman. Jo went over the developments, from what she'd learned from the order of service and her conversation with the Joneses. She expected him to react angrily – but instead he took out his pocketbook, grinning.

'*Stephen* Carruthers, you say?'

'Something promising?' said Jo.

'Pool chap gave us the names he could remember.'

He flipped open his pocketbook, and pointed to the page. There were six Christian names, and the fifth was 'Steve? Stephen?'

'You think it's Carruthers?' asked Carrick.

'Don't you?' asked Ben. 'Jo, can you go back in and keep her talking while I make a call?' He glanced over at Ferman. 'Thanks for your help, Detective Ferman,' he said brusquely. 'But I think we can take it from here.'

Ferman suddenly looked like an actor who'd stumbled out onto the wrong stage. 'Right you are,' he muttered.

Jo gave him her best apologetic glance, then returned to the interview room while she waited for Ben. She left the recorder off while it was just the two of them.

'Can I go now?' asked Sally meekly.

'Soon,' said Jo.

'What's happening?'

'Sally – there are some leads we have to follow up,' said Jo.

Sally nodded, as if the act of bobbing her head imparted some resolve. 'They sent me an invitation, you know – Dylan's parents. There was a service.'

Jo saw no reason to lie. 'I was there,' she said. 'It was rather nice. There was some Chopin. If I'd known about your connection, we could have travelled together.'

Sally looked sad. 'I'd have liked that.'

Jo was about to ask why she hadn't attended, when Ben came back in. From the bounce in his step, she knew it was good news. He started the tape, introduced himself, and began seamlessly.

'You were talking with my colleagues about your husband's work,' he said.

Sally, still looking wistful, replied simply, 'Yes.'

Ben beamed. 'You might or might not be aware that Dylan Jones' remains were discovered in the garden of a house some sixty-five miles from Oxford,' he said. 'We've spoken to the building contractor who was working there at the time.' He looked at his pocketbook. 'A Mr Henshaw – and he's confirmed that your husband – Stephen Carruthers – was in charge of landscaping a section of the garden beside the pool.'

Sally didn't answer. Her eyes were glassy and unfocused. Jo was silent too.

'Do you understand what I'm saying, Mrs Carruthers?' asked Ben. 'We think your husband buried Dylan's body at his place of work.'

Sally's hands crept to her face. 'What? No! Why would he?'

'You tell us,' said Ben.

'Why are you doing this to me?' asked Sally, her eyes welling up. 'Why are you saying these things? My husband didn't kill Dylan . . . he just wouldn't.'

'You said he was violent sometimes,' Jo muttered.

'The odd bust-up,' said Sally. 'He wouldn't hurt a child. He was a good . . .' She stopped herself. 'Have you interviewed Dylan's father? He used to hit him, you know?'

Jo couldn't tell if she was just playing for time. 'We're aware of that.'

'Poor lad could hardly sit down sometimes. He was terrified of the old brute.'

'Lots of parents smacked their children thirty years ago,' said Ben. 'It doesn't make them murderers.'

'So why would my Stephen kill Dylan?' said Sally, more forthright. 'Answer me that!'

'Mrs Carruthers,' said Ben. 'The motive – whether it was sexual, or related to some other pathology – is irrelevant at the moment. The condition of Dylan's remains is such that discerning the cause of death is likely impossible. I know this will be hard for you to understand, but we've seen it hundreds of times before. We don't know what people are capable of, even those closest to us. All we can do as investigators is follow the prima facie evidence – what happened, where it happened – which in this case suggests your husband first met Dylan at your address, then later kidnapped him. Subsequent to that, Dylan died at an unknown location. We can't say for sure that he was murdered, or why, but that would be our assumption.'

'No . . .' said Sally. 'No, no, no . . .'

'Mrs Carruthers,' said Ben, 'at this stage, you're not under arrest, but we may choose to arrest you at a later point as more evidence comes to light. Do you understand?'

Sally looked at Jo. 'I haven't done anything wrong.'

Jo leant across the table and took the old woman's hands in her own.

'Interview terminated,' said Ben, and stopped the tape.

Jo sat with Sally for the next half-hour, passing her tissues, and trying to reassure her that she wasn't in trouble herself. Several times her old neighbour muttered, 'It's not true', and Jo didn't know what to say. In a case that seemed riven with coincidences, the fact of Dylan's piano lessons and the discovery of his body at Stephen Carruthers' place of work was one too many. Her only regret was that they could never question him. While the disparate fragments of the case were coming together, Sally's life was in pieces. Stephen Carruthers had a lot to answer for. And he never would.

And of course, it somewhat blew any connection between Dylan and Niall, the theory of the two clowns, out of the water. Stephen Carruthers was dead, confirmed by the register office, so he could never have been at RAF Bampton three days earlier.

In her pocket, her phone began to ring. Salisbury. She answered.

'Detective Masters speaking.'

'Hi Jo.' It was Dr Mike Wilson, the senior lab technician – Jo had known him on and off for eight years. 'I was trying to get Detective Coombs, but he didn't pick up.'

'He's on another call, I think,' said Jo. 'Can I help?'

'Detective Coombs wanted us to check back, as soon as the DNA came through.'

Jo was still catching up. *Dylan Jones. The samples.*

'Can you hold for just a sec?' she said. She placed her hand over the microphone, and muttered to Sally, 'Excuse me a moment. I need to take this outside.'

'Where are you going?' asked the old woman tremulously.

'I'll be back in a mo. We'll get you home soon.'

She felt terrible shutting the door to the IR on the broken face.

Jo couldn't see Ben anywhere in CID. Carrick was at his desk, chatting with Harry Ferman. She was glad he hadn't been bullied into leaving by Ben, but she wondered why he was still here.

'Go ahead, Mike,' she said. 'We've actually identified a prime suspect.'

'Oh, right. Well I hope this doesn't throw a spanner in the works.'

'How's that?'

'There was no match between the DNA from the remains and that of Mrs Jones.'

'Pardon? You're saying it's not Dylan?'

'Strictly, I suppose, we're saying the boy isn't the biological offspring of Mr and Mrs Jones,' said Wilson. 'You'd be surprised at what turns up in these tests. Adoption. Infidelity.'

He sounded quite jovial. Jo was still struggling to take the info on board. The fact that there were people in the world not dealing with something life-shattering seemed somehow unreal.

'We're still running the B samples, but given the other preliminary findings, I think we're on the surer ground here.'

'What preliminary findings? You said it was a boy, right age roughly. What's changed?'

'A pity we didn't have dentals – would have been able to give a definitive within twenty-four hours. No, I'm talking about the defects in the spinal column.'

'You'll have to explain.'

'So we found significant distortions in the bones of the lower spine. A pre-mortem condition – a severe dorsal arthritis.

Without a full set of remains it's hard to determine with much more certainty. Do you know if Dylan suffered with such a condition?'

She thought about the boy kicking the football at the carnival. Sitting up at the piano stool in the still image from the order of service.

'I don't think so.'

'Well, it's the DNA that's important,' said Wilson. 'Hope we've been a help. You want the report copied to you?'

'Yes, please,' said Jo.

She placed the phone in her pocket, her mind a jumble.

So if the skull in that digger's claw didn't belong to Dylan Jones, if the boy dressed in the Liverpool shirt wasn't the one who'd been taken in Yarnton, who was he? Either Stephen Carruthers was a serial killer, with a thing for kids in football shirts, or they were dealing with something else entirely.

Jo looked at Sally through the viewing panel, hunched over in a daze, the tea untouched.

And then she began to see it more clearly. The arthritis. *It runs in the family*, Sally had said. And the note. The connection with Stephen . . .

'You okay?' asked Carrick.

'I think so,' she said. 'Can you have a dig around in the file for Stephen Carruthers? See if there's anything about a son?'

'Er . . . sure,' said Carrick. 'Did she mention one?'

'No,' said Jo. 'But I think I know why. Where's Ben?'

'No idea. He took a call and headed outside. Want me to go and look?'

'If you don't mind. Send him in if you find him.'

Jo opened the door to the IR.

'Am I going home now?' asked Sally.

'Not just yet,' said Jo. 'I have a few more questions.' She started the tape again, and recorded their presence.

'I've told you everything,' said Sally. She was wringing her hands. 'Stephen's not here to answer questions. I really don't see—'

'You said you regretted not having children,' said Jo.

The fidgeting stopped, and Sally froze, almost as if Jo had cast a spell. Then a single blink.

'Sally?'

'Why are you asking that?' she replied.

Jo lowered herself into the chair opposite.

'I just learned that the body we unearthed isn't Dylan Jones,' she said. 'Which begs the obvious question . . .' She left it hanging. Sally glanced at the door longingly, as if considering a getaway. 'The little boy we found – he had a deformed back-bone,' she continued. 'Arthritis, just like you.'

Ben opened the door. 'What's going on?' he asked. 'I just got a message from Salisbury—'

'Come in and take a seat,' said Jo. 'For the record, Detective Inspector Benjamin Coombs has entered the room.'

'Can we talk outside?' he said.

'It's all right – I know it's not Dylan. Mrs Carruthers knows too. She knew all along, didn't you Sally?'

Ben entered, obviously confused. For a few seconds it was quiet, then Sally took a deep breath.

'His name was Martin,' she said quietly. Jo noticed she wore the beginnings of a small, strange smile.

'Your son?'

Sally nodded. 'My son.' She shot a direct stare Jo's way. 'He wasn't an easy child, right from the start. Bad sleeper, bad eater, always crying. We didn't know until he was four that it was because he was probably in pain. They found it in an X-ray – *ankylosing spondylitis*. Funny name, isn't it? It doesn't normally affect children so young, but I remember my grandfather suffering with something similar.' She laid her hands flat on the table, showing the odd bulging joints straining under paper-thin skin. 'Stephen didn't want to accept it. He thought the best thing was fresh air and exercise. Toughen him up, I suppose. He thought he could fix him, you know?' She laughed weakly. 'He always said he wanted a *normal* child, whatever that's supposed to mean. He pushed Martin hard. But he did it because he loved him.'

'What happened to Martin?' asked Jo.

Sally let a breath out with a visible shudder.

'I was never really sure. I got home one day and Stephen had been crying. I could tell from his eyes. He told me there'd been an accident. I called for Martin straight away, but I think I already knew. Stephen never cried, you see.' She was gazing at her hands still. 'He said that Martin had fallen down the stairs. I wanted him to show me, but he said it would upset me too much. Well, that just upset me even more. I wanted to see my little boy. But Stephen, he was stubborn. He wouldn't let me. I told him he was a liar, that he'd hurt Martin, but he swore blind it was an accident. He said he could take care of everything.'

'You didn't phone the police? An ambulance?'

'I wanted to,' said Sally. 'But Stephen had been in trouble with the police before, you see. He said they'd never believe it was an accident. Later, I wondered, but by then it was too late. Stephen took charge. He said we had to move away. Martin had done a year at school, but it was the holidays.'

'Where were you living at the time?' asked Jo.

'Wiltshire,' said Sally. 'We didn't have a lot of friends. Not real friends anyway. Stephen said we wouldn't have to go far. It seems silly now, but I just went along with it.'

'It doesn't seem silly,' said Jo. She looked across at Ben, who sat impassively listening. He understood that his input wasn't needed for the moment.

'So you moved straight away?'

'Within a month or so,' said Sally. 'I don't remember exactly – it was a confusing time.'

'I imagine,' said Jo.

'Stephen found the cottage in Horton. He took care of everything.'

'Including Martin's body?'

Sally nodded. 'He said he knew a place. A beautiful place overlooking fields, in the garden of a house where children played. I made him bury Martin in his favourite shirt.'

A DNA sample from Sally would settle it conclusively, of course, but Jo had no reason to doubt what the old woman was saying. If anything, it seemed like she was relieved to get it off her chest. A grief she'd carried for thirty years.

'And you sent the note, didn't you?' Jo asked. '*Bury him properly*.'

Sally smiled. 'I had to. I knew the spot where Martin was buried. The exact spot. I made Stephen tell me that. When I could, I'd drive past, and sometimes leave flowers in front of the house. It broke my heart when I saw what happened to the place. I thought of my little boy, alone, with no one around. Stephen was ill by then. Bed-bound mostly. We never spoke about Martin. Sometimes I wondered if he even remembered him at all.'

Ben leant forward. 'You do know that not registering a death is a crime, Mrs Carruthers?'

Sally drew back her hands to her chest. 'But I couldn't! Don't you understand? Stephen said they'd put him in jail.'

Jo gave Ben a jerk of the head that said, *outside*.

'Please wait a moment,' she said to Sally.

They left the room.

'What do you think?' asked Jo.

Ben shook his head. 'Not sure there's much point arresting

her at this stage. Any half-decent lawyer would say she was coerced into silence. We'll need to get a formal statement.'

'So you believe her?'

Ben looked deflated. 'Don't you? If the prints on the note come back as hers, that only corroborates her story and mitigates. She was too scared to tell the police until Stephen was practically in the ground himself.'

Jo shrugged. 'I don't understand why she didn't mention it before. She let us accuse her husband of murdering Dylan Jones when she knew the body in Bradford-on-Avon wasn't him.'

'What does it matter? In all likelihood, Stephen Carruthers probably was involved with Dylan too. We'll need to bring her in again. And maybe get a warrant to search the house.'

Jo baulked. 'Don't you reckon her life's been turned upside enough without doing it literally?'

Ben wasn't the sentimental sort though. 'Not sure we have a choice. Christ, what do we tell the parents? They had a fucking funeral!'

At that moment, the air changed, and Jo twisted around to see DCI Stratton stalled in the doorway. Beside him there was another woman, in senior uniform, with cropped grey hair. They were both looking her way, plainly hostile, as Stratton muttered something close to the woman's ear. She nodded, and made her way to his office. Stratton beckoned to Jo with a finger, and followed her in.

'What's that all about?' asked Ben.

'I have no idea,' said Jo.

She made her way between the desks and into the office.

'Shut the door behind you, please,' said Stratton.

Jo obeyed. She saw from the other woman's insignia that she was chief constable rank.

'Ma'am. Sir,' she said.

'Take a seat, detective,' said Stratton. He was tapping at his keyboard, eyes on the screen.

She felt like she was in the headmaster's office. Stratton faced her, steepling his fingers for a moment.

'We recognise that you probably haven't had time to file a report yet,' he said, 'but we'd like to get your version of events that occurred yesterday.'

'Specifically, sir?' asked Jo. It was McDonagh. Had to be. He'd made a complaint.

Stratton smiled for a split second, then it was gone. 'Let's start after I last saw you and gave you a direct order to keep a low profile.'

Jo swallowed. 'I went to deliver a message to Harry Ferman – an invitation to the memorial service I've just attended for Dylan Jones. Following that, I visited the John Radcliffe hospital, where I spoke with Niall McDonagh . . .'

Stratton raised his hand, frowning. 'On whose authorisation?'

'I wasn't aware I needed authorisation, sir.'

She shot an innocent glance at the chief constable. If there was any chance of sisterly support here, she needed it.

'And what did you learn there?' asked Stratton.

'He said he believed that he'd met a second kidnapper. An accomplice.' She kept talking, trying to ride it out. 'From there I discovered through another source that Alan Trent had been attending a support group for victims of sexual abuse that met regularly in South Oxford. I followed that lead, hoping to gain intelligence on the possible accomplice. Things went . . . awry. The group wasn't quite what I expected, and the surveillance was compromised by a member of the press. Subsequent to that . . .'

Stratton reached across and spun around his flat-screen monitor.

The headline was clear enough – WHAT ARE THEY HIDING? – but it took Jo a moment or two to realise that she was looking at a picture of herself outside the Quaker Meeting Hall. She looked wild, sliding across the bonnet of Saunders' car, while Lee Burgess' face was staring from the door, and an angry-looking man in a leather jacket was launching himself towards the lens.

'When you say, "awry", what you actually mean is an almighty fuck-up?'

The word 'semantics' rose rebelliously to the tip of her tongue, but she didn't say it. She took in the subhead: *Paedophile ring in the heart of historic city*. And further down, *Can we trust our police?*

Stratton turned the monitor back around. 'I'll save you reading,' he said. 'This piece has been sent to us for comment by lawyers at the paper in question. The only reason they have done so is because they're afraid of jeopardising an ongoing investigation. Our lawyers have gagged it, for now.'

'Quite right, sir,' said Jo.

Stratton leant back in his chair, eyes flaring. 'Is that all you've got to say for yourself?'

'Sir,' said Jo. 'I think there might be something in it. When I spoke to Niall . . .'

'You can go,' said Stratton.

'Sir, his father was okay with it. I believe what Niall said. There's someone else out there.'

'If I may say, detective, you seem rather hard of hearing,' said the chief constable, speaking for the first time. 'DCI Stratton has filled me in regarding your links to this journalist and it's almost uncanny how your opinions coincide with her own.'

Not this again . . .

'Ma'am, I—'

'That's *all*, Detective Masters,' said Stratton. 'I'll expect that report first thing in the morning.'

★　★　★

She left Ben and Andy Carrick to share the information about the Dylan Jones conclusions, and took Sally home in her own car. Hopefully, some of the shine of actually solving a case might reflect her way, even if it was hardly a happy ending.

All the way, the old woman stared out of the window. A light rain had begun to mist the air, muting everything. And for all the self-pity and anger Jo felt – at the injustice of her treatment, at DCI Stratton, at Ben for somehow getting through this mess unscathed – the reflection of Sally's shattered countenance in the rear-view mirror put it all in a kind of perspective. She'd get through her difficulties, though maybe the promotion would have to wait. Sally's life, or what remained of it, was ruined.

'I'm sorry,' she said, as she pulled up outside Cherry Tree Cottage. 'Today must have been very difficult for you.'

'I know how it looks,' said Sally. She was sitting stiffly. 'But Stephen didn't kill Dylan. I know he didn't.'

She sounded so sure, almost defiant, and Jo climbed out to avoid answering. There'd be harder conversations to come, and Jo was simultaneously relieved to be spared them and sorry that she wouldn't be around to protect her former piano teacher from the bruising experiences heading her way. Ben had told Sally at the station that they'd need to speak with her further, under caution. He hadn't mentioned the possibility of a house search though. The thought of a forensics team ripping up old carpets and taking apart the pine furniture almost brought tears to Jo's eyes. Perhaps it wouldn't be necessary. In the parlance of DCI Stratton, the *optics* would be terrible. An old woman's life ransacked by an overzealous police force reeling from humiliation. She could only imagine what Rebekah Saunders would make of it.

Jo opened the rear door and hoisted an umbrella.

'Would you like me to come in for a while?'

'No, thank you,' said Sally. 'I think I'd rather be alone.'

'Well, I'm just up the hill,' said Jo. 'I'm only babysitting my nephew, so if you want some company, ring the bell.'

Sally began to walk up the path. She didn't seem bothered by the rain at all.

Chapter 22

At her brother's, Will was doing cartwheels in the hallway, his hands smeared with something brown. Amelia was putting in a set of earrings in the mirror by the front door, and wearing a long blue dress that accentuated her slender physique. She'd always been out of Paul's league – even their mother had said so.

'Don't be alarmed at his appearance,' Amelia said. 'We're not sure if it's the worms he was digging in the garden, or the entire chocolate muffin he discovered in my handbag, but a seven o'clock bedtime might be a tad optimistic.'

'Don't worry – we'll just slide up and down the bannister until he gives up the ghost,' said Jo.

'I never give up!' roared Will. He almost collided with a pot plant as he skidded across the floor in his socks.

'Em's gone already,' said Amelia. 'She's at a house party in Jericho and we'll swing by after and grab her in a cab.' She called up the stairs, 'Paul! It can't take this long for you to get ready? You haven't even got any hair to think about!'

Jo's brother descended the stairs in a dinner jacket, thumbs hooked into the waist.

'I can't find a belt,' he said, halfway down. 'Bloody things are falling down.'

'Did you look on the tie rack?'

'Yes.'

'Did you look properly, or like a bloke?'

Paul chewed his lip, then turned on his heel and trotted back up. 'I'll have another peek.'

Amelia rolled her eyes and smiled fondly. 'And how am I looking?' she asked.

'Too good for my brother,' Jo replied.

'Exactly what I was aiming for,' said Amelia. 'Listen, thanks again for this, Jo. The details of the restaurant are written on the telephone pad. New French place in the High Street.'

'It's no problem. It'll be fun.'

A crash came from the living room, followed by an 'Uh-oh!' from William.

'Fun is one word,' said Amelia. 'But seriously, don't disappear for ages again. It's been great having you over, and you're welcome any time.'

'Sorry I've been keeping funny hours,' said Jo.

'You must come and visit properly, when you're on leave. You know, Paul and I have rented a place in Spain for the October half-term. It's got an extra bedroom . . .'

'You just want a babysitter!' she said.

Amelia winked. 'That as well – but think about it, won't you?'

Jo was preparing a polite deferral when Paul emerged again, looping his belt.

'Your prince charming is here!' he said.

Jo wished them both a good night, and closed the door. She realised neither of them had asked her about her day, and for that she was grateful.

'Right, Billy-O,' she said. 'We need to burn some calories.'

★   ★   ★

267

At close to half eight, after several dozen more cartwheels, a cartoon about a family of pigs, a bath-time game of submarines with plenty of nail-scrubbing, and two and a half bedtime stories, Will fell asleep propped up in the crook of her arm. Jo waited for a few minutes, staring at the glow of his night light, before prising herself out of position, and pulling his Spiderman duvet up to his chin. She kissed his strawberry-scented hair, and left the bedroom.

She checked her phone, but there were no missed calls.

On the way downstairs, she passed the staggered portraits of her brother's family. All of them artfully posed, black and white, blissfully happy. Jo felt utterly dejected. Wretched. She couldn't help thinking it had gone wrong for her somehow – that she'd taken a wrong turning.

She made herself a stir-fry, then ate it in front of the TV, only half following the twists of a soapy drama. It came across as even more fake and contrived than normal. As far as she could tell, someone who was supposed to be dead had reappeared at the eleventh hour to prevent a marriage, and a fight outside a church ensued. The police were called, and at that stage Jo switched off. Even fake police work was too much of a drain tonight. And she still had the bloody report to write.

She opened her laptop, and while it took an age to boot up, she selected a magazine off the table – something about home renovations – and flicked idly through it. Every house looked like her brother's, with some arrangement of artisan lighting, soft furnishings and neat storage solutions. The thought of returning to the flat in Bath was beyond depressing.

Her phone rang. *Ben.*

'Hi there,' he said, as she answered. 'Wondered what you were up to?'

'Nothing much,' she said.

'Snap,' he said. 'I didn't want to ring the bell – I'm outside.'

She sat up straighter, pulled aside the curtain a touch. It was only her car in the drive.

'Car's in the garage. Cylinder's just gone again. I cabbed it over.'

'What are you doing here?'

'I thought you could do with some moral support,' he said. 'Tough day, right?'

'Ben, I . . .'

'One drink, Jo. Come on. I'm getting drenched, by the way. No brolly.'

She found she didn't quite have the energy to fight. Not tonight, so she climbed off the sofa, padded to the front door, and there he was with a bottle of red wine in his hand, hair plastered to his head.

'One drink,' she said, and stepped aside so he could enter. As he did, the ghost of his aftershave followed. 'We've got to be quiet,' she added. 'Will's asleep.'

'Roger,' said Ben. 'Let me go and get dry.'

He handed her the bottle, and set off towards the downstairs cloakroom.

Jo wandered through to the kitchen, where the rain was pattering on the glass roof. A strong wind was blowing the branches of the trees above. Ben emerged a minute later, hair sticking up and in just his jeans and Berlin Marathon T-shirt. They'd run it together, four years before. He took the bottle he'd brought, unscrewed the lid and poured it down the plughole.

'Er . . . what are you doing?'

'That was just my ticket in here,' he said, grinning. 'I know for a fact your brother's got something much better.'

Jo laughed and slid a bottle of Tasmanian Pinot Noir from her brother's wine rack and gave it to Ben while she fetched some glasses. He pulled the cork deftly.

'Seriously, though,' he said, as he poured for both of them.

'We're both writing up reports on the last twenty-four hours. I thought it might make sense to talk it through. Make sure there are no, y'know, discrepancies.'

'You don't have to do that,' she said. 'Just tell it like it happened, and I'll do the same. I'm a big girl.'

'I know that,' said Ben. 'I just don't want you to get any more heat than you have to. You did the right thing. You showed initiative. Christ, if more detectives did the same thing, instead of chasing their tails, and filling in risk assessments . . .' He waved a hand. 'Oh, don't get me started! It'll be a long night if you do.'

She caught his glance as he said it, embarrassed but inviting at the same time. Despite herself, despite everything, she felt a stir down the inside of her thighs. *Don't be an idiot, Josephine Masters. You've not even had a drink yet.*

The moment passed.

'What do you make of the Thames Valley lot then?' he said, pushing a glass towards her. She sat opposite, on the other side of the island.

'They're okay.'

'Even Stratton? I thought Bridges had a rod up his arse, but that guy's something else.'

Jo sipped and smiled, and the alcohol reached its soothing fingers down her neck and across her chest. 'I guess you don't get to DCI by bending the rules.'

'Carrick seems a nice bloke,' said Ben. 'You think he's gay?'

'No way. I saw a picture of his family.'

'Really? I was ninety-five per cent sure.'

'Your gaydar was always a bit ropey though. You thought Paul was checking you out when you first met.'

'That's true,' said Ben, raising his glass, before taking a swig and licking his lips. 'To Paul, a heterosexual, and his remarkable cellar.'

'To Paul,' said Jo. It was very good wine. 'He needs something to spend his fortune on,' she added.

Ben looked around. 'Yeah, he's doing all right. Hey, you remember the plonk we used to drink? Three bottles for a tenner, wasn't it?'

'I think I've blocked it out,' said Jo. 'I remember the hangovers were something else.' She pointed at his T-shirt. 'I can't believe you're still wearing that. Talk about faded glories. Bet you couldn't run a five-K now.'

Ben smiled. 'Steady on – I'm not that bad!'

She'd finished her glass already. Ben leant across to refill, but she put her hand over the top. 'I'd better not.'

He remained in place, the bottle extended. 'May as well finish the thing. It's stolen property – we have to destroy the evidence and I'm *not* pouring this one down the sink.'

Jo took her hand away and he poured.

They talked on, about Berlin, about a disastrous cycling trip to the Pyrenees, about his parents' surprisingly loud sex life one Christmas. Jo saw what he was doing, whether it was deliberate or not, but she let the conversation take her along like a lazy river. After days of work, of keeping herself buttoned-up, of secrets and half-lies – just to sit with someone she didn't have to hide from was such a release. An unburdening.

An hour passed. They finished the bottle, and this time she didn't even protest as he opened another.

'Hey, what about Ferman?' said Ben. 'They don't make 'em like that any more, huh?'

'I like him,' said Jo, then feeling the need to explain herself, added, 'Carrick said he'd lost a daughter.'

As soon as she'd said it, she wondered why that was the detail she'd picked. Ben sat back in his chair, looking down.

They lapsed into silence, and several conversations drifted through the ether, waiting to be spoken into existence. Any joviality had been sucked out of the room. All roads led mentally back to the same place, to those horrible moments after the sonographer left them alone, her stomach still slippery with the lubricating gel.

'Paul said you were getting help,' said Jo at last.

Ben put down his glass, looked at her, and nodded. 'It's early days, but they make a lot of sense. Christ, you think I'm bad, some of the other guys who come along . . .'

'I'm glad,' said Jo.

Ben sipped his drink again. 'Wish I'd done it a long time ago, to be honest.'

Jo cocked her head. *Don't we all.*

She turned her back on him, slid from the stool and headed under the panes of the orangery to the patio doors. The room felt claustrophobic, but the blackness of the windows only reflected it back at her. She turned the heavy handle and slid back the doors, letting in a gust of cool air. The rain was falling still, but in light sheets, peppering the leaves on the garden plants.

Ben, she saw in the glass, had stood from his stool as well. 'Jo, I know I fucked up. Fucked everything up. But I'm sorry.'

'I know. You've said it. A hundred times.'

'And this time I mean it. I mean . . . I always meant it. What I mean is, I guess I understand it now. I've . . . I've learned a lot about myself in the last few months. More than I thought possible, and more than I ever knew was even there, if that makes any sense. God, I can't even get my words out . . .'

Jo turned to him. He was standing with his hands pressed against his cheeks, as if the very act of massaging his jaw could somehow coax his mouth to shape the phrases that came tumbling out.

She went to him. Couldn't help herself. Put her arms on

272

his. He wasn't crying, but he looked so deep in despair she pulled him closer. Felt his head rest on hers.

'Ben, it's all right,' she said.

'. . . That person,' he said. 'I don't even recognise him now. That selfish, arrogant . . . loser. If I could go back, and if I could grab him by the shoulders and shake some fucking sense into him—'

'You can't,' she said. 'We can't.'

She felt a tremor through his body. He hugged her back, and his head lifted a fraction.

'Can't we?' he said.

She tipped her head up. She knew it was the booze, but she hadn't felt so close to anyone in so long. She was so tired of struggling. Of fighting work, and her landlord, of duty and expectation, and just the grind of her bloody life. Ben's lips came down to meet hers. And the warmth in her loins was one of anticipation. Because it would be easy. So, so easy. The bed was just upstairs.

She pulled away.

'No,' she said. 'We can't.'

'Why not?'

'Because I'm drunk,' she said. 'And so are you. We both need to move on.'

He looked at her, desperately. 'I'm trying,' he said. 'I'm trying, but I can't stop thinking about you, about how good it was, and about how that person I was then made everything bad.'

He reached for her and she took another step. 'Ben, it's over,' she told him.

'It can't be,' he said.

And even then, she still wanted him. 'Ben, don't.'

He showed no sign of hearing what she was saying. His eyes were manic.

'I'm different,' he said. 'I'm not *that* person now.'

'*I'm* different,' she replied, shrugging his hand off.

He looked put out, and didn't reach for her again. 'You can't just stop loving someone, even if they do something terrible.'

She thought, for a brief moment, about Stephen Carruthers, and poor Sally's obstinate denials about what her husband had done to their son. Perhaps Ben was right. Perhaps, in the part of her heart she couldn't control, she did still love him in some desperate way.

But that didn't mean she had to be with him.

'I want you to leave,' she said.

And there it was, as his face hardened – the gaze of wretchedness gone as quickly as a mask whipped away – the old Ben.

'No,' he said. 'Not until you hear me out.'

'There's nothing else to say,' she replied. 'This is my house, and you have to leave.'

He shook his head. 'It's your brother's house and you're going to listen to me. You owe me that.'

She snapped, and pushed him in the chest. 'I *owe* you?' she said. 'I owe you *nothing*.'

He tried to block her way, and his face wore a look she'd seen before, but only in the interview room. The lips open a fraction, the eyes impatient, distant and cold. Not getting his way. Not understanding how that could be. And it only made her angrier. He hadn't changed. He couldn't. Any more than he could turn back time and make a different bet or choose a different stock to trade.

For the first time in the conversation she felt physically vulnerable. Ready to fight.

'Get out of my way,' she said.

He didn't move. This time when she shoved him again, he caught her arm and spun her around, encircling her with his reach and pressing her body tight to his.

274

'That's assault,' he said in her ear.

'Oh, grow up,' she said, and lifting a foot, raked her instep down his shin. He let go at once, with a howl, and she marched towards the kitchen door.

'Don't!' he said. 'Come back!'

Jo was about to swear, when she saw William at the bottom of the stairs in his pyjamas. *God, he must have heard us.*

'Billy-O!' she said. 'What are you doing up?'

'The clown's outside,' he said.

Ben came to Jo's side, and she moved away. 'I can handle this,' she said coldly. 'You can go.'

'What's the matter, buddy?' said Ben, ruffling Will's hair.

'I said, I can handle it!' She'd raised her voice, and instantly regretted it.

'He's outside,' said Will. 'He's watching me.'

'He has night terrors,' said Jo, impatiently. 'Come on, I'll tuck you in.' She picked Will up, and glared at Ben over his shoulder. 'Uncle Ben will go and make sure the clown's gone, okay? And then he's got to go home.'

Will mumbled something. His breath was warm on her cheek.

As she carried him upstairs, she wondered if he could feel her heart thumping against his chest. She didn't know what she'd do if Ben was still there when she came back down. Phone the police?

In Will's room, she carried him across to the window where the curtains were slightly ajar. She looked out.

'See – no one there.'

Will unfolded his face from the nape of her neck and stared out too.

Jo closed the curtains, her arms aching already, and carried her nephew across to his bed.

'Sleep tight, captain,' she said, pulling the duvet up again.

'Can you stay?' he asked. His eyes were glittering silver in the semi-darkness.

She touched his cheek. 'Of course,' she said. Actually, staying upstairs suited her just fine. Give Ben time to cool down too. Let him make the right decision.

William rolled over, so he was facing away, tugging the blanket tighter around himself, and she continued to stroke his hair. She wondered, absently, how the clown stuff had percolated through to such a young mind. He must have heard Em talking, or maybe Paul and Amelia.

As her anger seeped away, Jo tried to think calmly about what was next. Ben would be contrite, as always, but what had happened downstairs was simply unacceptable. He had to realise that. They couldn't work together any more. Even being in neighbouring forces felt a bit too close for comfort.

Downstairs, the smash of a glass. Will sat bolt upright, wide awake.

'Auntie Jo?'

Jo left her hand on his head. 'It's nothing. Stay here.'

She stood up.

'No, I want to—'

'Stay here, Will,' she said sternly.

She crossed the room quickly, paused at the door. 'Ben?'

No answer.

If he'd lost his temper and broken something . . .

But that wasn't Ben. Or at least not the Ben she knew.

'Ben, are you down there?'

'Auntie Jo?' said Will, still sitting up.

'Shh, captain,' said Jo, extending a hand. Her phone was downstairs, still in her handbag. Maybe there was one in her brother's bedroom, two doors up.

The lights across the landing went off suddenly, and William sucked in a gasp.

'You're scaring Will, Ben!'

'It's not Ben,' said Will, his voice almost a theatrical whisper. 'It's the clown.'

'Don't move,' said Jo, more harshly than she intended. 'You stay in your bed, and you don't move an inch.'

She darted across the landing and shoved the master bedroom door open, fingers reaching for the light switch. She found it, and saw the phone beside the dresser. She forced herself to dial calmly, entering Ben's number from memory. He could only just have left.

It rang, every tone dragging out for seconds, and on the third she realised she could hear the corresponding jingle downstairs. He was still in the house.

'Ben!' she shouted. 'This isn't funny!'

She hung up, and dialled 999 instead.

'What's the nature of—'

Will screamed, not once, but in a series of fear-fuelled wails unlike anything she'd ever heard outside a horror movie. It paralysed her, shooting electricity from her neck down to her knees, and she dropped the phone. On legs that barely worked she ran to the door and saw half a figure, just some wraith of skin and bone, disappearing into William's doorway.

'Leave him alone!' she shouted and her own voice was odd, alien, throaty. Everything felt too slow, and she was aware of a pungent, foul odour, like sour milk or overripe cheese. And as she ran into William's room, fighting the impossible weight of her limbs, she saw his pale shape right there. An arm, thin, the fingers long, whipped across from her right, and though she felt nothing, it felt like everything suddenly switched off. She was on the ground, and she couldn't move. That made no sense at all.

Will was screaming and crying and begging, 'No!' and saying, 'Auntie Jo! Auntie Jo!'

She managed to roll onto her back, but she couldn't lift her arms, or her head, and her feet felt untethered, like useless flippers on the end of her legs. The cries of her nephew became muffled, and more distant, and she realised he had left the room. Her mind screamed at her body to *Move, just fucking move!* and then the switch flicked on again and she could. She found herself on her knees. Reaching for the wall, she clambered to her feet and the room spun. She couldn't help but retch as her stomach revolted like the worst sort of seasickness. She puked across the carpet, then staggered through the door. There were two sets of stairs, one next to the other, and she picked the wrong one, smashing into the balustrade. Feeling with her hands, she made it onto the steps and descended, slipping several times to the bottom. The front door was wide open. That *smell!*

'Will?' she called, and pain shot through her jaw. It felt massive, unwieldy, and there was blood in her mouth.

She wheeled around and stumbled through to the kitchen, the double vision phasing in and out in time with her pulse. She had to grab at the door frame to steady herself. As she did, her eyesight sharpened. There was red wine on the floor, and up the wall, deep red, and half the tulip of a glass rested in the centre. At the end of the island, the stool on which she'd hooked her bag lay on its side, and more wine was pooling around the leather strap.

Only it wasn't wine. It was thick, and too copious, and she could smell something else, seeping across the room on the summer evening breeze. That rich iron tang of the butcher's block on a Saturday morning, when she and her dad had gone to get the meat for Sunday's roast in the Covered Market.

She edged into the room until she could see Ben's shoes, then the rest of him, slumped against the other side of the island. His shirt along the left side of his body was saturated red, and the top of a wine bottle hung from a tear across his throat. And though she moved right into his line of sight, right into the open glare of his eyes, he didn't see her at all.

Chapter 23

The next ten minutes were confusion and chaos, and when she thought back to the events later, Jo struggled to recall the order in which things had happened. Certainly, she checked Ben's pulse, ascertaining that there wasn't one, but she couldn't say for sure whether she went out of the house first, calling for William, or if she called the police straight away.

After a time, a squad car arrived, then an ambulance. The paramedics tried to calm her down, saying something about looking at her face, but Jo had been too busy marshalling the officers, repeating only the essentials they needed to know. On autopilot, she gave them a description of William, in clear, concise terms, and told them to start looking. When asked about the man who took him, she found herself floundering, her mind stubbornly refusing to give up more than the faintest impressions of his appearance. Tall, certainly. Pale. Unclothed. But that couldn't be right. A naked man couldn't simply walk the streets. She didn't remember seeing a vehicle.

The first clear thought she had was on seeing Dimitriou in the hallway of her brother's house as she was sitting, wrapped in a blanket, at the bottom of the stairs. He looked completely incongruous, but her surprise was nothing compared to the shock on his face when he saw her.

'Jo, are you okay?'

'He took my nephew, Dimi. You've got to find him.'

'Jo, Ben's dead,' he said.

A sound escaped her lips. A sob. 'I wasn't there. I didn't see.'

'We're looking. We've called everyone in. We'll find him, Jo.'

She nodded, mutely.

'Is there someone we can call?'

Somehow she hadn't even thought about Paul and Amelia, and it was almost too painful to do so now.

'My brother – I need my phone.'

'Let us do it,' said Dimitriou.

She shook her head quickly, and the pain shot across her face. 'No – I've got to.'

He put his arm around her. 'Jo, you need to go to hospital. You've got a head injury. You're in shock.'

'I'm bloody fine,' she said, and tried to stand, but she reeled as soon as she did and Dimitriou supported her.

'Jo, you're not fine. You either get in that ambulance of your own accord, or I will put you in by force. We'll speak to your brother.'

'They're having dinner at some company thing,' she said weakly. She pointed to the table by the door. 'It's on there.'

'Leave it to me,' said Dimitriou. He led her outside, where blue lights were spinning across the leaves of the trees, and the ambulance waited with its rear door open. Jo followed the paramedics' instructions compliantly, as they made her lie down on the stretcher and went through the motions she'd seen dozens of times. And though it was a comfort to be a patient, to obey commands, to let her body sink into the mattress, the

281

truth of the matter consumed her every thought and sensation, a great tumour of guilt filling her body.

William was gone. And every second he was away, he'd be filled with terror; a sweet, innocent, precious young boy who couldn't possibly understand.

'We're going to take you to hospital now,' said the paramedic. 'Do you want something to calm you down?'

'No,' said Jo, trying to sit up. There was some sort of strap across her chest, another on her knees. 'Let me out . . .'

'We need to secure you for the journey,' said the paramedic.

Someone closed the back doors of the ambulance and Jo sagged back on the stretcher. She felt the rumble of the engine as the vehicle stirred into motion, taking her away from the scene of the crime.

* * *

They must have given her some sort of sedative, because when she woke up it was in a hospital bed. She wore a gown, and her jaw was throbbing. When she tried to move, her neck was stiff. Reaching up, she realised she had a brace on. Slowly, the jumble of thoughts reassembled, and with it came the wave of nausea. *Will . . . Ben . . .* Her tongue felt thick, her mouth dry. But there was a glass of water on a tray table, and she reached across for it.

'Here, let me,' said a voice.

She turned, stiffly, and saw Heidi Tan. The sight of her face almost brought tears to her eyes.

'Have you found him?'

'No.'

Jo tried to get up, but the sheets over her body were pulled tight, and she felt so, so weak.

'You mustn't,' said Heidi.

'I have to . . .'

'We've got units all over the city,' said Heidi. 'We're looking everywhere.'

'What time is it?'

'Just after one,' said Tan.

Jo guessed the attack had been somewhere around ten. Three hours already, and no word. She felt a tide of puke climbing her throat and managed to swallow it back.

'Will said he saw him, and I didn't believe him.'

'Saw who?' said Heidi.

'The clown – he's not a clown. He's something else. Oh God, he's something else, Heidi. He takes children and he . . . Oh, God. He's got Will. He's got my nephew.'

'Forensics are at the house now,' said Tan. 'They'll get a dog unit too.'

'My brother . . .'

'Andy's looking after them at the station,' said Tan.

'And Em?' Tan hesitated. 'My niece.'

'She's with them too, Jo. She's safe.'

Jo tried to think straight, like a police officer. But, each time, her mind revolted, and she was running into the bedroom, seeing that white *thing*. Carrick's words came back to her: *monsters in the forest*. There were no such thing as monsters though. Not like that. Not outside night terrors and stories.

But it couldn't be a coincidence. It came for her. For Will. To *that* house. And that meant it knew her. It was connected to the case, to Alan Trent.

'You've got to bring Burgess in,' she said with a sudden flash of clarity. 'It's someone from that group.'

'We're on it,' said Tan. 'He's in custody already.'

'And?'

'If he knows something, we'll get it out of him.'

'*I* need to talk to him,' said Jo. It took all her strength, but she managed to pull the sheet off, and swing out her legs. She was wearing a gown.

'Where are my clothes?'

'I don't know,' said Heidi. 'Jo, you're in no state.'

Jo managed a few steps, feeling like an old woman, when she saw a face she recognised at the door. It was Emma.

She stopped. 'I'm so sorry,' she said.

Emma ran towards her, and Jo fell heavily into her embrace. It felt wrong, her niece holding her up, but Jo felt like a puppet with the strings cut.

Heidi Tan was there. 'Jo, sit down, for God's sake.'

Jo let the two of them lead her back to the bed.

'Where are your mum and dad?' she asked, her head on the pillow.

'They wanted me to go to a friend's, but I made the taxi stop here first.'

'Em, you shouldn't. They'll be worried.'

Emma put a hand to her face, as she broke down. 'They said Uncle Ben's dead.'

Jo reached out, touched her niece's arm, and nodded. She stopped herself from crying, just. Emma didn't need to see that. Her niece shook her head in disbelief.

'Why would anyone take Will?' she said. 'He's just a little boy.'

'I don't know,' said Jo. 'But we'll find him.'

The tears were spilling down Em's face. 'You promise?'

And though Jo wanted more than anything to cry too, to release the fear that churned inside her like poison, she managed to hold back and force out the words with conviction.

'I promise.'

WEDNESDAY

Somehow, she slept again, and when she woke, it was to clear daylight, startling panic, and a sharp guilt that she could have ever drifted off. She was in the same room, but she was alone. Her head was pounding. Beside her bed, there was a plastic bag. She recognised her clothes inside. Tan must have found them. Her shoes and handbag were in a separate transparent sack. She took out her handbag, then found her work phone, switched off. She tried to bring it to life, but the screen remained stubbornly black.

She pressed the call button among the array over her bed, and within thirty seconds a female nurse came through the door.

'How are you doing?' she said.

'My head kills,' said Jo.

'We'll get you something,' said the nurse.

'And a charger,' said Jo, holding up her phone.

'I'll see what we can do,' said the nurse.

Jo grabbed her wrist. 'I need one,' she said. 'It's important.'

The nurse nodded, pulled her hand away, and left. Jo realised she'd forgotten to ask the time. Had Paul and Amelia been in? She couldn't believe she'd fallen asleep, even though she'd seen a hundred head traumas before and knew the effects well.

The nurse brought a small cup containing two pills and the charger. Jo inserted the plug first, then swallowed the pills before the nurse had even told her what they were.

'They might make you drowsy,' she said.

After she'd gone, Jo watched the phone screen, willing it to come to life. When it did, after a couple of minutes, she called Andy Carrick. He didn't answer. She left a message, asking for him to call her, then got out of bed. Her legs felt much firmer than before, and she opened the clothing bag.

Her trousers were a creased mess, and her blouse was saturated with damp blood at the collar. But her knife was there. She began to get dressed and was pulling on her shoes when Andy Carrick came into the room. The expression he wore made her stomach churn. He'd taken off his tie.

'You've found him, haven't you?'

Carrick shook his head, beside the door. 'No, Jo, we haven't.'

'Andy, you've got to let me do something.'

'Jo, can you sit down a second please?' He pointed to a chair.

'I saw him,' said Jo. 'He was just like Niall described.'

Carrick pulled across a chair of his own and sat down. 'Describe him to me,' he said. 'Take your time.'

There seemed no rush about him, and Jo knew he was keeping something from her.

'You've found something,' she said. 'Just tell me.'

'We're doing everything we can,' said Carrick.

'Where are Paul and Amelia? I need to talk to them.'

'Your brother and sister-in-law are being looked after,' he said. Jo found his voice disconcerting – it was slightly impatient.

'He's their kid, Andy. My nephew. I *need* to speak with them.'

'We're not sure that's the best idea at the moment,' said Carrick.

'Why the fuck not?'

'They're very distressed. So are you.'

'Of course I am,' she said. 'He's gone, and that sick fucker killed . . .' The tears grabbed her, and she stifled them. 'He killed Ben.'

Carrick took out his pocketbook. 'Tell me, Jo, what happened. Please, as clearly as you can.'

She took a deep breath, and closed her eyes, but all she saw was the white shape drifting into the bedroom. Had she even seen his face?

'It was dark. Will had woken up. I was putting him back to

bed. Then . . . I don't know . . . he was here. He must have hit me with something.'

'This was upstairs? We found blood in William's bedroom. On his sheets.'

Jo broke down under a barrage of flashing images. The pirate ship, the Spiderman sheets. *Captain Billy-O.*

'One of the neighbours said he heard a disturbance,' said Carrick.

Jo wiped her eyes. 'There was a smash. When I was upstairs. I think it was the wine bottle breaking.'

'No,' said Carrick, running his pen along the page of his notebook. 'A disturbance as in raised voices. An argument between a man and a woman.'

As he looked at her, Jo felt strange unsettling currents in the air.

'Ben and I had a row,' she said.

'A row?' Carrick's eyebrows jumped. 'Your brother mentioned you two had history. What was the row about?'

'He thought we could get back together, I didn't. But listen, none of that's important. This guy, this *freak* – he didn't have any clothes on. He can't have—'

'Jo, let me do my job,' said Carrick. 'We're looking for Will, but if we establish an accurate timeline leading up to him disappearing, it will help everyone. You too.'

Jo wasn't sure what that was supposed to mean. *What do I have to do with any of this?*

'Someone targeted me,' she said. 'What's Burgess said? It has to be linked.'

'Burgess has been helpful,' said Carrick, without really explaining what that meant. 'Tell me about the row with Ben.'

'Okay, okay,' she said. 'I remember now. It woke Will up.'

'It must have been quite a blow-up,' said Carrick. 'You'd been drinking, I think?'

'Barely.'

'We found three bottles.'

'We poured one away down the sink.'

Carrick frowned. 'Why would you do that?'

'Can you put that fucking book away and listen to me?' she said.

Carrick folded the notebook closed. 'Detective, I am listening, but you're not making a lot of sense at the moment.'

'I just want you to do your bloody job and find William!' she said.

Carrick gave a consoling nod. 'The neighbour said the argument happened at 21.45 – does that sound right to you?'

'I suppose so.'

'And it woke up your nephew.'

'Yes. He came down the stairs. I took him straight back up, and told Ben to leave.'

'But he didn't?'

Jo breathed a sigh. 'Evidently.'

'Do you know where his car is?' asked Carrick, flashing a glance at her.

'Er . . . yes, in a garage. The cylinders are always going.'

'You know which garage?'

'No, why the fuck would I?'

'There's no need to be aggressive,' said Carrick. 'We're just trying to find his car. We thought whoever took William might have . . .'

'Well they didn't,' said Jo. 'It's in the garage.'

'Okay, back to the timeline,' said Carrick. 'The attack, you think, happened a while after Ben arrived? Say before ten?'

'Yes, it must have.'

'So why didn't you ring the police?'

'I . . . I did.'

'*Someone* rang the police from the property at 21.51,' said

Carrick, 'but they hung up. Later, a car attended the scene at 21.56, but that was in response to the neighbour's call about a disturbance.'

'No, I must have . . .' said Jo.

'You didn't.'

And through the fog of troubled, incoherent thoughts, Jo realised with clarity what was happening.

'You can't think . . .' She was shaking her head. 'Andy, don't even . . . I . . .'

Carrick let her lapse into silence.

'It was the clown, Andy. It was him! Will even said it.'

She stood up, and Carrick echoed her movement. 'Jo, you should stay put.'

'Why aren't you listening to me?' said Jo desperately. 'He's out there. He's got him. We got to Niall in time. He's going to kill him this time. You fucking know that!'

'Jo, I'm going to ask you to stay in this room,' said Carrick. A uniformed officer emerged behind him. 'And we're going to need to take your phone.'

'What? Why?'

'You know why.'

The officer took her phone.

'Am I under arrest?'

'Jo, don't make this harder than it needs to be. We're just being thorough. You're too close.'

'You're saying I murdered my fucking nephew. Are you insane?'

Carrick frowned. 'Jo, no one mentioned murder. Why would you even say that?'

She felt weak again, light-headed.

'Leave things to us,' said Carrick. He started towards the door, then turned around. 'Actually Jo, there's one more thing. Rebekah Fitzwilliam – when did you last see her?'

The question came from nowhere, and it took Jo a few moments to think. 'The press conference. Yesterday morning. What's that got to do with anything?'

'She's been reported missing,' said Carrick. 'I'm sure it's nothing. You sit tight, okay?'

He left the room, and Jo caught her own reflection in the glass. Bloodstained, neck-braced, hair wild. She looked like a madwoman.

Chapter 24

The uniform on the door had his back to her. Just doing his job. She didn't recognise him from the station.

No one else entered the room, and with no clock on the wall, she had to guess the time. She couldn't even imagine how Paul and Amelia must be feeling – they'd never have been allowed back into the house, so she guessed they'd be at the station, or maybe at a friend's house, one of the parade of happy guests at her brother's party. It seemed like years ago, but it had only been a few days. That night her biggest frustration had been the fact she was off the Dylan Jones case, that Ben had somehow come through everything unscathed. She could never have dreamed it would end here, like this. That Ben, for all the pain he'd caused her, would be . . .

She closed her eyes, trying to fight back the tears again.

Had she really not called the police after finding Ben? She tried to think back, to the moments after she stumbled out of the kitchen. Maybe she hadn't. And if they'd come . . .

They couldn't really believe that she had anything to do with it. It was preposterous. She tried to put herself in the shoes of an investigator. What was the theory? That she killed

Ben and drove away with Will somewhere in his car? It made no sense.

The problem was, as Ben himself used to say, sometimes life didn't. Sometimes all you needed were the whats and wheres.

And even as she struggled with her own incredulity, she knew Carrick's line of questioning shouldn't have been such a surprise. In nine out of ten cases of child murder, the suspect was known to the family already. The step-parent, the uncle, the sibling. The trusted, or not so trusted, friend. She saw exactly where Carrick was coming from, and why he wanted her here. Because the alternatives were even harder to fathom. That an attacker somehow chose her brother's house. Chose Will to be his victim, the nephew of an investigating officer.

And Carrick was right. She *was* too close. Had been from the start. Stratton could be a prick, blowing hot and cold, but he'd seen it too. From the moment she'd arrived from Avon and Somerset, trouble had trailed in her wake like the scent of a rotten corpse, and all because of her past, right back to her first mistake – one she always told herself was innocent, but which she knew in her heart was a sort of cowardice – walking on by while a man in a clown outfit took Dylan Jones. It felt like she was at the centre of an infection, the carrier and the cause. Everyone else was just trying to keep away. *And why not?*

Somehow even Sally Carruthers had been caught up in it, an old lady who'd deserved to see out the remains of her life without being dragged into a police station. Every missing child case within fifty miles from the last thirty years would be re-examined for potential links to Stephen Carruthers. The wheels would turn – every site Carruthers had worked on would be examined, perhaps excavated, whether there was a confessional note or not. And under those wheels, poor Sally Carruthers would be crushed. She'd have to hire a lawyer, probably sell what was left of the house at auction. At least people like Trent and Burgess and Matthews got sentences they could measure, parole. For Sally, there'd be no respite, not until the day she died, and her only crime had been to try to teach children to play the piano and fall for a bloke who'd probably seemed great at the time, but had a sick pathology.

Stop, Jo. Just stop.

Worrying about Sally Carruthers wasn't going to help her find Will. Stephen Carruthers wasn't preying on kids any more. Dylan Jones was the past, wherever his body was resting.

She needed to be present. To focus her mind and think like a detective. *What am I missing?* She didn't blame Carrick for coming to the conclusions he had. He wasn't there when it happened. But *she* was. She'd *seen* the man, albeit briefly. But it was *just* a man. Not a ghoul, or a spectre, or a monster. Niall had seen the man too. And Will. She sat up sharply.

He came from the garden.

Will's bedroom was beside the guest room in which she had stayed. The vantage point was almost identical. The pitch of the roof and the extended orangery precluded any line of sight to the side gate, so if Will saw someone, that person came up *through* the garden, from the rear of the house. He'd set off the security light. And there was nothing that way, apart from . . .

The barn.

Jo's skin tingled. The officers would have gone to Sally's house straight away – they'd have knocked on the doors of all the neighbouring houses. They'd got a dog squad, Heidi had said. But she wondered – if Carrick was working on the assumption of Ben's car being used . . . any car . . .

And Will's scent would be all over the garden anyway.

And Christ – the river, the fence – would they have gone further? It was a wilderness down there. They might not even have seen the barn.

Jo took a deep breath, trying to stay calm. To analyse. Sally had been down at the barn, the night of Paul's party. Feeding the cat, she said. But why at night? She was an old woman – why take the risk of a fall?

Jo knew she wasn't thinking straight, whether it was the drugs in her system or the swelling of her concussion, or simply the discordance that had seemed to accompany the last few days. She closed her eyes, struggling to process the niggling coincidences and the vying complexities of the investigations, of her and Ben, of the body that wasn't Dylan, of Alan Trent and the pale fiendish creature that Niall's father was only too happy to think of as a figment of his son's imagination.

The barn.

In her mind's eye, the confusion of signals phased quite suddenly into something different. She saw it, dimly, like a face through rain-streaked glass, or the eyes of a face hidden behind a mask. And though she didn't understand completely, she knew where she would find her nephew.

She walked to the door and opened it, then the officer turned to look at her. He was impossibly fresh-faced.

'Sorry, ma'am,' he said. 'Detective Carrick said you've got to stay here.'

'I need to speak to him,' she said. 'Can you call him for me?'

'Sorry, ma'am – I don't have his number.'

'Anyone in CID then.'

'I can ask my sergeant,' said the officer. 'He'll be up in a few minutes.'

Jo looked at his insignia. 'Constable Owens,' she said, addressing him by name. 'Now, please.'

He radioed through to someone called Sergeant Frankel.

'Say it's important,' she said.

'Sir, the detective in hospital . . . she wants to talk with someone in CID.'

Jo heard the sergeant's response. 'Everyone's up to their ears. Someone will speak with her later.'

Owens looked apologetic.

Jo felt like screaming, but instead she simply walked along the corridor.

'Ma'am, you can't,' said the constable. 'Please, stop. Stop there.'

Jo reached the bank of elevators and pushed the button.

'Ma'am, I need you to come with me.'

He gave her arm a little tug, and she resisted.

The elevator doors opened, and she climbed in, squeezing alongside an orderly with a stacked trolley of bedding and a young couple holding a child's car seat. Owens didn't look at all sure, and got in too. He got on his radio again, and told his sergeant, 'The detective has got into a lift.'

The sergeant's voice, slightly bewildered, said he'd get in touch with CID and ask what to do. Jo could've laughed, but she was already wondering how she could get out of this.

As the lift stopped on the first floor, the doors opened, and another doctor squeezed in. Everyone jostled. Jo waited until the doors were closing, then slipped out sideways, hearing a cry from the constable as he was caught inside. She rushed along the corridor, following the fire exit signs until she reached barred double doors. She pushed through, finding herself in a concrete-floored stairwell, then dropped a flight quickly. As she went, she flexed her neck, deemed it satisfactory, and unfastened the brace. Through another double door and she was out behind the hospital. She tossed the brace into a bin.

With no obvious bearings, she crossed a staff car park, heading for traffic lights in the distance. She broke into a half-arsed run, but felt knackered at once. The occasional driver gave her an odd look, and she thought about flagging one down. And then she realised where she was. Back on the London Road. Plenty of other pedestrians looked like they were heading to work. Some were getting onto a bus, and Jo climbed on too. The bus driver looked at her with a hint of interest.

'Where to?'

'City centre.'

'Two quid please.'

Jo realised she didn't have her purse. She fished for some cash in her pocket, but all that came out on her hand was her warrant card.

'Shit . . . I'm sorry. I haven't—'

The driver clocked her badge and gave her a nod. 'On you get,' he said.

She flagged a cab as soon as she reached St Giles, gave her destination, claiming a police emergency. She wondered briefly about asking to borrow a phone, but she wasn't sure exactly what she would say to Carrick, or how the cabbie might react in the front. He'd barely batted an eyelid at her appearance, but if she started talking about kidnapping that might change.

She just hoped that she wasn't too late.

★　★　★

Sally opened the door wearing an apron, looking more alive than ever, and wiping her hands with a tea towel. Her eyes widened at the sight of the bruising around Jo's jaw.

'Josie! Oh, look at you! What happened? The police came round.'

Jo's certainty, the clarity of it all, threatened to waver. 'Can I come in?'

Sally looked past Jo, to the path. 'Yes, yes. Of course.'

Jo entered, and waited for Sally to close the door. 'What did the police tell you?' she asked.

'They said a little boy was missing, from a house up the hill.'
She blanched. 'It's not . . . It wasn't William, was it?'

Jo nodded, and she didn't have to feign the tears that came
to her eyes.

'Oh, Josie. No. He's probably just run off.'

*They didn't tell her. No surprise. They're controlling the flow of
information.*

'Did they ask to search the house?' asked Jo.

Sally shook her head. 'No. Why on earth would they?'

No, why would they? Old woman living alone, widowed . . .

'Y'know – the gardens. Will might have come this way.'

'At night?'

Did they tell her he went missing at night?

Jo's eyes travelled to the small desk beside the bookshelf.
There was a black A4 diary on there.

'You couldn't put the kettle on, could you?'

Sally smiled and headed through to the kitchen.

'His poor parents must be beside themselves,' she called back.

Jo went quickly to the desk. The current day was marked.
She looked back through the last few weeks, skimming. Sally
had mentioned that she hadn't had many clients, and there
were only a couple each week, or fortnightly, inscribed in
Sally's neat writing. Names and times. Frieda Barnstaple, Aurelia
Wager, Carl Lomax. She flicked the pages. Sally had a row of
box files on the desk too. One labelled 'Referrals', another
'Private clients'.

She was about to pull out the latter when she realised a page
had been torn out of the diary. June 16th. A Monday, six weeks
ago. She skipped back further. A week before, June 9th, was
gone as well. Jo rewound another seven days. Same. The day's
appointments excised from the records.

*Or a person . . . someone who, according to his boss, never worked
Monday mornings at Gloucester College.*

'What are you doing?' asked Sally. She was standing in the doorway to the kitchen. And in her hand was a tray, with a teapot and two cups and a milk jug. 'I'd just put the kettle on before you arrived,' she said, in way of explanation.

Jo kept her hand on the page. 'You're missing some pages,' she said.

'You shouldn't be looking through my private papers,' she said. 'There are client details in there.'

'But nothing for Alan Trent,' said Jo.

'Alan who?'

'I think you know who I mean.'

'Josie, you're frightening me a bit,' said Sally. 'Is this something to do with yesterday? About Stephen and Martin?'

'Perhaps,' said Jo. Sally didn't say anything. The only sound in the room was the clock ticking. 'Sally, do you know where Will is?' she asked quietly.

'I'm going to call the police,' said Sally. 'You can't harass me like this.'

She went towards the phone, but Jo intercepted her. She grabbed both Sally's thin shoulders and held her firm.

'He's in the barn, isn't he?' she said.

Sally started to cry. 'Please leave me alone. Please go.'

'Dear God, if you've done anything to him . . . Stop crying, and just *tell* me!'

She let go, but must have pushed at the same time, because Sally stumbled back and hit the ground hard with a moan. Her lips parted with shock, then she buried her head in her hands and wept.

'I know you blackmailed Alan,' said Jo. 'Who's the other one? Is he down there now?'

She went along the hallway towards the back door, but found it locked.

'Where's the key?' She advanced again, meaning to lift Sally to her feet, but she heard a door somewhere else in the house and stopped.

'Will?' she shouted, spinning on the spot.

'He can't hear you,' said Sally, sniffing.

'Who's in the house?' she snapped.

Sally was looking up from the floor. All kindness had gone from her eyes and been replaced with pity. That, and a look she knew from the interview room. Resignation. Acceptance. Jo grabbed her and hauled her to her feet. She weighed nothing.

'Who's in the fucking house?'

'I didn't want this,' said Sally. 'I always liked you.' Her eyes shifted a fraction to look at something behind her.

When she turned around, Jo saw there was a third person in the room. Right in the middle, as if he'd materialised there, manifested from a child's nightmare. He stood a good six-foot-three, even with the hunch that made his head protrude forwards. The proportions of his body were wrong – almost ape-like, with long legs, knees slightly bowed inwards, and narrow hips. His chest was much broader, with fleshy pectorals, and well-muscled arms. A giant goblin, not a clown, and if a man, the sort of man who made no sense in the world Jo knew. He looked like two different bodies combined, then painted all over with the same pigment – a sickly grey, with the thread of blue veins beneath, a kind of living marble. His head was almost perfectly round, hairless, with swollen lips that were cracked and sore. The eyes were pale, set deep in bruising shadow, the irises misshapen, like two shucked oysters, and she knew instinctively that he was close to blind.

But strange as he was, there were telltale signs – that unmistakeable cleft of the chin, the long eyelashes, a few bristles of red hair.

Dylan Jones.

'He won't hurt you,' said Sally, moving aside.

Jo, isolated, took a step back, sensing with the instinct of a prey animal that the thing meant to do her harm, whatever Sally said. She couldn't work out where he'd suddenly come from – but then saw the door to what looked like a downstairs bedroom was slightly ajar. It had been shut when she arrived. He must have been hiding in there.

He moved towards her, wide nostrils twitching and ape arms jerking out. There was nowhere to go, and he pressed her into the corner. His mouth gaped, fishlike, but there was no sound other than the wet muted contractions of his neck muscles, his tongue a shocking red stump that pulsed in the back of his throat. His breath was rancid and pungent, his teeth just a mess of yellow-black shards. Jo gagged involuntarily.

'Dylan, it's all right,' she said.

His eyes changed, pupils sharpening, and her brain was just telling her to lift her hands in defence when he threw his weight into her, one hand on her chin. Her head hit the wall behind so hard that she feared her skull would crack. Her mind became unmoored, drifting.

The second blow blackened everything.

Chapter 25

When Jo woke, lying on her side, it was to dim light, the smell of rust and the taste of blood. They'd moved her. The air was warm and choking, and she realised, as a groan escaped her lips, that she was gagged with a piece of material.

She tried to move, and found her hands were fastened too, tied behind her back. Looking down, she had gaffer tape on her ankles, so it was likely the same on her wrists. Her whole body felt leaden. The roof was spanned by cross-beams of gnarled dark wood. *I'm in the barn.* Three quarters of the way along the ceiling was a shallow mezzanine level, maybe for storage. A rudimentary rope ladder hung down. There were workbenches along one wall, with shelves of paint and other containers. The carcass of an old motorbike rested against a drum of some sort, and the floor was covered in old pieces of cardboard, stained with engine oil. Thick metal hooks hung from the wall, from which held an assortment of tools. A mallet, a saw, a pair of tongs. There were a couple of tiny, shuttered windows, but the only light came from an old oil lamp beside Sally.

A whimper made Jo twist her neck, and her eyes found

William. Her nephew was sitting in a corner, gaffer tape across his lips. His eyes, saucer-like, were fixed on something in the distance. But he was *alive*, and the rush of love and terror exploded across Jo's chest. She tried to call his name, and it came out as a strained mumble. She wondered why he didn't come to her, then saw his ankles had cord tied around them. His arms were free.

Jo heard a cough and jerked her head back the other way. Sally Carruthers was sitting down on a battered leather armchair. She had put on a coat.

'I saw the look in the car,' she said. 'When I *told* you Stephen didn't kill Dylan. You thought I was a silly old woman. Deluded, no doubt.'

Jo managed to manoeuvre herself into a sitting position. As she did, she saw the thing that Dylan Jones had become. He was sitting on his haunches, dipping a sponge in a bucket, then lifting it and slapping at something on the ground. *What the fuck did they do to him?* It looked like he'd never seen sunlight. Had he been here, in this barn, all that time?

Jo tried to use her shoulder to roll the gag out of her mouth, flexing her neck. It hurt like fuck, sending crippling waves of pain across her jaw, but she just needed to speak, to get through to Sally. She managed to prise it partway out.

But her former piano teacher was barely paying any attention.

'I think Stephen thought we could just move here and everything would be fine. But it wasn't like that. I missed Martin so very much. He was difficult, but he was still my boy. I wanted another child, but by then it was too late. I suppose I hated Stephen, for what he'd done. And he knew it too. So when we met Dylan, it seemed like fate. He was such a sweet thing, and so *expressive*! Martin never could be bothered with music. Dylan though, he was a dream.' She turned back towards him. 'Weren't you, sweetheart? You always practised hard.'

302

Dylan was still playing with the sponge, but nodded vigorously.

Jo spat out the remains of the gag.

'Don't scream, please,' said Sally. 'Dylan hates loud noises. The other woman wouldn't stop.'

Jo had no idea what she was talking about.

'It's going to be all right, captain,' said Jo, looking at Will.

He didn't move.

'Are you hurt?' asked Jo.

'He's not hurt,' said Sally. 'Dylan likes him.'

'Will, talk to me,' said Jo.

'Where's Mum?' he said.

'We're going home soon,' she said.

'I'm scared.'

'We had a difficulty,' said Sally. 'Poor little mite got a shock, didn't you, sweetheart?'

'You need to let William go,' said Jo, as earnestly yet gently as she could.

Yet if Sally heard her, it didn't sink in. She looked at Dylan. 'Leave her, darling. She's all clean now.'

Jo couldn't see what it was he was cleaning, but there was a definite pink tinge to the sponge. And now she understood that Will wasn't looking at Dylan at all.

'Will, don't look over there,' she said. 'Look at me.'

His gaze flicked to her.

'Good. Will, don't worry about that man.'

She shifted her legs, and felt that the utility knife was still in the ankle strap. She wondered if she could reach it with her bound hands. Certainly not without being seen. She needed time. She needed to keep Sally talking.

'Stephen took Dylan from the carnival that day,' she said. 'He was the man in the mask.'

'We *rescued* Dylan,' said Sally. 'I mean, *really*, what sort of mother lets her child wander off alone like that?' She chuckled.

303

'It was Stephen's idea to do it at the circus. He'd helped to set up the generators, so he knew the place well. When Dylan said he was going, it seemed like fate.' She held out her arms to him. 'Come here, sweetie. Come to Mummy.'

Dylan, on his knuckles, swung his legs beneath him, and made his way, monkey-like, across the floor. She heard Will cry out in the corner, pressing his head into his hands. But Dylan stopped beside Sally, and presented her with a pair of pale shoes that Jo recognised from somewhere.

'Oh, silly!' said Sally. 'I'm too old for these!'

She wrapped her arms around his shoulders and kissed the top of his head.

Close up, Jo saw that his body was covered in fine hairs. His hands were large, with long, elegant fingers. She understood now who'd been playing the piano when she visited a couple of days before. The sheer audacity of letting him come up to the house shocked her.

'It was hard for him in the beginning,' said Sally. 'A new place, different rules. It took a while to find something he would eat.'

Jo felt sick as she remembered the tin. 'You gave him *cat* food.'

'Not at first. We gave him all the sweets he wanted, but the little tyke wouldn't brush his teeth properly. After that we just had to find something he could chew, something nutritious.'

Jo grimaced.

'Spare me the sanctimony,' said Sally. 'At least we loved him. I'd seen what his so-called father did to him. Taking his belt off for the smallest thing. And Stephen never lifted a hand to him unless . . .' she looked sad for a moment '. . . unless he had to. We got him everything he wanted.'

Dylan was smiling. Jo looked around. How long had he been in here? Was there a bed somewhere?

'I want to go home,' said Will.

Dylan cocked his ears towards the sound and took a couple of leaping strides, passing Jo and heading towards her nephew.

'No!' she said. 'Leave him alone!'

She threw herself after him, but only succeeded in sprawling.

'No shouting,' said Sally. 'Please, Josie.'

Will had his hands over his head, not wanting even to see. Dylan stretched closer, and the ridges of his spine were jagged under his almost translucent skin. He sniffed at Will's hair, his neck, then lower. A pool of urine darkened the floor. With a hand, Dylan smashed the wall above Will's head and turned to Sally.

'Again?' said Sally, her mouth turning upside down.

Dylan's mouth contorted, and the half-sounds emerged.

What happened to his fucking tongue? And as soon as she thought it, she knew. They'd had to keep him quiet. A seven-year-old would have cried and screamed, and if they'd shouted at him, he would only have screamed more.

'I know Dylan's probably a bit different to his other friends,' said Sally. 'But they'll get used to each other. Children are more adaptable than you give them credit for.' She chuckled. 'Just look at Dylan.'

Jo had never felt so utterly powerless. She wanted to scream that if he hurt Will, if he scared him any more, she'd kill him, but she stopped herself. Instead, she wriggled like a worm, trying to get closer. Just to be with her nephew if anything happened.

'I'm coming, captain,' she said.

Dylan took hold of William's arms, prising them from his face. William started to scream, and Dylan used the little boy's hands to cover his ears.

'Don't, captain,' said Jo. 'There's nothing to be frightened of. He doesn't understand.'

But William didn't stop. He couldn't. She wondered if Dylan was actually screaming too. His mouth was gaping.

'William, stop!' shouted Jo. It was the first time she'd ever raised her voice to her nephew and it seemed to do the trick. He stopped, and looked at her through his tears. 'That's right, captain,' she said. 'Just look at Auntie Jo.'

Dylan's gaze went back and forth between the two of them, then he spoke in his guttural jabber to Sally.

Sally laughed.

'He says you're pretty,' said Sally. 'Come back here, Dylan. You're scaring William. Give him time.'

Dylan snapped something at her, then took a couple of loping hops to get closer to Jo. She didn't care if he hurt her. As long as he was away from Will. He reached out and touched her hair. She flinched away, but he didn't register it, and let his hand trail down her front, squeezing her left nipple hard.

'Dylan!' warned Sally.

He looked sulkily at her, and smiled at Jo. He leant forward, and she froze, lips clamped together but not able to stop the moan of terror. She felt the heat of his breath on her cheek, and then the sharp tips of his teeth on her ear. The pressure was only light.

'Dylan – not now,' said Sally. 'Come over here *at once.*'

This time he obeyed, and as he moved out of her line of sight, Jo saw what he'd been doing on the floor. A woman's body, naked but for a pair of jeans, lay sprawled on the ground. It was Rebekah Saunders. One half of her head was caved into a bloody pulp.

Oh fucking Christ.

She wriggled the last few feet until she reached Will's side, and pressed close to him. His clothes were soaked with a panicked sweat.

'It's okay, captain. I'm right here and I'm not going anywhere.' Sally was stroking Dylan's hand in her lap.

'He's sensitive,' she said. 'Always has been. It's what made us choose him.' She looked at Jo conspiratorially. 'He didn't like Niall at all. That whole thing was . . . unfortunate. He wasn't a nice boy, despite what Alan promised.'

'You went to the RAF base, with Dylan?'

Sally looked cross. 'He was so excited,' she muttered. 'He'd been talking about a friend for years. Getting really quite *stubborn* about the whole thing. You know children. I tried to tell him it wasn't safe, going out, coming up to the house all the time – *Stephen* would never have allowed it – but he struggles with his temper a bit, does our Dylan.'

Jo realised that the bruise on Sally's cheek might not have been a stumble after all.

'I thought a friend might keep him happy, and Alan seemed a capable enough man. Looking back on it all though, I don't think he really tried. I'm glad we did it on neutral ground, so to speak. I hate to think what Dylan might have done if Alan had brought Niall straight here. Some of the *language* that boy used.' She smiled broadly, her eyes shining with delight. 'Not like our William.'

'Sally, listen to me,' said Jo. 'You have to let William go. The police will come here. They'll find him. And when they do, they'll take Dylan away from you too.'

Dylan sat upright, snatching his hand away. He gave a few grunts.

'No, they *won't*,' said Sally. She shot Jo a scolding glance. 'And really, you shouldn't say things like that in front of him.'

A buzzer went off suddenly, and Dylan crossed the floor quickly. With both hands on the rope ladder, he hauled himself onto the mezzanine above with remarkable speed, before pulling the ladder up behind him. He had to crouch up there – it

307

couldn't have been more than five feet high. Perhaps *that* explained the hunch in his back. If Stephen had kept him up there, all this time . . .

'I have to go for a moment,' Sally said, standing up and brushing down her skirt. 'Josie, this is serious now, so listen please. If you make a sound, if you try to escape, Dylan will kill you both. I know you're a clever girl, so you understand, don't you?'

Will was shaking beside her, and Jo said simply, 'Yes, Sally.'

'Jolly good. If you'll excuse me.'

She hobbled speedily towards the door, letting herself out.

Jo pressed her face to Will's. 'It's all right, captain. I'm not leaving you.'

A few seconds later the buzzer went off again. Jo realised it was the doorbell. It could well be the police. Maybe even the dog squad. But they wouldn't be looking for her, not here. Carrick would assume she was on the run, not back round the corner from the scene of the crime. She tried not to let her eyes dwell on Saunders' corpse. She couldn't work out why the hell she was here. Not that it mattered for the moment.

From the mezzanine opposite, Dylan watched them, poised in a crouch. *Can he see this far?* she wondered. If she shouted for help now, what would he do?

Of course, it might not be the police at all. And if she screamed, and if Dylan attacked . . . If she'd been on her own, she might have risked it, but with Will beside her, it wasn't an option.

I've got to get my knife. Got to cut this tape off.

She looked at the tools on the wall. If she was given the chance, she'd use anything she could.

She imagined Sally was almost at the front door by now. Depending on the visitor, she might be back in one minute, or twenty. This might be the first and only opportunity. She rocked up onto her heels beside Will, and with her hands hidden, strained her arms until she could hook the hem of her trousers. Dylan didn't move. He looked like a living gargoyle, completely motionless.

They trained him, she thought. When the buzzer goes, he freezes.

She eased up the trouser leg, and her fingers found the knife. Still Dylan remained, and under his unflinching, unseeing gaze, she tugged it out. Will had seen though, and was shooting glances downward. There was nothing to be done there. She guessed, for all Dylan's deficiencies in sight, he more than made up for it with his other senses. Her mind struggled to fathom how long they must have kept him in the darkness for him to end up looking like this.

She unfolded the blade awkwardly, her hands still bound. It was two and a half inches long. She flipped it in her hands, and laid the edge of the blade against the tape on her left wrist. With tiny, difficult movements, she began to saw. As she worked the blade back and forth, even the small noise sounded amplified in the empty barn.

She estimated the time passing. Forty seconds. Fifty. A minute. Sally could be back at any moment, and she couldn't fail to miss what Jo was doing. Suddenly, she felt the tape give a little and heard a tearing sound. On the mezzanine, Dylan twitched, head cocked. But he remained where he was.

Jo continued cutting. *Come on. Come on . . .*

The door rattled and Sally came back in. 'There we are. Nothing to worry about.' She looked upwards. 'Come on then, sweetpea.'

Dylan tossed the rope ladder down, and it unfurled to the ground.

Now or never.

Jo ripped her hands apart, shredding the last of the tape, then drove the knife into the tape at her ankles. Through it in a couple of seconds, she clambered up.

'No!' cried Sally.

Dylan lowered himself like Tarzan, hand over hand, and dropped the last ten feet to the ground.

Jo was running, heading for the mallet, as he came the other way, but she was just too slow. With his teeth bared, he slammed into her, and they both rolled across the barn floor, fetching up against the base of a cabinet. He was on top of her and brought down a fist towards her head. She did her best to block, then drove the knife into his ribs. Dylan arched his back, reaching for the wound, but she pulled it out and stabbed again. She felt hot blood gushing over her knuckles, spattering her face. She stabbed and stabbed, not really thinking where, but driving the blade as hard and deep as she could. Then he must have struck her arm, because it went completely numb and the knife skittered away.

'What have you done?' wailed Sally. 'My poor boy!'

Dylan's hands found her throat, and he lifted his hips, pressing down his whole weight. Jo squeezed her chin, but it was useless against such a force. It felt at once like her neck would simply give way, crushed under his bulk. She tried to buck her legs to toss him off. He grimaced, lips spooling blood and saliva. It poured between the stumps of his teeth, all over Jo's front. Her head was heavy, dislocated from the wild stampede of panic in her chest, and blackness swept across her eyes. She reached up with her hand, searching for the wounds in his side, but it was all so wet that she couldn't find the cuts. Jo tried to plead, because she knew she was going to die, but she couldn't speak at all, and in the back of her mind, that seemed so terribly unfair. The world was shrinking, its sounds muffled and colours muted, until all she could see were Dylan's eyes, the irises as luminescent as glowing pearls.

And then they gave an odd tremble, before rolling together sideways. The hands on her neck slipped loose and Dylan rocked for a moment. Sounds came back in a rush, and it was a scream she heard. Sally's scream.

Then a dull thud. Dylan's head lolled, and he toppled forwards, face smashing into the wall. Standing behind him was William, holding a mallet in both hands, hopping for balance with his ankles still bound.

Jo pushed Dylan's weight off her, forced to move in what felt like slow motion. She reached out and took the mallet from her nephew's hand.

Sally, arms outstretched, hobbled past them both, dropping to the ground beside Dylan's body and saying, 'Oh! Oh! Oh!'

He was lying flat on his stomach, completely still, but for the twitching of one hand. For a second or two, his elegant fingers tapped a syncopated rhythm that told of nothing more than his brain's dying thoughts. And then they too were still.

Jo scooped Will to her, hoisting him into her arms, and walked as quickly as she could to the door without looking back. She carried him out into the light of an impossibly sunny day.

'Are we going to see Mum?' asked Will. His voice was quiet, stupefied, but he wasn't crying any more.

'That's right, captain,' she said. 'I need you to be brave for a bit longer.'

At the top of the garden path, she entered Sally's house again, stopping in the living room by the piano and picking up the phone while still holding William. She dialled three nines then calmly asked for the police.

As she was waiting to be put through, she watched the back door in case Sally decided to follow, though she suspected it would be a long time before the old woman emerged from the barn. She identified herself to the dispatcher, gave their address, and requested an ambulance, CID attendance plus uniformed back-up, as well as a forensics team.

Then, and only then, did her knees buckle. She sank to the carpet, with William clinging limpet-like to her chest.

Epilogue

Four days later, Jo picked Ferman up from his house. He was in a dark suit, clean-shaven.

'You look smart,' she said, as he lowered himself into the car.

He fastened his seat belt. 'You look a mess.'

'You old charmer,' said Jo. It was true enough, though. Her neck and face were coloured by an assortment of bruises – purple where hands had almost strangled her life away, fading to green and yellow around the left side of her jaw.

They drove towards John Radcliffe hospital around the perimeter of the city. It seemed like another place entirely now the case was over. Families out enjoying themselves, students laughing without a care in the world. Life going on.

'How's your nephew doing?' asked Ferman.

'Under the circumstances, well,' she said. 'The whole family have gone camping for a few days in Devon – trying to put it to the back of their minds. He'll need help though, going forward.'

'Don't we all?' muttered Ferman. 'So what about you?'

'I'll heal,' she said. 'Chewing hurts.'

'I didn't mean physically. You went through something bloody nasty, so I hear. Have they offered you any counselling?'

Jo nodded, eyes on the road. 'I didn't think you'd be a fan of all that touchy-feely stuff.'

Ferman stretched out his legs. 'You should take them up on it,' he said.

'Didn't do Alan Trent much good,' said Jo, then regretted the flippancy.

But Ferman laughed. 'Hopefully you'd get one who's not a psychopath.' They were almost at the hospital, and an ambulance streaked past in the other direction. 'She's been sectioned?' said Ferman.

'Under evaluation for thirty days,' Jo answered. She'd periodically thought about visiting, but dismissed it. Cherry Tree Cottage was still surrounded by police tape. It felt too fresh. And from her brother's house that morning, looking over the back of the garden towards the barn, she really couldn't untangle how she felt about Sally Carruthers. Couldn't separate the kindly piano teacher from the crazed woman who thought it was okay to steal another family's child. Who'd used Alan Trent, a vulnerable, scared man, in the worst possible way, taking his fragile trust and smashing it with no thought for compassion or professional ethics. Who still, even now, was oblivious to the perverted upbringing she'd inflicted on poor Dylan Jones. Apparently, according to the team assessing her, she kept asking after Dylan, telling the staff to make sure they fed him properly. And this from the woman who'd given him cat food for three decades.

'Chances of her doing time look slim,' she said.

'Some might say she's suffered more than most,' said Ferman. 'She's lost two kids now.'

He was speaking seriously, she realised. And there was a sort of truth to it.

But still. Tell Mr and Mrs Jones that . . .

They drove on in silence, and Jo wondered if Ferman felt the same weight of dread growing in the pit of his stomach as the first signs came up for the pathology lab.

'So are you heading back to Bath soon?' he asked.

'For a while,' said Jo. 'I've put in a transfer request for Thames Valley. Oxford hopefully.'

'All this hasn't put you off then?'

'DCI Stratton's actually put me up for a commendation.'

Ferman scoffed. 'I'd say congratulations, but that fella blows with the wind.'

'Things like this make you appreciate family too. I don't see them enough as it is.'

She didn't mention her mother, because she still hadn't quite decided what she'd do there. She'd gone as far as buying some geraniums, Mum's favourite, and rung the place for visiting hours, but whether she'd actually go was another thing.

She took the last exit off the final roundabout and pulled up by the mortuary building. Andy Carrick's car was there already.

'Ready?' she said.

'I suppose so,' said Ferman.

They went inside and found Mr and Mrs Jones waiting with Carrick in the reception area. Both were dressed smartly.

Mr Jones stood up. 'Thank you for coming,' he said, shaking their hands in turn. Mrs Jones had a handkerchief clasped in hers.

'I've explained what will happen,' said Carrick. 'If you change your mind at any time, that's quite all right.'

'Let's get this over with,' said Mr Jones. He held out a hand and helped his wife to her feet.

Carrick led the way down the white corridor, with Jo and Ferman following at the rear.

Jo had been through the process several times, but this was different. It had been made clear to Mr and Mrs Jones by the liaison officer that a formal identification wasn't required in light of DNA confirmation, and she knew Carrick would have tried to persuade them, understandably, not to come. But they'd insisted, and from the way Mrs Jones took the lead, Jo guessed it was more the mother's decision than the father's.

They reached the mortuary suite, and through a glass viewing window, Jo saw the gurney in the centre of the room. A white sheet covered the body. A lab-coated woman was sitting at a desk, and she stood up when she saw them. Carrick opened the door.

'Doctor, Mr and Mrs Jones are here.' He moved aside. 'Dr Dubrovski will take you through things,' he said. 'We'll wait outside.'

Mrs Jones was staring into the room. For a moment, Jo thought she'd have second thoughts and turn back. But with a deep breath, she went inside. Carrick let the door close behind the parents. Jo watched as the doctor spoke to Mr and Mrs Jones, just a few words. They took a position about a metre from the gurney. Mr Jones' chest was visibly heaving, but his wife appeared rather calm. She wiped her eyes a final time, then replied with a single word, 'Yes.'

The doctor took hold of two corners of the sheet, and slowly folded it back to reveal Dylan Jones' face. His eyes and mouth were closed, and his head had been shaved. Jo found herself relieved, because there was nothing of the horror she'd witnessed in the barn. His skin was still pale, but he was just a dead man in the bleak, artificial light of the mortuary room.

She knew it was fatuous, but at least he looked at peace.

I'm sorry, she told him. *I'm sorry I didn't say anything. I'm sorry I let him take you away.*

Mr Jones took only the briefest of glances, jaw clenched, but Mrs Jones broke away from him, approaching closer, transfixed. She asked the doctor something and received a nod.

Reaching out, Dylan's mother touched his cheek lightly with her fingers, then stroked his brow. Then she leant forward and kissed his forehead. It was much the same spot as Sally had placed her lips in the barn. Jo swallowed, and realised that beside her Ferman was trembling. She looked across and saw he was fighting back tears.

After they said goodbye to the parents afterwards, and Ferman was getting back into the car, Carrick called Jo over.

'Thanks for that, Jo. It must have been tough.'

'It's no problem.'

'Listen, are you going to Detective Coombs' funeral tomorrow?'

'Yes.'

She hadn't wanted to. Ben hadn't told his parents or the rest of his family anything about the split, so she'd had to do so herself. She'd said she'd understand if they didn't want her there. But they had asked her to come.

The exact circumstances of his death were becoming clearer. Dylan had entered through the open doors to the orangery, the doors Jo had opened. Fingerprints on the neck of the wine bottle belonged to Dylan and to Ben, but it wasn't clear if Ben had tried to use it first and been disarmed, or Dylan had taken him by surprise. The argument overheard by the neighbour had been excised from all but the official police statements, so it wasn't hard to paint his murder as tragic heroism. He would likely have fought – of course he would – and Jo knew if he hadn't been there that night, it might have been her on that kitchen floor.

'We found something, on Rebekah Fitzwilliam's phone,' said Carrick. 'We're not one hundred per cent sure at the moment, but it looks like it might have been Ben leaking to the press.'

Jo let the information sink in, surprised it didn't have all that much impact.

'Right.'

'They were in regular contact, since a couple of months or so before the Bradford-on-Avon exhumation. He called her the day she was killed, just after Sally Carruthers was at St Aldates. We've no way of knowing the contents of the conversation, but given Fitzwilliam ended up where she did, it looks likely he tipped her off about Sally.' The information should have shocked Jo more than it did, but after everything that had happened, she absorbed it like a punch-drunk pugilist.

Carrick went on, 'The good news is that neither Thames Valley or Avon and Somerset have a lot of appetite to investigate further. Both parties are deceased, so it's low priority. And let's face it, we could do without the embarrassment.'

She'd wondered where Ben was getting his money from and this explained things. *You stupid, stupid bastard*, she thought, but it wasn't with any conviction. She'd found it hard, until they split, to accept he was an addict – that really there was a side to him she would never truly understand. Carrick's news only proved that Ben had been in the grip of pathologies he couldn't control. If he was willing to gamble away their future, was playing such a high-risk game with his career any worse? He'd been desperate. Saunders had been ambitious. Both of them had paid a price, and it had been too high. She wondered if there was anything she could have done to stop him; if there was a point somewhere in their past when they both could have taken a different route, where they'd be living happily in Bath, trying again to start a family.

You could torture yourself with this stuff. People made decisions, there were consequences.

'Just thought you'd want to know,' said Carrick.

'Yes, thanks,' she said, absently lost in her own thoughts.

★   ★   ★

318

The Three Crowns was twice as busy as the previous time she'd come, meaning there were two people at the bar, and as Ferman went to his usual table, Jo ordered the drinks – vodka for herself and brandy for him.

'Better make them doubles,' she said, then carried them over.

'You all right?' she asked.

'Aye,' he said. 'Sorry about that, my getting upset back at the mortuary.'

'No need to apologise,' she said. 'It's a difficult case.'

He took a sip of his drink. 'It wasn't that,' he said. 'Not only that, anyhow.' He sipped again, eyes distant. 'They told you, I suppose, about me. My daughter.'

Jo took a drink herself, and relished the burn. 'Andy said she died.'

'Car accident,' he said. 'Sort of thing you attend all the time. Ruins your day, but you move on. Have to, don't you?' He looked at her, very directly. 'She was twenty-two, coming back from uni, car stuffed to the gills. Jess – my wife – she'd cooked a big meal for dinner . . .'

He blew out his cheeks, eyes misting up again as he glanced up at the beer mats on the ceiling.

'We were expecting her at two-ish. No mobiles then, of course. Some silly fella, insurance sales, driving too fast after a boozy lunch. He came round a corner on the wrong side . . .'

He stopped talking, took a determined gulp and held it in his mouth for a second before his Adam's apple bobbed.

'I'm sorry,' said Jo.

'She was trapped, after. They tried to cut her out, but she was losing blood. She managed to tell them our number. Too late by then. Wouldn't let us see her until the morgue.'

'God,' said Jo. 'Harry, you should have said. You didn't have to come today.'

'You know, it didn't really hit me until we got there. Lindsay,

319

that was her name. It was the anniversary, a couple of days ago. I thought I should tell you, in case you thought I was being rude. I get a bit grumpy this time of year.'

'There's no need to apologise, but thank you,' said Jo. He'd almost finished his brandy. 'You having another?' she asked.

'Better not,' he said. 'You don't want to be hanging round with a miserable old codger all day.'

She grinned. 'I like miserable old codgers.' She swallowed the rest of her drink. 'Your round though – make mine a single. I've just got to nip out and make a call.'

'If you insist,' he said.

Sitting on a bench outside, Jo scrolled through her numbers and pressed call, taking out her diary and placing it on her lap.

'Bright Futures. How can I help you?'

'It's Josephine Masters,' she said. 'I was in about ten days ago. I need to sort out a date for a hormone infusion. I've got a pretty empty schedule for the next few days.'

The receptionist took her through it, with the same sleek professionalism as she'd encountered on that first consultation, like Jo was the same person she'd met that day. Which she was, of course, in the most obvious ways.

Jo went through the details, arranging that she'd go in on the Thursday following.

Back inside, Ferman was placing the drinks on the table.

'You look a bit more cheerful,' he said.

'Do I?' she said. 'Must be the booze.'

Acknowledgements

I'd like to thank, first and foremost, my family: my wife Rebecca for her infinite patience, support, and for making me take a break when I was quite literally losing the plot; Martha (6) and William (2) for their frequent interruptions and sense of perspective – the sound of little footsteps outside the study door is always welcome, even when there's a chapter to finish.

Though the process of writing a novel can be quite solitary, publishing one is anything but. All the team at Avon have been wonderful. When I came blinking into the light out of the first-draft cave, their words of encouragement lifted me enormously. A special mention to my editor – Phoebe Morgan – for her wisdom, industry, and calm under pressure; and to Oli Malcolm for taking a punt on a debut, and for his generous support thereafter.

And thanks to my friend and agent, the magnificent Julia Churchill of AM Heath, who's stuck with me through years of never actually finishing any book I said I'd started, and for throwing more opportunities my way than a hack ever deserved.

Finally, my gratitude to Detective Constable James Wilson of Greater Manchester Police, for his guidance on elements of police procedure. Anything that smacks of authenticity is down to him. Any errors in that regard are my own, whether they arise through misunderstanding or lazy research (or 'plotting expediency', as we writers like to call it).

**If you enjoyed *Hold My Hand*,
try the #1 bestseller C.L. Taylor**

Sometimes your first love won't let you go . . .